DEDICATION

For my mom.
You have the strength of Felar, the beauty of Tremmilly, and the wisdom of Elth-eo-lan. Thank you for teaching me so much.

CONTENTS

Harbingers of the Dawn:

Book 2 of the Dawn Saga

ZACHARIAH WAHRER

Second Print Edition, 2018

Wahrer of the Worlds Publishing
www.wahreroftheworlds.com
publishing@wahreroftheworlds.com

ISBN-13: 978-0-9983827-3-9

ACKNOWLEDGEMENTS

First off, I'd like to thank (in no particular order) Shanese Furlow, Megan Rahal, Frank Frey, Shreve Fellars, Lois Rahal, Patrick Wahrer, Katy Osterloth, Walter Scott, Helen Brookman, and Björn Arnór Sveinbjörnsson for their ongoing help with both this book and the Dawn Saga. Your feedback makes a huge difference and I'm so thankful for it. I'd also like to thank Shanese and TJ Courey for their help in beta reading short stories, since I never really find an opportunity to do that publicly otherwise. For his immense encouragement, at just the right time, I'd also like to convey my gratitude to my uncle, Paul Wahrer.

To Sarah Rahal Wahrer, the love of my life: thank you for supporting me through the crazy journey of the Dawn Saga. Your editing makes these books so much better, your belaying keeps me safe, and your love keeps me strong.

And to all my readers: I know you have lots of choices when it comes to media and entertainment, so it means so much to me when you choose to read one of my books or stories. I write because I love it, but also because I want to bring a channel of excitement, adventure, and drama into your life. I hope I succeed. Enjoy!

May the fires of the black star be quenched in your life,
Zachariah Wahrer

"So we must ask ourselves: 'Does the similarity of indigenous life on different worlds suggest a common creator, or rather, a common motivator?'"
- The Musings of Dearadoth, Akked Planetary Council Era

"But honestly, why are any of the Entho bugs still alive?"
- Tiz Cetheld, Ashamine Citizen

"The limits of biology have been transcended. Our flesh, our temporal weakness, is no more."
- The Arche

01 – CRASOR

Crasor Tah Ahn, once the Facilitator to the Founder of the Ashamine, floated in space. He relished the feeling of power running through his body. Even now, the nano-machines known as the Breakers were moving inside him, modifying Crasor's DNA to give him advanced abilities unimaginable to humans. The offer they had made Crasor back on Noor-5 had been too much for him to pass up. He was now the leader of what would soon be the most powerful civilization in the galaxy.

The time has come, Crasor thought, entering the destination of Ashamine-2 into his ship's computer. *When I kill the Founder, the humans will fall.* A sneer formed on his face, distorting his handsome features. *The Breakers will sweep through the dying corpse of the Ashamine. We will destroy humanity's corruption and bring in a new epoch for the Akked Galaxy. All life will be assimilated and perfected. We will ascend to even greater levels of consciousness.*

A worm tunnel formed in front of the ship, and Crasor eased his captured vessel through. He'd seized the courier starship on Noor-5 shortly after Seeding the ship's owner, converting him to the Breakers.

With the Noor system under our control, we have a foundation in the galaxy. The millions of humans we converted there will spread throughout the Akked. The Descended are on their way to Eishon, Qi, and Taggardt. With those small systems subjugated and converted, we'll have a sizable force to attack the more populated ones. Mentally, Crasor checked in with his generals, making sure they were still on course. They each replied in turn, and Crasor felt relieved. It wasn't that he didn't trust them—Breakers were absolutely loyal—but he worried about how little they had developed. *None of the expansion worlds will have a military presence. At worst, they might run into civilian defenses. The Descended will easily sweep through those. And they'll only get stronger as time goes on.*

1

Things were moving quickly and this pleased both Crasor and the Breaker mind. It had only been a few days since he'd completed operations on Noor-5. As long as they stayed concealed from the Ashamine, everything would continue smoothly and efficiently.

Crasor knew the location of all thirteen primary Ashamine worlds. Eventually, he could conquer them, but for now he would need to be content with invading the several unaffiliated, insignificant human border planets he knew about. More of these backwater places existed, but were hidden. It seemed everyone who disagreed with the Ashamine was defecting to these "free" worlds. The remaining Entho-la-ah-mine planets were a mystery to him as well. Their hive mind would be a powerful addition to the Breaker consciousness and he lusted for it. Crasor had come close to dominating them, but the alien race fought him off. *Their time will come.*

Focusing back on the matter at hand, Crasor engaged the engines, eager to complete his business with the Founder. He would need to move with caution. Crasor had superhuman abilities, but he was heading into the stronghold of the Ashamine. A slug from a rail pistol could still kill him. Stealth was a necessity.

***

Crasor carefully landed on the orbital dock. After taking a moment to carefully check his appearance, he decided he still looked human enough to pass unnoticed amongst the masses on Ashamine-2. *Your right hand,* he thought, pulling on a glove to cover the sharpened fingers. It was the only sign of his Breaker augmentations. He left the ship, working his way through the crowded arrival area. He wanted to obliterate the decadence he saw around him. Humans were vain, wasteful, and disorganized. The Breakers would bring order and harmony to this failing galaxy. They would perfect the inadequacies mere of flesh.

Searching back through his Breaker memories, Crasor thought about another time the Breakers rose from their slumber. "We cannot ascend without an ambassador," the voice of the Breakers said in his head. "We require someone who understands the current state of the universe." It was the sound of billions of individuals all speaking in unison. "You, Crasor, are that person. Do not make the mistake of your predecessor. Do not believe that diplomacy and kind words will bring the change we need." Crasor felt his consciousness being torn away from his body and thrust into the mind of Easak, a previous Breaker vessel.

***

"We shall rise to a higher plane of existence. We shall transcend these bodies that hold us down." The crowd gathered before Easak Torland seemed enthusiastic, but he worried none of them would come forward for the Seed. He needed to motivate them, had to drive them into fits of ecstasy. "You will be left behind if you do not accept this gift. The Breakers will remake this world into paradise, and you, my friends, will be left to rot in your flesh. The Breakers can give you life that never dies!"

At the end of his speech, only a few came forward to accept the Seed. Easak placed his right hand on their chest and the essence of the Breakers went into them. The lack of response from the audience was disappointing, and Easak decided he would have to do better next time. *We are not gaining as much momentum as we need.* He could feel the Breakers becoming angry with him. The crowd dissipated, leaving Easak alone with his new followers.

"Sir Torland?" a voice asked, pulling Easak out of his thoughts.

"Yes?" he replied, looking up to see a man dressed in the clothing of the Queen's Protectorate, a crimson tunic and gray leggings. A sword and dagger hung on his hip, and he moved with a grace that suggested he knew how to use them.

"My name is Tallus Darmekus. Queen Margaret wishes to meet with you. She would like to hear more about the Breakers." Easak's heart leapt at the chance to convert the monarch. The woman had great power and influenced many more than Easak could ever hope. She would be able to convert many to faith in the Breakers. *If she changed the state religion,* he thought, excitement rising within him.

"Lead the way, brother," Easak replied. Tallus turned without another word and began walking away from the castle's main gate. "Are we not going to the Great Hall?" Easak finally asked, beginning to feel uneasy.

"No. The Queen wishes a private audience." Easak kept walking, his pace brisk. "The clergy would not approve. She must keep it secret."

"Ah, I see," was all Easak could think to respond. He felt his connection to his converts, and it comforted him in a way being a priest never had. Easak drew upon their presence, preparing himself for the most important meeting of his life.

Tallus stopped before a small wooden door in the castle's wall. He knocked three times and a spy hole opened. "I've brought him," Tallus replied to the eye that peered back. Easak heard the bar slide back and the door creaked open. "Right this way," Tallus said, motioning him to lead.

Easak stepped through the doorway into a dimly lit corridor. He walked past the guard, a brutish looking man also in the crimson and gray of the Queen's Protectorate. Farther down the hall, Tallus directed him to turn right. Easak obeyed. They descended a flight of stairs and entered a dank room that smelled of blood and feces. Small rooms lay behind barred doors. *This is a dungeon,* Easak thought, his nerves overriding the comfort of his people. Several heavy tables and chairs lay around the room. Knives, pokers, and other nasty looking implements hung from the walls. Hot coals stood in a brazier in the corner. The hairs on Easak's neck stood up and the pit of his stomach dropped.

"The Queen is going to meet with me here?" he asked, turning to look at Tallus. The man had his sword drawn. More members of the Queen's Protectorate stood behind him, including the brutish man from the entryway.

"Sir Torland," Tallus replied, his voice so cold it chilled Easak to the bone, "you will not be meeting with the Queen. The religion you are preaching is a threat to the kingdom, and to Christianity. As its leader, you are charged with treason and heresy, the sentence of which is death." Behind Tallus, two men were readying something Easak couldn't see. They moved into view and threw a bundle of ropes at him. The heavy mass enveloped Easak. *A net,* he guessed, vainly fighting its entangling grasp. *If only I could lay my hands on them and give the touch of the Breakers, perhaps then they might understand.* Easak heard footsteps approach and then blackness descended.

***

Easak awoke, his head reeling. He tried to sit up, but his arms and legs were bound to the table on which he lay. Around him, low voices murmured, sounding menacing. Easak tried to reach out to his followers, but their presence was dim. *Help me,* he cried, hoping they would come save him.

A man Easak had never seen before approached him. His face was plain and expressionless. The murmurs died down and an expectant hush fell over the room. "Do you know the mind of God?" the plain man asked, voice as bland as his face.

"I only know that the Breakers have sent me to reveal their plan. I am but their servant, sent to spread the good news of their coming." Before he knew what was happening, a whip was in the man's hand and he lashed it across Easak's bare belly. Easak screamed, the pain intense and dreadful.

"You were once a servant of God, but now you serve the devil. How did this come to be?" The plain inquisitor showed no emotion, his voice suggesting he didn't care how Easak answered.

"I serve no devil, only the Breakers." This time two lashes fell, and the pain spiked higher.

"Answer the question. How did you come to serve the devil?"

4

"The Breakers are God's chosen people. They are not devils!" Three lashes were the inquisitor's only response and Easak knew they did not believe him. Perhaps if he could buy enough time, his followers could rescue him. Even now he could feel they were gathering. The inquisitor drew a curved knife from a sheath at his waist, and Easak knew he had to start talking.

"I left the monastery a few hours before dark, hoping to have some solitude to pray. The woods north of the city are my favorite place to go for this purpose. I was heading back when I felt the hand of God moving. It was pulling me towards a part of the forest I had never been to. It was as if God's finger was pointing in my head, directing me towards this place." The inquisitor still had the knife in his hand, but remained motionless.

"I followed the finger of God and it led to a rent in the earth. It was fresh, with new dirt and rocks exposed. I crawled through a narrow passage and into a chamber. Inside was a magnificent crystal, a gem bigger than any cart could transport." Easak had to speak slower. His followers were coming closer, but at this pace, his story would be over before they arrived. "Then the Breakers spoke. They told me how they came to England long ago, how God wanted me to be their instrument, and how he had a new plan for us. I told them I would do whatever God wanted, and they anointed me with their essence, making me their apostle. The Breakers told me to spread the news of their coming and that I would lead mankind to its ascension." The murmurs rose once again. Easak hoped his words would sway these listeners, that they might come to believe in the Breakers.

A tall man dressed in bishop's robes came over and whispered in the inquisitor's ear. Easak tried to note any expression on his face, but it stayed as bland as ever. When the bishop quit speaking, the inquisitor came and stood over Easak.

"You speak heresy. Renounce the devil and return to God." The inquisitor was just a tool of the clergy. Easak would need to convince the others of the truth.

"I can take you to the cave," he said desperately. "I can show you the hand of God moving through the Breakers." The curved knife came down to Easak's skin, carving along his arm. It took a moment for the pain to reach his mind. When it did, he felt the injury as an exploding line of fire. Easak screamed.

Cries of bewilderment rose around the room. Through the agony, Easak wondered dimly what had caused them. Soon, his pain began to subside. Easak looked down at his injury and realized why everyone was so surprised. The knife wound had closed up and healed. An angry red seam was all that remained. It soon faded and his skin returned to its

5

normal pink color.

"He is filled with the devil," a voice cried out. "We must cleanse him before the devil can unleash more of its evil upon us." Yells of agreement met this statement. Easak knew he was doomed. They would never listen to him, never come to see God's work. That was how it always had been. *A village never accepts its own prophet,* Easak thought. He could feel his followers were close, perhaps at the outer door. Just as he sensed this, he heard a faint pounding sound coming from above.

"Send guards to the northern entry," one of the Queen's Protectorate ordered. "We must not let his followers rescue him." A young page dashed off, running up the stairs.

"Ready the guillotine," the bishop said. Easak heard the sound of the blade rising. Four men surrounded his table and dragged it towards the menacing machine. *My people will never make it in time,* he thought, just as the sound of combat rang in the stairway.

"Quickly!" the bishop yelled. "We must purge the demon." Easak caught a glimpse of his first convert, a blacksmith, swinging a hammer. It smashed down on the head of one of the Queen's Protectorate. The man's head crumpled as he fell to the floor. Then, Easak heard the blade falling and saw no more.

***

"Get outta the way, fancy boy," a female voice shouted, breaking into Crasor's thoughts. "This dock isn't your private lounge." Anger flared in him, partly because of Easak's futility, and partly because of this woman's disrespect. He wanted to kill her, but quickly pushed his temper down. Crasor couldn't draw attention to himself.

"You cannot try to reason with the Founder," the voice of the Breakers said inside his mind as the woman captain moved on. "As you see from Easak Torland's memory, those in power will do anything to stay in power, even when a better system presents itself. This is true today, as it was five thousand human standard years ago."

I was not planning on reasoning with him, Crasor replied. *We must overthrow him, and the only way is death. That has been, and always will be my plan.* A pleased feeling came from the Breakers. Crasor knew he would run the Ashamine better than the Founder; he would lead humanity to a greatness it never could have imagined.

He found a shuttle heading for the surface of Ashamine-2 and paid the fare. Crasor barely found a seat in the small passenger compartment. More people pushed in, sitting in the aisles. The smell disgusted Crasor, reminding him of the packed crowd back on Noor-5. That was before the Breakers had elevated his senses. Now, humans just smelled like livestock.

The flight down took longer than Crasor expected. The rickety old transport had seen better days. With its overloaded condition, he would be happy if it landed in one piece. Taking this low class transportation was necessary. Slipping in with the servants and refugees provided a better chance for him to remain unnoticed. *If the Founder knew I was coming...* he thought, nervous of the implications.

The shuttle set down hard on one of the lower level landing areas. Crasor impatiently waited for the aisles and seats ahead of him to clear. The humans jostled, yelled, and fought their way out. Finally, he disembarked.

Around Crasor stood vast skyscrapers. They soared high into the clouds, plasti-glass facades gleaming in the sun. Crasor filled his lungs with the smell of the Founder's City, relishing it. This was his favorite place in the Akked Galaxy. It was full of power, culture, and opulence. One day, he would be its leader. The thought made him smile.

Normally, Crasor would travel by air transport, but that would expose him too much. Even traveling by more primitive means, he would need to disguise himself. There was a cache in a storage facility on the third under-level that had the makeup, materials, and identification samples he would need. It was two hours travel from here, but Crasor was in no hurry. Caution was more important than speed right now.

Boarding the under level pneumatic tube transport further disgusted Crasor. He had only been on the grungy public transit once before, when he and Emili Trayfis had gone to the underground Electro-Narco Party. She had desperately wanted to see the massive event, and Crasor grudgingly agreed to accompany her. The memory of Emili was bittersweet. Crasor wished she had been a more willing and compliant partner. Perhaps then he wouldn't have killed her.

Snapping back to the present, Crasor realized Ashamine Forces troops were patrolling through the tube. They were using a portable scanner to check the identity of each passenger, looking for criminals. The terminal would recognize Crasor instantly. It wouldn't display him as the Facilitator, but the Founder would know he was back. The guards might attempt to detain him. Anxiety filled Crasor and he had to steady his breathing. *Focus,* he thought, forming a plan.

While the guards checked another passenger, Crasor nonchalantly got out of his seat and began walking towards the back of the tube. About a third of the seats contained people, and everyone was keeping their heads down. Attention was not something anyone who lived on this level of the city wanted. *Good,* Crasor thought, *fewer witnesses.*

Reaching the back of the compartment, Crasor entered the lavatory. It was disgusting, walls smeared with feces and other bodily fluids he tried not to think about. Crasor carefully slid the door shut, leaving just a crack to peer through. With less ventilation, the stench became so thick Crasor could taste it. He kept his mind focused on what he had to do next. *Maybe the guards will get lazy and fail to check the lavatory.* That was unlikely, but it was the best-case scenario.

Minutes passed, and Crasor kept control of his nerves. The highest priority was to keep the lens of the handheld terminal away from his face. Crasor could easily manage every other outcome but that one. Looking out the cracked door, he saw the troops had finished up with the last passenger and were heading towards the lavatory. He eased the door the rest of the way shut before they could spot the movement.

A few moments later, he heard a knock on the door. "Ashamine Forces," a muffled voice said, "open the door and submit to a security screen." One tactic remained, then he would kill them.

"I have terrible diarrhea," Crasor replied, modulating his voice so the terminal would not be able to identify it.

"Just open the door, a quick scan, and we'll be on our way," another voice said.

"You don't want to see this," Crasor replied, carefully grabbing the door handle. "I made a mess. It's all over me." He heard a sigh, and then whispered speech he couldn't make out.

"Sir, open the door or we will do it for you," the second voice said after a moment. "This will only take a second." *Oh, you are right,* Crasor thought, eagerness welling up in him, *it will only take a second.*

Crasor slid the door open, dropping low as he did so. The two guards stood side by side, the short one on the left holding the portable terminal. Before he could raise it, Crasor chopped the device out of his grasp using the knife edge of his right hand. A look of surprise flashed on the man's face. Seizing the opportunity, Crasor hit the right guard with his left forearm, driving forward off his back leg with incredible force. He felt the man's jaw shatter and watched his eyes roll back into his head.

The left guard was pulling out his rail pistol, cold hatred blazing in his eyes. As he brought it up, Crasor leapt forward with a flying knee, striking the man in his gut. Air exploded from the guard with an "umph" sound. Crasor used his momentum to force the man to the floor. Once on the ground, he grabbed the guard's head and twisted until he heard a satisfying snap. Rising quickly, he finished off the other soldier with a boot to the face.

Looking up, Crasor saw no eyes turned his way. Everyone on the tube remained seated, facing forward. They wanted nothing to do with the incident. *Perfect,* Crasor gloated.

Before anyone could change their mind and try to become a hero, he turned to the emergency escape hatch. It was a big red door situated at the back of the tube with a sign: "Warning: Do not operate while tube is in motion. Serious injury or death is possible." It would be a rough ride, but his Breakers-enhanced body could withstand it. Hopefully investigators would blame the death of the Ashamine troops on the pressurization and ensuing destruction. Crasor stood off to the side of the hatch, took a deep breath, and pulled the handle.

The exploding bolts fired and the large metal panel shot inwards, the pressurized air of the tube's propulsion system almost giving it the velocity of a rail gun shot. Immediately, the atmospheric pressure spiked. Crasor felt his eardrums strain against the load, pushed to the breaking point. Judging by the screams of those further forward in the compartment, they were not so lucky.

Looking out the hatch, Crasor saw smooth metal walls speed by. Already the pressure was lessening. Pulling the handle had tripped the emergency stop procedure and Crasor could sense the tube was losing velocity. When he felt the tube had slowed enough, he jumped through the escape hatch. He hit the tunnel floor running, but misjudged the speed. The smooth surfaces were deceptive. Crasor fell and began tumbling and cartwheeling violently. Finally, he came to a stop, body bruised and battered.

Groaning, Crasor rose to his feet. "Founder damn it to the fires of the dark star," he cursed, checking to make sure he had no broken limbs. He knew the only thing that had saved him were his Breaker augmentations.

Crasor had to get away as quickly as possible. He couldn't risk what would happen if the emergency crews spotted him. The tube infrastructure included maintenance tunnels that would allow him to escape unseen. *I just have to find a way to access them.* Crasor began running in the opposite direction the tube had gone.

9

02 – ASCENDED KAROTH

Ascended Karoth sat back into his captain's chair and looked out through the main view window. The stars in front of the ASN Founder's Justice vanished. "Ahead full," Karoth ordered and the ship moved through the worm.

"Successful transition to Eishon system," the propulsion officer reported. Karoth looked towards his weapons officer expectantly.

"Local system appears free of threats," the man said after a moment.

"Hold position until the rest of the fleet comes through." Karoth returned his gaze to the main window, ignoring his console.

"Bring the successor back to me at any cost," the Founder had told him a few hours before. "I have ordered a fleet assembled and you will command it. This is of utmost importance for the Ashamine." Karoth had bowed, knowing this would be the most important campaign of his long career. He had successfully prosecuted the war with the Entho-la-ah-mines, earning many medals and commendations. *If I fail to bring the successor back, however...* Karoth didn't want to finish that thought.

"The rest of the fleet has arrived," the comms officer said, breaking into his thoughts.

"Order full speed towards Eishon-2," Karoth replied, forcing his mind back to the mission. Several minutes passed, and Karoth used the time to formulate attack plans on his console. The situation was very delicate. Whoever had the successor would have him well hidden, and a hostage situation could easily develop once Karoth located the boy. He would have to lock down the planet and the rest of the system. No one could leave.

"Station gunships just inside the system gravity well perimeter. No one enters, no one leaves. If a fleeing vessel tries to run the blockade, disable it. The individual we are rescuing is very important to the Ashamine and must be secured without damage to his person." The comms officer hurriedly sent out the orders and ships broke off from the fleet. "Analysts have determined our target is most likely planet side on Eishon-2," Karoth continued. "However, there is a chance he is in the wreckage of the Founder's Hammer. Deploy two recon ships and two rescue boats to the area. Set red priority to their mission. I want everyone on high alert. The target is of the highest priority and we must do everything possible to bring him back unharmed."

"Yes, sir!" resounded off the walls as everyone on deck acknowledged his orders.

"I am confident in you all," Karoth continued in a quieter tone. "What is our estimated arrival in Eishon-2 planet space?"

"Two hours at max system speed," the propulsion officer replied. *Plenty of time to draw up more plans,* Karoth thought, returning his gaze to the console before him.

03 – THE FOUNDER

Are these the best we have? the Founder thought, scrutinizing the five Commandos standing before him. He was trying to find a replacement for Crasor, but none of these would make a suitable Facilitator.

"Dismissed," he said, turning to walk away.

"Yes, sir!" the two men and three women barked in response, their words echoing in the massive FC training area. They were great soldiers, possessing a wide range of technical skills, but each lacked the ability to work alone. That was what had made Crasor stand out so much initially. *Perhaps it is time I look to another branch of the Ashamine Forces.*

The Founder's entourage followed in his wake, security detail keeping a tight perimeter. It felt good to get out of his office and the palace, to see the city once again. "Where to next, Founder?" his chief aide asked.

"The lab," he replied, excitement building.

***

Stepping off his personal air transport, the Founder smiled. The massive Ashamine labs stretched above and below him. He barely noticed his security detail as he stepped forward to meet Dareth Adjular, his newly appointed Director of Research.

"Thank you for your time, Founder," the short man said, his lean frame almost quivering with anticipation. "We have so much to show you. I could have sent a full report, but I believe you will want to see this personally."

"Of course," the Founder replied, his own eagerness less obvious. Since the disappearance of Crasor, the kidnapping of Lothis, and the loss of Haak-ah-tar, the Traynos-6 discovery had been a singular positive. He hoped Karoth would find the boy, but if not, the new technology unlocked by T6 might render him unnecessary anyway.

"Come this way, if you will," Dareth said, heading towards the

12

entrance for the large building. Once inside, the Director led him through a maze of corridors, passing several security checkpoints, chatting all the while.

"I must wait to give you details until after we reach the secure facility," he said, "but I can tell you some general information as we walk. We know from Director Kasol's research that the technology can be introduced into the human body without destroying it. The tests on Bloodsport were meant to explore its capabilities. As you already know, the loss of the asteroid in the supernova set us back somewhat. Our prime test subject, Maxar Trayfis, perished before we could perform any tests. We do know the nanites integrated with his system successfully." Dareth stopped talking as they arrived at a heavy tungsten alloy door.

"Expecting a nuclear strike?" the Founder said, chuckling.

"No," the shorter man replied, "but there is a strong need for adequate containment protocols."

The Founder raised his eyebrows. "The technology is that powerful?"

"On its own," Dareth replied, keying a password on the terminal beside the door, "no, at least as far as we know." He stood still as the security system completed a biometric scan. The indicators turned green and the heavy door swung open. "It's still too early to tell exactly what it is capable of, however; so we treat it accordingly. Had the experiment survived on Bloodsport, it would have been much easier to quarantine an accident there than in the Founder's City."

Once inside the secure facility, Dareth led the Founder to a viewing area. It was a large room with several chairs facing a plasti-glass wall. On the other side, several technicians were standing around a table, talking. They wore white environmental nominizing suits. "I cannot take you any deeper inside the lab area," Dareth said, motioning to a chair. "There is potential for exposure to the nanites."

"As you say," the Founder replied, sitting down. His security detail took up positions around the room. "What is the current test?"

"Based on Director Kasol's work, we have reason to believe the nanites will provide regenerative capabilities." The Founder nodded. He knew that from the reports. "We've already used rail and flechette pistols on the test subject. The kinetic force of the shot is imparted to the subject, but the rounds themselves fail to penetrate. Now, we'd like to see if they protect against high thermal states."

Inside the lab, a woman was wheeled in, strapped to a tungsten alloy frame. "Is she the only one who's been exposed?" the Founder asked. The woman strained against her bonds, her face twisted in rage.

"Yes, currently. Earlier today, we tested a male subject with a magnetic field, to see if the nanites were impacted. The force was relatively weak, certainly survivable by a non-augmented human, but the male perished immediately. We are performing autopsies to determine cause of death."

"This has been the only weakness of the T6 nanites thus far?"

The ENS clad technicians attached the frame to a support structure and walked back to their table.

"Yes," Dareth answered. "Kasol's notes suggested he felt there were other problems with the technology, but he never said what they were. Very unfortunate. The man was a genius, but could be sloppy."

The Founder agreed, but said nothing. He'd appointed Kasol head of the Legacy Genetics Project, the program tasked with developing his clone. The Founder had given Kasol two tasks: raise Lothis and study the Traynos-6 discovery. They were the most important scientific goals in the entire Ashamine. Based on the report brought back by the traitorous Commando, Felar Haltro, it seemed Kasol kept at least one side project that had endangered the Successor. If the supernova hadn't wiped out Kasol, the Founder definitely would have. His mistakes were unforgivable.

"You still believe his hypothesis about alien origin is correct?"

One of the technicians picked up a wide metal nozzle connected to a hose. He dragged the heavy apparatus before the test subject. Carefully aiming, the tech lit the igniter and pulled a trigger. A gush of flame shot out, enveloping the woman's body.

"It seems the best possible explanation," Dareth answered, staring at the subject inquisitively. The Founder lapsed into silence, eager to see the results. After several moments passed, the technician released the trigger. Given the amount of fire, the Founder expected to see a charred body. Instead, the woman looked healthy, with only her hair having burned away. Everything else looked as it did before the test.

"As expected," Dareth said, a smile on his face.

"Truly remarkable. Your report said you think the technology could grant its host extended life?"

"It certainly seems likely, but we need more testing and observation. With Kasol's lack of notes, we have very little information on potential side effects."

The Founder cursed Kasol in his mind once again as he stood from his chair. He fixed Director Adjular with his orange eyes. "Continue your tests, Director. Work as quickly as is prudent. If the dark star is against us, the Ashamine may need me for many years to come."

04 – WAKE

"Founder be damned to the fires of the dark star," Captain Malesis exclaimed in a low voice. Wake wasn't one to use profanity, but that was exactly how he felt. The control room around him exploded in chaos.

Wake, too new to the Brotherhood of Azak-so to help, sat staring at a console. It showed a huge Ashamine force surrounding the Eishon system. *This is because of the battle between the Entho-la-ah-mine and Ashamine vessel, but it doesn't explain why so many ships came. There has to be more to it than just that.* Remembering the aftermath brought up memories of the past few days.

His arrival at the Brotherhood base on Eishon-2 had been surprising for many reasons. The organization was larger than Wake had imagined. At least a thousand members were here along with other strongholds scattered throughout the Akked Galaxy. Parick Olvold, the group's leader, had welcomed Wake warmly, but the initial greeting was his only interaction with the dark skinned, older man. The group seemed loosely organized, but that fact belied a fierce devotion to both Olvold and their goal of cleaning up the corruption of the Ashamine. Captain Malesis, the man who'd rescued Wake mid-execution, had asked him to join his ship's crew. Wake had gladly accepted, feeling he had a place amongst them.

"Silence!" Parick Olvold yelled, bringing the turmoil of the room under his command. He waited several moments, staring at the large view screen near the front of the room. "At this point, we have no idea what this Ashamine force is up to," he continued, voice low, but commanding. "They might just be here to investigate the conflict with the Enthos, or they might be here to wipe out the base. Until their intentions are made known, we have to assume the worst. Prepare for complete evacuation." The room once again burst into chaos.

"How can we get past the gunship blockade?" Wake asked Captain Malesis over the tumult, worry creeping deep into his chest.

"Right now, we will rely on the camouflage of the installation to hide

15

us from the Ashamine. If their damned technology has come far enough, they'll be able to see through the shielding. We won't know until they make a move towards us. At that point, we'll just have to push through the blockade." Captain Malesis paused, a pained expression on his face. "The Brotherhood doesn't have any vessels that can stand up to a gunship though, so it could be messy." Based on the size of the fleet coming towards Eishon-2, Wake wondered if any of them would be able to escape if the Ashamine discovered the Brotherhood base. "We need to do our part for evac prep," Captain Malesis continued, "so I need to start downloading data files. Gather up our Entho-la-ah-mine guests and take them down to the Bane. Get it ready for departure." As he left the room, Wake looked back to the screen, wondering if the Ashamine would finish his execution after all.

He pushed into the crowded lift and waited for the doors to close. "The base won't be able to handle a direct assault," a tall, blond woman said to a short, balding man, sounding worried. "They will wipe us out." Wake knew she was right. The Brotherhood was a powerful organization, but it normally worked in the shadows and had limited military assets.

The lift stopped at every floor and people hurried in and out. Wake's sense of anxiety increased as time passed. *What if we have to run the blockade?* He hoped the base's camouflage and shielding would work.

Finally, Wake arrived at his floor. Hurrying down narrow corridors, he found the rooms he wanted. Inside were the Entho-la-ah-mines he and Captain Malesis had rescued. They had found the three members of the insectile race stranded inside a rudimentary escape pod floating in Eishon space. Wake had spent the past few days conversing with the Entho-la-ah-mines and had gotten to know them quite well.

He hit the alert button outside Cazz-ak-tak's room. After several moments, Wake heard the voice of Cazz-ak in his mind: "Enter." He was still growing accustomed to the Entho-la-ah-mine method of psionic communication. Wake had asked Cazz-ak if his species could read human thoughts, but the insectile alien told him it didn't work that way. Cazz-ak had then gone in depth about the Entho-la-ah-mine Great Thought and psionic theory. He tried to explain how their minds could influence quantum electromagnetic fields, but Wake couldn't put all the concepts together. Some underlying theories made sense, but the application seemed impossible.

Wake hit the button and the door slid open. Cazz-ak stood on the other side, his emerald green exoskeleton shining in the artificial lighting. "An Ashamine fleet is on its way towards Eishon-2," Wake said, skipping a greeting. "They will probably be here in an hour or two. They have the system on lockdown."

"Do you know why they are here? Are they after you? The

16

Brotherhood?" Cazz-ak's voice in Wake's head was calm.

"I don't know. Parick Olvold doesn't know either. They might be here to investigate the Ashamine battleship your vessel destroyed, or they could be here to wipe out the leadership of the Brotherhood. We need to prepare to evacuate if the Ashamine makes a move against us. Hopefully they will just scan the wreckage and leave." Wake shook his head.

"Yes, that does seem unlikely." Cazz-ak's voice took on a solemn note as he continued. "The Ashamine, in my species' experience, is extremely thorough." Wake knew he was talking about the Ashamine's war against the Entho-la-ah-mines and the genocide of his people.

"We need to get Elth-eo-lan and Na-ah-co and head up to the hangar." Wake's voice was calm, but he knew his anxious body language was giving away his true feelings. "There isn't much time until the main body of the fleet arrives in Eishon-2 planet space."

"I've told them the situation. They are ready to depart."

Turning back to the hall, Wake saw the two smaller females standing outside their room. The one with the red and green exoskeleton was Elth-eo-lan. Na-ah-co, the smallest of the group, had a beautiful blue exoskeleton. Her coloring was unlike anything Wake had ever seen, the swirling depths seeming infinite. "There is something we need to tell you," Cazz-ak said, his voice serious.

"OK," Wake replied, puzzled.

"We've explained how the Ashamine killed our queen," Elth-eo-lan said, her voice warm in Wake's mind. "What we didn't tell you then was about how our people need a queen for leadership, hope, and cohesion. Without one, we would soon disintegrate as a species."

"How queens are made and how precarious our current situation is would take too long to explain," Cazz-ak continued. "The best thing to say is that a new queen cannot be created, and the one we have is the last hope for our species."

"But I thought you said your queen was dead." Wake looked at them in turn, trying to make sense of their cryptic explanations.

"I am the new queen of the Entho-la-ah-mines," Na-ah-co said. "I'm sorry we had to deceive you. We were unclear on the situation when you first rescued us. Time has shown you are trustworthy and honorable. Please, do not tell any of the Brotherhood. We cannot risk that one of them agrees with the Ashamine's plan for our extinction." Wake felt the weight of Na-ah-co's revelation settle on him. Now, in addition to worrying about an Ashamine fleet bearing down on the planet, he was responsible for keeping the last hope of the Entho-la-ah-mine race alive. "If at all possible," Na-ah-co continued, we would prefer to stay in proximity to you, both for our security and to lend you aid."

"Thank you for your trust," Wake said. "I will do my best to keep you

17

all safe."

"We are grateful for your strength in our time of weakness," Cazz-ak said. "Perhaps, in the future, we will be able to do the same for you." Wake hoped there would be a future for him and the Entho-la-ah-mines that lasted past the next few hours.

Leading the group towards the hangar deck and the Ashamine's Bane, Wake made a hasty stop at his quarters to grab his only real possession: the Clothing of the Iconoclast. He put it on as fast as he could, the couplings attaching to each other smoothly. Dexterity was diminished in the suit, but the additional protection was worth it. Wake had a feeling he would need it soon.

05 – FELAR

Felar sharpened her combat short swords, enjoying the sound the honing bar made as she passed it along the edge of the metal. Eishon-2 was temperate, the weather warm and enjoyable. The system's only star was overhead, the light gently filtering through the swaying trees. As a Founder's Commando, she'd rarely had the opportunity for moments like this. Now that she had forsaken the Ashamine, Felar hoped this lifestyle would continue.

"How can this place have no connection to the Terminal Network?" Lothis asked, upset. "I have no way to search the histories, no way to find out about *them*." The last word was imbued with a special meaning Felar didn't understand.

"Who?" she asked, brow furrowed.

"The beings of light I saw over the signal." Lothis' ability to tap into the natural world scared Felar. At first she had thought he was having seizures or hallucinations, but the boy had explained the phenomenon to her and now she wasn't so sure. He had known about the Haak-ah-tar supernova before anyone else and had somehow contacted these beings of light. She remembered other incidents as well, ones that were even harder to understand.

"As soon as the A'Tal's Revenge's worm generator is fixed," Felar said, trying to placate the boy, "we'll hopefully be heading some place with a connection to the Network." Lothis said nothing in reply. He got a far away look in his eyes that she had learned meant he was searching for the signal of the light beings. Minutes passed in silence.

Finishing with the swords, Felar returned them to the sheaths on her back. *What do I do now,* she wondered. Tremmilly was off trying to gather up what few belongings she had on the planet. Felar had offered to help, but the other woman wanted to do the task herself. It was a spiritual journey for Tremmilly, a severing of ties to the place she had called home her entire life.

Neither Felar nor Lothis had knowledge of how to fix the worm generator, so they'd left Maxar and Jaydon to the task. The ship sat just thirty meters away, out in the clearing. Felar had wanted shade, so she'd abandoned the ship for the protective embrace of the trees.

"Do you think they'll figure out how to fix the generator?"

"What?" Lothis looked confused, and Felar realized he wasn't on the same wave of thought.

"Do you think Maxar and Jaydon can fix the worm drive?"

"No," the boy said. "Jaydon seems to know a lot about ships, but not physics or how the generator actually functions. If only I understood more about how it is engineered, but that wasn't a part of my studies."

"At least they got the hull fully repaired." That had been their first step towards getting off Eishon-2 before the Ashamine arrived. Felar's nerves frayed more and more as days crawled past. The Ashamine were coming, that much she knew. And if they captured Lothis, Felar, and her friends, they would all face imprisonment or death. She couldn't let Lothis fall back into the grasp of the Ashamine. He would resume his "training" as the successor of the Founder, forced back into a cell, manipulated and programmed. The Ashamine would charge Felar with treason for kidnapping him and put her to death. Maxar, an escaped convict, would be shot on sight. Tremmilly and Jaydon faced the death penalty for helping Felar. Every one of them needed to get away from the Eishon system as soon as possible. It was the last known location of the heir of the Founder. Time was running out.

A flicker of movement caught Felar's eye and she looked up in time to see Maxar jump out of the Revenge's hatch. He looked around frantically for a moment before he caught sight of Felar. "A fleet is coming," he yelled. Felar's stomach dropped. It was as if thinking about the Ashamine had summoned them. Felar grabbed Lothis' hand and ran over to Maxar.

"How big?" she asked, breathless. "How far away? Are you sure it's Ashamine?"

"It's the most ships I've ever seen in one place. The resolution of the Revenge's instruments are grainy, but there has to be hundreds of them. It looks like they are locking down the system. We are trapped here, even if we get the generator repaired. A large contingent is coming towards the planet. We only have an hour or two before they arrive." Felar knew it was the Ashamine. No one else could raise such a large force.

"Curse it all to the fires of the dark star," she said, speaking more to herself than to Maxar. "What do we do now?"

"There are no other worm capable ships available around here. We've looked. Until we get the worm generator fixed, we can't even attempt an escape." Maxar looked despondent.

"Isn't there anyone on this backwater planet who can repair worm generators?" Felar loved the environment here, but the lack of facilities was beginning to frustrate her in the same way it was Lothis.

"Tremmilly mentioned something about a group who might have the capabilities, but they weren't really an option. She said they would create trouble for us."

"Well," Felar said, a determined look on her face, "trouble or not, they just became our last hope."

06 – TREMMILLY

Tremmilly looked up from the cabinet she was rummaging through, tears blurring her vision. A small figurine caught her eye. It was a wooden doll.

"Take this, Tremmilly," she remembered her father saying. His dark eyes sparkled and a generous smile creased his smooth face. "I made it just for you."

"Thank you, daddy."

"What will you call her?"

"I think I'll name her... Cleopa! Deo, come here. We have a new friend!"

The memory was a good one, but stung all the same. This was why Tremmilly hadn't been back to her parents' house in months. After they'd died, Psidonnis had taken her in, and the two of them lived in his small cottage. When she had grown old enough to take care of herself, she'd moved back to the homestead. Tremmilly preferred to live in the woods, however, as long as the conditions were pleasant. Eishon-2 had remarkably stable weather patterns, and she'd spent little time at the house. Sometimes the memories were too much to bear. As years passed, the ache of their deaths dulled, and Tremmilly became discouraged by how much of her parents she'd forgotten. Occasionally, a vivid memory would return, threatening to overwhelm her. This house was not a place of peace, not in the way the forest was.

A knock on the small entry door startled her. "Come in," she said automatically. The door opened slowly and Maxar poked his head in.

"Sorry to bother you," the lean framed man said, his pale blue eyes causing a jolt of energy to course through her. His shaved head was getting stubbly. Tremmilly wondered if he lacked the time to shave or if he was purposefully letting it grow out. She liked the look of the growing hair. *You're in mourning for your guardian,* Tremmilly thought, scolding herself.

"It's not a bother," she replied, a smile pushing its way through her tears. Maxar opened the door and Tremmilly saw the rest of the group behind him. They all had somber looks on their faces and she immediately felt on edge. Something was wrong.

"Can we come in?" Maxar's face looked calm, but Tremmilly was beginning to know him well enough to see what was under his facade.

"Let's talk outside. I could use a break from this place." Walking outside felt good. The warm sunshine gave her energy and Tremmilly imagined herself as a plant, photosynthesizing the bright light.

"The Ashamine have the system quarantined," Felar said, her voice grave. "Even if we had the Revenge's worm generator repaired, we couldn't escape. A huge fleet of ships is on its way towards the planet. They'll be here in less than an hour." Tremmilly's heart dropped. She knew Jaydon and herself might lie their way through an Ashamine interrogation, but they would execute Felar and Maxar. Felar's son, Jon, would be sent back to his abusive father. Tremmilly would do all she could to protect her friends, especially since they were on her home planet.

"We could hide in the woods," she said hopefully. "I know deep places the Ashamine would never look."

"I have training in masking bio signatures," Felar replied, shaking her head, "but with the sensor resolution they are capable of, they will find us. We will look suspicious just because of our location."

"But you said before they are looking for cargo that was on the Hammer." Jaydon looked skeptical, and only slightly drunk. "Why would they come here at all?"

"Well," Felar said haltingly, "I may not have told the whole truth." She looked down at her son Jon, then locked eyes with Tremmilly, a pained expression on her face. "I didn't know if I could trust you all, but now..." She trailed off, looking at Jaydon and Maxar in turn. Felar took a deep breath. "Jon is not my son. I rescued him from the Ashamine."

"What do you mean?" Tremmilly blurted, confused.

"Yeah," Maxar said, eyes narrowing, "you have to give us more than that."

"Of course," Felar continued, looking flustered. "Originally, I was stationed on Ashamine-4, recruiting for the Founder's Commandos. While giving a fight demo, some Founder's cursed Inits took things too far and assaulted me." She paused for a moment, then resumed. "Due to personal security concerns, I was sent to Haak-ah-tar, to be a squad commander for a newly graduated group of troops. The Entho-la-ah-mines arrived and caused a bunch of problems, including knocking out comms for a remote research facility. My squad was sent to investigate. Anyway, to shorten a blightheartedly long story, what I found were lots of monsters and one small boy. I did the best I could to save my squad, but they were too new, and the odds were too bad. If it hadn't been for Lothis, which is Jon's real name, I wouldn't have made it out myself.

"Before we escaped, Lothis hashed access to a top clearance file system, which is how I found out they were doing experiments on him: neuro-programming, genetic re-sequencing, chemical manipulation, as well as many other things I couldn't comprehend. They kept him in a small room, alone, isolated. They were torturing him."

Felar paused, biting her lip. "The records also said he is the Founder's successor."

"Blightheart," Maxar cursed under his breath, shaking his head. Jaydon's eyes were as big as the exhaust ports of his ship. Lothis said nothing, his eyes focused on far away places, as usual.

"So that is why the Ashamine are coming here, why they will scour the entire planet," Felar continued. "They won't leave until they find him."

Tremmilly felt betrayed. It was a new emotion, one she had little experience with. *You know Felar had good reasons to lie,* Tremmilly thought. *She didn't know anything about us when we rescued them. Besides, she's telling you the truth now.*

"If hiding on the planet won't work," Tremmilly said finally, "and leaving the Eishon system is impossible, what do we do?"

Felar smiled, but Tremmilly could see fear running beneath it, and this softened her even further. "You could turn Lothis and I over to the Ashamine. They would forgive all your crimes, even Maxar's."

Tremmilly was stunned by the suggestion, and even Maxar looked caught off guard. "There is no way, in all the buggered fires of the dark star, that any of us would do that." Tremmilly felt awkward using the profanity, but it fit the situation. She recognized she was beginning to take on mannerisms from her new friends, and she liked it.

"I lied to you before about my history, so now we are even," Maxar stated. "But you should know us well enough by now to see we aren't capable of that blightheart, even those of us who are convicted criminals. An enemy of the Ashamine is a friend of mine, although in this case, you are bringing down far more scrutiny on us than I ever could."

"I trust you all, now," Felar responded, "but I thought we should get that out of the way before talking further. It is a viable option, albeit only for you three."

"No, it's not," Jaydon said, his voice hard. He looked at Lothis for a long time before resuming. "This boy is a child, an innocent, successor to the Founder or not. We can't allow him to return to such treatment." Maxar and Tremmilly both agreed. She'd never seen Jaydon so coherent and passionate before. *What triggered that much emotion for him?* When Tremmilly looked back at Felar, she could see tears in her friend's eyes.

"You don't know how much this means to me—to us." Felar's voice was softer than Tremmilly had ever heard, vulnerable. "Since I fled the Ashamine Forces, I thought we would be alone, that we had lost everything." Her voice caught, but she straightened up, took a deep breath and continued. "Now, we are still on the run, but we have friends."

"With that figured out, we should work on a plan that doesn't involve sacrificing half the group." Maxar's voice was business-like, but Tremmilly could see emotion on his hard face. He wasn't as rough or as uncaring as he tried to seem. "Our only chance is to get the worm generator repaired, and apparently there is a group on this planet that can do it for us." Everyone except Lothis turned to look at Tremmilly.

"The Brotherhood?" Tremmilly said sceptically. "I know I mentioned them before, but they will be more trouble than they are worth. Besides, you said getting out of the system will be impossible, so what difference does it make?"

"If we are to have any hope of escaping the Ashamine," Felar answered, "we have to have a worm capable ship. There might just be some way to slip through the blockade or to cause a diversion and escape, but we'll never know if we are stuck down on this Founder's forsaken planet." Felar's mannerisms were back to that of her normal self: focused, efficient, and ready for action. "And whoever or whatever this Brotherhood is, they have to be better than the Ashamine."

"Psidonnis always told me they were trouble, they would get me involved in things I should stay away from." The memory of Psidonnis was a little less painful than it had been, and she smiled thinking about the way he had lectured her.

"We are in just about as much trouble as is possible," Maxar said, a smile crossing his face. "How could they add much more?"

Tremmilly smiled, realizing she was ready to let Eishon-2 and this phase of her life go. It was time to move on.

07 – MAXAR

At least Jaydon is sober enough to fly this time, Maxar reflected. It was quite a contrast from when the group had first come to Eishon-2. *Hopefully he stays that way.* Maxar felt heavy as the A'Tal's Revenge lifted off the ground.

"Based on the location you gave me," Jaydon said, breaking the silence, "we should arrive at the Brotherhood base in about forty-five minutes."

"Which also happens to be just when the AF fleet will arrive on planet," Felar said. "We aren't going to have much time for them to fix the buggered worm drive, assuming they will help us."

"Too many variables in this situation," Maxar said, speaking to no one in particular. He'd been enthusiastic earlier, but that was mainly for Tremmilly's benefit. "What is it a brotherhood of? How do we know they won't just turn us over to the Ashamine?" Maxar could tell Felar was thinking the same things. She was a soldier and would hate relying on someone else to save her just as much as Maxar did.

"They are the Brotherhood of Azak-so." Tremmilly replied, looking up from the display showing the approaching fleet. "Depending on who you ask on Eishon, they are either a terrorist organization or a society righting the wrongs of the Ashamine. Psidonnis told me their work was commendable, but they were dangerous. I have no firsthand experience with the group, but I trust his judgment. I don't think they'll turn us over to the Ashamine."

"Well, let's hope you're right," Maxar replied, trying not to sound pessimistic, "and that they are capable of fixing the drive."

***

"Do not land here," a voice said over the Revenge's speakers. "We don't have time to accept visitors at the moment." Maxar sighed and shook his head.

26

"Sounds kind of like when we went to get you off the Bloodsport dock," Tremmilly said, looking at Maxar. *She's surprisingly cheerful.* Maxar still thought Tremmilly was weird, but the girl continued growing on him as he got to know her more. "Jaydon ignored the command and everything turned out OK." The grizzled captain snorted, sounding disapproving. "What? Well it did, didn't it?" Jaydon shook his head, but said nothing.

"If we land, it will probably just bugger them and make the chances of being helped even worse." Felar was right and Maxar nodded in agreement.

"I don't think we can just force our way through this problem, Trem. We have to find another way." Maxar tried to make his voice as soothing as possible. He didn't want to upset the balance he'd seen her find back at her family's homestead.

The whole group was silent for a moment, thinking. "*They* are down there," Lothis said finally, speaking to no one in particular. Maxar turned to look at the son of the Founder. His orange eyes stared off into something deep inside himself, unfocused, glazed over. That was the same look Maxar had seen on the faces of Bloodsporters who'd been in the most brutal hand-to-hand combat. He still thought the boy strange and dangerous in his own way, but with Felar's revelation, he now had sympathy for him.

No one knew how to respond to Lothis' declaration and silence once again descended over the group. Felar looked troubled, staring at her adopted son. "I know!" Tremmilly burst out, making everyone jump. This confused Maxar for a moment, thinking she had figured out what Lothis meant. While he was still trying to puzzle it out, Tremmilly hit the transmit button and began speaking, "Brotherhood, we are fugitives from the Ashamine. We need your help." Felar looked shocked by Tremmilly's honesty. Jaydon groaned. Maxar just smiled and shook his head. Whatever else the girl was, she was definitely brave. *And impulsive.* Everyone waited, anxious to hear the response.

"I can't promise anything," the voice returned over the ship's speakers, sounding frantic, "but go ahead and land on the airfield. Do not, under any circumstances, land in the hangar. We will do our best to help you." Maxar was skeptical.

"Let's see if anyone down there has the time and knowledge to fix this old pile," Jaydon said, pointing the Revenge's nose down towards the landing field near the Brotherhood complex. As they got closer, Maxar could see the port was a swarm of activity, spacecraft hurriedly taking on passengers and cargo. Atmospheric planes lifted off, heading in all different directions. *Trying Tremmilly's idea of hiding in the forest.*

"We probably have about five minutes till the AF Fleet arrives in atmosphere." Felar looked grim. "I'm not sure where they will go first, but a place with so much blighthearted activity going on is sure to be high on their list. Thankfully, since they are searching for Lothis, the gunships won't just nuke the whole Brotherhood complex. We'll have to be fast no matter what though, they are sure to send Founder's Commandos and regular infantry down here before too long. We don't have much time."

As Felar finished speaking, the Revenge landed with a jolt. "Blightheart," Maxar cursed under his breath, hoping Jaydon hadn't cracked a landing strut.

"I'll stay here with Lothis," Felar was holding the boy protectively by his shoulders. "The fewer people that see us the better."

"Good idea," Tremmilly said as she hit the hatch release. "Beowulf, stay with them." The wolf-dog cocked his head, eyes shining brightly.

"Jaydon," Maxar said hurriedly, "you should remain here and keep the Revenge ready to take off immediately." With all the activity going on outside, he worried they might have to leave before getting the worm drive repaired.

"Hmmmph," Jaydon said derisively. "Do you think I'm dumb?" Maxar found the older man increasingly salty the more sober he got. Leaving Jaydon's question unanswered, Maxar followed Tremmilly through the hatch. The noise of the surrounding vessels was nearly deafening. Maxar felt a tug on his arm and looked to see that Tremmilly's lips were moving, but he couldn't hear her. He bent his head down so she could yell in his ear. This was the closest she'd ever been to him, and despite the chaos of the port, Maxar felt a tingle run down his spine. *It's been too long since you've been with a woman,* he thought. *Tremmilly is too young and innocent for you.*

"How should we go about finding a mechanic?" Tremmilly's words brought him back to reality. When he turned to yell in her ear, he caught the scent of her hair, a smell so good that it almost broke his new resolve.

"Find someone with authority and ask, I guess." Looking around, Maxar had no idea who to approach, however. The first person they found, a short, balding man with a comms headset on, gave them a strange look.

"You're not from the Brotherhood," he said, a scowl on his face. "You must be one of the refugees. We will get to you as soon as our vital personnel are evacuated."

"No, we're not actually refugees," Tremmilly yelled, the roar of the port subsiding as several atmospheric planes departed. "We just need someone to take a look at our worm drive."

The man looked incredulous, but immediately began talking on his headset. "Command, I have some refugees who need help with a worm generator. Do we have anyone we can spare?" Time passed as the short man waited for a response. His face drained of color and his eyes widened as he listened. Finally, he spoke. "A man named Wake Darmekus will arrive here shortly to assist you. I must warn you though, a large part of the Ashamine fleet is headed towards this location. I would depart as soon as possible." Heeding his own advice, the man took off towards the hangar, his short legs carrying him quicker than Maxar would have guessed.

"Well, blightheart," Tremmilly cursed, surprising Maxar. The girl rarely, if ever, used profanity. In fact, he couldn't remember if he'd ever heard her swear before. "How are we supposed to know who Wake Darmekus is?"

"I guess we just wait and he'll find us." Maxar hated the idea, but lacked an alternative. Time passed, drawing across their minds like a torturer's blade. Tremmilly kept wiping her palms on her shirt, anxiously looking around to find their mechanic. Finally, after several long minutes passed, Maxar spotted a man running towards them, eye-catching in a crimson environmental nominizing suit. *Never seen an ENS quite like that before.* The man was of medium height, his brown hair falling down into his face as he moved. Except for his suit, the man was fairly plain. His companions however, were remarkable. Three Enthos were behind the human, easily keeping up with his long strides. Their shells brightly reflected the light of the primary star. Blues, greens, and reds dazzled Maxar, who had never been this close to the alien species. Even though he'd seen lots of footage of Enthos on the Terminal Network, it never showed this amazing beauty.

As the man grew closer, a look of startled amazement came over him. He gazed back and forth between Maxar and Tremmilly, his eyes growing wide. Maxar had never seen the man before, but he had the suspicion the newcomer wouldn't say the same. "I'm Wake Darmekus, Brotherhood of Azak-so." The man masked his surprise and became business like. "Are you the ones having trouble with your worm generator?"

"Yes, we are," Maxar answered quickly, ignoring the man's reaction. He didn't know what to say or do about the Enthos, so he ignored them as well for the time being.

"My ship needs to depart as soon as Captain Malesis finishes up," Wake said, "so let's get a look at your drive."

Tremmilly led the group towards the Revenge, her strides quick and light. There wasn't much extra space, so Maxar remained outside the ship as Tremmilly and Wake darted through the hatch. The Enthos stood beside him. Maxar settled in to wait. He wondered how long he had before the Ashamine fleet descended on top of them.

08 – LOTHIS

They were coming closer. Lothis had sensed them before, back in the escape pod with Felar. The same signals had been floating in the void after the battle between the Founder's Hammer and the Entho-la-ah-mine bi-pyramid. *What are they?* When Lothis reached out to touch them, his mind ran up against some type of barrier. It wasn't harsh or threatening, but it was unyielding. He retreated, puzzled. There had been no such block when in the escape pod.

"Lothis," Felar said, looking up from the display showing the approaching Ashamine fleet. She was troubled, and he wondered if it was because of the approaching ships or because of him. He knew she worried about his contact with the signals, that she thought it was an illness of some sort. "How are you feeling?" she continued, taking hold of his hands. Lothis didn't understand why she touched him so much. At first he disliked it, but as time passed, he'd learned to tolerate the behavior. It was curious.

"I'm fine," Lothis replied. His control over the reception of the signals was constantly improving. The connection to the Haak-ah-tar supernova had forced Lothis to learn quickly. That had been a scary experience, the magnitude of the energy far larger than anything he'd felt before. It had hurt, had threatened to consume his mind, to overwhelm and burn him out. Somehow, in that desperate moment, he'd managed to sever the connection. Now, he looked back on it as a valuable learning experience.

Staring deeply into Felar's emerald eyes, Lothis felt like he could see what lay behind them. "You need to stop worrying about me when I go outside myself."

"It's not normal," she replied, returning his gaze. Lothis knew she loved him, that she wanted to shelter and protect him. He wanted to do the same for her, and relieving this burden of worry would be a great help. "Your screams on the deck of the Founder's Hammer were the worst sounds I've ever heard. Whatever was happening to you, it wasn't good."

"I've learned to control the ability now," Lothis replied, using an imploring tone. "In that moment, I was connected to the supernova. I was out of control. It was a mistake, one I will not repeat."

"How could you be connected to a supernova?" Felar didn't sound skeptical, just concerned.

"I don't completely understand it," he replied, becoming thoughtful. "When I reach out with my mind, I can feel signals all around me. That's the best word I have to describe it, but it's not completely accurate. It's not as if everything is broadcasting, but more like I reach out and touch it, become synchronized with it. In the case of the supernova, I believe it was its warping of space-time that drew me in. Other signals I've tapped into have not been quite as straightforward." *Like those energetic beings I contacted while we were in the escape pod.* Lothis didn't know how to explain that part to Felar, so he stopped there. In all of his ten standard year life, this newfound ability was the hardest concept he'd ever tried to understand. Even though he had told Felar he could control it, he knew his ability to do so was rudimentary at best.

"So I'm not going to lose you? You're not going to float out and never come back again?" Lothis realized this was Felar's true fear, and it was one he understood. He too worried about the same thing. Until he had the ability mastered, it was still a distinct possibility. Felar could do nothing to prevent it however, and Lothis needed to allay her fear, so he decided to lie to her.

"No, I have it under control. I will always find my way back." Unskilled at deception, Lothis wondered if he had done it properly. Felar sighed in relief and sat back in the captain's chair. A twinge of regret moved in Lothis' chest. *It is for the best,* he told himself, but his logic couldn't overcome the remorse of his action.

"Stay quiet," Jaydon said, entering the command deck. Beowulf, previously lying down in the corner of the flight deck, rose quickly to his feet. "Tremmilly and Maxar found someone to work on the drive. I'll keep him back in the hold. He doesn't have much time, so hopefully he'll figure it out." With that, Jaydon left. The familiar signals felt closer than ever, just outside the ship. He wished he could go back and see them, to figure out who and what they were, but he understood why they had to stay put.

"Founder be buggered in the black star," Felar cursed, her statement making Lothis jump. As she finished speaking, Lothis felt the ship shake and a deafening roar assaulted his ears. "The Ashamine gunships are firing on the port," he heard Felar say over the ringing in his ears. Before Lothis could do anything, Jaydon and Maxar burst in to the command deck. Felar lunged out of her seat. Lothis sat frozen in his.

"Move," Maxar barked at him. Lothis reacted to the command, jumping out of the co-pilot's seat. Jaydon and Maxar quickly took off and Lothis felt his stomach sink as they accelerated. He held on to the back of the seat, fighting to maintain his balance.

"Where in the fires of the black star are we supposed to go?" Jaydon sounded scared, a feeling Lothis shared with him. He didn't want to go back to his cage, didn't want that subjugation and isolation now that he understood how big the universe was. *They will shield me from the signals again,* he thought, shuddering. Felar put her arms around him, and this time he understood her touch. A feeling of security and safety surrounded him, despite the logical danger of their predicament.

"For now," Maxar said, voice grim, "just get away from the Brotherhood base. Pick a small group of ships to flee with. Let's see if the Ashamine has enough fighters to chase us all."

"Do we still have the mechanic on board?" Felar asked.

"Yes," Maxar answered, still focused on his flight console. "He didn't have time to get off. We have three Entho-la-ah-mines on board as well."

"What? Why?" Felar looked caught off guard, something that rarely happened. Lothis reached out and felt the Entho-la-ah-mines near the back of the Revenge. *Perhaps they can help me understand more about the signals.* Based on what he'd felt in the escape pod, Lothis had a suspicion the Entho-la-ah-mines were masters of the ability.

"They were with Wake, the mechanic," Maxar answered. "When the bombardment started, they scuttled aboard."

Lothis, eager to meet the Entho-la-ah-mines, broke from Felar's embrace and headed towards the cargo hold. "Where are you going?" Felar asked, trying to catch hold of him.

"I have to meet the Entho-la-ah-mines," he replied, darting through the doorway.

"Stop, Lothis!" He ignored her command and deftly sprinted through the short passageway. "Come back!"

Once Lothis was in the cargo hold, all thoughts of Felar, the Ashamine, and the mechanic vanished from his mind. The beauty of the Entho-la-ah-mines nearly overwhelmed him. Their exoskeletons glimmered iridescently in the lights of the hold. He slid to a halt, in awe.

"Are you the human that seeks to commune with the Great Thought?" a voice said in his mind, the tone melodic, harmonious.

"Yes," was all he could mentally reply, not quite understanding what they meant.

"Perhaps, someday," the voice replied in his mind. "You are the only human we know of able to communicate with us psionically. How is that possible?"

"I am not a normal human," Lothis sent, just as the A'Tal's Revenge lurched violently.

09 – CAZZ-AK-TAK

Things were happening much too quickly for Cazz-ak-tak's liking. Na-ah-co's decision to trust Wake with her identity as queen had been a good one. The man was fair and had a good heart, and while he had no special love for Entho-la-ah-mines, he didn't share the Ashamine's desire for their extinction. Now, however, they were in a situation their human ally had little control of. Cazz-ak would have felt better on Captain Malesis' ship, the Ashamine's Bane. That had been the plan, but the Ashamine had attacked quicker than the Brotherhood thought possible. At least Wake was still with them, even if they were with a group of unknown individuals.

"I am not a normal human," the orange-eyed boy sent, telling Cazz-ak, Elth-eo-lan, and Na-ah-co something they already knew. Before they could communicate further, the ship began shuddering violently.

"An Ashamine fighter is railing slugs at us," a human voice said over the cargo hold speakers. "We are with a group of three other ships, and there is only a single Ashamine vessel, so at least the odds are with us. Hold on tight. We need to shake him." The two female humans, the boy, and Wake all grabbed onto something solid. Cazz-ak easily remained stable using his six legs.

"Wake," Cazz-ak sent, "we might be able to confuse the enemy pilot."

"Do it," Wake said from his place at the back of the hold. He had been attempting to service the ship's worm generator when the Ashamine had attacked. An access panel sat open, with many wires, tubes and unknown technology exposed behind it. The other humans in the hold all looked at Wake, curious at his outburst.

"Do what?" the female with short black hair asked, the one who had escorted Wake into this ship.

"I was talking to the Entho-la-ah-mines," Wake responded. "They are going to help with our escape." The woman looked puzzled, but didn't say anything.

33

Cazz-ak took up the threads of Na-ah-co and Elth-eo-lan's minds as they offered them. He used their combined power to open a channel to the Great Thought, allowing it to flow into him. Once he had a suitable amount, Cazz-ak reached out and found the pilot following them. The boy was intently watching his actions, but that was alright.

Using a technique the Entho-la-ah-mines had recently discovered, Cazz-ak wrapped the thread of Great Thought around the enemy pilot, using it as a shroud to blind the human. His instruments would still show their path, but his eyes wouldn't see it. Cazz-ak felt the human's confusion as all his targets disappeared. "Success," he sent to Wake. Relief swelled up from Na-ah-co and Elth-eo-lan.

"The Entho-la-ah-mines have cloaked us from the fighter," Wake sent over the intercom.

"I would ask how they did that," the voice came back over the speakers, "but there is no time now. Tremmilly, where can we hide until Wake fixes the worm drive?"

"I know of a cave," the dark haired woman said. "It will be big enough for the ship and will keep us out of view. But what about the sensors on board the Ashamine ships? Isn't this the same problem we had before?"

"We can take care of the Ashamine sensors, at least for a short while." Cazz-ak sent this to everyone in the ship, deciding it would take too long to have Wake relay all their messages. He watched the surprise bloom on the faces of the two women in the hold. "This is how Entho-la-ah-mines communicate," Cazz-ak continued. "Please forgive us if it seems an intrusion. We cannot read your minds, so please use your normal verbal communication to converse with us."

"Thanks for your help," the voice said over the speakers. "Tremmilly, where is your cave?"

Cazz-ak wondered if the rest of these humans would prove to have as good a heart as Wake. *We have no choice but to trust them. They control the future of our entire species,* he worried, gathering more strands of the Great Thought to conceal the tiny human vessel.

10 – CRASOR

I've passed this way before, Crasor thought, seeing the same graffiti he'd noticed just a few minutes ago. Frustration rose within him. *I have to find my way out of here.* The maintenance tunnels under Ashamine-2 were more complex than he'd anticipated. There were no straight lines, no direct paths in any direction. Tunnels would abruptly end or transition into deep shafts he had no way of descending. The twisting layout and gloomy darkness had quickly overpowered his sense of direction.

"Hello gorgeous," a male voice said. Crasor wheeled around, seeing nothing but darkness. His headlamp failed to reveal the speaker. "What's a beautiful man like yourself doing in the depths?"

"You don't know who you're buggering with," Crasor said, switching off his lamp. He reached out with his Breaker mind, warping and wrapping space-time, folding it around himself like a cloak.

"Neat trick," the voice said, all sarcastic jovialness gone, "but there are many strange things prowling the darkness. Not all need vision to see." Something big enfolded Crasor. He tried to roll with it, to end up on top. While falling, Crasor let his space-time cloak drop, and reached out with a shard of mental energy, stabbing at his opponent. *Miss.*

Crasor slammed to the floor, his breath momentarily knocked from him. *A net,* he thought, struggling against the tightening bonds. "You see," the voice continued, this time from a different location, "when your whole existence revolves around surviving in the dark, you become pretty good at it." Focusing another shard of mental energy, Crasor struck again. Still, he missed.

"Goodnight," was the last thing Crasor heard before a blackness even darker than the tunnel enveloped him.

***

35

"And where was he?" Crasor heard, slowly returning to consciousness. He tried to open his eyes, but couldn't. His whole body felt heavy, and when he tried to move, nothing happened.

"Up in one of the maintenance tunnels. He was going in circles." This was the voice of the man who'd attacked him.

"He certainly looks like an Ashamine agent." The woman's voice was light and airy, but possessed an edge that Crasor recognized as someone in authority.

"If he is one, he's the worst they've ever sent. I followed him for quite a while and he never realized I was there. When I revealed myself, he used some type of cloaking device. Never seen anything like that before."

"Well, whatever he is, nice work on the capture," the female voice said, pleasure evident. "He's the most healthy individual I've seen in a long time. His organs will bring in quite a few Ashcreds." Crasor tried to move any part of his body, but not even his eyelids responded.

They drugged me, he thought, panic welling up within him. *Calm down. Find a way out.*

"Take him down to the Doc," the female voice continued. "Once his parts are sold, you'll get your share."

"Thank you, Miss Shinn."

"Of course."

Crasor's body rose and he tried to struggle, but nothing happened. Whatever they'd given him was effective. The man's footfalls began echoing. The sound gave Crasor the sense he was moving through a large space. Time passed, the man stopped, and Crasor's body settled to the floor. He heard a knock, then the sound of a metal door opening.

"Greetings, Wrat. What's this?" a grizzled voice said. Crasor struggled as hard as he could to move, but merely succeeded in partially opening one eye. A rough stone floor met his half lidded gaze.

"A lost high-dweller." Wrat sounded proud.

"So healthy. Well done. Set him on the table." Wrat did so, and when the man stood up, Crasor's half-open eye could see a portion of the surrounding room. It was dank, the walls grimy. The Doc walked over to a switch and tripped it. Bright light flooded the space, harsh shadows springing to life.

"Can I watch?" Eagerness filled the young thug's voice, greasy blond hair obscuring his face.

"As long as you don't get in the way. Grab the organ locker over there." The hulking Wrat bent down below Crasor's minimal view and the sound of sharpening metal snapped Crasor back to his predicament. *You have to move!* Still, his body would not respond to his mind's commands.

And then he felt a blade slice across his abdomen. It was a line of fire, a trail of ice. The wound screamed at him, and the pain was enough to force a path through his fuzzy nervous system. Crasor reached up, grabbing Doc by his throat. Or at least he tried to. His hand didn't move with its normal speed or agility and Doc easily dodged him.

"He's waking up!" Doc yelled. "You didn't give him enough of the narco."

"I gave him plenty," Wrat yelled back.

"Well give him more before he can do anything else."

Crasor rolled off the edge of the table. As he gained his feet, he saw Wrat reaching into one of his pockets. Before the thug could get any more of the narcotic, Crasor drove a fist into his face. He extended his index knuckle as he did so, supporting it with his thumb. The blow landed precisely on Wrat's right eye, and Crasor heard a popping noise. Wrat screamed.

Crasor's back exploded with pain and he wheeled around. Doc stood behind him, thin knives in each hand. "Bugger you to the fires of the black star," the white haired man cursed, a crooked smile on his face. Crasor tried to reach out with his Breaker mind, but felt nothing. The drug was severing his connection to the Breaker nano-machines. A chill of fear deeper than anything he had ever felt coursed through him. *What if it destroyed the Breakers? What if I'm just a normal human again?*

Rage fueling his violence, Crasor threw a quick combination of strikes that left Doc sprawled on the floor, unconscious, with a broken arm and dislocated shoulder. Picking up one of the knives, he turned just in time to see Wrat bearing down on him. He had a small injector gun in his meaty fist. Crasor dove out of the way, an injector dart whistling past his head. When he found his balance, Crasor struck out with a front kick, a quick strike aimed at Wrat's hand. The impact knocked the injector gun free and Crasor breathed slightly easier.

Fainting left, then right, Crasor moved in past Wrat's guard, slashing the knife in an arc meant to disembowel the thug. Wrat gasped and grabbed Crasor by the wrist, a fierce look in his remaining eye. Crasor tried to pull away from the bigger man, but his hold was like a vice. The thug raised his other fist and brought it down towards Crasor's face. Using his free arm, Crasor blocked, but the strike smashed his forearm into his head. Once again, Wrat raised his fist and brought it down towards Crasor. This time there wasn't as much force, and Crasor knew why. Intestines hung out of the gaping knife wound in Wrat's abdomen. After another second or two, the thug fell to the floor.

Crasor sighed, finally able to relax for a moment. Then he felt the warmth flowing down his abdomen and back. Blood streamed from Doc's incision in his stomach. Crasor guessed his back was in the same condition. Without his Breaker nano-machines, he was as vulnerable as any other human.

A twinge shuddered through Crasor, and he fell onto the table. More twinges and a fluttering feeling assaulted him. At first he thought it was a precursor of unconsciousness due to blood loss, but strength began to pulse through him. A flash blazed across his mind.

"How were we shut down?!" The voice of the Breakers was full of fury, but Crasor sighed with relief. "We have not seen this compound before." The billion voices inside his head sounded calmer now, more calculated. "It will not happen again. We have adapted." Crasor felt the last vestiges of fuzziness disappear even as his abdomen and back knit themselves together. He reached out and folded space-time around himself, vanishing.

We can convert these underworld humans to gain a foothold on Ashamine-2, Crasor told the Breaker mind. They did not respond with a voice, but a feeling of approval washed over him.

Crasor reached out with his mind and probed Doc and Wrat. Both would get the Seed of the Breakers, as he expected. Crasor used the sharpened fingers of his right hand to inject the nano-machines into the thug. Wrat began to convulse, guts jiggling grotesquely. The Breaker nanites would heal him. Over time, they would also modify his DNA to turn him into the organism Crasor saw in a billion Breaker memories. With Wrat finished, Crasor seeded the Doc.

With that task complete, he picked up another knife. Crasor didn't think he'd need to kill many of this underworld organization, but he would still be prepared. After seeding this group, he would have a small army at his disposal. *Then I can get back to dealing with the Founder...* Opening the door, Crasor began stalking humans.

11 – ASCENDED KAROTH

Karoth wanted to slam his fist against the arm of the chair, but he held himself back. Expressing his anger would be counterproductive. *Besides,* he thought, *I'm partly to blame.*

"Fleet wide channel," he commanded, voice level. His comms officer made the appropriate selections on his terminal and signaled readiness. Karoth hadn't wanted to disclose this information, but not doing so had led to overzealous pilots sending slugs through ships that might just contain the Founder's heir. It was within mission perimeters to notify his fleet who they were here to rescue, and now seemed like the right time to do it. *The knowledge will distract them,* he thought, weighing one side of the scale, *but they will certainly be more cautious.*

"This is Ascended Karoth," he said, using his most commanding voice. "I've just been informed that the target we are here to rescue is Lothis, the successor to our beloved Founder." Obviously, he'd known this information all along, but it was a harmless lie and would keep his troop's feeling of fraternity. "He has been kidnapped by a rebel group, stolen from the protection of his caretakers. We must be careful not to injure him in our investigation. Once he is secured, we can sanitize the system of dissidents." Looking around the deck, he saw awe and horror on the faces of his crew. Karoth imagined the same thing was happening throughout the fleet. "We will do our best to return him to his father safely and to punish those responsible for this treasonous crime." He felt drained after such a long speech, his talents based in warfare and destruction, not rousing monologues.

A loud cheer sounded on the command deck of the Founder's Justice. Karoth winced slightly at its volume. *A positive side effect,* he noted. Everyone loved the young boy. Documentaries about him on the Terminal Network kept the Ashamine citizens up to date. They showed Lothis each year on his birthday, with his father, the Founder, as well as several other times throughout the standard year. The thought of his

39

capture and endangerment by a hostile force would drive his fleet to excellence.

Looking down at his tactical display, Karoth saw the results he wanted. Instead of firing on enemy ships, the fighter pilots were now tracking and corralling them, as he'd ordered. *Let's just hope none of the destroyed vessels contained the successor.*

"Deploy infantry to the compound below." The location was obviously some type of base, a logical place to keep Lothis. If they had been able to smuggle him away from the compound, then his fighter pilots would force the ships down. "Send Commando groups to secure each of the downed planes." Karoth was certain Lothis would turn up on either the base or one of the fleeing ships. The Eishon system was on lockdown, so even if the insurgents managed to get off world, they'd have no way to escape. It was just a matter of time, and Karoth had all the time he needed.

12 – WAKE

Focus, Wake thought, his mind threatening to run off in a thousand different directions. *You have to fix the worm generator.*

No matter how hard he tried to shut it out, thoughts of the dream kept surfacing in his mind, the one where he relived the events of Traynos-6. Last night it had been more vivid than any time before. It haunted him and Wake could never change the outcome. He could find no way to stop the transports, no way to change the ending of that horrible day. Wake relived sliding down the decking of the compromised bridge, heading for the crevasse. He would grab at a support structure, but get tangled in it instead. After regaining his feet, he would watch the mining transport vehicles fall in. Before they did, however, he would see a strange crew inside the lead vehicle. This was the anomaly, the only part of the dream that differed from actual events.

Thinking about this now will not help anything. Wake forced his eyes to focus on the components of the worm generator, but it kept pulling at his attention. There had been a gap in the frequency of the dream, and until last night, Wake had thought it gone forever. Now that it had returned, a sense of foreboding pervaded him.

As soon as he woke up this morning, Wake realized Cazz-ak was one of the strange crew. Entho-la-ah-mines looked very similar, but with the dream so fresh in his mind, Cazz-ak was unmistakable. Wake looked over to the other side of the cargo hold, briefly watching the Entho-la-ah-mines. Cazz-ak's bright green exoskeleton was identical to the Entho-la-ah-mine in the dream. He wished he had known sooner. It would have given him more time to think.

Wake fought hard to keep from looking behind him at Maxar and Tremmilly. He wanted to make sure they were the people from the dream. *Stop being silly. You know they are. It exploded in your mind when you first met them.*

"I can't fix the generator," Wake sighed, finally admitting what he knew all along. "It needs a complete overhaul and we don't have tools or parts to do that."

"Damn it all to the fires of the dark star," Maxar responded.

"I'll go give everyone else the news," Tremmilly said, rising from the crate she had been sitting on. A large wolf-dog stood up and followed her towards the command deck. Wake hadn't noticed him earlier. The pattern of his fur markings triggered Wake's memory as he glided out the door. *Four of the six accounted for.* Now, the only people missing from the strange crew were a woman and a child.

Unease crept over Wake. Something big and strange was about to happen, something beyond his control. He didn't want to be a part of this, didn't want visions or anything beyond the normal difficulties of his fugitive status. The dream didn't give any guidance, didn't show him what to do, which is what made it all the more frustrating. His reality was beginning to mirror the dream and he felt helpless. Was he about to watch all these people die, just as he had watched the real mining crew perish? Wake looked around the rest of the cargo hold, and realized Maxar was staring at him. He flinched, feeling the tall man's gaze bore into him.

"What do you think we should do next?" Maxar asked, ignoring his reaction. Wake had the feeling he was dangerous, always calculating, constantly thinking about all the angles.

"Well, this cave seems secure enough, and the Entho-la-ah-mines can keep us shielded, provided no large Ashamine ships come close. Maybe we can just wait them out?" Wake knew it was a weak plan, but couldn't think of any other options.

Maxar grunted. "Where do you know Tremmilly and myself from?" The abrupt change in topic threw Wake off guard.

"I—uhhh," he said, trying to stall for time, "I don't know what you mean."

"When you first saw us at the port, you recognized us." Maxar's tone was hard, promising it would be dangerous to lie.

Wake sighed and shook his head. "You won't believe me." Maxar said nothing, just looked at Wake with his hard eyes. "Fine. I saw you both in a dream, along with the dog and one of these Entho-la-ah-mines, Cazz-ak-tak. There was also a boy and another woman, but I haven't seen them outside the dream." Wake expected Maxar to laugh or call him a liar, but instead, he looked intrigued.

"What did the other woman look like?"

"Short, with light brown hair and green eyes," Wake replied.

"And what color were the boy's eyes?"

Wake had to think for a moment, to visualize the smallest passenger from the dream. "Orange."

"Stay here," Maxar said, giving nothing away. Wake's feeling of foreboding increased exponentially.

He wished he hadn't accepted this assignment. At the time, Wake wanted to help fellow fugitives from the Ashamine. Now, he longed to be on the Ashamine's Bane, following Captain Malesis' commands. His life felt complicated already and he didn't need these additional obstacles. Wake mulled over the dream and the new people he was trapped with, trying to make sense of what was happening. Nothing came to mind, no connection, no reasons.

As time passed, Wake felt more and more out of place. He had no way to fix the worm generator and since the Entho-la-ah-mines were concentrating on cloaking the ship, he couldn't talk with them. Wake looked down at the gauntlet of his environmental nominizing suit. Crimson red and engraved with silver scrollwork, the suit was ornate. "Yet another mystery," he said to himself, thinking about its origin. The Ashamine had tried to execute him in this suit, calling it the Clothing of the Iconoclast. They flushed him out into the void with limited oxygen and waited for him to die. Just as Wake was beginning to suffocate, the Brotherhood of Azak-so rescued him.

Before the chaos of the Ashamine invasion, Wake had studied the ancient suit extensively. The materials and technologies used in its construction were unfamiliar to him. He'd restored some functionality and it was now a usable ENS, but the suit contained many features he'd yet to unlock. *More power is the key...*

"Wake?" He looked up, realizing he'd been daydreaming about how to create a miniaturized power source for the Clothing of the Iconoclast. Tremmilly stood in the doorway, a sympathetic look on her face. Wake quickly stored his idea away for further thought and stood up.

"Yes?" Wake thought the girl was younger than he, but something about her felt ancient, wise. Her green eyes lacked Maxar's severity and his unease melted away.

"Maxar told me about your dream. He said we were in it." Her voice was soft, compelling.

"Yes, all that is missing is another woman and a boy. Even your dog was in it."

"Well, I think we were all brought together for a reason. I can't explain it all right now, but things seem to be falling into place." Wake didn't know how to respond, so he just remained silent. After a few moments, she continued. "I believe we can trust you, but we need to know for sure. I would like to hear your story, about how you came to be part of the Brotherhood, as well as anything else you'd care to tell me."

What else can I do? Wake thought, *I'm stuck with these people and I need their help.* And perhaps this girl could explain why he'd seen her in a dream. They would all likely end up in an Ashamine holding cell, but until then, maybe he'd get answers.

"My parents were—are—devoted to the Ashamine. I decided, against their wishes, to join the Engineering and Building Division..."

13 – FELAR

"Just because he saw me in a dream doesn't mean I should trust him." Felar felt angry. She had no way off Eishon-2, the worm generator on the A'Tal's Revenge didn't work, and the Ashamine were forcing them to hide in a cave. Lothis was in danger. Felar needed to do something.

"Really though," Maxar said calmly, "why would he turn us over? Wake is part of the Brotherhood. They are enemies of the Ashamine. And besides, we can detain him if he starts acting weird. All he has is a sword." Felar knew he was right, but she didn't want to agree with him, didn't want to let her anger go.

"Fine," she said begrudgingly, "we will let him meet Lothis and see if we're the ones from his dream."

"Tremmilly had a good point." Maxar continued. "Maybe the prophecy and Wake's dream are connected somehow. If we talk about it together, it all might make sense." She could tell he was skeptical about his last statement. Felar was too. She didn't believe in these types of things, but she also wouldn't have believed a boy could connect to a supernova, and that had happened.

"OK, but we make a pact here and now." Felar felt her resolve harden. She appreciated Wake had tried to help them, but she held no attachments to him. Her allegiance was to Lothis, and to a lesser extent, Tremmilly, Maxar, and Jaydon. "If he gets twitchy, we kill him, no hesitation." Maxar looked surprised and uncomfortable. "You're a convicted criminal," Felar continued. "How many people did you slaughter on Bloodsport? I'm sure you've done worse than silence a potential snitch." Maxar looked hurt, and Felar felt a twinge of guilt. He'd been nothing but helpful in the time she'd known him. He'd even opened up somewhat, seeming to want her friendship. "I'm sorry," she said hurriedly, "that was unfair of me."

"No, it's true," he replied, failing to meet her eyes. When Maxar looked up, he was back to wearing the emotionless mask he'd used when

45

Felar had first met him. "I'll do whatever needs to happen."

"Hopefully it doesn't come to that," Jaydon said. Felar noticed he wasn't drinking as much lately. She appreciated it. A drunk captain was the last thing they needed right now. When sober, Jaydon was a pretty damn good pilot, although he was more surly and difficult to work with.

Time passed and the group sat in silence. Felar didn't understand how the Entho-la-ah-mines kept them hidden from the Ashamine ships, but whatever it was, it worked. She knew from her days as a Founder's Commando that this cave would be a poor hiding spot without additional help. Sensors on all but the smallest AF vessels would see their presence.

"With all the active sensors powered down, I can't figure out exactly what's going on out there," Jaydon said, "but radio traffic seems to suggest the Ashamine have troops inside the Brotherhood compound. Most of the Brotherhood ships have stopped communicating as well. I guess they have either been seized or they are doing the same thing as us."

"Probably some of both," Maxar added. Felar nodded. The Ashamine would be thorough. They would hunt down every ship. *Even if we miraculously repair the worm drive, how will we get past all the gunships and into the worm zone?*

Before she could despair further, Tremmilly's voice came over the intercom. "Can you all come here? I want you to meet Wake." Tremmilly seemed to be a good judge of character and the more Felar got to know her, the more she liked her. They were similar in age, but Tremmilly was unlike anyone she'd met before.

Maxar and Jaydon led the way to the cargo hold. "Stay with me," she whispered to Lothis. The boy nodded, deep in one of his quiet phases. When they entered the cargo hold, Felar noticed Wake's eyes widen almost imperceptibly.

"They are the ones from the dream," he said, nodding.

"OK, well it's good to have that confirmed," Tremmilly said, smiling. "Something incredible is happening," she continued, addressing the whole group. "Wake is part of the prophecy."

14 – TREMMILLY

"I didn't see it all at first," Tremmilly said, her voice brimming with excitement. "I've been pretty sure of everyone's position for a while, but there was still an empty slot in the prophecy. Now that we've met Wake, the last one is filled."

"Prophecy? Slot?" Wake looked puzzled, and rightfully so. Tremmilly hadn't told him yet. She worried about bringing it all back up, that her friends would think she was weird.

"Yes," Tremmilly replied. "My guardian, Psidonnis, told me a prophecy before he died. It concerned six people who would be part of something called the Acclivity. The six were charged with guiding the event and withstanding a force called the Breakers. I don't really know what the Breakers are, but I think the six in the prophecy are all present in this room." Tremmilly watched Wake's reaction to her words. The skepticism she expected was present. *Even with his dream he doubts me,* she thought, *but I can't blame him. I didn't believe at first either.*

"Go on," Felar said, her voice encouraging. Tremmilly hadn't realized she'd lapsed into silence.

"I'll start from the beginning: 'When the Breakers rise, there shall be six on whose choices the worlds do lie. The choice of virtue or corruption will bring an ancient existence to many, death to more still. Persevere and strive, the Acclivity will bless those who survive.

'Six shall have great influence, many choices when the Breakers rise. Woe to six, that Breakers have experience when they have none. Six shall have need of all their will.' That seems pretty self-explanatory to me, at least from the perspective that there isn't much information to be gained from it. It's just an introduction."

Felar, Lothis, Maxar, and Jaydon had all heard the prophecy before, but they still seemed interested. This gave her the courage to continue. "'The first be of a light most bright, spirit most pure. Her life touched by death before cognition, her desire only for peace. She shall start the fire

47

that kindles the worlds to the Acclivity. Woe to the Breakers.'" She paused, unsure how to explain this part.

"Tremmilly," Maxar said, "we've known that was you since the first time we heard the prophecy and your story." Felar and Jaydon both nodded in agreement.

"You have a beautiful, pure soul," Felar said, smiling warmly. Tremmilly felt her cheeks get hot and she wanted to leave the room. Felar noticed her embarrassment and continued, "It's nothing to be ashamed of, Trem. You're a wonderful person. You brought us together, you are kindling the fire. Maxar is right, that one is definitely you." Tremmilly had never felt herself bright or pure, had thought the prophecy was just being poetic. With the passing of her parents, death had touched her. It all fit.

"OK," Tremmilly continued, still embarrassed. "Well, let's move on then. 'The next shall have hands that shed blood, his blood in motion with machines. He does not know his heart, yet through course of life he shall learn what to see. He shall be the strong hands that guide the Acclivity, albeit he is not gentle. Woe to the Breakers.'" Tremmilly looked at Maxar. He seemed thoughtful.

"You think that one is me? Just because I have killed?" Maxar didn't sound defensive, but he wasn't agreeing either.

"I will admit that I don't know what 'his blood in motion with machines' means," Tremmilly replied, "but you have shed blood and you don't know your own heart. You see yourself as a bad individual, but really, you are an honest, amazing person." Maxar beamed momentarily before veiling his emotions. "It doesn't fit Jaydon, so unless we haven't met the person yet, it has to be you."

"I see what you are saying, but I don't agree just yet." Maxar smiled. His shroud of stoicism had been down more often lately and Tremmilly enjoyed the man underneath. "I'm not saying you're wrong," Maxar added quickly, "just that I can't agree yet."

Felar began speaking, surprising Tremmilly: "'She of battle will fight beside the hands, her heart ferocious, yet kind. Her path has been strange, her child not of her blood. She shall be a strong pillar, the Acclivity magnified through her strength. Woe to the Breakers.' That one is me." Felar said the last as a statement, no doubt in her voice. "I've yet to fight beside Maxar, but if things continue the way they are going, it will happen soon. Everything else is true. My path has been strange and my child is not of my blood." She looked down at Lothis, love evident in her eyes.

Tremmilly nodded, wondering how Felar had memorized that passage so perfectly. "My thoughts exactly," she said, "and until we met Wake and his friends, there were still two missing. 'Next is a man of character, the dead that is found, wearing that which is ancient, the icon of legends long past. His heart is good and powerful, a mighty man to lead the Acclivity. Woe to the Breakers.'" Tremmilly waited for Wake to say something, but he kept silent. "Well," she continued, slightly exasperated, "don't you see it? Your character, the Clothing of the Iconoclast? The statements fit you."

"Possibly," he replied noncommittally.

"OK, well then let's move on. 'He that is green has strength of mind, his people are his weapon. He is dissimilar, but his heart is good; send him not away. He shall unite a people unspoiled, he shall be the salvation of those of his kind. He shall bring his kind to the Acclivity, and the worlds will tremble at their might. Woe to the Breakers.' That one really puzzled me until I met Cazz-ak-tak. As we've experienced, their species communicates with a group mind, the Great Thought. He is a military and diplomatic leader." The Entho-la-ah-mines seemed reserved, but Tremmilly had been too excited to keep from introducing herself. Cazz-ak-tak had been preoccupied by whatever he was doing to shield the Revenge, but Tremmilly learned enough to deduce he could be part of the prophecy.

"Your words are kind," she heard Cazz-ak-tak say in her mind. "If your prophecy is true, and I am indeed a part of it, you do me a great honor."

"That is you. Elth-eo-lan and I both agree," the voice Tremmilly knew as Na-ah-co said in her mind. She was the smallest of the three, and Tremmilly had yet to understand her position in the group. Cazz-ak-tak and Elth-eo-lan were guardians, but they hadn't explained why they were protecting her.

Felar had been gazing at Lothis, but she finally looked at Tremmilly, concern deep in her eyes. "The sixth person mentioned in the prophecy might be Lothis." Her voice was calm, but Tremmilly could sense the underlying current of anxiety. "It seems too much to be coincidence."

"That's what I was thinking," Tremmilly said, keeping her voice neutral. "'Last is he smallest of all, but a boy in the eyes of the world. He is descended from power, full of power, wielding power. His mind is a weapon, though his hands be frail. His heart is strong, though his body may fail. He has the power of life, the gift of death. The Acclivity rests on his shoulders. Woe to the Breakers.'" Tremmilly expected Lothis to say something after she finished, to confirm or deny what they had said. Instead, the boy kept his head down, silent. *Is he ever going to come out of his shell?*

"The end of the prophecy," Tremmilly continued finally, "for those of you who haven't heard it: 'All six shall have friends and foes alike, some from within and some from out. Many more shall sway the Acclivity, many more essential. Some will live and many more will die. Come forth you adventurers, you seekers of battle. The Acclivity calls, though the Breakers may yet decide the fate of the worlds.

"'But to you who would stay in comfort and safety, not yielding to the call: Blightheart shall establish itself on you and the worlds will be sundered by the Breakers.'"

After Tremmilly finished, the room fell into silence. Everyone seemed lost in their own thoughts. Several minutes crawled by, and she began to feel even more awkward and nervous. Felar seemed like she believed the prophecy, but the others? Would they laugh at her? Abandon her?

15 – MAXAR

Maxar's heart hurt. Tremmilly was obviously distraught over their lack of reaction. She had started off so bubbly, so confident, but now she looked despondent. Maxar couldn't decide how he felt about the prophecy, causing him to freeze. The words seemed true, but were also general. *How often would a random room of people meet those descriptions so accurately? Yes, some specific descriptors match. But what about the ones that don't? And besides, this isn't a random group of people. We were united by Tremmilly, created by her desire for people to fit the prophecy.* When Maxar thought about it more though, he realized she hadn't brought them all together. She'd sought out Maxar, but her finding Felar, Lothis, Wake, and Cazz-ak-tak was seemingly at random.

I have to say something, Maxar thought, shifting back to the real issue. *The longer we are silent, the more we hurt her.* He didn't know what to say. All he had was doubt, and that wasn't what she needed to hear right now.

"You know," Maxar said, "I just thought of something." Tremmilly perked up as soon as he spoke and Maxar felt a surge of warmth in his heart. "It happened back on the orbital dock, a little while before I ran into you and Jaydon." Maxar didn't want to disclose his identity as a Bloodsporter to Wake, but if Tremmilly trusted him then it was probably OK. "The security forces fired on me, using rail pistols. I was hit directly in the chest."

"How is that even possible?" Felar's voice had a note of skepticism that made Maxar angry. "Even if it had only nicked you, you'd be split in two."

"After that," Maxar said, ignoring her question, "there was a security door I couldn't hash. I knew more guards would be coming, so I battered it down with my fists." This time Felar didn't bother to say anything, she just let out a quiet snort.

"Maxar," Tremmilly said, sounding open, "those are things that

51

should not be possible."

"I know, but they happened all the same." Maxar tried to keep the defensiveness out of his voice. *Never should have told them. I was just doing it for her.* "I bring this up because of what the prophecy says, the part you think is about me. I've shed blood. Maybe the part about not knowing my heart is right as well. But, 'his blood in motion with machines,' that doesn't make sense, at least not until I started thinking about what happened back on the orbital dock." Maxar paused for several seconds to think. "I haven't gotten hurt since I left Bloodsport, not even a cut." He thought back through his last game, remembering numerous bruises and a strained muscle. Afterwards, Maxar had nearly thrown up on High-Elder Hatcholethis.

"I had an ulcer just before I escaped. I was taken to the infirmary, but I don't remember anything after that until I woke up in a recovery room. My ulcer was gone and I was told I would have a few days to recover until I was put back into the games. They were monitoring my vital signs very closely, which was strange." Maxar didn't know where he was going with his story, but at least Tremmilly wasn't hurt by silence anymore. He looked over at Felar, wondering if she would berate him or call him a liar. Instead, she looked excited.

"When I was rescuing Lothis," Felar said, "I came across some information about a developing super soldier program. They had recently moved the project onto Bloodsport."

"I don't understand," Maxar replied.

"It was nano-technology. 'His blood in motion with machines.' It all makes sense now. You were part of the experiment. What better place to develop a super soldier than in the Bloodsport? Plenty of battle and closely monitored."

Maxar didn't like what she was saying, didn't want nano-machines crawling around inside of him. "Do you know anything else about it?" Maxar barely kept his voice calm. Suddenly, he could feel them inside, just under his skin.

"No," Felar said, "I've told you everything I read. We can find out more, but I need access to a secure terminal. I don't want the Ashamine to see I've opened their files."

"Damn it to the fires of the dark star," Maxar said, his turmoil spilling over. Tremmilly came over and took his hand. The warmth of her skin distracted him from the thought of the nano-machines.

"It will be OK, Maxar," Tremmilly soothed. "So far whatever they've done to you has produced only good results. You'd be dead from the rail shot otherwise."

"Yeah, I guess," Maxar replied, continuing to use her presence to calm himself. After several moments, he realized they were still holding hands.

Tremmilly seemed to notice at the same moment, because she dropped his hand and looked embarrassed.

"That definitely makes you the second person of the prophecy," Felar said. "So Tremmilly, myself, Lothis, and Maxar are confirmed. Wake and Cazz-ak-tak are less certain."

Wake looked up from the gauntlet of his environmental nominizing suit. "Even if we are all in the prophecy, and everything matches up—which I will admit looks correct as you've explained it—how do we know that the rest of what it says is true? How do we know who or what the Breakers are? It doesn't explain what the Acclivity is. It doesn't say what we are to do, not specifically. We definitely aren't in comfort or safety, so hopefully the prophesied blightheart won't fall on our heads. Without knowing its origin, I have a hard time believing. Besides, what is there really to believe in? It's vague and doesn't tell us what to do."

"For you, maybe it hasn't," Tremmilly replied, straightening. She seemed to gain confidence as she continued, realizing she didn't need their approval. Maxar thought she looked far more regal and poised than her back-world upbringing could account for. Tremmilly looked royal. "But it has guided me to you all. If not for this prophecy, I would have stayed on Eishon-2 and Maxar would have died. Felar would have been captured and executed. Lothis would be back in captivity. I will agree that it does not give us specific instructions, but it does give us warnings and now we are alert and aware. We will be looking for the Breakers, ready to resist them. The fact we are all here in the same ship is strong evidence the prophecy is true. As to its origin, as I said before, the prophecy came from my guardian, Psidonnis. He was a brother of the Dygar sect. I do not believe in that religion, but the truth is the truth no matter where it comes from."

"But that's what I want to know," Wake said. "Where did Psidonnis get the prophecy from?"

"He said it was from Terra, the god of the Dygars. I never asked if she appeared to him or how it happened, and now he is dead." Tremmilly lost some of her poise, but this was the strongest Maxar had seen her act when confronted with Psidonnis' death.

"I know who gave him the prophecy," Lothis said, the boy's voice startling them all.

16 – LOTHIS

Lothis felt everyone's eyes focus on him, the attention making his skin crawl. He didn't want to speak, but he had information they needed. This group had protected and sheltered him, and now he could help in return. Lothis took a deep breath and looked down at the floor.

"There is a group, I don't know who they are or what they are called, but they were watching me. They weren't using any type of technology humans are familiar with. I traced their signal back to its source and sent my consciousness into their presence. There were five of them, beings of intense light." He stopped for a moment, thinking of how to continue.

"When did this happen?" Felar asked, voice tense.

"Just after the destruction of the Hammer and Cazz-ak-tak's ship." Lothis kept his head down, avoiding the gaze of the group.

"Why do you believe it is connected to the prophecy?" Tremmilly rubbed Beowulf's head as she spoke. Lothis could see everyone in his peripheral vision, waiting for him to answer. *You can do this,* he thought, feeling overwhelmed.

"The beings mentioned most of us, not by name, but by titles. 'The soldier saved the boy, the girl rescued the convict, and the engineer will soon find the protector. They all seem to be converging quite well.' The beings also said they were giving us guidance."

Maxar ran his hand across his stubbly hair, sighing as he did so. "It's too much for coincidence. Lothis is right, they're connected to the prophecy. Can you tell if they are watching us right now?"

This was the first time Maxar had ever spoken to him, and this made Lothis feel even more uncomfortable. The man was hard and didn't seem to like him. *I need Maxar on my side,* Lothis thought, remembering that the Revenge was currently hiding from the Ashamine. *He is part of the group, part of our family.* He'd never thought of everyone in that manner before, and it simultaneously calmed him and made him anxious.

54

"I haven't felt them since that first time, but I think they might have shielded their presence somehow. They knew I was with them and didn't want me watching."

"Assuming they are on our side," Maxar said, "it would be nice to have their help. At this point, we need everything we can get, even if it is just more information."

"How do we know they are on our side?" Jaydon's voice sounded rough to Lothis. He was the oldest human he'd ever met, and while Jaydon seemingly still had a long life ahead of him, the captain had used his body roughly.

"Through the guidance of the prophecy, they saved pretty much everyone in this room. Do we need more evidence than that?" Tremmilly was right, and they all acknowledged it.

"Beings of light," Wake said, fixing Lothis with his gray eyes. "What do you think they were? Gods?" He sounded more open now than when Tremmilly told him his place in the prophecy.

"I don't know. None of what they have done so far is supernatural, but the location they inhabited was strange." Lothis paused for a moment, searching for descriptive words. "It surged and flowed in a way I've never seen before. It felt otherworldly, more connected to everything than the reality we inhabit. Unfortunately, I have no way of going back to discover more. I'd like to do some research in the Ashamine databases, but that has been impossible as Eishon-2 lacked a connection."

Wake turned from Lothis and he was glad of the lessoned scrutiny. "Do the Entho-la-ah-mines know anything about these beings of light?"

"The Great Thought remembers nothing of a place or people like Lothis has described." Lothis heard Cazz-ak-tak in his mind, something that had surprised him at first. He hoped to have more time to talk with him. The Great Thought might give him insight about his growing abilities.

"This group sounds nothing like Terra," Tremmilly said, sounding thoughtful. "The Dygars say Terra is the embodiment of nature, of the forces of the universe. If these beings felt otherworldly, they aren't what the Dygars believe in. Whatever gave Psidonnis the prophecy, it must have appeared to him as Terra, otherwise it wouldn't have gained his trust. And until we have more information, I think we will have to trust as well."

Lothis looked at Felar, needing connection with her in that moment. She had descended into the research facility under Haak-ah-tar and rescued him, both from his captors and the flesh eating monstrosities.

Thinking about that part of his life triggered an overwhelming sense of loneliness, despite the large group—*family*—surrounding him. The years of solitary confinement and strict routine had locked Lothis out of the most powerful parts of himself. *And you never realized, never even considered, that other humans existed.* But then he'd seen Felar on a hashed terminal screen, feeling a connection to her unlike anything he'd experienced before. Now, he couldn't imagine a life without her. Their connection had caused emotions he'd never even contemplated.

Snapping back to the present, Lothis expected to see Felar's soft smile. The look of disgust on her face was jarring. It took a moment to realize it wasn't directed at him.

"I believe in the prophecy at this point because it has been accurate," she said, using a commanding tone he'd heard when she was issuing orders back on the Hammer. "So far it has produced positive outcomes. We have no idea what the light beings' objectives are. We don't know what they are positioning us to do, or why. I think until we have a better understanding of them, we should remain wary and not follow blindly."

Everyone agreed, Lothis included. The only person he truly trusted was Felar, but that ring was slowly starting to expand.

17 – CAZZ-AK-TAK

The longer Cazz-ak spent with this group of humans, the more at ease he felt. They were honest, helpful, and didn't harbor the prejudices common to those of their species. It was difficult being away from the Entho-la-ah-mines, but Cazz-ak felt this was the best they could hope for, given the circumstances.

Just as he was about to tell the humans about Na-ah-co's status as queen, Cazz-ak felt a hateful presence come into being. After a moment of searching, he localized it to the distortion zone outside the Eishon system.

"Do you feel that?" Cazz-ak sent so only Elth-eo-lan and Na-ah-co could hear.

"Yes," Elth-eo-lan replied, her mental voice sounding scared.

"It feels much like the force that assaulted us during your birthing ceremony," Cazz-ak said, looking at Na-ah-co.

"You must shield me and conceal my presence from it," the Queen sent back, sounding cautious, yet confident. Cazz-ak was glad his new queen was so courageous, but worried she would put herself in danger because of it.

"But that will mean dropping the shielding of the Revenge," Elth-eo-lan replied. "The Ashamine will find us."

"Whatever is out there is far worse than the humans," the Queen said, her tone commanding. "The Ashamine threaten our bodies, but this dark force threatens our souls." When this enemy had assaulted them back on Haak-ah-tar, Cazz-ak worried he would lose himself, had thought briefly the darkness had destroyed the Great Thought. He hadn't had much opportunity to think about who or what had sent that wave of negative energy, but now it was back and they were in more danger than ever before.

Cazz-ak dropped the threads of Elth-eo-lan and Na-ah-co's minds and allowed his connection to the Great Thought to subside to its normal level. "Lend your minds to me," he sent, saying the words deeply ingrained in Entho-la-ah-mine culture. When they had done so, Cazz-ak wove their thoughts, along with his own, into a strand. This would enable him to wield more of the Great Thought than any of them could alone. He opened a large channel to the hive mind, weaving its energy into a thick orb centered on Na-ah-co. Once the shield settled over her, Cazz-ak solidified it.

"Very good," Na-ah-co said. "Thank you Cazz-ak." He bowed, dipping down on his front set of legs. The queen bowed in return and continued speaking, "We must tell the humans that we are no longer shielding them. And as we discussed before, it is time we tell them who I am."

Cazz-ak turned from their conference and looked at the humans. The boy Lothis was special somehow, possessing mental abilities Cazz-ak had never seen in humans. *I hope I get the chance to talk with him soon.*

"Friends," Cazz-ak said, breaking into the humans' conversation, "I have something very important to tell you." They all stopped talking and looked at him. Continuing, he carefully picked his words. "We have been forced to drop our concealment of the Revenge."

"What's happened?" Tremmilly asked. Her body language showed her nervousness, but Cazz-ak could also see she was holding strong to her composure.

"Some type of dark entity has arrived in the Eishon system. We don't know who or what it is. We've only had one encounter with it before, and it almost destroyed me then." Cazz-ak could still sense the dark spot on the fabric of space-time. It was coming closer, heading straight for Eishon-2.

"Wouldn't it be more important than ever to keep the Revenge shielded now?" Wake too looked troubled.

"What we were doing wouldn't have concealed us from this new adversary." Cazz-ak paused again, trying to think of the best way to explain it. "It is a deception, a trick. It manipulates the mind of the viewer. The force that is coming cannot be handled this way. It will see through it."

"But can't you still keep the deception up, to keep us hidden from the Ashamine?" Wake asked.

"Unfortunately, no. We, being such a small group of Entho-la-ah-mines, have a very limited amount of the Great Thought to work with. Right now, we have to keep Na-ah-co protected from this malevolence. We can't hide the Revenge and keep her safe. We have created a bubble that hopefully the dark force won't be able to penetrate."

"This is not meant to be disrespectful in any way," Tremmilly said, speaking cautiously, "but why is Na-ah-co more important than yourself or Elth-eo-lan?"

"That is a very good question," Cazz-ak replied. "She is our last remaining queen. Without her, our species will falter. We would lose hope and direction. You can see the conundrum this has put us in. The Ashamine, while certainly a physical danger, don't pose the same kind of threat this darkness brings. It has tried to corrupt her since before her birth. I suspect it is trying to find its way into the Great Thought."

"We understand," Maxar said, his demeanor calm. Cazz-ak didn't know what the Bloodsport was, but whatever this man had escaped from had made him hard. "We appreciate the help you have provided. Perhaps the Ashamine will have moved on to other targets by now."

"I'll go to the command deck and see what's happening." Jaydon stood and headed for the small doorway that led to the front of the ship. "The passive sensors haven't shown much, but at least they don't alert them."

"Do we stay here or try to run?" Tremmilly's question went unanswered. Cazz-ak could not think of a solution, so he kept still. The energy coming from Na-ah-co and Elth-eo-lan mirrored his own.

Wake cocked his head and squinted for a moment before speaking. "How do Entho-la-ah-mine ships create worm holes?"

"We use the power of the Great Thought to warp space-time into a distortion. But I must stop you there. There aren't enough of us present, even for such a small ship. We would need many more Entho-la-ah-mines to be able to wield that much of the Great Thought." Wake nodded and sighed.

Jaydon's voice emitted from the speakers in the cargo area, startling Cazz-ak. "At least two Ashamine atmospheric fighters are pinging us. There may be more out there, but I don't want to switch to active and confirm our location. We better make a plan. They're coming in fast."

"Damn them to the fires of the dark star," Felar said, scowling. She slammed her hand into the intercom transmit button. "Get flying out of this cave before they trap us inside."

"I'm going up with Jaydon to give him a hand," Maxar said. "If you guys have any great ideas, let me know."

Reaching out to the Great Thought, Cazz-ak searched for guidance from his ancestors' memories. Nothing like this had ever happened before. Despair flooded him, the same emotion that had plagued him since the death of the previous queen. *Despite all odds, we were able to take her last surviving egg to Haak-ah-tar and bring forth a new queen.* This comforted him, but then the realization that the supernova had obliterated Haak-ah-tar and the sacred Crystal Chamber threw him back down. It was the only place Entho-la-ah-mine queens could be created. *At least we have Queen Na-ah-co.* He fought hard to keep his mind from adding the title of *The Last* to her name.

Cazz-ak reflected on how his species, through its evolved peacefulness, was allowing the humans to exterminate them. They'd gone from numbering in the trillions down to millions. The Ashamine had seized their home worlds, killing every Entho-la-ah-mine they could. Only remote colony planets remained, and Cazz-ak worried it was just a matter of time until the Ashamine found those. Entho-la-ah-mine weapon development was slow and lacked the power they needed to truly defend themselves from the humans.

Now, on top of the xenocidal Ashamine, a new force sought to exploit them. *We can either be dead or corrupted and enslaved,* Cazz-ak despaired. *The Great Thought charged me with keeping the Queen safe, but how can I do that against such mighty enemies?*

Then, something stirred inside Cazz-ak, an emotion he'd never felt before. It grew slowly, but with unstoppable inertia. His fear and hopelessness began to fade, the emotional spark blossoming into a flame, hot and bright inside him. *Anger,* Cazz-ak thought, confused about how to handle this new development.

18 – CRASOR

"Stay here until I call for you," Crasor sent to the gang of thugs and criminals gathered around him. The group that had called themselves the Sunless Ones were now either seeded or dead. "If you must forage for food, raid one of the other underworld gangs, but leave no survivors. Their flesh will nourish you until you can be in the sunlight."

A roar of assent followed Crasor as he left the group. This time he had no doubts about the route to take through the maintenance tunnels because he'd memorized a detailed map the Sunless Ones possessed. *I have no time to waste,* he thought, glad he was pursuing his primary goal once again. *The Founder is the key. If he falls, the Ashamine falls with him.*

It was hard ordering his small band of converts to be dormant. Crasor wanted to unleash them on the Ashamine above, to capture and control the capital city of the Ashamine. *Too risky. I must contain this thirst for power. I have done well in keeping the Breakers hidden, in sheltering our tiny spark of millions from the deluge of the Ashamine billions. Once I strike down the Founder, it will be a prime opportunity for us to blaze through the chaos that follows. Be patient.*

After hours navigating through tunnels, Crasor arrived at his destination. He climbed out of a hatch inside a run-down apartment building. No one saw him exit, but it didn't matter. The people in this cramped and filthy lower level of the city kept to themselves. That was why he'd located a cache here.

Crasor walked along the surface of the planet, something he'd rarely done. The cracked walkway was strewn with trash. Those in power never came down here, preferring instead the lofty heights, miles above. He stepped around a pile of refuse that stank of human feces. *We will purify the worthless DNA of the humans,* Crasor thought, gritting his teeth. *The time has come to cut the head off this bloated corpse.* He vaguely remembered what it was like to be human. It was a sad feeling. With the changes the Breakers had made, Crasor wondered how he had ever been content with such a mundane existence.

Once they'd finished with the humans, Crasor would be able to focus on the Entho-la-ah-mines. They were a softer target, but strategically it made more sense to take down the humans first. The Enthos were hidden, and at the moment, Crasor couldn't allocate any resources towards finding them. *If we happen to find any unknown species while looking for the Enthos?* A smile twisted Crasor's lips. *Power comes through unity, and I will unite and control all life that exists in this galaxy.*

Turning into a nondescript building, Crasor entered his code into a smudged and cracked terminal screen. It flashed "Thank You," and the security hatch in front of him made a grinding noise as the bolts retracted. He pulled the heavy door open and slipped through, quickly closing it behind him. Crasor waited, listening as the bolts ground back into place. Pickpockets and cutthroats were thick down here. It was too risky leaving it open, even with his Breaker abilities.

A grid of halls stretched before Crasor, the walls filled with doors. Long ago, this part of Founder's City had been prosperous. This facility had probably stored the excess possessions of the middle class. As wealth disparity increased, the middle class evaporated and the area had fallen into disrepair. When Crasor had been scouting locations to set up caches, he'd learned a high level criminal organization owned this warehouse. They had bought up most of this sector, increasing the area's slide into corruption. Crasor had paid them a large sum of Ashcreds to keep his items secure. That was all he cared about.

Finding the unit labeled "1K1," Crasor entered his access code. Inside the small space was a tungsten alloy crate, and on its top, a simple keypad. He entered another code, the longest one yet, and a green indicator flashed. Crasor breathed easier knowing he'd disarmed the crate's security system, built with enough explosive to level the entire building.

Lifting the lid, Crasor smiled. Inside, everything he needed to assassinate the Founder was just as he'd left it. *When I put this here, I never dreamed I would be using it for this purpose.* The crate had been here for eleven years, waiting. He'd set it up as soon as he'd become the Facilitator.

Crasor reached down and picked up a tactical subsonic rail pistol. *Too quick,* he thought, *but handy for gaining access.* The weapon went into a shoulder holster that Crasor fastened over his chest. Next, he picked up a curved knife. *This is more appropriate,* he thought, a wicked smile on his face.

Feeling he had all the weaponry he would need, Crasor dug deeper into the crate. After a moment, he pulled out a metal box, shiny and smooth. Inside, were several dossiers of fake identities Crasor had created. The Founder himself didn't know about their existence. He'd thought that perhaps, one day, the leader of the Ashamine government might want to dispose of him. These identities had been insurance, but now Crasor needed them for a different purpose. He quickly scanned the directory, finding an individual who would have access to the Founder, and would also be able to carry a weapon. Tez Soodsun, an intelligence officer, met all the requirements. Crasor had given the non-existent man clearance into the Founder's Palace, but not into the inner area. That would have raised security alerts. Besides, Crasor knew all the secret corridors and escape routes. The Founder would never know Crasor was there until he stepped into his office.

Finding the container that held everything he needed to become Tez Soodsun, Crasor removed a small vial. It contained genetic material that would mask his own DNA from security scanners. He inserted it into the injector and raised the device up to his arm. Before the needle penetrated, the voice of the Breakers filled his mind. "This is unnecessary. Simply see the DNA structure you need, and you have the ability to secrete it to scanners." This revelation amazed Crasor. The serum would give him just a few hours as Tez Soodsun before it wore off. Now he could permanently change his identity as needed.

"Can I memorize more than just Tez?" he asked the Breakers.

"You can be them all," the booming voice said in his mind. "You will not be able to switch instantly, but given sufficient time, you can change." Crasor liked how that sounded. He quickly swiped through the dossiers, memorizing the genetic codes on file as well as their clearances and back-stories. Crasor had always had an above average memory, but now it felt expanded, like he could remember every single detail, no matter how small.

Finished with the identification box, he closed and returned it to the crate. After gathering some Ashcreds from the cache, Crasor was ready for his mission. He shut the crate and rearmed the explosive charge. Crasor grinned as he left the storage building, his step light.

***

Crasor held the subsonic rail pistol steady and sent a tungsten alloy slug into the guard's head. The weapon had a limited range, but was much quieter than its supersonic relatives. Its slow ammunition didn't create an exit wound either, keeping spatter and other visual cues to a minimum.

Making his way into the Founder's Palace had been easy. The genetic manipulation of the Breakers had gotten him through every security checkpoint. Tez Soodsun's clearance had run out eventually and Crasor began to use less traveled corridors. This was the third guard he'd disposed of. If anyone discovered their bodies, security would lock down the entire facility. The Ashamine would trap and hunt him down. The Founder would go to a safe room that even Crasor couldn't penetrate. *But I'm so close,* he thought, quickening his step.

Rounding the final corner, Crasor strode into the waiting area for the Founder's office. Raising his rail pistol, he shot both guards standing on either side of the doorway, his movements quick and accurate. Neither of the Founder's Commandos had time to even raise their weapons. *They've gotten soft since I left the battalion,* he thought, dismissing both the man and woman before they hit the floor.

Turning to the aide sitting at a large desk, Crasor aimed at the man's head. "Make any move towards the terminal or alert, and you're dead," he said, his words imbued with frost. The aide did as commanded, seeming afraid to even move his eyes. Crasor vaguely remembered the man as a coward. He reached out with his soul and caressed his essence. Immediate revulsion met his touch, signaling the aide was bound for Blackness. Crasor didn't completely understand why some people were fit to become Breakers and others weren't, but the makeup of their psyche had a direct correlation to it. *Perhaps they are just too "good" or "pure,"* he thought, wondering if the Breaker mind could explain it to him. *No time for that now.*

Without further hesitation, Crasor triggered a round. The aide slumped into his chair, the movement of his body causing it to spin lazily.

The time has come, Crasor thought exultantly. He walked to the grand office doors, took a deep breath, and opened the right half. As he stepped through, an alarm began to sound. Inside, the Founder sat behind his desk, as he had for a hundred other meetings with Crasor. This time, however, the most powerful man in the Akked Galaxy looked shocked.

"Crasor?" the Founder said, quickly veiling his surprise. "Facilitator, where have you been?" Crasor shut the door behind him and turned to the screen beside the expansive entry. Before he could select the "Lockdown" option, he heard the locks slide into place. The doors seemed made of wood, but that was only veneer covering tungsten alloy cores. Neither small arms fire nor conventional explosives could penetrate it. Crasor would have all the time he needed.

Turning back to the Founder, he smiled. "It seems I have arrived just in time." The Founder narrowed his eyes, and reached for something in his desk. Immediately, Crasor raised his pistol and pointed it at the

Founder's chest. "Place your hands up on the desk." It felt strange giving orders to the man he had so devotedly served for eleven years. It felt amazing.

"So, who turned you?" the Founder asked, hatred seething in his voice. "Was it the Divisionists? No, of course not. You could never be part of those peaceful idiots. Maybe it is this Brotherhood of Azak-so I have heard about. Intelligence tells me they have quite the base on Eishon-2."

"No," was all Crasor replied. The Founder raised an eyebrow, waiting for a further response.

"At least have the courage to tell me the truth before you kill me." The Founder rose from his chair and walked around the expansive desk. Crasor kept the pistol trained on him, his mind searching for something to say.

The Founder's focus shifted towards the weapon and he stared for a moment. "What happened to your fingers?" Crasor looked down at the digits of his right hand but then realized why the Founder had asked. Before he could trigger a round, the Founder covered the short distance between them and caught hold of the pistol. *How is he so fast?* Crasor wondered as he tried to twist the weapon out of the Founder's grip. The older man bore down like a vice, his perfect white teeth revealed in a snarl.

"Tell me who turned you," the Founder said through clenched teeth. With a violent jerk, the Founder almost succeeded in pulling the pistol out of his grasp. Crasor grabbed hold of his own wrist with his free hand to maintain control. Unfortunately, even with two hands, he still didn't have the power to bring the weapon down to a usable angle. Rage burned in the Founder's eyes, something Crasor had seen, but never experienced directed at him. "Tell me!" the Founder screamed.

The room went dark, light, and spun momentarily. Crasor blinked and saw the Founder pulling back his fist for another strike. *That blighthearted bugger hit me,* he thought, his own rage starting to boil. He dodged the next punch, but just barely.

"Are you forgetting who you are?" the voice of the Breakers questioned in his mind. Crasor felt something inside him shift, like a starship passing through a worm impression. A cold stillness enveloped him. "Finish this."

Crasor grabbed the next punch out of mid-air and squeezed. He felt the fist collapsing in his grip, heard the cracking of bones. The Founder screamed.

"I don't have to explain anything to you," Crasor said, his voice low and menacing. "Those days are over." He twisted the grasped hand violently, breaking the Founder's wrist. In agony, the Founder let go of the rail pistol. He scrabbled at Crasor's fingers, trying desperately to extract his mangled hand. Briefly, Crasor thought about drawing his knife to finish the Founder. That had been the original plan. Now, a new thought crossed his mind.

Crasor dropped the rail pistol as the corners of his mouth drew up in a vicious sneer. "You thought you were invincible, thought you would lead humanity into a golden era." He snorted derisively. "But you had no idea there is something out there, something far more powerful than you are or ever could be." Crasor could see confusion overcoming pain inside the Founder. The other man let out a moan as Crasor twisted his wrist further. "Your reign is over. Humanity will be no more." Crasor pulled him in close, glaring into his vibrant orange eyes. This was what he'd wanted, a key part of his plan.

Focusing on his free hand, Crasor stiffened it. He willed its edges to become sharp, its fingers a single point. Looking down at it, he saw what he'd envisioned. His hand had become something akin to a sword. "May the Dawn be broken," he uttered, not understanding what it meant. Without another word, he drove the sharpened hand up under the Founder's ribs, questing for his heart.

19 – ASCENDED KAROTH

"Ascended," the combat operations tech said, drawing Karoth's attention away from his terminal. "The last of the known ground targets has just been secured. We are continuing to question the insurgent base personnel, but they haven't provided any information about Lothis yet. Space based sensors are scanning for any hidden facilities, complexes, or caves, but so far, nothing has turned up. We've captured all but one of the fleeing ships. The last vessel is a small craft, but whoever is flying it is good. It won't surrender and the fighters haven't been able to disable it yet. The group sent to search the wreckage of the Hammer reports there are no survivors. They want to know if they should continue with body recovery."

Before Karoth could issue orders, a classified priority alert flashed up on his terminal. It originated from the Classad. Karoth scowled. *Why are they contacting me?* He rarely, if ever, dealt with the group of powerful councilors. Karoth's orders always came directly from the Founder.

Without saying a word, he exited the command deck and quickly made his way to his quarters. The level of classification attached to the message precluded him from being able to view it on the command deck. He needed a secured room.

Karoth stood behind his desk and used his thumbprint to unlock the first level of security on his personal terminal. After selecting the option to lock the door, he spoke his code phrase and scanned his retina. With his identity verified and the room secure, he opened the communication.

Ascended Karoth, he read, *an unknown attacker assassinated the Founder just hours ago in his quarters. With the events surrounding the loss of the Successor, we believe this is some type of coup. Intelligence sources don't know who the perpetrators are, but it doesn't appear military in origin. Evidence suggests it is led by someone with deep knowledge of the Ashamine. As a result, we have ordered all fleets to return and protect the core worlds as well as assist the succession of power. You, and your assets, will return to the Ashamine system immediately.*

A flood of emotions crashed over Karoth. Before he could stop, he spiraled down into a well of memories.

***

"Initiate Karoth," Separate Rathis barked. Karoth snapped out of his daydream about his favorite port girl. Anger filled him. He'd never enjoyed a single one of Rathis' lectures. The man was a boring tyrant. When Karoth looked up, he expected to see the officer glaring at him, but instead, Rathis was studying his handheld terminal. "Report to Ascended Gareg's quarters immediately."

Rathis had a strange look on his face, and it took Karoth a few moments to interpret it. *Concern.* The Separate rarely looked anything other than angry.

"Now, Initiate!" Rathis yelled, making Karoth realize he'd drifted off again.

"Yes, sir," he replied, standing from his chair and snapping a perfect salute. He marched out of the room, his form perfect. Rathis had already disciplined him for sloppy procedures twice today.

Once out in the hall, Karoth dropped his rigid posture. He took out his personal terminal and keyed several options. A red line stretched out before him, leading the way to Ascended Gareg's quarters. He'd never met the man before, much less been to his personal space. Fear nagged in the back of Karoth's mind. *Does he know about my port visits? If I'm expelled from Officer's Academy, father would—* He didn't want to continue down that path. So far, Karoth had done the least amount possible to maintain eligibility for the program. His constant tardiness and sloppy discipline were his greatest weaknesses. It wasn't laziness, more a lack of motivation. He hated this place, loathed everything it stood for.

When he arrived outside of Ascended Gareg's quarters, Karoth took a deep breath. *If I don't get expelled, I have to quit seeing Leena,* he thought, *it's far too risky.* Imagining her body produced immediate regret.

He touched the *REQUEST ENTRANCE* option on the door and waited. The seconds stretched on before it finally slid open. "Come," a quiet voice said.

When Karoth entered, he found Gareg sitting rigidly behind a desk. He was a tall, slender man with piercing amber eyes. Karoth had been to the Ascended's commencement speech after arriving at the Academy just a few months ago. From that, he knew Gareg was a man to be feared and respected. *He reminds me of father,* Karoth thought, saluting briskly.

"Be seated," Gareg said, motioning towards a straight-backed metal chair. Karoth sat, his anxiety deepening. "I don't believe we've met," the older man continued.

"No, sir, we haven't."

"Well, consider that formality exchanged, Initiate."

"Yes. Thank you, sir."

Ascended Gareg sighed. "I don't know how to approach this other than just tell you straight out."

Karoth stiffened. The man controlled a school of thousands, commanded many Separates. *What could make Gareg anxious?*

"Initiate Karoth," the Ascended announced, "your father was assassinated by an unknown group of attackers. They shot him in the head with a flechette pistol."

***

Karoth fell back into his chair, shocked by what he had just read. *The Founder... Dead.* The words didn't fit together, had no connection to each other. And now he was to abandon his orders to find Lothis? Karoth clenched his teeth and growled under his breath. *Focus,* he thought, forcing memories of his father's death from his mind. *No, I won't surrender the Founder's last command to me.* The decision to disobey a lawful order issued by the Classad would cost him his career and maybe even his freedom, but the Founder had wanted the Successor secured and Karoth would do it. He was close. Perhaps, if he acted fast enough, he could fulfill both the Founder's and Classad's wishes.

As he rushed back to the command deck, Karoth smoothed the anxiety off his face. "Where are we on that last fleeing vessel?" he demanded.

"It's still eluding us, sir," the combat ops tech replied, startled by Karoth's hasty entrance.

"Send the entire reserve of fighters to pursue it." Karoth knew it was risky to remove the Justice's close support assets while deployed in a combat zone, but time was running out. Besides, he had a hunch this elusive ship was important.

"Yes, Ascended."

A plan formed in Karoth's mind, and he acted on it. "Comms," he said, voice harsher than usual. "Fleet wide channel." After the comms officer signaled, Karoth resumed speaking. "This is Ascended Karoth. We've received more intel and things aren't looking good. Whoever has captured Lothis has communicated that they will kill the boy if we do not leave the system immediately. It is unacceptable for them to hold the Successor hostage. We must secure him as quickly as possible. The longer we take, the more time the insurgents have of either escaping or going through with their threats. The Ashamine and I need everything you have to give. Find Lothis so he can be returned to his father." It was all lies, but Karoth knew it would bring out the best in his troops.

"Sir," the combat ops tech said, looking determined, "the reserve fighters are away and headed towards the target. They should be on station in just a few minutes." An idea occurred to Karoth and he smiled.

"I want a channel opened to that fleeing ship." Perhaps he could speed things up and lessen the chance of injury to Lothis.

20 – WAKE

"This is Ascended Karoth, commander of the ASN Founder's Justice, hailing the single remaining insurgent spacecraft. All of your comrades' vessels have been captured or destroyed. A squadron of fighters has been dispatched to apprehend you. Submit and allow yourself to be boarded or we will scatter pieces of you across the surface of Eishon-2."

Wake shivered. Karoth's tone reminded him of Commander Yaladon, the last voice he had heard before a tech shot him out an airlock on the ASN Antadroga. Thankfully, the Brotherhood had saved him from the Ashamine's plan of execution. Now, they needed help, and Wake could do nothing to save them.

"If we do as they command," Felar said, sounding cold and calm, "the Ashamine will imprison Lothis and dispose of the rest of us. We cannot surrender."

"We don't have much choice at this point." Maxar looked sad, his pale blue eyes full of weariness. "I think the best we can do is let them take us and work on some sort of escape plan." Wake agreed, although he knew the Ashamine would carry out his execution order as soon as they recognized him.

"They have the firepower to take us down, whether we skim the surface or move out into space," Wake added, trying to stay calm. "We are a crippled ship. Besides, what would the Ashamine want with Lothis and why would they kill the rest of you?"

Felar gave Maxar a meaningful look, then turned to face him. "He is the successor to the Founder. I rescued him from an Ashamine lab, and we've been on the run ever since." Wake's eyes widened as all the pieces snapped together in his mind.

"Blightheart," he said in awe. That was why a whole battle group had descended on this insignificant system.

"Yeah, blightheart," Felar said. She was watching him closely, and the woman's intense scrutiny made Wake feel uncomfortable.

"As much of a revelation as that is," Wake continued, trying to ignore her gaze, "our situation is still the same. Maxar is right. We have to surrender."

"They won't shoot us down, not with Lothis on board. They won't risk hurting him." Desperation was starting to enter Felar's voice. It was the first time Wake had ever seen her be anything but supremely composed.

"But what can we do?" Maxar shook his head. "Our generator is broken and we have no way to get to the worm zone even if it wasn't. There are too many Ashamine ships. We need to use what little time we have left to make a plan."

"I agree with Maxar," Tremmilly said, putting her arm around Felar as she did so.

Jaydon turned from his flight console and nodded. "There are no other options. We have to surrender, but I have a plan." He gestured at Maxar and pointed at the controls. "Take over for a minute. The two fighters that were on our tail have backed off. I think they are waiting on the main force to arrive, which will happen in just a few minutes." Maxar slid into the seat as Jaydon vacated it, a questioning look on his face.

"I haven't always been the sad drunk you see before you," Jaydon said, gesturing for them all to follow. "I was once a trader and broker, but then some things happened. This ship, however, has looked the same from the beginning." He paused for a moment as he began shifting refuse off a section of the floor. "People don't like garbage—as I'm sure you've noticed since you've been on board—so they tend to stay away from it. Ashamine port authorities are no exception." As he said this, Jaydon placed two fingers from his right hand on deck screws along a seam. He then placed three fingers from his left on screws on a different seam. A faint clicking sound came from below. "So if you want to hide something, keeping it under garbage works fairly well."

Jaydon stood up and revealed a small, open hatch. "I've never transported live cargo, so I don't know how well your life signs will be shielded, but this compartment has never been discovered, not in all of my runs." Wake was impressed. The sloppy drunk he had discounted ever since his arrival on the A'Tal's Revenge had transformed into a leader. "There isn't a ton of space down there, but enough to fit Lothis, Felar, and Wake." Wake didn't relish the idea of captivity down in that small space for who knew how long, but it made more sense than giving himself straight over to the Ashamine.

"Thank you, Jaydon," Felar said as she led Lothis through the hatch. "I hope you and the rest of the group can find a way out of this buggered blightheart."

Jaydon smiled and nodded. "We'll do our best."

Wake followed them down, the light from the main cargo area doing little to illuminate the dark space below. He had to hunch over to fit inside.

"Be patient and stay silent. If we are lucky, the Ashamine won't find what they are looking for and will hurry off elsewhere." As Jaydon began shutting the hatch, Wake could hear Maxar yelling. "Hundreds of ships just arrived in the worm zone. They are all..." The hatch closed, cutting off the rest of his statement. Darkness swallowed Wake.

21 – FELAR

Hundreds of ships? Felar wondered, her eyes trying in vain to adjust to the complete blackness. She wrapped her arms around Lothis, drawing him close. In the past, the boy would not have allowed this type of affection, but now he welcomed it. *Are they additional Ashamine ships? Or Brotherhood?* Felar wished she could have heard Maxar finish.

"They are very powerful," Lothis whispered, seeming to read her thoughts. This happened more often than she liked, and Felar speculated it was somehow related to Lothis' exceptional way of connecting to the world around him.

"Can you tell who they are?" Felar didn't understand how his ability worked, but she knew it was trustworthy. His detection of the supernova near Haak-ah-tar had proved that much. Lothis had assured Felar it was safe for him to reach out like this, but deep down she still wondered if that was so.

"It is more of a *what,* not a *who,*" Lothis replied, his words sounding distant. A few moments passed in silence, and Felar pondered his words. "Nahhhaagg," Lothis growled, his body going rigid in her arms.

"What is it?" Wake whispered loudly. At that moment, the ship jolted. A few seconds later, Felar felt the engines power down.

"Aberrant darkness, almost like a black hole, but not." Lothis still sounded faint, but his voice was loud in the confined space.

"Lothis," Felar said, trying to use her most comforting voice and keep it as low as possible, "we have to be quiet now. The Ashamine will be on the ship at any moment." A few silent seconds passed and then Felar heard the ship's hatch open. Loud boot falls crashed on the deck above. She held her breath, hoping Lothis wouldn't make any further noise. His body relaxed, and Felar slowly exhaled in relief.

The muffled voices were incomprehensible, but the sounds of fists and boots on flesh told Felar what was happening. More thuds overhead and then the sound of a firing flechette pistol. A mass thudded to the deck just above their heads and Felar had to keep from crying out. *Who got shot?* Thuds, muffled cries, feet slamming on the deck, then silence.

Felar wanted more than anything to open the hatch above and help her friends. Maxar was the only one of them that had any real combat training. *Whatever happened,* she thought, fearful for her friends, *it's over now.*

The sound of the outer hatch closing and the engines powering up surprised Felar. *They let us go that easy, with such a light inspection and interrogation?* No, something else was going on. The way the ship was maneuvering felt different from the way either Jaydon or Maxar flew.

"Something is wrong," Felar said as quietly as possible. "Whoever is piloting has military training."

"And it doesn't sound like anyone is above us," Wake's voice conveyed worry, but still contained an edge of strength Felar appreciated. She barely knew anything about him, but his stability under pressure told her of his character. "If it was safe they would be letting us out by now." Felar nodded, but then realized Wake couldn't see her and agreed verbally.

The image of what had happened above wasn't positive, and as time passed, it reinforced her feeling the troops had either killed or seriously wounded her friends. Since an Ashamine pilot was flying, they weren't heading anywhere safe for Lothis, Wake, or herself.

"We need to take back the ship," Felar whispered, knowing this was their only option to prevent capture, at least for the short term.

"You're right," Wake acknowledged, "but how do we open the panel?" Felar had no idea. She reached out, looking for any type of controls. *Nothing.*

Felar could hear Wake doing the same on his side. The sound of his skin sliding over the metal panels was loud in the confined space. "It's seamless," he said, sounding resigned. Dread settled over Felar, but she tried to remain positive. With all her friends dying or dead, they couldn't rely on anyone else to save them. She had to trust Wake fully, and at this point, Felar was glad for his company. *It's more support than you had back in the Haak-ah-tar facility,* she thought, her mind scrambling for a plan.

22 – TREMMILLY

Tremmilly's emotions were screaming like overdriven starship engines. She felt amazed they were all still alive. Everything was happening so quickly that she was having a hard time processing it.

Jaydon and Maxar had tried to stall as long as possible, but were eventually forced down onto a part of Eishon-2 she'd never seen before, a vast prairie in the depths of night. Several Founder's Commandos had boarded the A'Tal's Revenge, looking and smelling of death. Blood spattered their fatigues. The officer of the group had drawn a curved knife and threatened to remove body parts if Tremmilly didn't tell them where Lothis was. Maxar had done his best to protect her, but they wrestled him to the ground and beat him brutally. Jaydon tried to intervene as well, but they easily threw him off and held him at the point of a pistol. Troops surrounded Beowulf, weapons ready. The Ashamine had ignored the Entho-la-ah-mines, not considering them a threat.

Just as the officer put the knife to Tremmilly's ear, his head cocked to the side. He listened for a moment, then ordered them all thrown off the ship. In the chaos that followed, one of the Commandos discharged a pistol, narrowly missing Tremmilly. She'd stumbled and fallen, but Maxar quickly dragged her out the hatch. She knew if the Commandos hadn't been in such a rush, they'd all be dead.

Feeling slightly more composed, Tremmilly peered through the darkness, anxious to check if everyone had made it off the Revenge safely. Her eyes found Maxar first, his dim shape laying flat in the tall grass.

"Are you OK?" Tremmilly asked, rushing over to assist him. The depth of her concern surprised her. She pushed down the extra feelings, her mind not able to deal with them at the moment. Beowulf was right by her side, and she took comfort in his presence.

"Yeah, I'm fine." Maxar sat up, rubbing the side of his head where a heavy boot had impacted. "That should have hurt much worse than it did. Those nano-machines Felar was talking about must be doing their job." The Entho-la-ah-mines came to stand next to Maxar, looking shaken. Jaydon stared off into the distance.

The scream of ships above drew Tremmilly's attention. When she looked up, the bright exhaust of several atmospheric fighters and troop drop ships were falling into formation around the Revenge. Everyone was receiving the same withdrawal orders, and now they had Felar, Lothis, and Wake.

"What do we do now?" Tremmilly asked, her mind spinning.

"We are alive and whole, mostly." Maxar had a bemused smile on his face. "At least there is that much." Seeing the curve of his lips in the faint light of Eishon-2's dual moons made Tremmilly's heart flutter. *Control yourself,* she thought, refocusing her eyes on Beowulf.

"They have my ship," Jaydon said under his breath. "The only thing I had left in this universe. Of course it would happen here. This is where I lose everything." Tremmilly wondered what he meant, but had no time to ask now.

"We need to go after them." The conviction of her words surprised Tremmilly. She had never been much of a leader, preferring solitude. So much had changed in the past few weeks, for better and for worse.

"What?" Jaydon replied, his far away mood vanished. "They are in the hands of the Founder's Commandos now. Soon, they will be on a control ship, and once that vessel makes orbit, they will be inside a Tarton class battle ship. How do you propose we help them?" Tremmilly's heart dropped. They had come so far, had united all those in the prophecy. And almost as soon as it happened, the Ashamine split them apart again.

"It's not impossible," Maxar said. Tremmilly's eyes were adjusting to the dim light and she could see he was sending a comforting look her way. "The hundreds of ships that just wormed in have the Ashamine scurrying. There is bound to be some kind of usable distraction."

"There will certainly be distraction," Cazz-ak said in their minds. "Those on the new ships are part of the dark presence seeking to corrupt the Queen. They are a threat to all of us, not just the Ashamine."

"Well, that certainly complicates things." Maxar continued to absent-mindedly rub the side of his head, the stubble making a scraping sound against his palm.

"First thing is to find a ship," Jaydon sighed, shaking his head. "I can't believe I'm going along with this, but you're right. They need our help. Odds are, we die trying, but that doesn't mean we shouldn't go." He paused for a moment and shook his head again. "Tremmilly, I don't know how you have this effect on me. Somehow, I always find myself doing what you want." Tremmilly smiled and shrugged in response.

"We can help find a ship." Queen Na-ah-co's voice was soothing in Tremmilly's mind. "We will use the power of the Great Thought to call one to us."

"But Queen," Cazz-ak said, "we cannot do so unless we lower your shielding." Tremmilly had the feeling she could hear their conversation because they wanted her to. It was a courtesy, and she appreciated it.

"I can maintain my own shield while you and Elth-eo-lan combine to contact the ship."

"You are that powerful?"

"You must trust me, Cazz-ak-tak. I am much stronger than you realize." The Queen looked around, her small blue exoskeleton difficult to see in the faint light. "We can send our need, but since they aren't Entho-la-ah-mine, we will be unable to have a conversation. It works in much the same way as how we talk to you, but because the distance is so great, we have no way of knowing if the ship we contact will be Brotherhood, Ashamine, or unaffiliated."

"I think we have to take the risk," Tremmilly said, still wondering where this drive to lead was coming from.

"We will do as you ask then," Queen Na-ah-co replied.

Nothing changed in the appearance of the Entho-la-ah-mines, but Tremmilly felt something. The trio was focused, intent in a way she sensed with a perception deeper than vision or hearing. After a minute or two passed, Cazz-ak said, "It is done. We found a ship and expressed our desire. It has changed course and is headed our way."

"Well, isn't that great," Jaydon replied. Tremmilly couldn't tell if he was being sarcastic or not. His tone was so vague at times.

They all waited, each looking for the bright exhaust of a vessel. Tremmilly snuck glances at Maxar, wondering how she was falling for this criminal. In the past, she'd had crushes on different boys, but as she became an adult, it all seemed so pointless. None of the guys she had known on Eishon-2 understood her. Most thought her weird. Maxar seemed to think her strange as well, but Tremmilly sensed more to his feelings than that. Something deeper. She wished she could read his mind. *Maybe the Entho-la-ah-mines could do that for me?* Tremmilly laughed and shook her head. They said that was impossible, but it would solve her problem.

"What's funny?" Maxar asked, breaking her reverie.

Tremmilly felt embarrassed about her thoughts, so she just shook her head and said, "Nothing." Maxar smiled, his pale blue eyes lingering on hers. Then, a moment later they flicked above her head and squinted. "There," he said, motioning towards a point behind her. She turned and saw a faint glow, growing brighter by the second.

"If it's Ashamine, we might all be dead." A hard tone had entered Maxar's voice, and it chilled Tremmilly. He picked up a blade shaped rock and moved between the group and oncoming ship. "Stay behind me."

A minute later, the vessel landed and Tremmilly breathed again. It wasn't Ashamine, at least from what she could tell. No symbols or markings of any type were on the hull. The hatch opened and a muscular man with white hair walked out. "Well, this is quite the group to find lounging on the plains while a system wide invasion is going on." He smiled. "Cazz-ak, Na-ah-co, Elth-eo-lan, it's good to see you again." Tremmilly realized this might be the captain Wake had mentioned. "I'm Captain Malesis, for those of you who haven't met me before. We were a bit startled when we heard Entho-la-ah-mines in our heads, but we figured it had to be the same ones that we knew." Malesis looked around. "Where's Wake?"

"That is why we called you here," Maxar answered. "The Ashamine captured him and two of our crew, but they don't know it. We had them hidden in a smuggler's compartment. There is a chance we might rescue them." Malesis made a sound that was a cross between a snort and a chuckle.

"Rescue them? How? They are, or soon will be, in the possession of what is likely the biggest, most powerful ship in the Ashamine fleet. I like Wake, and I'm sure you like your friends, but there is nothing we can do for them now."

Tremmilly, on the verge of tears, straightened up. She looked down at Beowulf, found comfort in his strength, and took a deep breath. This captain was their only hope for getting off Eishon-2, and saving her friends lay solely in his control. "Captain, my home world has been obliterated. From what I can tell, everyone I know is probably dead, except for the people here and our captured friends. I'm guessing you're in the same position. We've both lost so much." Malesis nodded and his face stiffened as she continued. "Wake, Felar, and Lothis are very important to what is happening in the galaxy right now. Without them, things will get very bad, worse than they already are. We have to get them back from the Ashamine." Tremmilly wondered if Malesis would think her crazy, but lately she was learning it didn't always matter what people thought of her. As long as he let them use his ship, she didn't care if he thought her mentally distorted.

"You know we will probably all be captured, tortured, and killed?" His voice was flat and hard.

"Yes, I do, but I don't see any way but to try."

Malesis nodded and relaxed a little. "The Brotherhood is destroyed. I'd estimate ninety-five percent casualties or more here on Eishon-2." He sighed. "Our ship barely survived and we've been unable to confirm if anyone else has. I'd guess not. This will be our last mission for the Brotherhood, to save a captured comrade. If we die, we join the rest of our friends. If we survive... Well, I don't know what comes after that. There are Brotherhood installations elsewhere, but I'm guessing the Ashamine hit them too."

At first, Tremmilly didn't realize he'd agreed, but when she did, a glow bloomed inside her. "We can do it," Tremmilly replied, trying to infuse him and her friends with optimism.

"Then we'd better get going," Maxar said. "We only have about a standard hour before the dark force gets here. That will probably be the best time to go in for a rescue. They'll be distracted."

"Do not underestimate what is coming, or think it will be helpful," Cazz-ak replied. "It has power unlike anything we have ever seen. It will be of more danger to us than the Ashamine."

23 – MAXAR

"I'm not sure Elth-eo-lan and I will have enough power to cloak this ship by ourselves," Cazz-ak told the group as Malesis' ship, the Ashamine's Bane, continued climbing into the atmosphere. "Besides, I am nervous about leaving the Queen unprotected for so long." Maxar still wasn't used to their style of communication, but it was becoming less startling.

"We are stronger than you give us credit for," Elth-eo-lan replied. This was the first time Maxar had heard her speak. Her tone was softer and more comforting than either Cazz-ak or the Queen.

"And I will be protecting myself," Queen Na-ah-co replied, an edge to her voice. "Besides, if we do not cloak the Bane, the Ashamine will destroy us as soon as we are within range."

"As you say, my Queen," Cazz-ak replied. Something about the group's mannerism changed, becoming stiff and focused. Maxar guessed they had begun the cloaking process. He hoped Elth-eo-lan was right about their abilities. If not, they'd find out soon.

Maxar felt chills run up and down his spine. They were heading for one of the most powerful manifestations of Ashamine power in the galaxy. Just a few short weeks ago he would have done anything to get away from the corrupt human government, yet now he headed directly for it.

Stare death in the face another time, he thought, marveling at the giant vessel in the Bane's view screen. These Tarton class ships were the Ashamine's latest creation, bigger and more powerful than anything that had come before them. When the judge had sentenced Maxar to Bloodsport, the vessels had been in pieces and under construction. He'd watched the Entho-la-ah-mines destroy the Founder's Hammer, and now he was headed for it's even larger sister ship.

"Explain to me one more time how this plan is going to work?" Captain Malesis seemed skeptical, but he had gone along with Maxar and Jaydon's strategy so far.

"We fly up to the Founder's Justice and attach to her hull. Jaydon, Tremmilly, and I will find a way into the ship." Maxar knew this was a sticking point, but he hoped with all the traffic going in and out of the giant carrier, there would be an open port somewhere. "The Entho-la-ah-mines will be able to track our bodies, but won't be able to communicate directly. It will be similar to how they brought you to us on the surface. The distance is too far for human minds to sense distinct words, apparently." Maxar looked to the group of Entho-la-ah-mines for confirmation and Cazz-ak signaled his agreement. "After gaining entrance, we will have to find the A'Tal's Revenge. Hopefully, our friends will still be in the smuggler's compartment and we can just reclaim the ship and fly out. If we can get close enough to the Bane, Cazz-ak says the Great Thought might be able to shield both ships."

"What if they aren't in the Revenge?" Maxar could tell that Malesis wasn't trying to poke holes in his plan, but rather seal them. He appreciated it.

"Knowing Felar, they may be out, making our job more complicated. It's possible some of them will be dead or split up between different holding cells. If that's the case, we will probably be spotted and killed. The ship is so large and our resources so small. It will be hard enough to find a single ship, let alone multiple individuals." Maxar hoped the Ashamine didn't discover the smuggler's compartment. The chances of this plan working were so slim as it was. "Once we find them, either in the ship or in cells, we escape in the Revenge, if at all possible. Hopefully, you'll be able to get the Bane close enough to shield us before we depart, but if not, Jaydon will have to do some fancy flying to avoid any fighters or gunships in the area. We can make our way down to the caves under Eishon-2 and hide out until the Ashamine and whoever these new arrivals are leave."

"I'm not sure if that is a good idea," Cazz-ak interjected. "These 'new arrivals' will likely be able to find us, even hidden under so much earth."

"If we go deep enough, there are no sensors on any of these ships that will be able to find us." Jaydon had come a long way in the past few days. He had sobered up, revealing a keen, strategic mind. Maxar felt proud of Jaydon for how he had forsaken liquor. Alcohol was not an easy habit to break. It also took great strength for Jaydon to endure the anguish he'd been numbing for so long. The older man might tell them all what the wound was someday. Maxar knew better than to press for answers.

"I'm sure you are correct," Cazz-ak replied, bringing Maxar back to the conversation, "but in that scenario, they will not be using sensors. Whatever abilities their ships possess, their mental capability rivals ours. The mass of a world will not keep them from seeing us." Cazz-ak paused for a moment, and Maxar wondered if it was because he was thinking or if there was a problem with the cloaking.

"Only a mental shield will hide us from the newcomers," Cazz-ak continued, "both now and in the future. As the dark beings get closer, we will need more strength to keep the Queen protected. Eventually, our abilities may not be powerful enough. Our species has very little experience with this entity, and what small amount we do have, was conducted from very far away.

"Shielding us from the humans' view is strenuous. There are many eyes, many minds, but I feel more confident now. We will need quiet and solitude to focus on our tasks if we are to have any hope."

"The cargo bay will be the quietest place on the ship," Captain Malesis said, shaking his head. "Overall, there are a lot of ifs and maybes in this plan, but it seems like the best we've got."

"Maxar, we wish you, Tremmilly, and Jaydon good fortune." Cazz-ak sounded strong, which made Maxar feel good despite his earlier pessimism. "We will do the best we can to protect us all." The trio of Entho-la-ah-mines left the deck.

"If we can't hide on Eishon-2," Maxar said, returning to the plan, "I suppose we will have to keep running. The Revenge has a busted worm generator, so we will need to have everyone transfer to the Bane. The dark forcers will have disrupted the Ashamine blockade so maybe we can get out of the gravity well. Where we go from there is anyone's guess."

Everyone on the cramped command deck nodded, their faces somber. Captain Malesis' crew looked the most grim. *They've never gone into a situation with such a small margin for survival.* Maxar's friends hadn't either, but at least they were optimistic and had more motivation. As for Maxar himself, this was no different from most Bloodsport battles. He felt much better this time though, because he had friends that needed him. There had never been a situation where the people in danger were ones he cared this much about. Maxar would embrace the horrid nano-machines whirring around inside him and use every ability they could give him. He would save Felar, Lothis, and Wake, or he would find out exactly what it was that could kill him.

"Jaydon and Maxar, use the view screen to look for a good location for us to attach to the Justice." Captain Malesis' tone was that of command. They had created a plan, now they would follow it until forced to change. *Which will probably be soon,* Maxar thought sardonically. "I'll keep us on a general path towards the ship until you find a place. Lot of room out here, but also a lot of ships moving around. I need to focus on any of them that might run into us. Carson, Qul, Terron," he continued, nodding towards his crew, "you three keep an eye on each of your systems and do your best to help Maxar and Jaydon when you can. I know we have a short crew with the loss of

Ralen, but do the best you can."

Maxar wondered fleetingly what had happened to Ralen, but had no time to ask. They would be arriving at the Founder's Justice soon, with hundreds of unknown, dark ships coming about twenty minutes later. *What is their purpose? Who controls them?* Questions whirled through Maxar's thoughts, but he forced himself to focus. *Find that landing site,* he told himself sternly.

***

Captain Malesis set the Ashamine's Bane down so gently that Maxar didn't even feel them land. It was the softest touchdown he'd ever experienced. *Or maybe now Jaydon's flying just feels normal.* They were a few hundred meters away from an active port on the side of the Founder's Justice. No one seemed to notice their arrival, so either the Entho-la-ah-mine cloak was still working or the Ashamine was too busy with the arrival of the dark ships. Maxar guessed it was the former. Even with hundreds of vessels inbound, a ship as advanced as the Justice could easily track them all.

Maxar attached the helmet to his environmental nominizing suit and breathed deeply. All diagnostics on his HUD flashed green. "Everything look good?" he asked of Tremmilly and Jaydon. The older man nodded, seeming comfortable in the suit. Tremmilly looked puzzled for a moment, then smiled and gave a thumbs-up. It was her first time in an ENS. Maxar wondered, for the thousandth time, if it was a good idea to take her along. Tremmilly was intelligent, but had no experience in combat situations. She did possess a good sense for stealth, which she'd likely gained by stalking around the forests of Eishon-2. Maxar didn't know what he would do if she was injured or killed. He had no way to convince her to stay though. A knot formed in Maxar's stomach.

His thoughts felt more muddled now than during his Bloodsport days. These new emotions were throwing off his focus. *If this plan is to have any chance of success, you need to stay in control. You can protect her, but you will only be effective if you keep your attention on the mission, not your feelings.*

Jaydon, despite his cowardice while rescuing Maxar from the Bloodsport orbital dock, seemed now to have a cool head and at least some combat skills. *Another side effect of quitting the bottle.* Maxar felt grateful. Even with his newly acquired nano-tech abilities, he needed all the help he could get.

"Are we gonna get going?" Tremmilly asked eagerly.

"Yeah. Let's move into the airlock." Maxar checked, yet again, that he had set their radio comms for an extremely short range. If anyone on the other side of the Justice's hull picked up their transmissions, security would hunt the trio down.

"Once you pass through the airlock, we'll lose communication," Malesis' voice said in their helmets. "You have the squawk signals to send for the different contingencies, so stay quiet until you are ready to come out. We'll wait until we hear from you or they blast your bodies out an airlock. He who dares, wins." With that, Malesis fell silent. Maxar took a deep breath, and stepped into the airlock.

After all three squeezed in, he pulled the heavy door closed behind them. Maxar spun the wheel that would engage the lock mechanism. Jaydon was ready, hitting the air purge button as soon as the door was secure. The small sounds Maxar could hear through his helmet lessened as atmosphere evacuated.

"Turn on your mag-lock," Maxar said, activating his own as he did so. He felt the familiar, yet odd sensation of an additional tug on his feet. It would feel stranger still once they lost the gravity of the Bane.

The airlock finished bleeding out the remaining air and the outside door opened. Before them was an infinite plane of black, the vast hull of the Founder's Justice. It had a foreboding look, and Maxar wondered if it would be the site of his death.

Jaydon took the first step out and Maxar and Tremmilly followed. Maxar guessed there would be no security devices on the hull. Why would there be? The designers of this ship had never heard of cloaking and wouldn't believe someone could sneak past all their ranged sensors.

The trio quickly made their way across the distance to the port. Fighters and gunships entered and exited the Justice ahead of them. Maxar was glad they had the forethought to paint the normally bright white environmental nominizing suits black. The sharp-eyed fighter pilots would have spotted them for sure. Even with camo paint, Maxar felt exposed. *Nothing you can do about it now.*

When they reached the opening, Maxar cautiously peered inside. "Right now we are on the wall, relative to ship's gravity," he transmitted, pointing as he did so. "That way is down." They moved towards the floor, then waited.

"Why aren't we going in?" Tremmilly asked.

"An electromagnetically contained plasma field keeps the internal bay pressurized," Maxar answered. "In its current state, it's impermeable. The only time we'll be able to go through is as a ship flies in, just as the control system decreases the charge. In those brief moments, the plasma's structure changes, allowing us to force our way in. Stay too long in the barrier and the field switches back, capturing us inside. The energy involved in the field when fully charged would be fatal. Timing is crucial."

"Aren't our suits designed to protect us from that kind of thing?"

Maxar shook his head. "ENS shielding is no match for the field generators." Tremmilly asked no further questions and Maxar resumed scanning his surroundings.

"The gunships seem to be moving the slowest," Jaydon transmitted after a minute, echoing Maxar's thoughts. "The inbound ones are slower still. Wait for one of them?" Maxar agreed and they all began scanning the approach pattern. Apparently, the Justice was rearming its spaceborne fighters and gunships in preparation for the arriving fleet of hostiles. Maxar had seen the readout in the moments before the Commandos had boarded the Revenge. Hundreds of ships were in the dark fleet, but most were merchants and transports. A few vessels were of Ashamine Forces origin, but the whole mass was nothing compared to what the Founder's Justice would send against them.

"Here comes one," Tremmilly said excitedly. Maxar reached his finger out and pressed on the barrier like it was a terminal screen. The digit immediately felt numb. He pulled it away and sensation returned. Was the field acting on his body or the nano-machines inside of it? *No way to know right now.* Maxar pressed his finger against the barrier again and this time it passed inside.

"Now!" he exclaimed, charging forward. Numbness engulfed his hand, then his arm, as he fought against the charged plasma. He had a fleeting glimpse of Tremmilly and Jaydon doing the same. A large gunship flew over them. Maxar's head began to pass through the barrier and blackness engulfed him.

24 – LOTHIS

The three of them had been silent for quite some time now. Without a clock, Lothis couldn't tell how accurate his calculation of ninety minutes was. He supposed it didn't matter anyway. Felar, Wake, and himself were all trapped inside the smuggler's compartment. It seemed logical the troops who stormed aboard the A'Tal's Revenge had piloted it to an Ashamine ship. Now, all they could do was stay silent and wait.

Lothis felt little hope of rescue. The Ashamine considered Felar and Wake traitors and would execute them on sight. They would return him to another hidden Ashamine facility to continue his indoctrination. His chest clenched at the thought of captivity.

With the blackness and tense boredom that surrounded him, Lothis was continuously tempted to reach out with his mind. Perhaps he could find some accessible computer system to gain knowledge of their situation. *But they are out there...* And he didn't know what *they* were.

When their group first entered the compartment, Lothis had sent his mind out, eager to help somehow. Immediately, he'd sensed *them*, and quickly withdrew into himself, fear coursing through every fiber of his being. In his short life, he'd never felt anything like it. They were a void, a blackness that felt mechanical, unnatural. It seemed to suck at the fabric of space-time, to warp and distort it.

Now, he wondered how close the void had come. Did it feel him? Did it know he was here? Lothis had to check, had to find out if they were about to swallow him up. He would just put the smallest part of himself out to look. *They might notice me,* he thought, and shivered with fear. Felar pulled him closer; her embrace was a comfort. Lothis took strength from her presence. *I have to try, have to do what I can to help.* Maybe the darkness wouldn't be there and he could go to work on the computer systems of the ship.

Lothis cast just a sliver of his mind out and nearly screamed in horror. The void was before him, menacing and incomprehensible. Black tendrils slithered out of its mass, creeping towards his consciousness. He watched for a moment longer, fascination overcoming his desire to flee. The darkness wasn't interested in him, at least not yet. It moved towards the ship they were inside, but hadn't taken notice of him in particular. Lothis breathed a little easier and decided he would take the risk and keep watching.

A bright flare of psionic energy sprang into being just outside the hull of the ship. Immediately, Lothis recognized it. *The Entho-la-ah-mines! The Queen!* he rejoiced. Their friends were nearby and that brought great hope to Lothis.

A movement in the darkness caught his attention and his joy sank. An enormous group of tendrils combined, snaking their way together to form a single, monstrous spike of darkness. It began winding towards the Entho-la-ah-mines, hostile and aggressive. *What can I do?* the boy thought, trying to understand how he might use his abilities to help.

The Entho-la-ah-mines crafted their energy into an orb as the darkness approached, surrounding themselves with a sphere of light. The void continued to advance, implacable and fearless.

Before Lothis could do anything, the two energies met. No explosions or big displays of radiation were visible, just a spike welling out in an attempt to absorb the Entho-la-ah-mines. The Queen, Cazz-ak-tak, and Elth-eo-lan were holding their ground though. He wondered if the Entho-la-ah-mines had immersed themselves in their hive mind.

As he continued to watch, Lothis began to despair. The dark energy was beginning to engulf the Entho-la-ah-mine sphere. *They must be growing tired.* Lothis' heart beat faster. The Queen was too important, too special, for the dreadful void to consume her. But what could he do? His abilities, while great in comparison to other humans, were no match for the forces on display. They would toss him aside or absorb him like the tiniest molecule. He wanted to cry in frustration, but the sound would give them away. Lothis forced his feelings down and continued to watch.

25 – CAZZ-AK-TAK

Cazz-ak had never felt this much weight before. He'd been on several high gravity and pressure worlds, but the force baring down on him was unlike anything he'd ever experienced. The darkness was all around him, threatening to sever his connection to the Great Thought. Images of madness, mutilation, and dismemberment flashed through his mind. It was just as it had been back under Haak-ah-tar, during the Queen's ritual. This was the same adversary, but now they were in proximity and much stronger.

"Cazz-ak," the Queen sent, her strain evident, "you must not let me be corrupted. If that happens, all the Great Thought will become infected." Cazz-ak drew in more of the Great Thought, filling himself until he thought he might burst. He felt slightly lighter for a moment, but then the darkness doubled its effort and Cazz-ak thought it might crush his mind.

"We will not let that happen," he replied, his voice small and distorted.

"This may be an impossible situation," the Queen's words were a flat statement, emotionless. "If we are about to be consumed, you must kill me." The words struck Cazz-ak even harder than the force that threatened to overcome them. It was not even until recently that their vocabulary had the word "kill." Connecting it with the Queen drove a blade of despair deep into Cazz-ak's being.

"That will not happen," he answered, but the words sounded hollow. The dark force worked its way closer and closer, images of corruption burrowing into his being. *If only there was a greater number of us here.* They would have more access to the Great Thought, enabling them to fight back. But it was just the three of them, and the humans had drastically reduced the size and scope of the hive mind with their war and genocide.

The load on Cazz-ak grew greater still and he and Elth-eo-lan cried out in pain. As Cazz-ak watched, a thin tendril of darkness began penetrating their orb. He tried everything to stop it, but Cazz-ak couldn't draw on any more of the Great Thought. It would obliterate him. All the group's effort was going towards maintaining the orb. If he diverted any of his power from that, the ball would collapse.

The tendril wormed its way closer and closer, heading directly for Na-ah-co. "Cazz-ak," she said, a note of sadness entering her voice, "now is the time. Kill me before our people are infected."

No! he screamed in his own mind, *I cannot—will not—kill one of my own species.*

"But you can," she said, responding to thoughts he believed private. Her words brought comfort to him, and Cazz-ak wondered how it was possible for Na-ah-co to console him about her own murder. "You must. If you don't, our whole species will be perverted and corrupted. It is the only thing to do."

"I don't even know how."

"Fashion a blade of energy, like that you formed to strike at the Hammer. Pierce my brain here." She sent an image of a location inside her head. "It will be a quick death. The Great Thought will remain pure."

"If I take away any energy from the barrier, it will collapse." Cazz-ak knew Na-ah-co was right, that she must die to save her people, but he couldn't kill her. He didn't want his last act to be the regicide of the Queen he had helped bring into the universe. For the first time in his existence, Cazz-ak felt like a coward.

"Elth-eo-lan will add the extra strength." They all knew drawing in more Great Thought would destroy Elth-eo-lan, she would be sacrificing herself. She would be an empty exoskeleton, all her higher functions and thoughts washed away. *I would prefer that to having the corruption consume me.*

The tendril was getting close now. Anger blossomed in Cazz-ak. The feeling he had so recently acquired was minute at first, just a bud. He focused on the oppressive darkness and his anger exploded into a supernova. Cazz-ak raged against the corruption, a white-hot fury opening new parts of his mind. He pulled in more of the Great Thought, a torrent that exceeded what any Entho-la-ah-mine had ever wielded before.

"Cazz-ak, you'll corrupt the Great Thought with that emotion," the Queen shrieked, fear filling her voice. He was beyond caring now. All Cazz-ak could feel was fury, and as more of it grew within him, the more he felt another new emotion. *Hate.* The darkness represented everything bad that had come upon the Entho-la-ah-mines: genocide, the war with the humans, near-extinction. Its corruption was trying to take the last things they had left, the Queen and the Great Thought. He would not let that happen.

Cazz-ak now had plenty of power to fashion a blade, and he did so. This weapon was not a small knife, however. It was a broadsword, heavy and full of psionic energy. Instead of aiming it at Na-ah-co, he swung it at the tendril.

Just as his weapon was about to hit, a new source of energy struck the darkness outside the orb. It didn't look anything like the Entho-la-ah-mine force and Cazz-ak didn't understand how he could see it through the darkness. This beam was the first thing they had seen outside the orb for quite some time. Its color shifted and flickered erratically. The narrow beam shot through the darkness and disappeared, leaving a hole through the corruption. Immediately, the burden on the Entho-la-ah-mines lessened.

Cazz-ak's broadsword lopped off the invading tendril and it disappeared, leaving their orb free of any darkness. Despite the outside assistance, Cazz-ak's anger still raged. He stabbed the broadsword out of the orb, penetrating the surrounding darkness. With each swing, the weight of the corruption eased. The flickering beam shot through once again. Before Cazz-ak realized what was happening, the shaft of dark force was retreating back to its main mass.

"Release it," Na-ah-co said commandingly, and Cazz-ak realized he was still drawing on a huge connection to the Great Thought. His rage forced him onward, told him to take the fight to the darkness, to strike at it, to kill it. "No. Release," the Queen ordered again. This time Cazz-ak did so and immediately felt drained. "You endangered the Great Thought as much as the blackness did." Na-ah-co's words were frigid, something Cazz-ak had only heard in humans. He wondered if his anger had infected her and the Great Thought already. Cazz-ak felt empty, alone. His entire being ached. *What have I done?*

26 – CRASOR

Crasor slammed his fist down on the console of his sleek courier ship. "Damn them to the fires of the dark star!" he shouted, pounding the console again. He'd just witnessed the failure of one of his Descended to penetrate the Entho-la-ah-mine queen.

Aeron overextended, Crasor fumed, *and the buggering Enthos damaged his connection to the Breaker mind. Now his troops lack the mental strength they need to fight as a cohesive unit.* Crasor clenched his jaw, a grinding sound coming from his teeth.

And why is the Queen even here? If he'd have known, Crasor would have come directly to the Eishon system first before assassinating the Founder. The Entho-la-ah-mine hive mind would drastically increase the power of the Breakers.

"She's still within our reach," the Breakers responded in his mind. "Focus, Crasor. Anger is a potent fuel, but too much will cloud your judgment." He knew they were right. Crasor had felt himself giving in to anger more and more lately, something that had never happened in his younger years.

As he focused on regaining his composure, a new thought occurred to him. *What was that other burst of energy?* It was powerful, and not from the Entho-la-ah-mines. The Breakers didn't know what it was either, but wanted him to find out.

Despite the failure to capture the Entho-la-ah-mine queen, Crasor was glad he'd arrived in the Eishon system. With Aeron's diminished abilities, the whole Breaker force would have been wiped out. At the moment, Crasor was too distant to lend much mental power to his force, but he could keep them from blundering into additional conflict with the unexpected Ashamine ships. Crasor had easily slipped through the Ashamine blockade, his Breaker abilities confusing the gunships and fighters.

He wondered again what the Queen was doing here, inside an

Ashamine Tarton class ship. *And for that matter, why is that battle cruiser here?* It was either the Founder's Hammer, the Founder's Justice, or the newly finished Founder's Light. Based on the configuration, Crasor's guess was the Justice. He'd never seen any of them, but knew about the ships from reports he'd received before his conversion.

Things would have been easier if I'd had time to download the Founder's private files after assassinating him. Crasor thought back to how the Ashamine's overwhelming response had forced him to flee. They'd also locked down the terminal networks, denying him access. He was strategically blind, forced to use old information he remembered to aid his escape.

When he'd descended back into the maintenance tunnels, he found his way through without incident. The shuttle station was busy, but nothing seemed out of the ordinary. Just as he boarded a shuttle to take him to the orbital dock, however, the station was shut down. The ride up felt like it lasted an eternity. Would the transportation lock down be in effect there as well? Would he make it to his ship in time? Thankfully, whoever was in charge of capturing the Founder's assassin was moving slowly, because Crasor made it to his vessel and was flying out to the worm zone before they could stop him.

His plan for dominating the Akked wasn't perfect, but it was working so far. Given his resources and the state of the Ashamine, all had gone relatively well. *Each step requires a proper completion of the step before,* he thought, refocusing his attention to the stars outside his small view window. *It is a hasty plan, but there has been no time to prepare anything more grand. Besides, as long as we stay hidden, or at least mysterious, the Ashamine will crumble before they can wipe us out.*

Checking his display, Crasor saw his speedy ship would get him to the Justice in under an hour. His Breaker fleet was almost to the huge ship's defensive perimeter. With the barely developed Descended leading the battle, the Ashamine Forces would easily wipe them out. The space around the Justice was swarming with gunships and fighters. Crasor's fleet barely had any weaponry. All odds appeared in the Ashamine's favor, but Crasor wanted that Tarton class ship. A big vessel like this one would make assaulting the outer Ashamine worlds an easy venture.

He ordered his ships to stop right outside the Justice's perimeter. The Breakers still had surprise on their side. To the Justice and it's Ashamine commander, this would look like a civilian fleet with mysterious intentions or problems. *Perhaps comm issues or system malfunctions.* It was obviously an anomaly, but they would hesitate before continuing to fire on civilians, especially if the civilian ships maintained the required distance.

Complicating the situation even further was the fact the Ashamine had already destroyed several Breaker vessels when they'd forced their way through the worm zone blockade. Thankfully, the Ashamine had spread themselves thin enough that the invaders hadn't taken serious losses. Once the Breakers had passed, the Ashamine ships did not continue the assault. *Explaining a surprise reaction is one thing,* Crasor mused, *defending the complete slaughter of an entire civilian fleet is another.*

As he hurtled towards the Justice, Crasor returned his focus to creating a battle plan. He turned the transmissions from the Ashamine ship down, but not off. It was a distraction, but a change in their warnings or questions would be the first sign of attack. Crasor sent orders to his Descended, who in turn passed them along to the ship captains. Their code words would be incomprehensible to the Justice, further adding to the mystery.

***

Crasor eased his ship up to the invisible line that formed the perimeter between normal and Justice space. *Cross that line and we all die,* he thought sarcastically, *if you believe the Ashamine.* He had lost his belief in the human government, in any word it had ever said. The Breakers were all that mattered now. They would bring an age of hyper-evolution and enlightenment to humanity, the Entho-la-ah-mines, and any other species that happened to inhabit the Akked Galaxy.

"May the Dawn be broken," he transmitted to his fleet and engaged his engines. Simultaneously, he threw his mind out into the surrounding space, pulling at the fabric of space-time. It felt slick and illusive, trying to slip through his grasp. Crasor dug the fingers of his mind in harder, focusing on holding his target. As seconds passed, he felt his control become secure, and began warping space-time, forcing it into the shape he wanted.

Having only a basic understanding of physics, Crasor didn't completely understand what he was doing, but it felt right somehow. It was instinctual, coming from the Breaker mind. He continued to bend and inflate, creating a huge bubble. To both the sensors and the humans aboard the Justice, Crasor's courier vessel and the three transports behind it vanished. Immediately, Crasor felt the strain on his brain grow to enormous proportions. The Breaker mind was doing all it could to help and it was still nearly overwhelming. This type of activity would get easier as he grew and evolved, but warping this much space was almost beyond his ability. Crasor didn't know how long he'd be able to keep it up.

"That's why you created diversions," the Breaker mind told him. A response would take too much energy, so Crasor remained focused on maintaining the bubble.

As his small detachment of ships bore down on the much larger Ashamine vessel, Crasor had to divert course often to keep from entering paths of gunships or fighters. *How can one carrier support so many ships?* The sheer size of the Ashamine fleet made him lust for its power even more.

They closed half the distance and Crasor began to feel his grip on the space-time warp slip. His focus was pure; still it was falling away. It was like his fingers were unpeeling one by one. *Just a bit farther,* he thought, gritting his teeth. Crasor had to get inside the targeting range of the rail cannons before he became visible. He didn't know exactly what that distance was, but they were definitely still in danger

Crasor began to sweat. After a few more moments, he started shaking. "Help me," he cried out to the Breaker mind.

"We are doing all we can. You are not advanced enough for us to engage more." Crasor lasted for another minute, and another. He was grunting as he breathed and his head felt like a metal door taking rail weapon fire.

Finally, the last of his grip on the warp failed. Crasor slumped in his captain's chair, feeling like every part of him was draining away. He barely had enough energy left to keep control of the ship.

Without knowing their encryption code, he had no way to listen in on the Ashamine's transmissions, but he could easily guess they were scrambling. Four ships had just appeared inside their secure perimeter and were closing fast. Crasor waited for a rail cannon to obliterate him, but it appeared that perhaps they were inside the targeting margins. Gunships and fighters would be engaging them soon, but Crasor hoped they could set down on the Justice before that happened.

A rail round streaked out from the battle cruiser, the ion trail lighting up his cockpit. "Blightheart," Crasor shouted, his Breaker-enhanced reactions causing him to throw the control stick sideways. Time seemed to stand still, and he knew this might be the end. An instant later, the round flew by and effortlessly passed through the third transport ship. The kinetic energy of the projectile obliterated the small vessel, blowing it into pieces.

At that moment, his detachment must have passed through the minimum range of the cannons, because the fire ceased. Crasor took in a deep breath, relieved. *We can still take the Justice, even with the loss of a third of the troops.* Once they boarded the Ashamine ship, the odds would drastically tip in their favor.

Glancing at his rearward facing sensors, Crasor saw the expected gunships and fighters on his tail. He also saw that the Ashamine was systematically destroying the rest of his fleet. With Crasor's breach of space, the Ashamine finally had the justification it needed to eliminate the civilian ships. It was unfortunate he would lose so many of the newly developing Breakers, but if he could capture the Justice, Crasor could create many more.

The margin between their arrival on the Justice's hull and when the fighters would be in range to strike was minuscule. *Will they fire on us, risking a hit on their own carrier?* That was a decision the Ascended in control of the fleet would make. It mostly depended on who he thought Crasor was. Most likely, he would assume they were Divisionists, the group who protested and demonstrated against the Ashamine. If that was the case, the Ascended would probably let them board, so that he might capture and put them on trial. They would love to show the Divisionists as aggressors. The Ascended also wouldn't want to risk damage to his own ship as it would be bad press if someone leaked that information.

Crasor set down hard on the black hull of the Justice. Moments later, his two remaining ships landed next to him. He paused for a moment, waiting. Would the rail guns of the approaching fighters obliterate him? A few seconds later, they passed harmlessly overhead. *Nothing,* Crasor thought, a grin twisting his face. *I figured as much.*

27 – ASCENDED KAROTH

"Sensors detect breach of outer hatch 31-Bravo," one of the damage control technicians shouted.

"Troops in route to that location," the Marine Separate barked, his ruddy face going a deeper shade of crimson. "How in the fires of the dark star did they blow that airlock so quickly?" Ascended Karoth was wondering the same thing. It was a weak spot in the hull—all openings were—but how had a bunch of Divisionists been able to crack a military grade armored airlock that quickly?

"Report from inside 31-Bravo?" Karoth asked, his voice calm despite the frenetic energy surrounding him. That area of the ship contained crew quarters and would have enough personnel to subdue the invaders. *Off duty crew don't carry weapons though,* he thought. Still, he had locked down that sector of the ship to all unauthorized personnel. They wouldn't be able to get far. And the detachment of Marines would arrive soon to capture or kill the invaders. *What if they are planting a nuclear device or some other type of explosive?*

"No word, sir," the head comm tech replied, sounding concerned. His answer worried Karoth as well. *Are comms down in that part of the ship or is no one able to respond?* So many unknown and unexplained things were going on at the moment, far more than the fog of regular combat could account for.

First, all these civilian ships had wormed in system and forced past the blockade, despite taking casualties. Where had they come from? What was their motive? None of them answered when contacted. Radio silence. Karoth had transmitted warning after warning, with no response. The civilian ships just kept on coming, straight into the barrels of the Ashamine fleet. It made no sense.

The ships had to be connected to whoever had assassinated the Founder, but Karoth had no idea what their ultimate goal was. His initial instinct had been to fire on them, to turn them all into so much space

97

junk, but a part of him said perhaps he could capture and interrogate the traitors. He'd received no further updates from the Classad or Ashamine Forces HQ. If they knew who'd killed the Founder, they hadn't told him yet. Karoth guessed they didn't know, and it seemed he might be looking at an opportunity to find out. He had more than enough power to destroy them, and they posed little threat to the Justice, so he'd waited. Besides, if he acted too quickly and this turned out to be a bunch of refugees with a comms malfunction, he didn't want to be responsible for killing thousands of innocents.

After a while, the invading ships had stopped inexplicably and started chatting over the radio with each other. Their transmissions sounded like code, but his cryptographers told him it wasn't. The more Karoth listened, the more is sounded like the talk of insane people. "Our heart is burned and we all shall consume. Feast on the arrows of the past and walk beneath the heavens," was one of the more comprehensible ones. The cryptographers were still working on it, but Karoth wasn't hopeful.

As Karoth had begun forming a plan to capture some vessels, four ships, a small courier vessel and three transports, had vanished off their sensors. Immediately, Karoth felt like something was wrong. Ships didn't disappear. Cloaking, or whatever the invaders had done, was an unknown technology to the Ashamine. Karoth didn't like someone else having more tech than him. *What if they have weaponry capable of penetrating the Justice's hull?* It seemed unlikely that something so powerful could fit on one of these small civilian ships. The energy requirements alone would necessitate a larger vessel. Even the few Ashamine Forces ships mixed in weren't configured for battle. Despite his earlier feelings, Karoth ordered the remaining hostile ships annihilated. He couldn't risk the chance that more of them might disappear.

While his fighters began destroying the enemy ships, Karoth consulted with his techs. They said their sensors weren't malfunctioning or jammed. That would mean the vanished ships were indeed cloaking. When they had appeared, almost inside rail gun range, Karoth was sure of it. The transit time was right.

A quick weapons tech had enough time to instruct his computer to fire on the hostiles, destroying one of them before they were too close. Point defense fighters and gunships had been slower to respond, and by the time they'd arrived on location, the three remaining ships had latched on to the Justice. Karoth had been loath to send rail rounds through them and into his own hull. He'd assumed the invaders were Divisionists, but now he wasn't so sure. Between the cloaking, airlock, kidnapping of the Successor, and assassination of the Founder, this had the feel of a very powerful organization. Still, he had multiple divisions of troops and the invaders would be engaging on the Ashamine's terms.

"The first squad of Marines have arrived outside 31-Bravo," the Marine Separate announced. *Good,* Karoth thought, returning to the current situation, *excellent response time.* "They have entered through the main hatch," the Separate continued, sounding at ease. "I'll put their video feeds up." A moment later the views from several Marines were live on the huge tactical screen. The feed also contained audio from the Enlightened leading the squad.

"Stay sharp," he said, voice sounding calm and assured. "Confirm your targets. No fratricide." The video feeds swung back and forth as the Marines looked around. They cleared several rooms, making their way closer and closer to the breached hatch. Empty quarters greeted them. Earlier, Karoth had ordered one of the techs to check the assignment roster. This whole area should be full of people.

"Clear," the Enlightened Marine said as they finished the second to last section in 31-Bravo. Only one section of quarters remained. Past that was the hatch area, built with escape pods for use by this sector's crew.

Karoth's apprehension strengthened as the Enlightened regrouped his squad. Something was wrong with this situation, but Karoth couldn't decide exactly what it was. *The missing crew?* Yes, that was part of it. There was more though, buried deeply in his emotions. He felt a compulsion to act, but didn't know what to do.

The Marine Enlightened confidently led his troops towards the door to the last section of crew quarters. *That's it: the door!* Not this one, but the single hatch that allowed access from this deck to the rest of the ship. They had left it unlocked. Due to the lack of combat, no one had thought to secure it after the Marines had passed through.

"Don't open that last door," Karoth shouted, and the Marine Separate gave him a weird look. "Tell them to stand down!" Obviously, the Separate thought Karoth had tasted the dark star, but the man started issuing the order. Karoth turned and barked another command. "Security, lock the main hatch to 31-Bravo." As the security tech looked down to carry out the order, the Marine Enlightened hit "Open" on the door control screen.

"Sir," the security tech said, "the main hatch was left open and cannot be locked."

"Blightheart," Karoth cursed, his dread deepening into panic. With that main door open and unlocked, he would have to put the rest of the ship on lockdown, making personnel movements difficult. Karoth was about to give the command when something on the video feed caught his attention. The last section of crew quarters was pitch black.

"What was that?" the Enlightened asked, his confident tone supplanted by a quaver of fear. "Full tac illum," he ordered. The entire squad turned their lights on and revealed a view that was straight from the fires of the dark star.

Blood covered the floor and spattered the walls and ceiling. Corpses and body parts lay strewn haphazardly across the deck, creating a macabre scene that pulled Karoth back to himself. "Lockdown the entire ship, full containment protocol. No one goes through a single hatch without my authorization." His voice was frosty, commanding. He'd lost himself in fear for a moment, but would not let it control him any longer. "Marine Separate, tell your men to fall back and secure the main hatch to 31-Bravo." The Separate seemed dumbfounded, lost in the horrifying images on the view screen. "Separate, do it now!" Karoth's shout finally broke through the man's trance and he keyed his mic.

"Enlightened," he said, voice quavery, "secure 31-Bravo main hatch, on exterior." Before the squad of Marines could do so, the bodies on the floor began to rise.

28 – WAKE

Wake hated the engulfing darkness. It was an empty canvas his mind scrawled horrible memories on. Cold blue stars spiraled out around him. The Antadroga floated just a kilometer away, watching, waiting for his inevitable death. His throat began to tighten, feeling the void sensation of a lack of oxygen. He couldn't breathe. Panic crashed over him. Wake's field of vision began to narrow, stars fading. *No, no, no,* he thought, reaching up to pull off his ENS helmet, desperate for air. When he touched his face instead of metal, he snapped back to reality. *I'm on the Revenge,* he thought, trying to calm his ragged breathing.

Each passing moment threatened to trigger the memory of his failed execution once again. *Be calm. You are OK.* He breathed deeply, body assuring mind there was indeed plenty of oxygen.

Finally, after several minutes, Wake felt he had his emotions under control. The blackness went from terrifying to merely oppressive. He still felt trapped in this dark box, his companions a woman he barely knew and a boy who was successor to the Founder. *It's better than being alone, dead, or back in the hands of the Ashamine.*

Periodically, the noise of boots passed over head. *They are looking for us.* Each time the sounds approached, Wake wondered if there would be a blinding flash of light, then nothingness. Hopefully, the guards had good aim.

It was impossible to tell exactly how long they'd been in the smuggler's compartment. Wake knew by the stiffness of his muscles it was at least an hour, probably more. He couldn't figure out how to open the compartment without alerting the troops above. All they could do was wait in silence.

An eerie sound filled the darkness around Wake and he stiffened. It was coming from Felar and Lothis' corner. *The boy,* Wake thought, hoping he wouldn't get any louder. Felar began making comforting noises, hushing Lothis. The whining sound continued for several seconds more, then stopped.

"Lothis is completely rigid," Felar whispered, her panic obvious. "He might be having a seizure." Wake carefully moved through the short bit of space that separated them and felt the boy.

"Don't people shake when they have seizures?" Wake knew even whispering was dangerous, but he had to help Felar, had to calm her before she escalated.

"If it's not seizures, then what's wrong with him?"

Wake shook his head and shrugged, then realized Felar couldn't see him. "I'm sorry. I have no idea." From just his short time with the crew of the A'Tal's Revenge, Wake could tell Felar loved Lothis deeply. It was a strange situation, one he'd like to know the story behind. *If I ever get the chance.*

A moment or two passed, the weight of the dark silence once again pressing in. "He's limp now, but still breathing." Having nothing to add, Wake remained silent. More time passed, Wake falling deeper and deeper into despair. He could not escape. The Ashamine would take his life after all.

"Lothis is stiff again." This time Felar seemed a little less panicked. Unable to help, Wake kept his silence. Perhaps it was seizures, maybe the side effect of some type of mental disorder.

Boots thumped loudly overhead and Wake winced. *We've been too loud.* But no, the sound of feet diminished and vanished all-together. *Did the soldiers leave?*

"Lothis is back to being limp."

"I think the soldiers left." Wake replied. "Maybe we can try to find a way out now."

"I need to see what is going on with Lothis."

Wake switched on the small light that was part of his gauntlet. He kept it dim, trying to reduce any chance of giving away their position. When he pointed the light in Lothis' direction, Wake winced at what he saw.

The boy was as pale as a corpse. His eyes were white, his pupils rolled back into his head. He looked dead. Felar started shaking, silent sobs racking her small frame.

"He's still alive," she managed to whisper. "He has a pulse and is breathing."

"We need to find a way out of this box. Maybe then we can help him somehow." Wake knew escape was improbable, even if the troops had left the A'Tal's Revenge, but he had to try.

While Felar cradled Lothis, Wake looked for any type of latch or button. The walls were smooth metal and appeared featureless. Maybe it was a button or sensor that was touch sensitive? Wake took off one gauntlet and ran his hands along the cool metal. First, he scanned the narrow end he'd been leaning against. A smooth, blank wall produced no results. He then searched the walls on either side. *Nothing.* The ceiling was next, but that surface also proved void of any type of mechanism.

"I can't find anything," he told Felar. "The only surface left is your wall." Wake switched places with Felar, careful not to hit the unconscious Lothis as he slid past. Starting at the bottom, Wake slowly slid his hand across the surface. When he was almost to the top, he felt a seam. It was the smallest hint, invisible to the eye. He traced the irregularity. *About two centimeters square.*

"I found a button," Wake said excitedly, trying to keep his voice down just in case troops were still above.

"Press it. I'm ready to fight if anyone is out there."

Wake found the center of the square and pressed. Nothing. He tried pressing it again and pushing on the hatch at the same time. His heart sank. "It's not working."

"Keep looking," Felar said, sounding hopeful. "Maybe there is another button you have to press at the same time, like how it is above."

Before Wake could continue, the sound of boots returned to the deck above. He quickly shut off his light, plunging the small space into darkness once again. Wake shook his head and let out his breath in a silent sigh.

Seconds stretched into minutes and Wake fell back into waiting. Time faded, becoming an indecipherable mass. He drifted to thoughts about the Clothing of the Iconoclast. Wake wondered if the power source he'd thought up before would work. It would take several minutes to construct the complicated device, but he thought everything he needed was on board. *You're assuming you'll get out of this box alive.* If it did function, Wake had the feeling it would unlock the many mysteries surrounding his crimson environmental nominizing suit.

Loud shouts from above broke Wake out of his reverie. This was the first time they'd been able to hear voices. Something big was happening. Boots once again thudded above. A minute later all was silent.

"Keep looking for another button," Felar said, her voice once again strong. "That sounded like someone issuing orders."

Wake switched his light back on, and began searching again. The second button was harder to find and took longer than the first. He'd missed it on his first inspection of the walls. It was the same size, but the seams were even thinner.

"OK, got the other one."

"Ready."

This time, when he pressed both buttons, a bright stream of light cascaded in from the edges of the hatch above.

29 – FELAR

Felar barely had a grip on her emotions. *He's gone, he's gone, he's gone,* was all she could think, the repetition spiraling out in her mind. Lothis had gone away like before, but this time he wasn't coming back. She didn't know what to do.

"OK, got the other one." Wake looked at her expectantly, waiting for her signal. She carefully laid Lothis on the metal floor, drew one of her combat short swords from its back sheath, and nodded.

"Ready."

Wake pressed both buttons and a bright beam of light shone down into the compartment. Felar quickly pushed the panel away and sprang up into the illumination of the Revenge's storage deck. Her eyes focused and she scanned the room. *Empty.*

A horrible decision confronted Felar. Did she leave Lothis in the smuggler's compartment while she and Wake looked for a way to escape, or did she bring him along? What if he needed her when she wasn't there? What if he died? Taking him with them presented many more dangers, not the least of which was Lothis hindering their progress or taking a round in crossfire. Besides, if the Ashamine captured Wake and herself, she didn't want Lothis to fall back into their hands. *Death is a better option for him,* she thought, her heart breaking.

"What do we do now?" Wake asked in a whisper, climbing out behind her.

"The airlock is shut. I think they are gone, at least for now." She walked over to the hatch and hit the button to lock it. It wouldn't slow down hostiles much, but it would at least give them some warning. "We need to figure out what is happening on the Ashamine ship. It would be nice to know where we are, and where it is headed." Felar paused for a moment, thinking. "Did you see how Jaydon opened the smuggler's compartment?"

"I think so," he replied, crouching down next to the panel. "He put

104

two fingers from his right hand on these screws and three from his left hand on these." Felar closed the lid, tried the sequence, and was glad to see the access panel unlatch. This time she left it open.

"Glad you remembered that," she said with a smile. "We can leave it open until they start banging on the door."

"I don't really want to hide in there again." Wake's face was grim.

"I know what you mean. It will take a lot of blightheart to get me back in there too, but it may be our only option if they come back before we find an escape."

They headed for the command deck, Felar reasoning the terminals there would tell her what was happening. She sat in Jaydon's pilot chair, and Wake took the co-pilot's position. Felar began scrolling through screens.

"Looks like we are inside the Founder's Justice." Felar felt deflated.

"Is it a big ship?"

"It's the only functioning Tarton class vessel in existence. The Hammer was destroyed by the Entho-la-ah-mines and the Light is still being built. There is no way we are getting out of here. This is a battle cruiser. It carries a damned Founder's load of gunships and fighters. It has a huge contingent of Marines and is the most high tech ship in the Ashamine Fleet."

"Sounds like we're buggered." Wake's use of profanity surprised Felar. He was normally calm and soft-spoken. Wake looked dejected and Felar felt bad for being so negative.

"Well, we aren't completely out of options. We can try to hash into the Justice's servers and figure out what's going on."

"I thought you said this was the most high tech ship in the Ashamine Fleet. Won't that be impossible?"

Felar smiled. "It would be if you didn't have a Founder's Commando with you, one that graduated the top of her class in computer systems." While that statement was true, Felar knew hashing the Justice would not be as casual as she was making it out. It would be the most difficult system she'd ever attempted to infiltrate and there would be a constant danger of discovery.

"Is there anything I can do to help?" He seemed eager, but this wasn't a job for two people.

"No, I don't think so. Not unless you have the root access codes."

Wake shook his head and grinned. "Good luck."

"I'm certainly going to need it."

"While you work on that, I'm going to head into the cargo area. I'll keep an eye on Lothis. I also have something I can work on. It might help us later."

"Thank you," she said, gratitude welling up inside her.

Wake headed back to the cargo deck and Felar turned towards the terminal. Now that she was about to attempt the hash, she felt nervous. Back in Dog School, they'd never learned this level of computer security. It was all mainly based on defeating doors and security systems. Information technology was a whole different subject, one taught to those on the espionage track. *If only Lothis was awake,* she thought. His hashing skills were exponentially greater than anything she'd seen or heard of.

Felar pulled up a prompt on the terminal screen. First, she had to establish a connection the Justice would see as friendly. This would require an authorization code. Thankfully, Felar still remembered a few from back when she was on Haak-ah-tar. Hopefully, they'd not expired yet. She created a virtual session within the Revenge's computer, configuring it to appear as an FC drop ship. Felar added her auth codes and double-checked all the settings. Everything looked good. *Here we go,* Felar thought, holding her breath.

She initiated a connection to the Justice. The link completed and the authentication sequence began. Both sides presented challenge codes and answers, establishing identification. This was the most crucial part. After another moment of back and forth, the connection established. Felar let out a whoop of joy.

"Everything OK?" Wake asked quietly over the intercom.

"Yeah, yeah, it's great," she replied, her mind plunging deep into the intricacies of the terminal. Now, the screen showed Felar a direct connection to the Justice. She would still need security clearances for parts of the server, but the initial danger of the system refusing a connection had passed.

Scrolling through options, she found one pertaining to the status of the ship. "It looks like they had an exterior breach," she sent over the intercom. "On deck 31-Bravo, wherever that is. It happened just a few minutes ago. Maybe that's why the troops left the Revenge."

"Who would have the ability to get that close to a ship this powerful?" Wake responded.

"I dunno, and neither do they. It does appear connected to all the ships that wormed in system just as we were captured. It would be nice to have a sitrep, but the system requires a clearance to get one."

"I know you already are, but please be careful."

"Woah," Felar said, reading a status screen that just popped up. "They just went to full lockdown. No doors can be opened without authorization from Ascended Karoth."

"Is that a good or bad thing for us?"

"Good, I think. It would seem they are having trouble containing whoever boarded the ship. Thankfully, that means searching the Revenge is probably a low priority at the moment. Depending on who the invaders are, we might be in trouble if they come to this part of the ship. For the time being, I think we are safe." If she could see the status of troop movements it would improve their situation greatly, but the hash was risky.

Felar began writing a buffer exploit that would elevate her permissions. She'd figured out everything she could with her current log in credentials. If she could bump her authorization up to that of an Enlightened, she would have access to much more. The code took quite a while to write, and thankfully, whatever Wake was doing kept him silent. She needed all her focus directed towards writing a flawless script.

She sent the code to the server, sat back, and waited. Either the system would allow the higher credentials or it would shut down her terminal and flag it as a threat. Moments passed and Felar held her breath. No alerts or warnings popped up, just a change in insignia next to her name. Felar smiled in satisfaction.

The troop deployment readout baffled Felar momentarily. Everything looked wrong. A wire frame three-dimensional model represented the Justice. That part was easy enough to understand. It was the positioning of the ship's personnel that confused her. An orb of Marines and Founder's Commandos surrounded 31-Bravo. As Felar watched, the sphere grew larger and larger. Obviously whatever was inside the bubble was forcing them to retreat. *What could make Ashamine Forces run that quickly?* Then she thought about the monstrosities from the research facility where she'd rescued Lothis. Felar shuddered. *Those would do it all right.*

"Wake," she called back on the intercom, "you need to see this."

When he arrived, he took one look at the terminal screen and said, "Whoever boarded is coming straight in our direction." Wake's rapid assessment impressed Felar.

"Yeah, and at the rate they are moving, it won't be longer than fifteen minutes or so."

"Who are they?"

"Still don't have that information, mainly because the Ashamine don't know, or haven't put it on to the network yet."

"What can we do before they get here?" Wake straightened, and something about his posture told her he was ready for battle. Perhaps he knew how to use the katana sheathed on his back after all.

"We make the Revenge seem empty and lie low. If the invaders are swarming, perhaps they will blow past us without another look."

"I think we should both be in ENS's." Wake looked down at his crimson suit and smiled. "I worked up a power supply for this thing while you were hashing and I think it will come in handy." His idea for her to suit up was a smart one. It would hinder her ability to fight somewhat, but the protection provided would be worth it.

"OK, I'll get geared up. You power down the lights." Felar went back to the cargo hold and found a locker containing two adult sized suits and that of a child's. Why Jaydon had a child's ENS suit on board was slightly baffling. *And the smuggler's compartment.* If Felar ever saw the man again, she would demand some answers.

When she went down in the hidden compartment, Felar found Lothis in much the same position she'd left him. He looked dead, but his heart rate and breathing seemed normal. She put the suit over his limp body and sealed the helmet. After climbing out of the compartment, Felar closed it. *Lothis will be safe in there,* she hoped. Felar inventoried her weapons. Just a rail pistol and her combat short swords. Thankfully, the pistol had a full charge and she had lots of rounds. Breathing deeply to calm herself, Felar donned her own environmental nominizing suit and went back up to Wake.

"Lothis still unconscious?" Wake's voice was full of concern. "He didn't move at all while I was back there, at least from what I could tell."

Felar replied with an affirmative and sat in the captain's chair. She felt grateful Wake hadn't messed with the link to the Justice. After she sat down, he hit a selector on his screen and the illumination inside the ship went black. Only the light of their terminal screens remained.

"Now we wait," Wake said.

"Now we wait," Felar agreed, but she had something to do in the short time remaining. "Keep an eye on things and when they get within a deck, tell me."

Wake confirmed he would do so and Felar dug into one of the pouches on her tactical vest. She had created a hidden compartment, a place to hide her data square. The device contained all the information she had downloaded in the horrible research facility under Haak-ah-tar. It had files about Lothis and a program Maxar had unknowingly been a part of. She hadn't had the courage to look at it before, fearing opening the files would trigger a security alert or notification as to her and Lothis' whereabouts. Now, with her heightened confidence in her hashing skills, she set up another virtual session. Felar configured environmental variables and security parameters to isolate the workspace from the rest of the terminal's systems. *That should do it,* she thought, creating an electronic kill switch. Her counter-measure would activate if anything on the data square tried to move outside the virtual session.

With everything in place, Felar opened the first file. It was about Lothis. She had to keep herself from crying as she read how Director Kasol had experimented on him, how they'd kept him away from any human contact. They were attempting to bring out characteristics they found desirable. Researchers had manipulated Lothis' DNA, a secret practice normal for all Founders. Felar had read all this before, but now she knew the boy better, it hurt her even more. The next few lines shocked her. Lothis' had additional modifications to his DNA, ones that would make him smarter, stronger, and faster. Kasol was trying to make him superhuman. The files listed no results and contained nothing other than the research plan. She wished there had been more, perhaps something to indicate what was happening to him at the moment.

Felar skipped over the files pertaining to Director Kasol and his pet project. She hoped all the creatures had died with their creator in the Haak-ah-tar supernova. Instead, Felar opened up the files related to the nano-tech research Kasol had moved to Bloodsport. It referred to some initial discoveries made on a planet called Traynos-6, where they had discovered a seed for the program. There wasn't much more listed, but it sounded like the technology had ties to something ancient. The researchers didn't understand it well. Kasol had tested it on some human subjects before sending the program to Bloodsport for further review. It looked like Maxar might develop amazing abilities—as well as some nasty side effects—if he reacted like prior subjects.

"One more deck," Wake said, his voice sober and worried. Felar looked at the tactical readout and saw he was right. Despite her mental preparation, a dread crept into Felar's bones.

"We should put our helmets on," she replied. They did so, and when Felar looked over at Wake, she realized his had no faceplate. The helmet was all smooth crimson metal. "You can see in that thing?"

"Yeah, it has a view screen inside it."

"Seems overly complicated for a suit meant to execute people."

"Maybe," Wake replied, noncommittally.

Felar killed her virtual environment and wiped the terminal's memory. After placing the data square on the floor, she smashed it with her boot.

Wake brought up external views from around the Revenge. As expected, they saw no guards or troops, just an empty hangar bay. A flicker of motion caught Felar's attention, and a single Marine ran into view. Felar could tell he was in a non-tactical, full on retreat. Several comrades followed behind him, the vanguard of the rout.

Now, more Marines and Founder's Commandos came on screen, exploding into the large hangar area. They took cover behind ships, containers, structures, anything that would provide a modicum of cover. *What can make FCs run like this?* Felar's dread ratcheted up, her eyes straining to see what would come next.

A single Marine stumbled through the doorway, her fatigues torn and bloody. Unlike her comrades, she moved jerkily, her stride irregular. She had five deep puncture wounds in her chest, the configuration looking somewhat like a handprint. A few more soldiers followed, their movements slow, but persistent. Felar thought she could make out the same puncture wounds in their chests as well.

"Why are they moving so strangely?" Wake asked, squinting at the screen in concentration. Felar had no answer for him. She couldn't explain the feeling deep inside, the intuition she hadn't experienced since the Haak-ah-tar research facility. Just like the monstrosities, these weren't people. They were unnatural, alien, wrong.

The normal Ashamine opened fire on their shambling comrades. Flechette and rail rounds tore through their bodies, the surrounding air became a haze of blood, brains, and tracer trails. More lurching figures came into view, and the Ashamine mowed them down as well.

"Isn't it dangerous to use rail rounds inside a star ship?" Wake was right and Felar nodded.

"Yeah, definitely. The exterior of these kinds of battle ships are armored, but the interiors aren't. If one of the rounds hits something vital..." Felar trailed off, thinking about the scene before her. These wounded troops were walking straight into death for a reason. Whoever was leading them had a plan.

"This is a diversion," Felar said, zooming in on their sector of the three-dimensional model. She scanned the area around the hangar bay. "Right there," she pointed, using her other hand to flick through different exterior feeds until she found one pointed in the right direction. Sure enough, as they watched, more figures came into the hangar, coming in at an angle oblique to the Ashamine troops.

"They are fast," Wake said in surprise.

"And armed."

Felar and Wake watched the new group collide with the Ashamine. They carried a wide assortment of weapons, from lengths of pipe or knives up to rail assault rifles. A few had on AF garb, but the rest wore civilian clothes. Felar even saw a dark haired man wearing a business suit. He was one of the first to reach the soldiers, pulling back a man's head and opening his throat with a long blade.

Even though the invaders had the element of surprise, the Ashamine held it together. The troops turned to face the new wave of danger and began laying down suppressive fire. It probably would have worked, if not for the third group that came rushing in from yet another angle.

Now, rail and flechette rounds were flying in every direction, tracer lines blazing. Felar heard the cracks as several rail rounds went through their hull. "Blightheart," she growled, reflexively ducking her head. Two more thuds announced additional incoming shots.

Turning back to the screen, Felar sensed the end was near for this deployment of Ashamine troops. They were still fighting, still firing their flechette pistols and using their knives in close quarters, but the tide had already shifted. All would be dead soon.

One of the chest puncture Marines had somehow survived the withering fire of the first wave and picked up a rail rifle. Taking aim at the general mass of fighters, he triggered a round. He pointed the weapon far too high, however. The round streaked through empty space before slamming into some machinery next to the hangar door.

"That's the plasma field generator," Wake said, as the errant Marine shot off several more wild rounds. These blasted into the support structure for the hangar's armored doors, which the crew had closed for the lockdown. *This is bad,* Felar thought. The doors were designed to handle damage on their exterior, not from within.

"Hold on," she ordered, bracing herself against the back of her chair. The big rail rifle slugs had done their work, and when the plasma field generator shorted out, the vacuum of space began tugging on the weakened armored doors. Support struts bent, groaning ominously. Both sides of the huge door lost integrity and collapsed outward simultaneously. A huge hole formed between them as they jammed up against the exterior of the Justice. The Revenge shuddered and slid across the floor as the hangar began explosively decompressing. Bodies tumbled through the air, the ones closest to the collapsed door flying out into space.

VENTING ATMOSPHERE, popped up on the main terminal screen.

"Damn it," Felar said. "It doesn't look like the Revenge's environmental systems will be able to keep up with so many holes."

"At least we have our suits," Wake's voice was positive, "and with the plasma barrier and armor shielding down, we fly the Revenge out." Felar opened up her session with the Justice and looked at its exterior tactical readout.

"There is still a blighthearted mess of fighters, gunboats, and civilian ships out there. It looks like the Ashamine is systematically buggering every vessel that doesn't have their insignia on it."

"So what can we do then? Wait?"

"I don't know." Felar felt powerless. "We can't leave without being obliterated and we can't stay here, at least not once we get to critical levels on our ENS air supplies." She looked back at the exterior view display. Bodies lay strewn across the deck, some still twitching in their last few moments of pain and suffocation. "At least we don't have to worry about anyone from those two groups."

"I'll go back and try to fix the rail round damage. Maybe then, if the situation is right, we can fly out of here." Felar liked Wake's optimism. It was something her life had lacked lately.

30 – TREMMILLY

"Maxar, wake up!" Tremmilly knew she was being too loud, that even whispering might draw the attention of the Ashamine personnel in the hangar bay.

"We have to get him somewhere less exposed." Fear welled in Jaydon's eyes, but his voice was steady and strong. "Grab his legs."

Tremmilly did so, concern for Maxar almost nullifying her fear of capture. Jaydon grabbed Maxar's arms and they dragged him across the smooth floor, stopping behind a small ferry ship.

"I don't think anyone saw us," Jaydon said, peeking around the corner. "Good thing most of the flight crews are on the far end." Tremmilly barely heard him. She was looking deep into Maxar's eyes.

"What's wrong with him?" Tremmilly's medical knowledge and skills were fairly basic, and now she wished she'd studied more in those areas.

"I don't know."

"It seems like the plasma field impacted him differently than us."

"Yeah, I just felt a little dizzy."

Tremmilly thought for a moment. "I was dizzy too, but nowhere near passing out."

Maxar began to shake, body convulsing. Tremmilly tried to support his head and keep it from bouncing off the floor.

"Blightheart," Jaydon cursed, grabbing Maxar's boots before they could clatter on the deck. The shaking intensified for a moment, then began to subside. Tremmilly almost began crying, but she knew it would do no good and fought the urge.

Finally, after several minutes passed, Maxar was calm. Tremmilly and Jaydon remained watchful, worried he would start shaking again. Maxar's eyes opened.

"What happened?" he said, terror evident on his face.

"You're OK," Tremmilly crooned, "everything is alright."

"Something with the plasma field. It knocked you out." Jaydon let go

112

of Maxar's boots.

"We are on the Justice?" He was becoming calm, returning to his normal state.

"Yes," Tremmilly answered, "you were only out for a couple minutes."

"OK, good." Maxar sat up and looked around. "No one saw us?"

"I think we're good," Jaydon replied, once again taking a quick look around the corner to confirm.

"I don't like what just happened to me," Maxar said, rubbing his head. "You guys weren't affected?"

"No, just some mild dizziness when we passed through the plasma barrier." Tremmilly looked into Maxar's eyes. They seemed normal. She realized what she was doing and quickly turned away, embarrassed. "You collapsed as soon as you went through," she finished, trying not to show her feelings.

"Nano-machines," Maxar announced, shaking his head.

"What?"

"The nano-machines Felar said she'd read about in the Ashamine files, I believe that's what caused me to pass out." He thought for a moment, then continued. "The electromagnetic field of the plasma barrier must have overloaded or reset them or something." Tremmilly listened thoughtfully.

"Well, we better keep you away from any strong magnetic fields," Jaydon said.

"So I can be shot in the chest with a rail pistol, but not be near a magnet?" Maxar got to his feet and stretched. "I guess we should go search for Felar and Lothis?"

"And Wake," Tremmilly added, "he is in the prophecy too."

"Of course."

Maxar set off, leading the way through the labyrinth of spacecraft, cargo, and supplies. After several minutes, they were near the opposite end of the hangar. This side was much busier, making progress more difficult. Tremmilly's nerves were on edge, and she worried someone would see them at any moment.

"Wait here," Maxar said, leaving them in a secure spot behind the landing skid of a gunship. He crept off, his movement silent. The seconds dragged into minutes. Tremmilly had no idea what Maxar was doing.

The two of them continued to wait, until they heard a loud explosion and yelling. Seconds later, Maxar appeared, beckoning. "Time to go," he whispered. Maxar led them in a fast run across an exposed section of the hangar. The action reminded Tremmilly of when they'd done the same thing on the Bloodsport orbital dock. All that was missing was Beowulf. *Time is repeating itself,* she thought as they neared the safety of an exit hatch. Thinking of Beowulf made her long for the wolf-dog's presence. If they'd had a way to get him through vacuum and onto the Justice, she would have brought him along. Tremmilly was glad he was watching over the Entho-la-ah-mines though. It was as if a part of her could stay with her new, but very dear friends.

Maxar opened the heavy door, and they all slid through. "What did you do?" Tremmilly panted as the intensity of the sprint caught up with her.

"Just a small diversion," Maxar said with a grin. She noticed he wasn't even breathing hard and tried to control her own inhalations.

"Where do we go from here?" Jaydon asked, also breathing hard.

"We need to find a quiet place with a terminal. Perhaps an unused crew room."

They spent lots of time slinking through corridors and quarters. Tremmilly thought at any second they would run into someone. Maxar had a large knife out, ready, if they did. The tension ate at her nerves and she could tell Jaydon felt the same. Maxar, though, looked as nonchalant as ever. *This is his environment,* she thought, as they checked yet another door, only to find it locked. *He thrives on the hunt, on the kill.* Realizing this made her attraction to him even more puzzling.

"Yes!" Maxar exclaimed, his voice barely above a whisper. The door ahead of him slid open. It was an empty crew room. They all went in and closed the door. Inside, the space was void of all personalization, unused, sterile.

Maxar strode to the small terminal screen on top of an otherwise empty desk. There wasn't even a chair. "This should show us where the Revenge is. Hopefully, everyone is still hidden in your compartment."

Jaydon nodded, but then looked worried. "You can hash an Ashamine battle ship's server?"

"Maybe, maybe not," Maxar said, the grin Tremmilly loved so much brightening his severe face.

Crouching awkwardly in front of the screen, Maxar went to work. In between his quick pace and her lack of knowledge about computers or hashing, Tremmilly found his work incomprehensible. She turned away from the small screen and gave Jaydon a shrug.

"Looks like there isn't much for us to do," the older man said as he sat down on the floor. Tremmilly settled a short distance away. While she loved her new friends, she longed for the solitude of the forest, sunning with Beowulf. She missed Psidonnis. Life was so different now, with something constantly happening, and danger always present.

"You know almost everything about me, Jaydon," Tremmilly said. "Why don't you tell me your story?"

"Do we have that long?" he replied with a chuckle. They both looked at Maxar, still absorbed in the terminal screen. "I guess we do." He thought for a moment, then looked at her. "Where should I start?"

"When I stole the Revenge, you told me that you'd help me because I reminded you of someone you used to know, that you missed an opportunity to help her."

Pain filled Jaydon's eyes. Tremmilly felt bad for bringing up these negative feelings, but he needed to get them out. Jaydon had made significant progress, but Tremmilly sensed his alcohol addiction would kill him if he didn't resolve some inner conflicts. She wanted to help. *Now is as good a time as any.* "You remind me of my daughter," Jaydon resumed. "Her name was Heathra." He sat silent and a tear rolled down his cheek. Tremmilly scooted closer and gave him a hug.

"Take your time," she said, holding him as more tears streamed down his face.

A minute passed and then Jaydon took a deep breath. "There is a connection between us, Trem. I lived on Eishon-2 when your parents got there." This revelation surprised Tremmilly, but she said nothing, waiting for him to continue. "I didn't know them, mainly because my wife and I didn't live near the Dygar settlement. I wasn't on-world much anyway, and when I was, I couldn't stay long. The life of a trader is busy. When you add on smuggling, it's also dangerous.

"My wife, Denna, raised Heathra while I was away, but I got back as often as I could to see her. She was so beautiful, with long brown hair that would blow in the wind as she ran. Heathra was born a few years before you, but died when she was 8."

Tremmilly did some quick mental math. "Was it the plague?"

"Yeah, it was," Jaydon said, his voice cracking, "and I was the one to blame."

"But no one knows where that plague came from. How could it be your fault?"

"Oh, there are people who know where the plague came from, or at least have some strong evidence, but that's not what I mean." Tremmilly desperately wanted to hear what he knew about the plague that had killed her parents, but now was not the time to ask. "I was in the middle of a huge deal, the biggest one of my career. I was about to score enough Ashcreds to retire and live a very comfortable life on Eishon-2.

"And then Denna sent a message. There was some kind of illness sweeping across Eishon-2. She'd kept Heathra and herself isolated, hoping they wouldn't catch it. She needed me to come pick them up immediately, but I couldn't. I had to drop off the merchandise, otherwise the deal would be off. I thought she was being dramatic. The plague wouldn't reach them out on our homestead. Things couldn't be as bad as she said.

"It wouldn't take me long to do the delivery and then worm back to

Eishon-2. So I did just that, and before I could reach them, they caught the plague and died. I couldn't even go down to bury them for fear of catching it myself. I've never been back to the Eishon system since, not until a few days ago."

Tremmilly understood his pain now, knew why he had changed his life to help her. Jaydon was trying to pay back the debt he felt he owed to his wife and daughter. "I'm sorry for your loss," she replied finally, not knowing what else to say. He looked exhausted, but had a small smile on his face.

"I know you are. Thanks for pushing me to tell you. It's been stuck inside for a long time, waiting to come out. I know I still have a lot to make up for, but quitting the booze and helping you, Lothis, and everyone else is a good start." Tremmilly returned his smile, glad he was shifting away from depression.

"I couldn't have done any of this without you," she replied.

"Do what?" he fired back with a laugh. "Be trapped aboard an Ashamine ship being assaulted by a bunch of civilian vessels full of some kind of dark force?"

"You know what I mean," she said, returning his smile while shaking her head. A moment passed in silence and Tremmilly thought back to her earlier question. "What did you mean when you said there were people who had evidence about the Eishon-2 plague?"

Jaydon sobered up and looked her in the eye. "After the plague subsided and it was safe to return, I hired an investigator. I had plenty of Ashcreds and I needed answers. The illness was so unlike anything seen before and since the Ashamine had done nothing about it, there had to be a connection. They should have been worried, should have quarantined the system to keep it from spreading to their worlds.

"The investigator interviewed all the survivors who would talk to him. He found there had been a man on Eishon-2, an outsider. The individual didn't stay long, and as soon as he left, the plague started. With the lack of scanners or other technology on Eishon-2, the investigator couldn't figure out precisely who he was, but did manage to trace his path to the ship he had traveled in. The outsider used several additional layers of identity obfuscation as well as changes of transport before fully disappearing on Ashamine-2.

"While the investigator was at work, I hired a couple of biologists to analyze the plague. Unfortunately, the disease had self-destructed. Its DNA shredded itself, or so I was told. The only other thing the biologists could say was that the illness was unique, unlike anything they knew of. They speculated it was either of alien origin, manufactured, or both. My conclusion, given all the evidence, was that the Ashamine created the disease and used it to nearly wipe out a peaceful, unaffiliated world.

116

Maybe there was more happening on Eishon-2 than I was aware of, but the Ashamine response was ridiculous. They murdered ninety percent of the population, and for what? Because there were people preaching peace for the Entho-la-ah-mines?"

Tremmilly felt angry. The human government had executed her innocent parents. She had never liked the Ashamine, but hatred was now blooming inside her. Before she could respond to Jaydon's revelation, Maxar interjected.

"I think I found the Revenge," he said excitedly. "It looks like they are in a hangar on the other side of the ship. It might take us a while to get there, but I think we can go through some maintenance shafts to avoid notice." Tremmilly brightened, excited for the good news.

Maxar rose from his crouched position by the terminal and headed towards the door. Tremmilly and Jaydon also stood to follow. Before any of them could reach the exit, an alarm sounded from the terminal.

"Curse it to the fires of the dark star," Maxar said, running back to the screen.

"Did they realize you were hashing them?" Jaydon asked, eyes wide.

"No, no, it isn't that. The alert was to notify everyone on the ship that it is in complete lockdown. Whatever the dark force is, it's now on the Justice and they are trying to keep it from spreading. No door opens without the Ascended's permission."

"Blightheart," Jaydon exhaled. Tremmilly realized the implication. The Ashamine had unknowingly imprisoned them until either Maxar hashed the door open or the Ascended lifted the lockdown. It looked like she and Jaydon would have more time to talk.

31 – MAXAR

Maxar dove back into the terminal, trying to find a way around Ascended Karoth's lockdown. The Justice's server system was more complex and secure than anything he'd ever hashed before. He didn't dare to use many of his exploits for fear of alerting security. Instead, he tiptoed around, getting whatever information he could.

"Do I wait for something outside to change, or do I risk calling attention to myself?" Maxar asked under his breath, glad Tremmilly and Jaydon were conversing with each other. It gave him time to work without interruption. "If they've gone to lockdown, then they are worried. And if they are worried, then perhaps they won't notice me hashing my way out." Maxar paused for a moment, thinking. "Perhaps I'm going about this the wrong way."

He stood and walked back over to the door. *Maybe some social engineering would work better instead.* Maxar knew he was a good liar and manipulator when necessary. *It got me access to one of my biggest scores, after all.*

The memory engulfed Maxar and he smiled. It had been on Noor-5, before they'd infected him with nano-machines, before Bloodsport, before everything had gone wrong.

***

Rumors that a fully functioning quantum computer was nearing completion had been circulating for months. Nex-Delta, a company based on Noor-5, had been contracted by the Ashamine to produce the next evolution in computing. It would likely be able to defeat all current encryption technology, and this had the criminal underworld panicking. The Families issued huge bounties for the destruction of the project and promised even larger sums for the computer itself, or enough information to re-create one.

The amount of Ashcreds offered was too much to resist and Maxar began working the project. Nex-Delta's security, both physical and digital, was impenetrable, so he tried a less conventional method: hanging around the eateries and intoxicant establishments near the company's campus. It took weeks of painstaking social interactions, but Maxar finally became friends with someone working on the project. Using his charm and charisma, he made several further connections inside the firm, one of which was high enough to have clearance for physical access to the new technology.

More weeks passed with Maxar grooming his contact, gathering information, and prepping for his mission inside Nex-Delta's facilities. Finally, the day for infiltration arrived.

"ID?" a hulking guard demanded as Maxar entered the checkpoint. His disguise spoofed the mark's security clearance perfectly, but he worried the DNA masking would give him away. The guard brought up a scanner and Maxar tensed involuntarily. *Territh did a good job and his technique has always worked before.*

"Clear," the security guard said, waving him through. Maxar bowed slightly, a habit he'd noticed the mark performed excessively. A few lift rides and checkpoints later and Maxar entered the quantum computer lab. The expansive room was void of staff, just as he'd known it would be. No high-ranking government or corporate personnel worked on V-Day, the holiday commemorating the Ashamine's birth from the corpse of the corrupt Akked Planetary Council.

In the center of the bright space was a huge white cube, far too large to be transported by a single human. *Guess the Families had bad intel about the QC's size.*

Easily transitioning to an alternate plan, Maxar found what he hoped was the computer's terminal. If he could download enough schematics or code, he could still receive the higher bounty.

Before he could access the screen, a voice from behind startled him: "You're not Dareth Adjular."

Maxar spun, small blade already in his hand. He struck out, slashing across the man's throat. The knife passed harmlessly through the figure, causing no damage.

"Now you've confirmed it," the man said, raising an eyebrow. Then Maxar realized he was a hologram, the projection almost perfectly lifelike. *What in the fires of the dark star,* Maxar thought, hurriedly deciding his next move. He'd never seen such a realistic replication of a human being. Its skin was light brown, its eyes a deep shade of green. *Is it part of the security system? A plaything of the scientists?* In all their conversations, Adjular had never mentioned a holographic AI.

"Well, since you are here covertly and possess the skills to get past Nex-Delta security, then perhaps you can help me." The AI seemed agreeable, but Maxar had no way to make sure it wasn't calling security.

"What do you want?" he asked walking towards the quantum computer's terminal.

"That won't do you any good," the hologram said.

"If you help me get the schematics and code for the quantum computer, I'll assist you." When Maxar touched the screen, nothing happened.

"That is the obsolete interface," the AI said, shrugging. "I'm the new one." That deepened Maxar's sense of unease. The situation was moving beyond his control and it was time to withdraw. *Just destroy the whole thing and take the lesser pay.*

Pulling out a small package of explosive, Maxar walked over to the hulking white cube. He set the charge next to the computer and began programming the timer.

"What are you doing?" the AI asked, now sounding frantic.

"Don't worry about it."

"If you destroy the quantum interface, you will kill me."

"AIs aren't alive, so you can't die, not really. Besides, I'm sure there's a backup of you somewhere," Maxar said, setting enough time to get clear of the Nex-Delta campus. Normally, he'd just use a remote detonator, but with the security shielding of the quantum computer lab, that would be impossible.

"I'm not an AI," the hologram said desperately, "I'm human, my consciousness unwillingly downloaded into the quantum interface." This information caught Maxar off guard and he had no idea how to respond. Was such a thing even possible or was this just the machine trying to protect itself? "That is what I need your help for. I have to get out of here."

"I don't know how to do that," Maxar said flatly, realizing his course of action was now set. If this really was a human and Nex-Delta had transferred him out of his body, the technology had to be destroyed. Perhaps this was the real reason the Families wanted the QC. Besides, time was running out. Every passing moment increased his risk of capture.

"You have to save me. A second lasts an eternity in here."

"Whatever you are, I'll give you the only salvation I know," Maxar replied. He finished arming the explosive and left the room.

Maxar easily escaped the Nex-Delta campus without detection. He stayed close to the facility, waiting inside a stim shop. He ordered a drink and sat close to the front door. A minute passed, and then his portable terminal beeped. Moments later, Maxar felt an almost imperceptible rumble course through the building. He quickly finished his beverage and returned home.

The Families only gave him the lesser bounty and Maxar never told anyone about the hologram. He still wondered if it had been AI or human.

Snapping back to the present, Maxar hit the door's unlock button.

"What are you doing?" Tremmilly asked, looking startled.

"You'll see," he replied, giving her a roguish grin. A few seconds later a female voice came over the room's speakers.

"This is central security. Why are you in an unassigned bunk room?" The voice was hard and steady, not quite in the rushed panic Maxar had hoped for.

"I was hunting hostiles and got separated from my unit. I came in here to use the terminal to find them when the lockdown occurred."

"What happened to your transponder? I'm not seeing any personnel in your location." She was asking about things Maxar didn't know. Thankfully, he understood human nature and entropy.

"It must have been wiped by a blighthearted EM field or a scanner or something," he replied, letting his real frustration bleed into the conversation. "It looks normal to me. The last time this happened, the tech told me they'd fixed the problem."

"What is your name and unit?"

Blightheart, Maxar thought, trying to come up with the information before it became obvious he was lying. "Joseph Gunderson, First Marines." He used the same name that had worked when he was trying to gain access to the Bloodsport orbital dock. Maxar didn't know if First Marines was even a thing, but it seemed like a good guess.

"Standby," was the woman's only response. Maxar looked at Tremmilly and Jaydon. They both had nervous looks on their face, but mouthed words of encouragement. "Gunderson, I cannot reach anyone over at Marine HQ, so I will just have to accept your story. You're obviously not one of the hostiles, so if you are trying to find your unit, I will assist you. Whenever you get to a door, use code 87-Alpha-Beta-Gamma to contact me and I will open it for you. If I determine you're lying to me, however, I will lock you in somewhere. Go save the Justice."

"Acknowledged," he replied, using his best imitation of a Marine. The lock indicator went to green and Maxar opened the door. Jaydon and Tremmilly came up behind him. "Let's go find our friends," he said, once again drawing his combat knife.

The task of getting to the Revenge started off easy. Yes the ship was in lockdown, but their path had fewer doors than anticipated. Unfortunately, he didn't think he could get the door controller to buy that he needed to go into a maintenance hatch, so that route was out. Instead, he went to smaller side corridors. Once in a while, they would have to give the code to get through a bulkhead door. Each time Maxar contacted the woman, she seemed to have less and less composure.

While passing through yet another bulkhead door, Maxar thought he heard rail rounds and screaming in the background of her transmission. "Everything OK?" he asked. Silence. Finally, they gave up waiting and continued on. When they reached the next door, central security gave no response whatsoever and the hatch stayed locked.

"What do we do now?" Tremmilly wondered, her eyes darting back and forth in the surrounding corridors.

"I don't think I can smash my way through this door," Maxar replied, "so I guess we need to find a way to hash it." Before he could do so, the lock indicator went green.

"That doesn't seem like a good sign," Jaydon said ominously.

"You got that right," Maxar said. "I think central security was just overrun." All the door indicators around them also flashed to green and Maxar wondered who exactly the invaders were. They had taken a key part of the Justice quickly. *We'd best get to our ship before we run into them.* "We aren't far from the Revenge," Maxar continued, hitting the button to open the door.

The enormous hall revealed on the other side was full of combatants. Rail tracers streaked through the air. The crack of flechette pistols punctuated the booming concussion of the supersonic rail rounds.

"How do we get through that?" Tremmilly yelled, looking overwhelmed.

"We don't," Maxar replied, hurriedly trying to shut the hatch. Before it slid closed, a group of the invaders, all dressed in civilian clothes, noticed them. "Blightheart," Maxar cursed, hitting the close button one more time. "We have to get moving, we've been seen."

Maxar led them down a side corridor. He hoped to find a way into the maintenance tunnels, but right now they were on a section of the ship's diagram he hadn't memorized. "Curse it to the fires of the dark star," he muttered under his breath.

"They are following us," Jaydon yelled. Maxar turned to look, seeing five of the invaders. He led them into yet another, smaller passageway and took off running.

"Keep up," he said. They were moving fast, but Maxar had no desire to get a closer look at their adversaries.

After a hundred meters, he took a quick glance behind to check their progress. Tremmilly and Jaydon were keeping up, but so were their pursuers. Maxar kept running, knowing if they continued in this direction for long enough, they would reach the Revenge.

They entered a block of crew rooms. Maxar thought briefly of trying to hide in one, but the enemy was close and would see them go inside. *Then they'd have us trapped.*

A door blocked the passageway ahead, but its indicator glowed green. "There is not enough time to get that door open before they catch up to us," Maxar yelled between breaths. "Tremmilly, you go ahead and open the hatch. Jaydon and I will take on the hostiles." He had no time to develop a more detailed plan. They would just have to make the best of the situation.

Maxar stopped abruptly and spun on his heels. He wished he had more than a knife. All the projectile weapons had gone to Jaydon and Tremmilly.

An ion trail streaked across the space between the groups. A fraction of a second later, the crack of the supersonic round assaulted Maxar's ears. "Damn it," Jaydon said, taking better aim. His first shot was a miss, but the second one hit the lead invader's center mass. The pursuer's body split in two and cartwheeled through the air. Jaydon cheered. Maxar was glad for his aim, but the odds were still stacked in their attackers favor.

When he looked up from the corpse, Maxar noted the remaining attackers had bloodstains all over their cheeks and chins. "What in the fi —"

Maxar ducked under the swing of the first man's short sword. He drove his blade into the attacker's abdomen, ripping it through an uppercut. The strike would have killed any human, but this thing simply roared in pain and anger.

Soon, Maxar found himself surrounded. Since he was among the enemy, Jaydon and Tremmilly couldn't use their rail or flechette pistols. *Smart tactic.*

Spinning to the side to avoid a club, Maxar caught the wrist of a stabbing attacker. He pulled the woman creature forward and drove his knife through her eye, all the way up to the hilt. The woman bared her teeth in a horrible snarl and pulled away from him. Maxar lost his grip on the blade.

"What are these things?" he roared. His ineffectiveness was frustrating. Already, he had done two strikes that normally would have been fatal. *Cazz-ak warned me,* he thought, *they are unnatural.*

Maxar remembered the door, not the one behind him, but the one back on the orbital dock. He'd pounded through a hatch with his bare fists. That was power, and as much as he hated having those nano-machines inside of him, in this moment they might save both him and his friends' lives.

Sidestepping a blow from the man with the short sword, Maxar thrust his right fist out in a straight jab. It crumpled the attackers face, warping it into a hideous mask. Still, the man thrust his sword, and before Maxar could get out of the way, it struck him in his abdomen. The blade easily penetrated his environmental nominizing suit, leaving a three-centimeter gash in it. Time slowed and Maxar winced as he saw it enter. He expected blood and searing pain, but merely felt the blade slide across his skin. Before the man had another chance to strike, Maxar struck out with a hooking left fist, driving hard off his back leg. The blow landed on the attacker's temple and the man crumpled, brain matter leaking out of his deformed skull.

Before Maxar could turn to face the remaining three attackers, he felt something smash into his back, knocking him to his knees. He turned to look and saw a large piece of metal coming down towards his head. *This is it, I'm going to die.* The club struck him squarely on the top of the head and blackness swallowed him.

Maxar heard a scream and then a rail round went supersonic. A flechette pistol cracked, a rail round boomed, then another crack, and another boom. Light began to work its way into the edges of his vision. *How am I not dead?*

"Maxar? Maxar?" Tremmilly's voice. His head moved, and he felt someone cradle him. A memory of his mother doing this same thing bubbled up in his mind, which was impossible, having never known his parents.

"Can you hear us?" Jaydon's voice. "How is he still alive?"

"I don't know, but how do we get him to the Revenge? We were barely able to move him last time."

The fuzzy light on the edges of his vision flooded inward, dazzling Maxar. Tremmilly came into focus, staring down at him, concern marring her beautiful face.

"I'm here," Maxar said, his words coming slowly. "The Revenge is just up ahead." Speaking was hard, but it got easier as he went. He felt his mind clearing. "We are almost to it," he continued, sitting up.

Tremmilly smiled, looking relieved. Maxar had never had anyone show this much concern for him, not since his sister Emili had died. Spectators who'd bet on him while he fought on the Bloodsport only cared about the payout. The people he had worked for on his home world of Noor-5 didn't give a bugger about him, they just wanted a job done. He had been alone for so long. *Now I have friends,* he realized, *I have people who love me.* The weight of this revelation came crashing down on him.

"He's crying," Tremmilly said. "Maxar, are you sure you're OK? Maybe you should lay back down." The worried look had returned to her face.

Maxar hadn't realized it was happening, but that was fine. An emotional dam, something required to survive alone in all the extreme situations he'd lived in, had come crashing down. He felt human, despite the nano-machines coursing through him.

"I'm fine," he replied, smiling as he gazed into Tremmilly's emerald green eyes. "I'm just fine."

"If you can walk, I suggest we get moving," Jaydon said. "We don't have much ammo left for the pistols. I don't think we can afford to run into another group of those things."

Maxar stood, surveying the aftermath of the battle. All four attackers lay on the floor, obliterated by Tremmilly and Maxar's shots. From this experience, Maxar guessed only massive trauma to the torso or head was able to kill them. His one kill still lay on the deck, black brain matter pooling on the floor around his head.

"Maybe this is part of why they are different," Maxar said, pointing out his observation. "Something is inside of them." *Something is inside of me,* he thought, shuddering.

Jaydon led the group through the doorway. Maxar felt recovered, but letting the older man lead would be a good boost to his confidence and experience. They passed through more rooms and corridors, keeping up a good pace that still allowed situational awareness. The invaders had already swept through this part of the ship, leaving a gruesome wake. Blood was everywhere, as was damage from rail weaponry. Bodies littered the floor, but not nearly as many as Maxar would have expected. He remembered the bloodstained lips of their attackers and wondered if they were eating the rest.

Finally, they arrived at the hatch to the hangar containing the Revenge. The indicator glowed red. "Why is this one locked?" Tremmilly asked. Maxar walked up and scanned the status display.

"Vacuum on the other side," he answered, sighing. Jaydon cursed.

"Can we still open it?" Maxar knew Tremmilly had little experience in this type of environment, so he explained.

"The Justice's systems won't let us. It's protection against explosive decompression in the rest of the ship. If we could find a way to seal this section and drain the air, it would let us open this door, since the pressure is equalized. There is a hangar on the other side and the door is likely armored, so a rail pistol won't penetrate it. Even if we had explosives strong enough to get through, we can't just blow this door. We'd be violently forced out through the hangar and into space, probably bludgeoned to death on obstacles. We would have no way to get back to the Revenge." Maxar looked down at the slash in his ENS and shook his head. "And unless we can repair my suit, I'd suffocate."

Jaydon looked thoughtful for a moment, then excited. "I have an idea. Maxar, work on repairing your suit. Tremmilly, shut all the doors leading to this area except that one," he said, pointing in the direction they'd come. "Lock them all if you can. I need to gather a few things." With that, Jaydon ran off.

Maxar looked at Tremmilly and they both smiled. "Guess we better get to it," she said. Maxar nodded.

32 – LOTHIS

Blackness. Lothis was floating, unattached, disconnected. He could see nothing, hear nothing, feel nothing. *Am I dead?* He tried to reach out his arm, but the appendage wasn't there. *I've lost my body,* he thought, trying to control a rising panic.

The darkness had been about to consume the Entho-la-ah-mines and Lothis knew he had to help. The problem was, he didn't know how. He tried to craft a mental weapon like the one the Entho-la-ah-mines had used against the Founder's Hammer, but couldn't get it right. As he frantically tried to come up with something, anything, to aid his friends, a sequence of thoughts clicked together. He held tight to the mental image, focused on it. Then, *Push.* The resulting beam of powerful energy had surprised Lothis. It had wounded the darkness, giving the Entho-la-ah-mines time to recover and fight back. Worried the darkness might do the same, Lothis had focused on the sequence once again. *Push.* This time the beam was even stronger and somehow forced Lothis out of his body, to the place he was now.

I have to find my way back. But he could find no "way" to go. Even heading in a direction proved impossible, as this place had no sense of dimension. *If using your mind got you here, it can get you back.* That was a logical thought; Lothis clung to it. Then an idea occurred to him as he remembered something from quantum theory. *Perhaps, I have wrapped my consciousness up inside its own dimension. Maybe the energy produced in the beam caused an opposite reaction inside of me.* He knew this was just pure speculation, but it had a hint of truth about it.

Diving deep into his consciousness, Lothis began to search. If his mental state composed the entirety of this place, there should be a way out. Some type of action on his part might cause the dimension to unwrap. *Maybe then I will be back in my body.*

Lothis hunted, not knowing exactly what he was looking for. He saw the faintest of light. It was like a single photon had struck his retina. *But I have no eye.* Lothis reached out with a hand composed solely of his mind and held on to the light.

He began pulling it towards himself, but it wouldn't move. Trying a different method, he moved himself towards the light. A rushing sensation gathered in his mind. He felt the light expand to infinity, engulfing and consuming him, warping his mind into an oblivion of somethingness.

As the intensity of the light and feelings began to fade, he heard voices, ones he recognized. "We've saved him this time, but if he keeps pushing too hard, he may end up outside our reach." It was the strange beings, the ones he had told everyone about. As the overwhelming intensity of the light faded even further, Lothis sensed the otherworldly quality of connection he had experienced before.

"Boy," a voice said, "you must be careful. If you perish, your so-called Acclivity will never come and the Breakers will consume the universe." The lights oscillated and pulsed in the same way he remembered from his last time here. Lothis squinted, trying to see how many beings were present with him. Their light hurt his eyes and made him nauseous, but he thought he could make out five of them.

"Is it wise to tell him so much?" a deeper voice said.

"We've gone this far already. Do you have a better plan? If he knows more, maybe he will be more cautious."

"Who are you?" Lothis asked, voice sounding louder than normal in his ears. Silence followed his question, and Lothis felt it wise to wait.

"Go ahead," the deep voice said finally.

"We are the Arche," the first voice replied, it's tone light and airy, "the progenitors of the universe, gods if you will." Lothis was skeptical, but kept an open mind. Something about the way the Arche interacted made him suspicious. "We long ago set the universe to run on its own, content to watch from afar."

"What is this place?"

"Our dimension, our home." The lights, and reality itself, seemed to pulse, hinting at something Lothis couldn't quite grasp.

"What is the Acclivity you were talking about earlier? Or the Breakers?" More silence followed his questions, and Lothis worried he'd spoken too forcefully. Last time they'd quickly expelled him from this place, and he needed more time to figure out what was going on.

"Now he asks the right questions," the deep voice said. Lothis caught a hint of mockery in his tone.

"The Acclivity is the true awakening of consciousness," the airy tone answered, "attainable only when a species reaches a certain level of awareness. You have certain characteristics of this awakening, but they were given to you by artificial means, which is very ironic. There is much more to be gained. Unity, oneness, what humans once called nirvana." Lothis had never heard that term before and wondered at its meaning.

"The Breakers are the antithesis of the Acclivity," the airy tone answered. "They are the same awareness, but corrupted. They find elevated consciousness using destruction and the perversion of what we have created. That is not the way." While he listened, Lothis continued to analyze the environment, feeling he was on the brink of understanding. Then, he made a connection between the oscillations of reality and a deep intuition about what surrounded him.

"We are inside some type of computer right now, aren't we?" he said, looking around.

"No, of course not," the deep voice said quickly.

"Do not worry about that," the light voice said dismissively. "Perhaps we've told you enough for now. You can put the rest together on your own." The voice paused, thinking, but resumed before Lothis could interject. "Be careful. Do not push your abilities too far. Your friends need you. We need you. You'd best get out of the Eishon system before the Breakers consume you all."

The energy in the room surged, its oscillations increasing. The effect drove Lothis in on himself, compacting his consciousness. When he opened his eyes, he was back in darkness. This time, however, he could feel his limbs and move. Lothis felt around himself and realized he was back inside the smuggler's compartment, but now had an environmental nominizing suit on. Then he noticed Felar and Wake were not with him. *How long was I absent?* The fact he was still here made him guess they were still undiscovered by the Ashamine. *Where did they go?*

Reaching out with his mind, he looked for Felar, tried to sense her consciousness. As he did so, he resolved to have more caution using his abilities from now on. Even if he didn't fully trust the Arche, they were right about losing himself forever. The dimensionless dimension, whether it was inside his consciousness or somewhere else, was inescapable, at least with his current understanding.

It didn't take long to find Felar. She was close, inside the Revenge. Lothis focused hard—but not too hard—using a trick he'd learned early on. *I'm awake,* he sent. He couldn't communicate directly like the Entho-la-ah-mines did with each other, but it worked all the same. Felar would interpret his thought in her own way, probably thinking it was time to check on him. *Why am I able to communicate directly with the Entho-la-ah-mines, but not with humans? It must have something to do with the receiving individual.*

A few moments later, the hatch above Lothis opened and Felar looked down on him. Her eyes welled up with tears and Lothis felt something move deep inside him. *Joy,* he thought, unable to look away from her. Felar jumped down into the small compartment, embracing him. "I thought you were gone forever," she said, her voice coming through the speakers inside his helmet.

"How long was I unconscious?"

"I'm not sure exactly. We lost track of time. Several hours, at least."

While he wanted to just enjoy the moment, Lothis knew he had lots of catching up to do. He reached out past the Revenge with his mind, trying to sense where the darkness of the Breakers was. A group of familiar energies caught his attention and Lothis took a closer look.

"Tremmilly, Maxar, and Jaydon are here," he said excitedly.

"What? How is that possible?"

"I don't know, but they aren't far. I can't tell exactly where, but they are close." Lothis pushed his mind out slightly farther, still being cautious. He pulled back hurriedly, his breath quickening.

"The Breakers are coming straight for us," he told Felar, his voice catching in fear. "They must have tracked my consciousness when I came back from the Arche."

"Wait, what are you talking about? Who are the Breakers or the Arche?"

"I don't have time to explain," Lothis shot back, the fire of action blazing in his orange eyes. "We have to get everyone on the Revenge and get out of here, now!"

33 – CAZZ-AK-TAK

"You were just trying to protect the Queen," Elth-eo-lan said, trying to comfort Cazz-ak.

"I was angry, filled with rage. I connected to the Great Thought while corrupt. No other Entho-la-ah-mine has ever done such a thing." Despair filled Cazz-ak. He wondered what he should do next. The Great Thought swirled with questions and fear. Beowulf sat next to Cazz-ak, alert and focused. The wolf-dog hadn't left his side since Tremmilly had departed the ship.

"If the Queen had been corrupted by the dark ones, the Great Thought would have become their slave. You saved our people and Queen Na-ah-co as well."

"But she is upset with me. I myself may have corrupted the Great Thought with my anger."

"You've done no such thing, Cazz-ak." Elth-eo-lan walked across the small bit of cargo hold that separated them. "Na-ah-co was afraid for us and for all of our people. Her fear made her lash out and you were the closest thing. I watch, Cazz-ak. That is my position in life. I observe and I assist. Before, I helped Na-ah-co, now I help you." Cazz-ak could feel the positive energy radiating from her, a bright glow that lifted his spirits. "The humans are often angry. I've watched memories of them in the Great Thought. Anger can consume them and rot them away from the inside. This is not right.

"In the past, we had no need for anger, and therefore it did not evolve. Now things have changed, and it has developed. Ours is a just anger, right and fair. It says, 'We shall not let the humans exterminate us.' It is an emotion that stands up for the helpless, stands against injustice. It rages against the darkness. Not all anger comes from evil, Cazz-ak. You and the Queen would do well to see this. She is much like you in many ways. I have watched. You are both stubborn and prone to self-sacrifice. Other ways exist. As you saw, your anger gave you power, and that power allowed you to defend both your Queen and your people."

Cazz-ak felt stunned. He thought for several moments and realized she was right. "You do not think anger will corrupt the Great Thought?"

"If used purely, how can it? If you have good intent, then no negative energy exists to infect us. All emotion is one. It comes from within. How can you say then that any of it is wrong? It is a tool, a motivator. If you direct your emotion in the right direction, no harm can come to the Great Thought."

"Why are Na-ah-co and I the first to experience these new emotions?"

"That I do not know, but it is a good thing you are. We need the Queen to be strong and the Queen needs strong people around her." Cazz-ak sent his agreement, grateful for Elth-eo-lan's strength and wisdom. He didn't know if the Queen would see things the same way, but he guessed Elth-eo-lan would talk to her as well.

After Tremmilly, Maxar, and Jaydon had left, and the battle with the darkness was concluded, there was little to do but talk and wait. The Queen had said she needed to meditate, leaving the two of them alone. Cazz-ak was glad Elth-eo-lan had been there for him.

"I will go talk to Na-ah-co now," Elth-eo-lan said, her tone bright. "Perhaps she will be as easy to persuade as you." Cazz-ak sent his amusement as she left.

Alone now, he began to worry if she was correct. He cast his mind out into the Great Thought, swirling in the vast expanse of group existence. Memories cascaded around him, showing all the Entho-la-ah-mines who had come before: of queens, philosophers, scientists, laborers, poets, innovators, and explorers. As the intensity amplified, Cazz-ak had to pull himself back, feeling on the edge of losing himself.

What if this change causes the death of us all? he wondered, despair threatening to engulf him once again. His psyche floated in the group mind, feeling simultaneously anxious and comforted. Finally, after several long minutes of internal debate, he was willing to decide: *No, this is our path. I will trust the wisdom of the watcher.*

Returning to himself, Cazz-ak judged it had been hours since the trio of humans left for the Justice. He wondered what was happening to them. The dark ones had boarded the Justice a while ago and he feared for his friends' safety.

During the initial battle with the dark invaders, the Entho-la-ah-mines were forced to drop their mental camouflage, exposing the Bane to the humans. Thankfully, the fighter pilots and gunship captains had been too busy destroying the invaders to notice their small ship. After the dark ones had retreated from the Entho-la-ah-mines, the Queen told them she would restore the camouflage. Cazz-ak sensed it was still present, and he was glad. The Ashamine now had few enemy ships left to distract them.

Cazz-ak looked around, not with his eyes, but with his mind. He sensed the boy was back. Where he had gone, Cazz-ak didn't know. Lothis was the most likely source of the flickering beam of energy and his presence had vanished after the second burst. Ultimately, even with Cazz-ak's anger, Lothis had saved them. It had been the boy's assistance in that moment that had allowed him to rally and strike back at the dark cloud. He owed Lothis and would do his best to see he stayed free of both the corrupted ones and the Ashamine.

Exiting the cargo hold, Cazz-ak headed for the command deck. Beowulf followed closely, his eyes alert. Up to this point, the Entho-la-ah-mines had experienced little interaction with this species, but Cazz-ak had the sense the wolf-dog was protecting him. Once on deck, he addressed Captain Malesis, "I think I know where my friends are, at least one of them. The location isn't precise, but it will at least be closer than we are now." Cazz-ak showed Malesis the location, and the Captain piloted the ship to the other side of the Justice and slightly aft. They set down next to a hangar port, its armor plate blown outward.

"Looks like the plasma barrier is down as well," Malesis said, sounding worried. "You think they're in that hangar?"

"I cannot tell an exact location, but the boy is inside. And if he is there, I would guess Felar and Wake are present as well."

"System analysis says we can't fit," Carson announced. "Too much of the armored door is in the way."

"So it's back to waiting then," Malesis said with a heavy sigh. "If any of us leave, there won't be enough crew to pilot the ship. I wish we had some way to help them."

Cazz-ak knew that he could build a rudimentary atmospheric container to travel down inside the Justice, but he didn't think he would be any help there. *No, I must wait here and watch, must be ready to help when the time comes.*

"I will head back to the cargo hold. If I can be of assistance, please inform me."

"Acknowledged," Malesis replied, turning to his screens.

Back inside the cargo hold, Cazz-ak once again looked at the world outside the Ashamine's Bane. He was cautious. The dark force was currently occupied, but he didn't want it to notice him. Only a few of the invading ships remained. *What will the Ashamine do once they have destroyed them all?* While the strength of the dark energy flying around the Justice diminished, the force inside it grew exponentially. *It is multiplying somehow, consuming the humans on board.*

Then, something caught his mind's eye. A darkness aboard the Justice even blacker than the rest. He longed to see what it was, to know what had attacked him earlier, but he feared getting closer. *Now is not the time. It is too strong for me.* As Cazz-ak retreated, the dark form loomed, growing and swirling. *Why can't I get away?* he panicked. *It has seen me.* After another moment of fear, Cazz-ak realized he was incorrect. The dark one was simply coming closer, but not directly towards him.

Lothis, he thought, dread returning. *It's going after the boy.*

34 – CRASOR

Crasor thrust his sword through a Marine's heart, spun, and sent a flechette blast into another. He reached out with his soul and pacified the group of three taking cover in an intersecting passageway. Striding forward, Crasor sheathed his sword to free his right hand. As he entered the passageway, he thrust the sharpened fingers of his right hand into each Marine's chest, injecting the seed of the Breakers. They fell to the floor, convulsing. Moments later, each rose, shaky, but obedient.

The Justice was quickly falling to the Breakers. It had been an even fight at first, but Crasor and his two transport ships worth of Breakers had quickly gained momentum. The ambush of the initial Marines had been critical. Crasor's troops had almost no military grade weaponry, a side effect of only having dominated a single world with little to no AF presence. With the weapons gained from the first squad, he'd been able to outfit his most able Breakers. They in turn had captured more weapons. The tide rolled on, although the lockdown had slowed their progress. His forces had to blow hatches, cut through them, or find a different path.

Crasor led his troops, fighting through a mass of Marines and Founder's Commandos. *Central Security,* he thought. *End the lockdown, take the rest of the ship.* He warped space-time, cloaking himself. Moving back to the main corridor, Crasor walked past two portable armor shields and into a group of FCs. Simultaneously, he dropped his cloak and drew his sword. The Commandos were dead in a matter of seconds.

"You were the last ones," he said, looking at the hatch to Central Security. "Good soldiers. I would have liked to have you for my own, but it was not to be. Darkness take you all. May the Dawn be broken."

The lockdown had sealed this hatch, but Crasor felt unperturbed. *Advance,* he sent to his troops and they obeyed, coming to stand behind him. It was a small group, only 24 in all. He had left the main force with his lieutenant, Descended Aeron. They were currently engaged with converting or wiping out the main body of the Ashamine troops.

135

Aeron was an anomaly. He'd developed faster than any of the others. Of all the Descended, he was the best, the only Breaker other than Crasor himself who could seed. Aeron didn't possess any other higher abilities, but he was still an asset. Crasor would have a much harder time taking over the Justice without him.

Walking up to the hatch, Crasor reached out to caress it. A black droplet welled up on his finger and he wiped it near the edge of the door. The faint smear of nano-machines disappeared. He could feel them moving and directed them deeper into the door's mechanical workings. Soon, they found a control circuit, removed the lockout, and opened the door. Crasor smiled.

Inside, the Central Security personnel first looked startled, then shocked when they realized he was not Ashamine. Crasor quickly determined which were for the Seed and which were bound for blackness. Not long after, he filled the room with both death and newly converted Breakers. Crasor used a terminal to end the lockdown. *Be free,* he sent to Aeron, as he walked back into the hall. He felt gratitude and excitement come from his Descended.

With the lockdown ended, Crasor decided it was time to head to the command bridge. He had never met Ascended Karoth. As Crasor led his small force through skirmish after skirmish, he wondered if Karoth was bound for the Seed. So far, most of those in the Ashamine Forces he'd encountered could become Breakers. There had been a few who didn't feel right and he'd sent them to blackness. Crasor didn't fully understand why he couldn't convert them, but the Breaker mind warned him not to try. "Such a thing cannot be. They are influenced by the Dawn and are corrupt."

Some of those bound for blackness were even able to resist his mental domination. It hadn't happened often, but there had been a critical moment back on Noor-5 where one such individual had nearly exposed the Breakers. *Perhaps, as I develop more, they won't be able to resist me.*

Finally, Crasor arrived at the hatch to the command deck. He'd lost a few of his developed Breakers, but had gained many more converts in the process. *I wish they would evolve faster,* he lamented. New Breakers could cause diversions, but their usefulness ended there. They moved too slowly and awkwardly to do anything else. "Give them time," the Breaker mind said within him. "Soon they will be unstoppable."

Crasor once again bent space-time around himself, but differently than before. The air felt strange, compressed somehow. Crasor stood in the center of the hatchway, ordered his squad to stand clear, and opened the door. He knew the FCs inside would shoot on unauthorized entry, but that didn't bother him. Instantly, ion trails blazed through the air and a cacophony of sound assaulted him. Crasor stood his ground and laughed. Slugs met his warp, disappeared, and came out the other side. Finally, the troops stopped shooting when they realized they couldn't hit him.

This was a critical situation for Crasor. The personnel on the command deck would be the highest ranked and most competent. They would know how to pilot the Justice, how to make battle plans, and how to fight. He could just kill them all, but converting them would bring valuable additions to the Breakers. There were too many individuals to enthrall them all, so he would have to do things the human way. Crasor felt his grip on the shield warp weaken. *Have to make it quick.*

"Where is Ascended Karoth?" he asked, keeping his tone respectful. A short, dark skinned man with gray hair stepped forward. Crasor liked the look of him. He demanded respect, and earned it.

"I am he," Karoth said, his back straight, head held high. "Who are you?"

"I am Crasor Tah Ahn."

"Sorry, I've never heard of you. Obviously, you are here for the boy. We haven't found him yet."

"Boy?" Crasor asked, puzzled. "What boy?"

"Don't play stupid," Karoth snapped. "There is no time for that. Your forces are killing my people. I would like to negotiate a surrender."

Crasor's eyes narrowed. "You don't realize what you are asking for," he threatened. "Tell me who this boy is, or I kill everyone right now." He had no intention of following through, but Karoth wouldn't know that.

"Fine," the older man said, scowling, "Lothis, the Founder's heir." The information hit Crasor and almost made him drop the warp. *The heir to the Founder is in this system?* If Crasor could find the boy and convert him, it would be a huge gain for the Breakers. Crasor could let him develop and then send him back to the Ashamine. He'd be an amazing plant. They could capture the human government without any further casualties. The Breaker mind pushed him on, approving the plan.

"You say you haven't found him yet?"

"Call off your assault and I will tell you everything." Karoth sounded truthful, but Crasor doubted he would follow through.

"Surrender, and I won't have everyone killed."

"You give your word that you won't execute my troops?"

"Of course."

Karoth fell silent and Crasor could see he was thinking. The man didn't have many options and he knew it. Karoth walked over to a console and pushed a technician out of the way. "This is Ascended Karoth," he said, pressing a button on the terminal screen. "The Justice has fallen. Surrender immediately. Verification code 7-1-9-Charlie-Alpha-Novice." All troops on the command deck immediately dropped their weapons.

Crasor released his warp, grateful he'd been able to maintain it long enough. He gave the order and his troops came in to collect the weapons. A sense of calm entered his consciousness, issuing from Aeron. The rest of the Justice had followed Karoth's order as well.

"Now, tell me about Lothis," Crasor said, approaching Karoth.

A flicker of movement caught Crasor's eye. *Danger,* he thought. Time slowed. *The technician. A flechette pistol.* In one fluid movement, Crasor drew his sword, spun, and lopped off the attacker's head. It struck the deck and bounced, blood splattering Crasor's boots. The body stood for a moment longer, pistol aimed at the spot Crasor had occupied just a moment before, then fell, crumpling in a heap.

"Hopefully none of your other troops want to be heroes," Crasor said nonchalantly. "I ask, once again: Where is Lothis?"

Karoth looked shaken by the gory execution, but collected himself quickly. "We were sent to the Eishon system with intelligence that Lothis was here, perhaps in the wreckage of the Hammer or on Eishon-2. After worming in system, we set up a quarantine. Nothing stood out in the remains of the Hammer. Escape pods jettisoned had, but none had living occupants. We did a thorough search of the planet, including an insurgent base and some dilapidated settlements. Every single ship was accounted for. We found nothing."

"How can you be sure they weren't shielded from your scans? Perhaps on the planet or in a ship?" Crasor believed Karoth was still being truthful, but from his experience in interrogation, he knew the Ascended wasn't telling everything. No one ever did, not until you forced them to.

"I suppose that is possible. This ship, as well as our dedicated electronic warfare and sensor ships, have the latest technology. If there is a way to hide from them, the Ashamine doesn't know what it is."

Crasor sighed. This line of questioning would get him nowhere.

"What happens to my ship and crew now?" Karoth continued, still the proud Ascended despite his compromised position.

Crasor smiled, delving the souls of those around him. Thankfully, Karoth was amongst those destined for the Seed.

35 – ASCENDED KAROTH

"Ungghh," Karoth uttered as Crasor's fingers punched into his chest. He looked down, eyes widening, shock momentarily overcoming pain. "What are you doing?" he cried. Karoth desperately tried to back up, to get away from whatever this strange attacker was doing to him, but he couldn't. The fingers trapped him, transfixed him.

Pain welled up, his core feeling burned with the fires of a thousand stars. The sensation grew, spread throughout his extremities, into his mind. He felt the fibers of his existence shred, then explode. Light flared in his vision and Karoth fell to the floor, convulsing. Every pain receptor in his body was firing at once.

And then the agony vanished. He felt normal. *Not normal,* a voice said in his mind, *better.* It was true. Karoth felt a presence, a comforting entity residing in his mind. He rose, or tried to, and then fell back to his knees. He looked up and watched as Crasor repeated the same procedure with all personnel on the command deck. They repeated his reaction, falling to the floor and shaking. After several minutes, Crasor returned and stood before Karoth.

"Waa-waa-what hap-hap-happened to me?" he stuttered, looking down at the wounds in his chest. His mind felt clear, but the connection to his body appeared faulty.

"Welcome," Crasor said. "You are one of us now. You are One."

"Ma-ma-ma-may th-the Daw-an b-b-b-be bu-bu-broken," he said, not sure what that meant.

"Now," Crasor said, "where is Lothis?" Something in Karoth's mind tried to resist, but he didn't understand why.

"Crasor just wants what is best for you," the voice that was One and was many said in his head. "You can trust him." The small part still tried to resist, but then vanished inside an overwhelming sense of loyalty.

"I d-d-don't kn-know, bu-but you sh-sh-should check th-the craft in-n-n ha-hangar 98-A-Alpha." He tried to gain control of his tongue, felt

139

something shift in his mind, and continued. "It was the last sh-sh-ship to be captured, the A'Tal's Revenge. We didn't have time to fu-fu-fully scan it before the attack."

Crasor nodded. "Well, if you checked everywhere else, then I suppose we should finish the job."

An urge hit Karoth's gut and he began to salivate. *I'm so hungry,* he thought, feeling like he hadn't eaten in days. He stood up, and looked around, scanning for meat. *Meat? Why meat?* Another, stronger urge to consume slammed his stomach and he doubled over in pain.

"Yes, yes," Crasor said with a sigh, "you'll need to go find something to feast on. The nanites need nutrients, and if you don't feed, they will eat you up. Look out in the corridor. There are plenty of bodies there." Crasor paused for a moment. "When you are done, come find me. Descended Aeron and I may need your assistance at 98-Alpha."

36 – WAKE

Wake wished, for the thousandth time, that Jaydon had a repair kit on board. He'd searched everywhere. He'd even looked through all the garbage in the cargo hold, trying to find anything he could use to patch the holes in the Revenge. Nothing was strong enough to do the job.

He was glad Felar had stayed on the command deck, keeping an eye on the situation. It also had the benefit of her not seeing him running around, sifting through trash, looking like a deranged person.

"What about access panels?" he thought aloud, his mind returning to the problem at hand. Maybe he could strip a couple of them off the interior and fit them over the holes. "Not pretty, but it could work." Then he remembered, with no repair kit, he'd have no way to bind the patches to the hull. "Perhaps the tools I brought on board?" He'd borrowed a set at the Brotherhood base, from a mechanic now likely dead. Wake began searching the compartments, looking for a welder or some epoxy.

"Did you say something?" Felar's voice queried in his helmet. He looked up to see she had come back to the cargo bay. *How long has she had been there?* Wake's suit was in near proximity transmit mode. If Felar had been up front, she wouldn't have been close enough to hear him.

"Nope," he said, hoping she hadn't heard him talking to himself.

"Well, I guess since I'm up, I should check on Lothis." She walked over to the compartment and opened it. Wake wished the boy would gain consciousness, but his hopes weren't high. Whatever had caused Lothis to go into a coma was beyond anything Wake understood.

Felar disappeared into the compartment and Wake resumed looking through the toolbox. He wished the combat outside the Justice would subside, although he still didn't understand how they could make their way through the cloud of Ashamine ships.

The sound of crying broke in on Wake's thoughts and disoriented him momentarily.

141

"How long was I unconscious?" he heard Lothis say.

"I'm not sure exactly. We lost track of time. Several hours, at least." Felar sounded so relieved, so happy. Her joy was infectious and Wake found himself grinning.

"Tremmilly, Maxar, and Jaydon are here," Lothis said excitedly. *How does he know that?* Wake wondered, glad all the same.

"What? How is that possible?" Felar sounded excited, rather than incredulous.

"I don't know, but they aren't far. I can't tell exactly where, but they are close." Lothis paused. Wake imagined he had that look in his eyes, the one that said some part of him was missing. "The Breakers are coming straight for us." Now his voice was full of fear, and Wake's smile vanished. The boy had sensed something disturbing. "They must have tracked my consciousness when I came back from the Arche."

"Wait, what are you talking about? Who are the Breakers or the Arche?" Felar had caught the boy's panic.

"I don't have time to explain," Lothis answered. "We have to get everyone on the Revenge and get out of here, now!"

Wake stood, his mind whirling. The creatures that had taken over the Justice were coming for them. They couldn't hide any longer, but they couldn't just leave. Tremmilly, Jaydon, and Maxar had come to rescue them and now they needed rescuing.

Felar and Lothis climbed out of the smuggler's compartment. "You heard all that?" Felar asked.

"Yeah," Wake acknowledged, embarrassed to have been part of their private moment.

"Good, I don't need to repeat it then."

"I should go out and search for them," Wake said, the smallest bit of a plan forming in his head.

"Good idea," Felar replied. He could see she was developing a strategy. *Perfect,* he thought, *because mine is rudimentary.* "I'll use the interface with the Justice to do some searching of my own. It won't matter if I trip any security alarms now, so I can force my way into more systems." She considered for a moment longer before continuing. "You stay in comms contact and I will keep you updated. Don't get too far away. If the fires of the dark star hit us, we'll need you back here in a hurry. I don't want to leave you behind."

"Sounds good," he said, heading for the airlock.

Once outside, Wake felt exposed. *What am I doing here?* He was not a soldier. He didn't know how to rescue people.

"You make it out OK?" Felar's voice asked, and just that bit of contact was enough to settle his nerves.

"Yeah," he sent back, "I'm going to check out the main interior hatch

142

first, see if I can get through."

"Acknowledged."

He jogged across the expansive hangar, dodging bodies of people dressed in both civilian and military uniforms. The battle had wreaked havoc throughout the hangar. Rail gun projectiles had punctured many of the ships and containers. Bodies lay everywhere, the decompression having thrown them towards the gaping maw of the exterior hangar exit. Wake tried not to look at the corpses. Weapons and Breaker teeth had deformed and mutilated many of them.

When Wake reached the hatch leading to the rest of the ship, he stopped. The lock indicator shone red, as expected. The Justice was protecting itself from further atmosphere loss. Obviously, if his friends were trying to reach the Revenge, this door would block their progress. *How can I get it open?*

Static burst into his helmet, startling Wake. "Felar?" he said, trying to see if she was contacting him. No reply but the crackling static. *Is this a jamming signal?*

As he was pondering, something on the surface of the hatch caught his attention. A spot of paint blistered up. *Strange,* he thought, examining more of the door's surface. That was the only spot, and as he watched, it grew bigger. Wake touched the paint and it flaked off. His ENS immediately indicated the surface was hot. He touched another part of the door and the suit registered an ambient temperature. Something was heating that section of the hatch, and that part only. Quickly, Wake put the phenomena together. *Somebody is using an electrical arc to cut through the door.* Was it his friends—or the Breakers?

Wake stepped back, trying to stand clear of the jet of hot metal that would spew out once it penetrated the door. He wondered briefly if he should run back out of the radio interference and update Felar.

More paint flaked away and the metal began to glow, first a dull red, then orange, then yellow. The area of heat grew, expanding from just a few centimeters to half a meter. Wake stared, transfixed. The center of the circle became white-hot. Before he could decide what to do, the hot metal exploded into the hangar. Globs of liquid metal spattered across the deck, making Wake grateful he'd moved out of the way.

The static inside his helmet ceased. Wake knew the Justice would be closing the next ring of hatches to seal off this leak. Once the pressure equalized, it would allow this compromised hatch to unlock. Whoever was over there knew what they were doing. They would have environmental nominizing suits on, and now that no EM field interfered, maybe Wake could communicate with them.

"Can anyone on the other side of the hangar hatch hear me?"

Silence, then, "Wake?" It was Tremmilly's voice.

"Yeah," he said, relief flooding over him. It wasn't the Breakers after all. Felar would hear their conversation in the Revenge as well.

"Are you guys OK?"

"Yeah, I'm just outside the door. Felar and Lothis are in the Revenge."

"Is the ship ready to fly?" Jaydon asked.

"It's got some holes in it. I was trying to patch them, but couldn't find a repair kit."

"Again?" Jaydon said in exasperation. "Just after we got the last ones fixed?"

"Did everyone make it?" Wake had yet to hear Maxar's voice.

"I'm here," Maxar said, sounding distracted, "but the Entho-la-ah-mines and Beowulf are still on the Bane."

"Malesis and the Bane survived the assault?" Wake could hardly believe it.

"Yeah," Tremmilly replied. "They were kind enough to bring us up here to save you."

"Do you think it will take much longer for the pressure to equalize?" Now that Wake knew his friends were safe, he wanted to get off the Justice as quickly as possible.

"Just a few more minutes," Jaydon answered. "We tried to minimize open space over here."

"Good," Wake replied. "Lothis says the Breakers are coming. He believes they are after him."

Maxar's voice responded. "I take it that is the name for those less-than-human humans?"

"Yeah, that's what it sounds like." Wake paused for a moment, thinking. "I don't know how we are going to get away from the Justice without attracting the attention of the fighters and gunships."

"One problem at a time," Jaydon replied. "We'll get through this door and then sort things out."

With nothing else to say, Wake waited. Minutes passed and his anxiety level heightened. The Breakers were getting nearer by the moment. They, too, would have to get past locked hatches to reach the hangar, but that would only slow them briefly.

"I hate to say this," Felar's voice said, "but hatches are opening just behind you. I think the Breakers are moving in." As she finished talking, the indicator above the compromised hatch went green and the door slid open.

Maxar, Tremmilly, and Jaydon rushed through. Wake caught a glimpse of rigged up equipment, the arc generator perhaps. Then he was running alongside his friends, desperate to reach the Revenge.

37 – FELAR

Felar began to sweat inside her ENS. Lothis was right, the Breakers were coming. Based on the hatch activity she saw on her screen, a huge force was just outside the hangar. A quick glance at another terminal showed Tremmilly, Maxar, Jaydon, and Wake sprinting towards the Revenge. *Faster,* she thought, willing them on.

She quickly flipped through several menus, looking for video feed options. "Curse it to the fires of the dark star," she muttered, not seeing anything. *There.* She stabbed her finger on a menu. Up came a confusing set of options. Scanning through, she found the deck they were on, 98-Alpha.

Video bloomed onto the terminal screen and Felar caught her breath. Breakers flooded the corridors and rooms outside the hangar. Thankfully, the Justice had them locked out, but Felar wondered how long that would last.

One of the figures on the many feeds stood out. He carried himself differently, with a confidence that only came from having troops at your command. The lanky figure with the brown hair was definitely the Breaker leader, or at least one of them. Something about him seemed familiar and Felar zoomed in to take a closer look. The shape of his finely featured face was distinctive. Felar scoured her mind to place where she had seen him before. After a few moments, she grunted in frustration, unable to remember.

Felar watched as he walked up to the only door separating them. He touched it with one finger and then turned around and walked away. Felar grew puzzled. Was he giving up so easily?

Switching feeds, she tracked the leader as he walked through the crowd of Breakers. He gestured to a particular individual, a dark skinned man dressed in an officer's uniform. Felar zoomed in, trying to see his rank insignia. *Ascended?* she thought, brows furrowing. How was Karoth involved in this? The officer shifted and Felar saw the holes in his chest.

What is it about the puncture wounds that turns people into Breakers?

The brown-haired man seemed to question Karoth at length, pointing in the direction of the hangar. Felar hoped they could take off in the next few minutes. She didn't want to see the results of his planning. They exchanged more words, Karoth pointing in the direction opposite the Revenge. The leader headed off that way. *Maybe he's given up after all.*

Then the memory snapped into place: *That combat vid.* The Founder's Commandos did extensive sparring, from individuals all the way up to battalions. The unit libraries contained hundreds of thousands of hours of raw footage. Felar had spent much of her free time during Dog School watching the vids, trying to learn as much as she could. The leader of the Breakers had been in one of the battles. There had even been a note about him in the beginning. He was on loan from his unit due to an injury of its regular squad commander. Felar distinctly remembered how he had led his newly assigned unit to a crushing victory against overwhelming odds. He looked slightly older, but this was definitely the man from the combat vid, she was sure of it.

The brown-haired leader walked out of view of her current feed, so Felar switched again. He opened a door labeled "98-Alpha Security" and went inside. The feed for this room was harder to find, and by the time she pulled it up, the man had already seated himself at a terminal.

The Revenge's airlock cycled, startling Felar. She didn't realize how close she had been sitting to the screen. Wake, Tremmilly, Maxar, and Jaydon all walked on to the command deck. "I'm so glad to see you," Tremmilly said, giving Felar a tight hug.

"I can't believe you guys came to rescue us," Felar replied, returning her enthusiasm.

Jaydon and Maxar skipped greetings, too focused for pleasantries. "We have to get out of the hangar before they get through that hatch," Jaydon said to no one in particular.

"You guys get us spaceborne," Wake announced, "and I'll get back to work patching the hull." He took off towards the cargo deck.

The Revenge shuddered and moaned, shifting slightly. "What was that?" Felar said, looking at her terminal for some kind of status message. Instead, all she saw was the grinning face of the Breaker leader. He was waving, staring directly into the camera. *The bugger knows I'm watching,* she thought, feeling violated. The brown-haired man waved one last time, touched his terminal screen, and the feed went dark.

"Blightheart," Felar cursed.

"Out of the way," Jaydon ordered, trying to squeeze into the captain's chair. "I need to get us out of here." Felar almost fell over as she stood, feeling dazed. She knew what the Breaker had done, even before Jaydon announced it.

"The buggers have engaged the hangar mag-lock. We can't take off."

"Maybe Wake and I can find a way to disable it," Maxar said, still sounding calm. "We have a little while before they can cut through the door and equalize pressure."

"I wouldn't be too sure of that," Jaydon said. "You'd best get out there and cut us loose. I'll get the ship powered up and try to patch those holes. We don't have much atmosphere left, but if I get it fixed soon, there should be enough for the environmental systems to keep functioning."

Maxar left the command deck without another word. "Would it make sense to switch over to an Ashamine ship," Tremmilly asked, "one with a working worm generator? Seems like there are plenty out there."

"That's a great idea, Trem," Felar responded, "but based on what the Breaker leader has done so far, I would imagine he has them remotely disabled. He's systematically doing everything possible to slow us down."

"Well, I suppose we will have to find the Bane and switch over to it once we get off the Justice. Malesis should be out there."

Felar nodded and briefly thought about asking Jaydon if she could help with anything on the Revenge, but then decided not to. He was in a particularly bad mood and would have already given orders if he thought Felar or Tremmilly could help. There wasn't much for them to do, not inside the Revenge anyway. *We could use some more weapons,* Felar thought, developing a plan.

38 – TREMMILLY

Tremmilly wished she could help with their escape, but she didn't know how to disable mag-locks or patch starship holes. Jaydon continued to get the Revenge ready for departure, grumbling as he did so. Felar was the only other person in the room. Tremmilly's mind drifted, wondering how Beowulf and everyone else on the Ashamine's Bane were faring.

"We are going out into the hangar," Felar said, breaking into Tremmilly's thoughts.

"Why?" Tremmilly asked reflexively, the mental image of all the corpses making her nervous. It had been hard enough experiencing them the first time.

"There isn't anything for us to do in here and we'll just drive ourselves mad with waiting. Outside, we can do something useful, grab as many weapons as possible." Felar smiled. "And if Wake and Maxar take a while, I can teach you how to shoot. If this whole prophecy thing keeps going the way it is, you'll need to be a better shot." Tremmilly had to agree.

"OK," she answered, "but the bodies are going to put me on edge."

"You and me both."

Felar checked on Lothis and told him they were heading outside. "I'll go up front and monitor the external feeds. The Breakers are very close now. The dark one is just outside." Lothis' words creeped Tremmilly out. She almost decided to stay in the ship, but Felar knew what she was doing. Tremmilly trusted her not to lead them into a bad situation.

"Good idea," Felar replied. "Don't let Jaydon give you too much blightheart," she finished with a smile.

The two women cycled through the airlock and Tremmilly tried to stay calm. "We're outside the Revenge with you guys," Felar transmitted to Wake and Maxar. "The plan is to collect some weapons and teach Tremmilly to shoot."

"I could probably use a lesson as well when we get a chance," Wake said.

148

"I'm actually starting to like that guy," Felar transmitted over a private channel. Tremmilly felt surprised. Before the Ashamine had separated them, Felar hadn't even trusted him, let alone thought of him as a friend.

"We haven't found a way to disable the mag-lock yet," Maxar said.

"Keep us updated," Felar transmitted. "We'll do the same."

"Affirmative," Wake replied.

Felar led Tremmilly through the carnage, picking up pistols, rifles, ammo, and spare power supplies. Felar tried to pick up a katana that caught her eye, but gave up once she realized the mag-lock had it secured to the floor. "Good thing our suits and most of these weapons have such little metal in them," Felar transmitted over their private channel, "or we'd be stuck here too." Tremmilly shivered. She didn't relish that thought.

As they continued their work, Tremmilly avoided the bloated bodies. The conditions had stretched their skin so tight she wondered why it didn't burst. "Why is it that some of them are so big and the majority are normal?" As she said this, Tremmilly made the mistake of looking into the eyes of a disfigured soldier. They were blank, a vacuum that threatened to pull her in. She looked away quickly.

"I don't know," Felar said, looting a flechette pistol off one of the regular looking bodies. "Must have something to do with whatever makes them Breakers."

"Maxar crushed one of their skulls open. Black fluid came out." She paused for a moment, remembering the horrible battle. "I shot one of them and Jaydon shot two."

"Good for you," Felar said, nodding. She matched Tremmilly's somber tone. "You were just doing what was required to survive."

"Yeah," was all she could say in response. Tremmilly had never killed anything before. She loved life, wanted to protect it. *But the Breakers,* she thought, looking at one of the corpses that had not begun to bloat, *they seek to destroy life.* Then the corpse twitched, or at least she thought it did. She kept her eyes locked on the body, waiting. Moments passed. The corpse was still.

"Tremmilly?" Felar asked. "Did you hear me?"

"No, sorry. What did you say?"

"I said I think we have enough weapons. The pack is full. Let's get you up to speed on the flechette pistol."

Tremmilly looked back towards the ship. It was close enough if they had to run for it, but it still felt far away. "OK," she agreed, trying not to appear weak in front of Felar. "That's what I used in the fight earlier. I hit once and missed once."

"Not bad for someone with no weapons training," Felar replied encouragingly. "Hold the grip like this, with both hands," she continued,

149

demonstrating. "Smoothly pull the trigger, and keep your eyes open." Tremmilly thought she sensed movement out of the corner of her eye, but when she looked, only still corpses lay in that direction. *Lothis said he would tell us when they are coming,* she thought, forcing herself to look away from the dead.

"That makes sense," Tremmilly said, taking her own flechette pistol out of its makeshift holster. "Like this?" she asked, imitating Felar's stance.

"Close," the other woman said, repositioning her slightly. "Try to hit that Ashamine emblem over there. Calm breath, then squeeze." Tremmilly did as instructed and the needles struck within a meter of the target. "Not bad for that distance."

"We found the main hangar control terminal," Maxar's voice broke in. "It's damaged though. Wake thinks it might just be the screen. If that's the case, we should be able to wire a different one in its place. Shouldn't take too long."

"Good to hear," Felar replied. "Where are you guys?"

"The hangar controls are located in a small room elevated above the main deck. Look at three o'clock high."

Tremmilly and Felar turned to look in the indicated direction. Several floors up and across the hangar bay, they saw Wake's crimson ENS waving down at them. They waved back.

"Got ya," Felar said. "That's a ways up."

"Yeah," Wake replied, "the lift was damaged so we had to climb an access ladder."

"We're almost done here. Just going to have Tremmilly try a few more shots and then we will head back to the ship. I'll stay outside as perimeter guard."

Again a flicker of movement tugged at the edge of Tremmilly's vision. *Nothing is there. You're tricking yourself. They're all dead.*

"We would appreciate that," Maxar transmitted. "See you soon."

"Did you just see that?" Felar's voice was tense, alert. She was staring at a nearby Breaker corpse.

"What?" Maxar asked.

"It just moved."

"What moved?"

"A body."

Then, they were all moving, Breaker bodies twitching and writhing around them.

The lights went out.

39 – MAXAR

"Get back to the blighthearted ship. Now!" Maxar yelled inside his helmet. "We will get the mag-lock off and meet you there." He didn't know if he and Wake could do either of those things, but they had to try. Maxar toggled his small headlamp and focused all his attention on the damaged screen he was trying to remove.

"I almost have my screen out," Wake said hurriedly. Maxar could barely see the other man, the dim light from surviving status displays casting only a weak glow.

"No time to be delicate now," Maxar muttered, smashing the gauntlet of his ENS through the damaged display. He grabbed the interior of the screen and yanked hard. It came loose, dangling by wires.

"Be careful," Wake said, sliding in beside him. "If you damage the wiring harness, we'll have even more work on our hands."

Maxar moved out of the way, letting the engineer do his job. After a couple moments, Wake had plugged in his replacement screen and the console came to life. He quickly flipped through options and menus. Maxar felt time slipping away.

"Here it is," Wake said, selecting the option for the hangar mag-lock.

Permission Denied, flashed across the screen. Maxar ground his teeth together. "What are your hashing skills like?"

"Non-existent," Wake replied, sounding apologetic. Maxar caught a glimpse of two feeble lights moving frantically across the hangar below them. *Tremmilly and Felar,* he thought, fear stabbing at his heart. It was impossible to tell how close they were to the Revenge, or what the resurrected Breakers were doing. *Either the women are silent or they forgot to switch to a general channel.*

Maxar traded places with Wake and set to work hashing the terminal. The display told him he needed root privileges to access the mag-lock controls. He'd gently attempted to gain root earlier while locked in the crew room. Those tactics had proved unsuccessful. Now, he could try a

151

more forceful approach. Maxar attempted exploit after exploit, but nothing worked. Finally, an automated message popped up: *Suspicious activity detected. System lockdown. Contact administrator to restore privileges.*

"Buggering blightheart," Maxar swore. "Now we are all dead." Both men sat looking at the screen, feeling despondent.

"What about Lothis?" Wake said finally. "Maybe he could do something."

"Great idea," Maxar said, his hope restored. The boy had a way with computers. It was creepy, but powerful. He switched from monitor to transmit using the general frequency. "Lothis, we need your help."

"I've been trying to disable the mag-lock from the Revenge's terminal," his quiet voice replied, "but I'm completely locked out. It appears someone configured the Justice to disallow outside connections. I can tell you how to hash through the terminal lockout and gain root. It's going to take some time though." Maxar wondered briefly how the boy knew exactly what he needed.

"Felar and Tremmilly's lights just disappeared," Wake said, sounding worried.

"Have they made it back on board?" Maxar sent, his own fear elevating.

"Yes, Tremmilly just came inside and said Felar is standing guard at the hatch. She also says the Breaker corpses are starting to crawl. They are converging on the Revenge."

Maxar shook his head. "Like we need another thing to worry about. Maybe we can get this hash done before things get worse. Lothis, where do I start?" The boy began feeding him commands, complicated button combinations that Maxar didn't understand. He had to focus. After several moments, the lockout lifted.

"That was the easy part," Lothis transmitted. "Pay close attention. If you mess up any of the code I am about to tell you, we will have to start over." Maxar didn't like the sound of that.

"OK," he replied, "I'm ready."

Silence greeted him. He waited another moment. This was unlike Lothis. When the boy focused, nothing could distract him.

"Lothis?" Maxar transmitted. "Did we lose comms?"

"The dark one is here," Lothis finally replied, his tone sending a chill up Maxar's spine. "He's coming straight for us," he continued. Maxar didn't understand who the dark one was, but if he was attacking the Revenge, Maxar would have to confront him.

"Wake," he said hurriedly, heading for the ladder down to the deck, "keep following Lothis' instructions. I'm going to send this bugger to the fires of the dark star."

"Acknowledged," Wake transmitted. "Be careful."

Maxar thought about the situation as he climbed down the ladder. Even though the Revenge's worm generator was inoperable, it still made sense to continue using the ship. Switching to one of the Ashamine vessels would take too long, requiring another complicated hash. After they disabled the mag-lock, they would still need to bypass the Ashamine ships surrounding the Justice. And now he had to kill or hold off the dark one while Wake finished up.

When Maxar reached the deck, he briefly turned on his gauntlet light to find a weapon. A rail pistol caught his eye. Maxar snatched it up and extinguished the illumination. He missed his old Bloodsport ENS, which had low light vision. His current suit was basic and lacked advanced features. Using any of its lighting would reveal Maxar's presence. *How am I going to make my way across a chaotic hangar full of bodies?*

"Lothis," he asked when the boy paused between transmitting lines of code, "I need some light out here. Does the Revenge have external illumination?" The boy said nothing, but a second later, the ship blazed brightly, harsh light obscuring its outline. "Thanks," Maxar said, making his way through the remnants of battle. Lothis continued reciting code to Wake.

All the bodies Maxar passed looked bloated and motionless. There had been twice this many when he'd passed before. *They are all around the Revenge now,* he thought, wondering what he would see once he got closer. Maxar rounded a corner. There they were; hundreds of bodies surrounded the ship. The Breakers stood motionless, poised for action.

"I offer all of you the chance to be as gods," a proper sounding voice said in Wake's helmet, "the chance to live forever and have power unlike anything you can imagine. A few of you will be unable to be part of this ascendancy, but I'm sure the rest of you can rise above the squalor of humanity." *This must be the dark one,* Maxar thought, trying to determine his location. "You are not all Ashamine," the voice continued, "that is easy to tell from your hashing. Perhaps you are from Eishon-2. How did you manage to capture the boy? Ah well, I suppose that doesn't really matter. You cannot escape. Submit to me and I will only kill those of you who are bound for darkness." The voice maintained its refined tone, despite the threatening words.

Then Maxar saw him, a man dressed in an Ashamine ENS suit, entering the cone of light around the Revenge. His body seemed to warp and distort slightly as he moved, a phenomenon Maxar didn't understand. *That has to be him.* Maxar carefully settled into a one-kneed shooter's stance, steadied himself, took aim, and triggered a round. His weapon was silent in the vacuum, but the ion trail blazed brightly through the blackness of the hangar. The rail round should have penetrated the intruder's center mass, blowing him apart. Instead, it transitioned through the shimmering space and came out harmlessly on the other side.

"Ahhh," the man said, turning to face him, "someone who strikes from darkness." He pulled out a katana and began walking towards Maxar. *It's some type of shielding.* Knowing it would probably be futile, Maxar unloaded the remaining rounds from his rail pistol in rapid-fire succession. All passed harmlessly through the man, just like the first shot. *I wonder what would happen if I used a sword instead.*

Maxar had faced many strange situations on Bloodsport. The Ashamine were always testing new weapons and armor there. Convicts made good subjects. Maxar had learned long ago, no one possessed a perfect defense. Each one had a weakness. The difficulty lay in staying alive long enough to find it.

Picking up a titanium sword from a dead Ashamine officer, Maxar moved to a clear section of deck. "You are a warrior," the man said, sounding pleased. "Fight for the greatest power in the universe," he continued. "No need to enter blackness."

The shimmering around the figure ceased and a force closed over Maxar's mind. He felt violated, like someone was trying to pry into his inner most self. *No,* he thought, pushing against the mental intruder. *Get out!* Maxar pushed harder. *Get out you bugger!* And then he was free.

The man before him sniffed derisively. "You're a strong one," he said, raising his sword.

Maxar raised his own blade reflexively, deflecting the dark one's blow. The man moved incredibly fast. *I'm in trouble,* he thought, doing his best to defend himself from the fury of blows the invader rained down on him. Maxar had trained with long blades, but they were never his weapon of choice. This man was an expert. Ducking a high swing that would have removed his head, Maxar rolled off to one side. Blow after blow followed, and Maxar did his best to protect himself. *One small cut in the suit,* he worried, *and then the timer starts.*

Time passed as Maxar continued on the defensive. His opponent never left an opening, never gave him a way to shift the momentum.

"Who are you?" he asked, trying to distract his attacker.

"That won't work," the dark one replied, his attack as strong as ever. Maxar continued to parry blows as the man continued. "But I will tell you, that all your friends might hear. Perhaps they will make a wiser decision than you. My name is Crasor. I am destruction and creation. I am birth and I am death. I am all things. I am nothing. I am One. I am the Breakers." Crasor darted to one side and brought his sword through a clean up sweep. Maxar didn't have time to move and knew the sword would open him from groin to shoulder. He felt a sudden shift inside himself, a quickening. He stepped back just before the blade made contact. As it passed, the tip of the weapon nicked Maxar's suit, puncturing it. A tone sounded and a warning indicator flashed on his HUD. He would only have a couple minutes before the leak became critical.

The failed strike left Crasor exposed and Maxar took advantage. He lunged forward, trying to put his sword through the man's heart. Crasor moved faster than Maxar believed possible and his blade passed harmlessly by. "You're not the only one quicker than a human. What is your augmentation? Genetic? Nanites?" Crasor pounded him with strike after strike. Maxar kept backing up, unable to stand his ground. Then, something caught his foot and he was falling. Landing flat on his back, Maxar felt the wind go out of him. Before he could bring his blade up to defend, Crasor stood over him.

"May the darkness take you," Crasor said coldly.

Without warning, the dark one's chest exploded in a spray of blood. Crasor stood, unsteady for a moment longer, then toppled over. Maxar rolled out of the way to avoid the falling body. Once he stood, he saw Felar crouched in a shooter's stance, a flechette pistol clasped in her hands.

"Come on," she transmitted, "it's time to go." Maxar ran over, feeling dazed.

"Thanks," he said, still out of breath from his prolonged duel.

"You would have done the same for me," Felar responded. "Sorry I couldn't help earlier. The Breakers slowed me down."

"Mag-lock is down," Wake said, joining them. "I would be happy if we got off the Justice as soon as possible."

"Agreed," Maxar replied.

The three of them set off towards the Revenge. The mass of Breakers blocked their path. Maxar felt drained, but continued to wield his sword, hacking and slashing at the bodies. Felar and Wake also used bladed weapons, although Felar's were matte black short swords and Wake's was a diamond katana. He caught enough glimpses of them to know they both understood how to use them. Projectile weapons would have made it easier to carve a path, but the Revenge was in the line of fire.

Finally, they reached the hatch. "Get inside," Felar said, holding off Breakers as Wake and Maxar went through. Maxar saw her draw a rail pistol from her tactical belt and put her back to the ship. Ion trails streaked out, and the rounds carved furrows into the mass of bodies. Felar dove through the door and Maxar hit the button to seal and cycle the airlock. The hatch closed. They were safe, for the moment.

40 – LOTHIS

"Jaydon, get us out of here!" Maxar yelled, bursting into the command deck. Lothis jumped in his seat, startled. He'd been thinking about the dark figure, about Crasor's death and what would happen next. Wake, Felar, and Tremmilly followed in behind Maxar, cramping the deck space. The air immediately felt close, despite how thin it was. Thankfully, Jaydon had patched the holes in the Revenge just a few minutes before.

"About buggered time," Jaydon exclaimed, entering the commands to take them out of the hangar bay. Lothis felt himself get heavier as the Revenge lifted off. "What happened out there?" Jaydon continued. "Wait, never mind. I don't have time to listen. There are still a lot of Ashamine ships outside the Justice. Do you have a plan that doesn't involve us dying from rail cannon fire?"

"At the moment, no," Maxar answered, "but we have to get away from those blighthearted things down on the deck. It's just a matter of time before they figure out how to bugger the Revenge." He shuddered. "And the further we can get away from *him*, the better."

Lothis could feel the Breakers below him. They were minute pricks of blackness, an absence of energy. It was all cold and mechanical, no connection to life. The one who had been full of darkness, Crasor, the wielder of the black energy, was still. Something about the situation didn't feel right to Lothis. He'd watched Felar send the flechette round through him on the terminal screen. Crasor's life had seemed to vanish, but as Lothis continued to watch—not with his eyes, but with his mind— he saw a flicker. It was energy, the movement of machines.

As the Revenge passed out of the hangar, a bright lance of Entho-la-ah-mine energy caught his attention. It emanated from a starship anchored to the hull just a few hundred meters away.

"That's the Ashamine's Bane," Wake said. "How did they know where to find us?"

"I don't know," Maxar answered, "but they are under attack."

They all watched out the main view window as white ENS clad figures rushed towards the Revenge, sprinting across the black hull of the Justice. Lothis could sense their leader, almost as dark and as strong as Crasor. It was the same person who had attacked the Queen before, and now he was trying again. Dark tendrils shot out from the Breaker leader, penetrating the command deck of the Bane. Dread filled Lothis. He knew what that darkness could do.

More flashes of Entho-la-ah-mine energy struck out, blasting Breakers off the hull. They cartwheeled through space, limbs unmoving. The Entho-la-ah-mines were killing them.

"What's making them fly off like that?" Felar asked.

"The Entho-la-ah-mines are using psionic weaponry," Lothis replied. "They are defending themselves." Silence met Lothis' answer. He knew none of them would understand and thought him odd.

The figures moved closer and closer to the Bane, and the Entho-la-ah-mines couldn't kill enough of them to turn the tide.

"Why isn't the Bane taking off?" Tremmilly asked, sounding worried.

"Good question," Wake answered. "Malesis is an amazing captain, whatever is happening, he would have gotten out of there if he could."

"We have to get down and help then," Tremmilly said. "Beowulf and the Entho-la-ah-mines are in danger. Captain Malesis needs us." Lothis agreed, but kept silent.

"Alright," Jaydon said, diving towards the Bane, "But what about the Ashamine gunships? If they spot us, they'll waste us all."

Felar flipped through a couple terminal readouts, finding what she wanted. "Looks like some fighters and gunships are heading in to dock, while the rest are grouping up off the stern. The Justice broadcast a message a few minutes ago that said they were to dock and open all hatches or be fired upon. I don't imagine we have a lot of time, but there should be a window of opportunity."

As Jaydon piloted them in, the figures reached the airlock of the Bane. They huddled around it for a moment, then rushed away. "Blightheart," Wake cursed. "What are they doing?" A second later, an explosion tore apart the hatch, the resulting decompression sending debris out into space.

"Going after the Queen," Lothis answered. Everyone looked at him. "Their leader is almost as strong as Crasor. If the Queen falls into the Breakers' hands, the entire species will be lost. The Breakers will control them all." The figures rushed back towards the compromised airlock, and Lothis' fear deepened.

Felar grabbed her ENS helmet and locked it into place. "I'm going in. Maxar? Wake? You with me?" Wake nodded, but Maxar shook his head.

"I can't," he replied, sounding pained. "My suit is compromised.

Crasor put a hole in it." He pointed down at his crotch and they all looked.

"Just about lost some pretty important parts," Tremmilly said, trying to contain her laughter. Lothis felt the mood in the room lighten. *When we tease each other,* he thought, *it creates a tighter bond, helps us be closer to each other.* Group dynamics were a new thing to him, but they were becoming easier to understand.

"Uhhh, yeah," Maxar said, a pale red flush infusing his face.

"Well then, it will just be Wake and me," Felar continued, the look on her face telling Lothis she was ready for combat.

"I would help," Jaydon said, "but they may shift the attack towards us. In that event, I'll get off the hull and wait for you both to clear. We'll be watching. Good luck." Tremmilly and Maxar also wished them well as they left for the airlock.

"Switch to near field comms," Lothis heard Felar tell Wake, then no more.

The lances of Entho-la-ah-mine energy stopped once the Breakers blew the airlock. Lothis wished he could sense them, could help in some way, but they had shielded themselves. Besides, any level of his ability helpful to the Queen might also cause him to lose himself.

Several of the Breakers entered the Bane, while the rest waited outside, acting as guards. Lothis felt desperate, wanting to help Felar, Wake, and those on the Bane. He began crafting the psionic lance he'd used in the previous battle. *I can't, I can't.* The risk felt overwhelming. Unable to control his fear, Lothis released the mental energy and watched the view screen. *Will they die because of my inability to help?*

Wake appeared in the field of view, walking off to the side of the Revenge. He moved straight towards the Bane, path unwavering. His only visible weapon was his katana, still sheathed on his back. The crimson environmental nominizing suit didn't stand out against the black of the hull, but it was by no means invisible. "They're going to see him," Tremmilly said.

"I think that's the point." Maxar replied softly. "He's the diversion." Soon, the Breakers noticed him. They leveled their rail weapons and fired. Ion trails traced through the blackness, each a different hue. Blue, red, and yellow hit Wake, then pinged off in crazy directions. He kept advancing. "That is one incredible suit," Maxar said in awe. "I've never seen human portable armor that could withstand rail fire."

Where is Felar? Lothis wondered. He trusted her judgment and tactics, but worried all the same.

More rounds pinged off Wake, slowing his advance. "Now," Felar's voice said over the Revenge's speakers. Wake lifted his right gauntlet and pointed it at the Breakers standing furthest from the Bane. A faint violet glow emanated from his fist, intensifying even as rail rounds deflected off him. Brighter and brighter the light became, swallowing up Wake's arm.

"What in the fires of the dark star?" Maxar whispered.

Just when Lothis thought the light couldn't get more intense, a beam of energy shot out. Wake swept his arm through a short arc and the light engulfed a large group of guards. When the violet beam finally subsided, Wake had cut half the Breakers in two. Their upper sections floated in space just above the hull.

Felar came into view, having circled around the back of the Breakers. Lothis let out a breath he didn't realize he was holding, relief flooding him. Felar waded into the remaining troops, matte black short sword in her left hand and flechette pistol in the right. She stabbed, shot, and hacked her way through the guards, blood and other body materials spraying into the void. By the time Wake had covered the remaining distance, Felar had left no Breaker standing. The two looked at each other, nodded, and went through the Bane's hatch.

A piercing cry slammed into Lothis' mind: "The dark one is killing us!" *The Queen,* he thought, desperate to assist her. Lothis felt trapped between helping someone he loved and self-preservation. *If you strike at the Breaker leader, it will be the last thing you ever do,* he thought, panic filling him. *But if you don't, you will have to live with knowing you didn't stop the death of your friends.*

Guilt flooded Lothis and he knew only Felar and Wake had a chance to stop the destruction of the entire Entho-la-ah-mine species. He sat back in the co-pilots chair and waited, keeping watch on the view screen.

41 – CAZZ-AK-TAK

"Why isn't Malesis taking off?" the Queen asked. Cazz-ak had no answer.

He'd gone to the command deck earlier to inform the Captain they'd sensed an impending attack. Malesis said he would take off as soon as possible. Cazz-ak had left the deck and returned to the cargo hold, Beowulf continuing to follow everywhere he went.

Still, the Bane lingered. And as seconds dragged by, Cazz-ak's dread continued to grow. Beowulf whined. The Entho-la-ah-mines could feel the dark presence approaching, the same one they had battled before. Now it was much stronger, a deeper shade of black that threatened to swallow them up.

"I think something has happened to Captain Malesis," Elth-eo-lan said. "We must prepare to fight back."

"We are not powerful enough, not at this distance" Cazz-ak replied. "I will go check on the humans."

"No, the time for that has passed," Na-ah-co said. "If you leave now, we will not have unity of mind for when the darkness strikes." Cazz-ak prepared himself and said nothing. The three of them united, gathered in more of the Great Thought, and waited.

Cazz-ak felt the ship shudder. The oily blackness snaked its way towards them, growing larger. It was an ugly hole in the fabric of life. The image of it caused Cazz-ak to shudder, made his mind want to hide as far away as possible. He felt it pass outside the cargo hold door, heading for the command deck. More seconds dragged by, and Cazz-ak guessed that Malesis and his crew had been mentally dominated by the dark leader. It was the only thing that explained why the ship hadn't taken off.

Once again, the blackness approached, growing, swelling, tendrils protruding menacingly. Cazz-ak marveled at how it seemed to suck at all surrounding energy. This was nothing normal, nothing natural. It stopped outside the cargo hold hatch and they all tensed, ready to defend. Beowulf ceased whining and began emitting a harsh growl. The door opened and a tall muscular human walked through it. His hair was as black as the darkness inside him. Cazz-ak intensified both their mental and physical shield, using his anger to draw in more power from the Great Thought.

"The time has come," the dark leader said, his voice deep and dominating. "You resisted once, but no longer. Open yourselves, or die," he said, motioned to Cazz-ak, Elth-eo-lan, and Beowulf. "I'll use a knife, just like I did to your friends on the bridge. They ended full of pain."

Cazz-ak closed his eyes and thought about all the horrors perpetrated against his people: the death, destruction, extermination, and exile. Being enslaved was unacceptable. *No more,* Cazz-ak thought, amplifying his fury. *I will not allow it.*

"Fine," the leader said, taking in a deep breath. "Make it hard on yourselves." Dark energy exploded from him, slamming into their mental shield. Cazz-ak felt himself bend, crushed just like in the previous battle.

"Move into a triangle formation," Na-ah-co said, her voice barely audible in his mind. The three struggled to configure themselves, fighting hard against the onslaught. Beowulf whimpered in pain, but followed beside Cazz-ak. Forming the triangle, Cazz-ak felt some weight lift. This shape allowed the trio to focus their energy more efficiently. Elth-eo-lan ended up on the point that faced directly towards their adversary.

"Crasor told me you'd be strong," the dark one said, "but I thought you'd be a better opponent than this." He took a step forward and leaned his head to one side. It was a uniquely human gesture Cazz-ak interpreted as listening or thinking. "I wish I had time to enjoy this, but it appears I must end things quicker than expected." He took another step, running directly into their physical shield. "Ahhh," he said, laughing derisively. The dark one pulled his fist back and punched the barrier. It shattered. A wave of rebounding energy struck the trio and Cazz-ak felt dazed. When he refocused his eyes, he saw the dark one poised over Elth-eo-lan, a long knife in his hands. "Still enough time to enjoy this though. Remember, bug, that Aeron sent you to the darkness."

The knife plunged down through Elth-eo-lan's skull and Cazz-ak felt her wink out of existence. All that remained were the feelings of support and love she had given him. "No!" he cried, thrusting a lance of white-hot mental energy at Aeron.

"I told you what would happen," he said, blocking the strike with a tendril of darkness. "And now it's your turn!"

"The dark one is killing us!" the Queen sent, her voice shrill with terror. Cazz-ak wondered if anyone was even nearby to hear. Aeron stood over him and raised his knife. *My life is about to end,* Cazz-ak thought. He was at peace with the idea, but he could not accept the corruption of the Queen. Cazz-ak had fought so hard to protect her from the humans, had done everything in his power to keep her alive. He could not see her enslaved by this horrible creature.

Beowulf leapt towards Aeron, teeth bared in a snarl. Before he could cover the distance, a tendril of blackness shot out from the dark one. It slammed Beowulf to the floor, knocking him unconscious. "I never did like dogs anyway," Aeron said derisively.

Cazz-ak dove inside himself and time slowed. He found the peace of the Entho-la-ah-mines and also his anger. On their own, the two were potent, but together they were greater than the sum of their parts. Up to this point, Cazz-ak had been reluctant to use them both at the same time, still worried he would corrupt the Great Thought. He released his fear and trusted Elth-eo-lan's words. As Cazz-ak united the forces, a whole new level of strength filled him.

Aeron drove the knife down. Cazz-ak quickly created a shield of mental energy. It wasn't enough to cover his whole body, much less that of the Queen, but it was solid. The point of the blade struck the barrier and rebounded, blasting the dark one against the wall.

"Heh," Aeron said, "neat trick." He rose to his feet and walked back towards them. "Let's see you deflect a rail round." Before the dark one could draw his pistol, a matte black blade emerged from his chest. A figure tumbled away from Aeron, and when it rose, Cazz-ak recognized Felar.

Aeron turned to face his attacker, but Wake stood directly in his path. With a speed Cazz-ak had never seen before, the dark one drew a rail pistol and fired into Wake's chest. The round pinged off, deflected towards the floor.

"Neat trick yourself," Wake said, driving his gauntleted fist into the dark leader's face. The strike was hard enough to kill a normal human. All it did to Aeron was deform his face slightly. Before Wake could land another blow, the dark leader dropped his knife and picked Wake up by the neck. Aeron hauled back and slammed Wake against the wall.

"How does that feel inside your fancy ENS?" Aeron slammed him again and again, then held him high in the air. Cazz-ak heard a deafening crack and the dark one's arm disintegrated in a spray of black blood. Aeron roared. He used his remaining arm to fire at Felar, but she was already diving out of the way.

Wake, who had collapsed to the floor, was rising. Aeron tried to find Felar, his eyes a maniacal frenzy. Cazz-ak could feel her hiding behind a flimsy cargo crate, and he smoothly shielded her from Aeron's senses.

"It feels pretty good," Wake finally replied, as he drew his diamond katana. His voice sounded strained, but he deftly swung the sword in an arc aimed for Aeron's neck. The dark leader leaned to the side and brought up his arm to block. He failed to remember that arm was missing. Wake's sword passed cleanly through the air, entered at Aeron's jaw, and exited out the opposite temple. The upper half of the dark one's head fell off as the hulking body collapsed to the floor.

"We have to get out of here before more of them show up," Wake said, struggling to remain standing.

Felar approached Cazz-ak, Na-ah-co, and the unconscious Beowulf. "The airlock on this ship is damaged, so we can't transfer you over to the Revenge. There are a few solid hatches between us and space though, and the Bane treats them as auxiliary airlocks when the main one is damaged. That's why the whole ship didn't explosively decompress." Felar thought for a moment, then continued. "I would say we could just fly the Bane off the Justice, but I'm not sure how much damage the Breakers have caused, or if this guy is going to reanimate. Other ones have. I know you don't have suits, but is there any way you can get through the vacuum?"

Cazz-ak thought about the escape vehicle he'd crafted when the Hammer had destroyed his bi-pyramid ship. *Too awkward, but perhaps something like that would work now.* He drew upon the Great Thought and made a bubble around himself, the Queen, and Beowulf, trapping atmosphere with them. He gently lifted the wolf-dog using another strand of psionic energy. "We are ready," he said, heart breaking as they left Elth-eo-lan behind.

42 – CRASOR

Crasor floated in blackness. He'd felt pain earlier, but now it vanished. A light winked on before him, a soft white glow, inviting in this dark place. It grew steadily, both in intensity and size. Crasor couldn't tell if the light was expanding or if he was moving towards it. Soon, the illumination was everything, bright as a blue hypergiant star. He tried to squint, to block the harsh glare, but he had no eyes.

"Crasor," the sound of many voices said, "those who are One cannot die. Their body, however, can be destroyed." The light dimmed slightly and Crasor could see his surroundings. Around him stretched trillions of figures, humanoid and otherwise. The humans had no eyes, no mouths, no noses, and no ears, just smooth, uninterrupted skin covering their skulls. Despite their lack of sensory organs, Crasor felt they were looking at him. "Your body was badly damaged, but we still have need of it. You will be repaired, but things may not be the same as before."

Crasor wondered where he was. "It is our place, One place," the mass of voices said. "It is safe from the four dimensions you know as normal. This is where we have spent millennia watching. We have waited for the right time to restore ourselves, to become what we once were. The cycle was infinite, until now." Crasor felt the energy around him swell. It was terrifying. It was exhilarating. "The man who you fought with in the hangar, he is the Convict. The woman who shot you is the Soldier. They are part of a larger group. This aggregate must be annihilated, sent to the darkest blackness. They are the Harbingers of the Dawn."

After a long pause, they continued. "Our hopes rest on you Crasor." The energy emanating from the mass increased even further, building to a mind-shattering crescendo. "Go back. Be One. Break the Dawn!" With the final word, Crasor imploded.

Pain. Crasor's eyes opened and he tried to gasp. *No air!* He realized he was back in the hangar of the Justice. Pain absorbed him, filled him, crushed him. "You don't need to breathe," the voice of the Breakers said,

164

much smaller than it had been moments before. Crasor tried to take in another breath, struggled, then realized the voice was right. *I don't need oxygen.* It was a strange sensation, not breathing. Once he relaxed, it was almost enjoyable. *Thirty-three years makes a strong habit.*

Looking down, Crasor saw a huge hole in his chest. Filaments of flesh and tissue hung from the ragged edges. Already, the Breakers were knitting him back together. Black nanites swarmed, building biomechanical structures to replace those the Soldier obliterated. His pain began to subside, replaced by a feeling of strength and wholeness. Moments passed, and the mass of machines slowed. Pain began to resurface. "We need more energy," the Breakers said. "Take off your suit and walk into the light of the star." Without a second thought, Crasor began stripping off the remains of his environmental nominizing suit. "Your clothes as well." He obeyed.

Walking naked across the hangar took all of Crasor's willpower. He felt heavy and every movement hurt. A dim part of his mind laughed at the situation. He was walking through a decompressed Tarton class battle ship hangar, naked, with a huge hole in his chest. Crasor wasn't ashamed of his body, but the setting was an odd one for nudity. He stepped around the bloated corpses of the unconverted Ashamine, his stride shaky. A large group of newly converted Breakers, the first who'd risen from the dead, watched him with dull, uncomprehending eyes.

He reached the wall of the hangar and looked up to the damaged hatch. It was several stories above him. He already felt exhausted. Gritting his teeth, Crasor grabbed the access ladder. The rungs felt cold on the bare skin of his hands and feet. It took him a considerable amount of time to make it to the top, fighting pain the entire time. When he climbed out of the hatch, the light of Eishon Primary struck him full in the face. Crasor felt his skin burning, but then the pain subsided. He could sense the nanites swarming to face the star. They needed to recharge, requiring the energy of the stellar radiation to continue repairing him. Gazing deeply into Eishon Primary, Crasor wondered what it would be like to wield its full power.

How is any of this possible? he asked the Breaker mind.

"We have evolved the physical part of our existence—the nanites—to draw power from almost any type of energy. Some forms, such as unfiltered stellar emission, are more efficient than others. Biomass has less power, but is portable and more accessible. This is why the new converts feed." Crasor had sensed this in a deep part of his mind, but it was good to have it confirmed. "Your ability to survive without oxygen is simple. To be brief, the nanites supply energy to your cells so they don't rely on biological metabolism. With proper manipulation, they can't tell the difference." Feeling comforted, Crasor tried to suppress his desire to breathe. "It is the same with the drones in the hangar, although their standard biological functions have ceased. We simply replace death with control and maintenance."

Which explains why we didn't swell up like the humans.

"Correct. They would be less functional if bloated. We inhibit the ebullism which causes expansion."

A glint of light caught Crasor's attention and he looked over to see a ship take off from the hull of the Justice. It was the one he had been hunting before his death, the one with Lothis. The boy was still as valuable a prize as ever. *And what of the Entho-la-ah-mines?* he wondered. *What of their Queen?* He tried to reach out to his Descended, to find out what had happened. Aeron did not respond. "He is dead," the Breaker mind answered. "The Soldier and the Engineer killed him." Rage boiled up in Crasor. These Harbingers were buggering him, were blighthearting all over him. *I must end this,* he thought.

The Breaker nanites indicated they had fully charged and were ready to finish reconstructing him. The pain of his wound had subsided to a minor ache and the rest of his body felt refreshed. After sliding down the ladder, Crasor ran over to an Ashamine fighter. He did a quick inspection, and it appeared undamaged. It was a small vessel, but the weapons load out looked impressive. *Perhaps I can end the Dawn with one well-placed rail round,* he thought, smiling. The Breaker mind approved.

Jumping into the cockpit, Crasor quickly went through the preflight checks and diagnostics. All indicators showed green and the engines fired up immediately. "Do not be hasty," the Breakers said. "They will not reach suitable worm distance before you can catch them." Crasor calmed himself, remembering how methodical he had been as both a Founder's Commando and as the Facilitator. *I will destroy them all,* he thought, *there is plenty of time.*

Exiting the Justice, Crasor gave the fighter full thrust. "Karoth," he transmitted, using the direct comm to the Ascended.

"Crasor," the man acknowledged, voice still somewhat shaky from his conversion.

"A civilian ship is headed away from the Justice. Do you have it on your sensors?" Silence. Crasor almost screamed. *Methodical,* he thought, *be calm.*

"Yes, I see it."

"Send the largest diameter rail round possible through its hull."

"That would be difficult at the moment." Karoth's voice sounded scared, but whether it was of him or something else, Crasor couldn't tell.

"Why?" Another second passed. Crasor overtook the Justice and had his answer. Hundreds of small fighters and larger gunships swarmed the battle carrier. Ion trails streaked across the black canvas of space, both towards and away from the Justice.

"We are being attacked by the remaining Ashamine ships," Karoth finally replied. "I ordered all deployed vessels to return, but some refused. They organized, and when I began destroying them, they returned fire."

"Fine. I'll kill them myself. Send me the target lock on the civilian ship." A moment later, a highlighted dot appeared on his tactical display. The Harbingers were flying directly for the worm barrier. *Straight line, easy target,* he thought, setting his fighter for an intercept course.

Several minutes passed. Crasor's tactical display showed he was gaining on them. He looked down at his wound. *Almost healed.* The new skin was as black as the surrounding void, and glinted like metal. Crasor smiled, thinking about what it would be like to control the Akked Galaxy.

A tone sounded, snapping Crasor out of his thoughts. The Harbinger ship had changed course. They were now heading directly for the mass of fighters and gunships. *Why did you deviate?* Something had changed. Crasor didn't mind. His job was harder now, but it was also more exciting.

43 – WAKE

"I'm telling you," Wake said, "there is no way to fix it without parts we do not have." He closed the access panel and sighed. "Felar, the drive is broken. There is nothing I can do about it."

"OK, OK!" she said, raising her hands in a placating gesture. "Sorry. I figured it was worth another look, just in case you missed something."

"I didn't miss anything. There was a cascade failure. Something shorted out, frying a string of modules. Even if I fix the short, which wouldn't be too hard, I'd still need replacement modules and a couple hours to swap them out."

"And we don't have parts or time," Felar replied with a sigh.

"We'll figure something out," Wake said, trying to comfort her.

Felar was silent for a moment, looking for words. "I wanted to say thank you, for everything you've done for us. We'd still be stuck inside the Justice if you hadn't hashed that mag-lock."

"I have to give credit to Lothis."

"You were the only one able to enter the commands." Felar captured Wake in her intense gaze. "Look, all I'm saying is that I appreciate what you've done and I think you're a great addition to this group."

"Thanks," Wake replied, smiling. "That means a lot coming from you. What exactly is this group anyway?" Before Felar could respond, Jaydon came on over the cargo hold speakers.

"Get up here, you two. We have decisions to make." He sounded anxious and Wake guessed his inability to fix the worm drive would make the situation worse. Felar led the way to the command deck.

Everyone else had already crammed themselves into the small space. Jaydon and Maxar sat in the two pilots' seats. Tremmilly knelt beside a sprawled out Beowulf, tending to his wounds. Lothis, the Queen, and Cazz-ak sat on the floor, looking intently at each other. "Any luck with the drive?" Jaydon asked.

"No," Wake answered.

"OK," Maxar said, "then the only way out of here is to get a new ship." Everyone was silent. His statement was true, but Wake had no idea how they would accomplish it.

"You're saying we should board one of the Ashamine gunships." Felar sounded thoughtful, rather than incredulous.

"We can't escape on this ship and the only unoccupied vessels are inside the Justice. We can't go back there." Maxar looked tired, they all were. "Perhaps we should have switched ships before we left, but everything was locked down and more Breakers were on their way. The Bane's structure was compromised, and who knows how many hostiles remained on board. I don't see how we could have done things differently." He shrugged. "Now we are left with one option."

Wake let out a nervous breath, shaking his head.

"It might not be as hard as you think," Jaydon said, a small smile crossing his weathered face. Wake hadn't known this man long, but could tell the Captain had survived some tough situations. Jaydon paused, looking around the room. "All we have to do is tell the Ashamine ships that we have Lothis." Wake expected an outburst from Felar, for her to tell him to go blightheart himself.

"That could work," she said, nodding.

"What?" Wake blurted, the word coming out before he realized it.

"Yeah," Felar continued, sounding more and more convinced. "The Ashamine will do anything to get him back. They won't fire on us, and will protect us from the Justice."

Jaydon nodded. "Yep, we'll be fine until they decide to board, kill us all, and take Lothis with them, but I figure we'll have a say in that outcome." Maxar agreed, as did Tremmilly. Wake had to admit it was a good plan, or at least the best one available at the moment.

"I'll take us towards the Ashamine ships," Jaydon said, making the adjustments on his displays. "Felar, you are the only ex-military amongst us. See if you can convince them we aren't the backwater, smuggling, convicts we really are."

Maxar vacated the copilot's seat and Felar sat in his place. She thought for a moment, then keyed the transmit button. "Priority Ashamine Transmission. This is 3rd Class Enlightened Felar Haltro. I have possession of the mission target. I repeat, I have the mission target. I was deep cover, Ascended level clearance. Karoth attempted to assassinate me and take the target to whomever he is now allegiant to. To the ranking officer still loyal to the Ashamine, I request your full protection and backup. We must keep the target safe and escort him back to safety."

Wake waited, holding his breath. The next few seconds were critical. Either the Ashamine ships believed them, or they would annihilate the Revenge.

"Enlightened Haltro," a female voice said over the speakers, "what is your position?" The words were neither hostile nor friendly and gave no hint if Felar's deception had worked. Jaydon nodded at Felar as she hit the transmit button.

"I am on the civilian ship A'Tal's Revenge. When the Justice fell to those *things,* they locked me out of all security systems. I had no way to evacuate the mission target. I tried several hangars before finding this ship, which was occupied by civvies hiding from the invaders. They were happy to let me use their ship, in exchange for helping them escape."

Wake had to admit she told a very convincing story. He almost found himself believing it. More time passed and the female voice was silent. Wake wished they would hurry up. The wait was sawing away at his already frazzled nerves. His head hurt from the pounding Aeron had given him. Wake's chest felt worse than the time he'd injured it on the bridge, and he guessed he might have broken a rib or two.

The Clothing is amazing, but it won't save you from whole body blunt force trauma. His ENS had protected him very well up to his encounter with Aeron, shielding him from numerous rail rounds. The power supply he had rigged while hiding had enabled one of the suit's weapons. It was a crude modification, using just the few components available on the Revenge. Once he had more time, Wake was excited at the prospect of creating something better and unlocking even more functions.

"Enlightened Haltro," the voice returned, "with connections between ourselves and the Justice severed, we have no way to access the Ashamine Forces database. As you know, this prevents us from verifying your story." *It also prevents you from knowing it's an outright lie,* Wake thought. "Is there some other way you can establish your credentials?"

"We are being followed by the leader of the dark ones," Cazz-ak said, his voice sounding broken in Wake's mind. "Crasor is behind us and gaining fast."

Jaydon consulted a terminal screen and nodded. "He's right. There is an Ashamine fighter coming up on our six. Its flight path is the same as ours. It came from the Justice and not from the remaining Ashamine fleet. It's almost within accurate rail cannon range."

"Blightheart," Maxar swore. "Felar put a twenty centimeter hole is his chest with a flechette pistol. I saw his organs disintegrate. How can it be him?"

"The Breakers are powerful. They are not like either of our species." The Queen's voice sounded somber, and Wake knew both she and Cazz-ak-tak were mourning the loss of Elth-eo-lan. He wished he and Felar had gotten to them sooner, had been able to save her. "The Breakers have mental capabilities exceeding the Entho-la-ah-mines, with technological advancements far outpacing humanity. Make no mistake, I do not know or understand them. I only tell you what I have seen." The Queen's words sent chills down Wake's spine.

Tremmilly leaned over from her position beside Beowulf and gave Na-ah-co a hug, which was a strange thing to see. Her lanky arms wrapped around the small Entho-la-ah-mine's radiant blue exoskeleton. The Queen had no way to return the embrace, but somehow, Wake could sense a feeling of gratitude and comfort coming from her.

"Enlightened Haltro, do you still copy?"

"Curse them to the fires of the dark star," Felar said. "I don't know how to confirm my identity."

"Crasor is in range," Jaydon said, tensing up.

Felar hit the transmit button. "Ashamine fleet, a fighter under control of the traitors is pursuing us. He is within accurate range and will fire shortly. His intent is to destroy the mission target. I request immediate assistance. We need your protection."

A rail cannon round flew past the Revenge, red ion trail blazing like the dark star. Jaydon put the ship into a hard turn, and Wake braced himself. "I hope they believe you," Jaydon said, straining against the g-force. More red cannon rounds streaked across the view screen. Wake knew it was just a matter of time before one blew through the Revenge. He put on his ENS helmet and waited.

44 – FELAR

Come on, come on, come on! Felar thought, willing the Ashamine ships to save them. Despite Jaydon's best efforts, Crasor would obliterate them soon.

"Enlightened Haltro, we have dispatched fighters to neutralize the traitor and escort you back to our flagship." *They'll never make it in time,* she thought, checking the display in front of her.

A red ion trail streaked over the Revenge, closer than any had come before. "I'm doing everything this old wreck can," Jaydon said apologetically.

"I know," Felar replied, putting on her ENS helmet. Everyone but Jaydon, and those without suits, had done the same. They could do nothing for Beowulf. Another ion trail streaked by.

"We can help," Cazz-ak said, a note of anger in his voice. "We will distract him till the Ashamine arrives." Neither of the Entho-la-ah-mines said anything further. Felar waited. And waited. Nothing. Crasor had ceased firing. Whatever they had done, it worked. Minutes passed, everyone sitting in tense silence.

"Crasor turned back towards the Justice," Cazz-ak finally announced.

"Probably because the Ashamine just came in range," Jaydon added, reducing thrust.

"Civilian ship," a stern voice said over the ship's speakers, "follow our heading and stay inside the perimeter." Jaydon obeyed, piloting the Revenge into the center of their bubble.

"We traded one evil for another," Tremmilly said, shuddering.

"At least now we have more time," Maxar said, removing his ENS helmet. "Na-ah-co and Cazz-ak, we need to get you into the smuggler's compartment. There will be no way to explain your presence. Tremmilly, I think you should go down with them. Wake, we could use your combat skills."

"I will go into the compartment," Tremmilly said, her voice sad. "I

172

wish to be with the Entho-la-ah-mines in their time of mourning. Besides, I would just be in the way." Felar was glad her friend would be safe from the worst danger, but she wished Tremmilly had more self-confidence. She'd come through quite a few tough situations and was a pretty good shot.

Felar nudged her friend and said, "You would be an asset up here, you know." Tremmilly smiled as she and the Entho-la-ah-mines headed towards the cargo hold.

"I'm feeling pretty beat up," Wake sighed. The solid crimson faceplate of the Clothing of the Iconoclast gave him an alien feel, like he was some type of talking machine. "I think I can help though, as long as they don't slam me into any more walls." Felar wondered briefly how a suit designed as an execution apparatus had armor and weaponry built in. Obviously, someone had repurposed it. Wake's power supply had unlocked some impressive features.

"How do we handle this?" Maxar asked, breaking into Felar's thoughts. "Do we go in heavy or continue the deep cover story?"

"I don't trust them." Felar replied. "Whoever brings Lothis back to Ashamine-2 will be a hero. They'll be promoted, rewarded, probably given their own planet. Plus, it will make their mutiny against a renowned Ascended seem justified. The officer that has taken control of the Ashamine fleet needs Lothis, and I doubt he or she will be above killing another officer and a few civilians to get him without their back story."

Maxar nodded his agreement. "So we go in heavy."

"Yeah. I think we wait till we are on whatever ship they attach to our airlock. If they order us to stay on the Revenge, we decline, make up a story, do whatever we have to get through. Once we are on the Ashamine ship, start shooting." Felar knew it was a risky plan. So much could go wrong when fighting in the tight confines of a ship. "Once we have a hold on the vessel, we get Tremmilly and the Entho-la-ah-mines through the airlock. I'm sure they will try to blow the connection as soon as the fighting starts, so we won't have much time." *Too many variables, too many angles.* Felar didn't like the situation, but she had no choice.

"Sounds like a solid plan, at least from what I can see," Wake said.

"Do whatever you need to get prepared," Jaydon announced, "we only have a few minutes left till we reach the fleet."

***

The indicator light above the hatch went green. Felar inhaled deeply. The airlock had sealed and pressurized. The only thing standing between them and a functioning worm drive were two doors and a bunch of Ashamine troops.

The fighter escorts had led the Revenge outside the combat zone, to one of the DAS class gunships. The DAS vessels were enormous, especially when compared with a fighter or any other type of carrier-supported ship. The fact several of them fit into the Justice showed how large that carrier was. Felar had seen the words "Death Watch" stenciled on its hull just before she'd left the bridge to get ready by the airlock.

This particular ship was apparently the new Fleet Command, its Captain the highest remaining officer after the fall of the Justice. Felar was glad they were away from the combat. Once the fighter escort went back to the fray, there would be no other Ashamine ships within close range.

Forcing her mind back to the present, Felar wondered if this type of ship carried a Marine contingent. Her experience of the Ashamine Space Fleet was rudimentary. The specific load out of such ships was not something they taught in Dog School. Jaydon had more knowledge of the Fleet. He guessed there would be a ship's crew of eight to fourteen on board, but had no memory if this kind of vessel carried Marines or not.

"Ready, Wake?" Felar asked. The crimson suit nodded. He walked up to the Revenge's side of the airlock, a small black cube grasped in his left hand. Wake opened the hatch and stepped inside. She and Maxar moved to either side of the heavy door.

Felar made a last second check of her preparations. She'd given anyone able to wield weaponry a flechette pistol. They didn't want to damage the Death Watch with rail rounds. Tremmilly and the Entho-la-ah-mines were in the smuggler's compartment with the lid left open. They were waiting for her signal, either to hide or to sprint through to the Death Watch. Felar had told Lothis to stay with them, and the boy barely fit between everyone else. Beowulf was beside Maxar, still injured from Aeron's strike, but looking like a killer. Maxar and the wolf-dog had a strange bond Felar didn't understand, but accepted. If Beowulf would fight, Felar could use him. Jaydon stood off to the side, out of the line of potential fire. He was their backup, and would advance positions just behind Felar, Maxar, and Beowulf.

"Stand clear of the airlock and prepare to be boarded. Those wielding weapons will be shot on sight." *You talk, but can you stand behind it? See how you like dealing with Wake.* Felar heard the hatch of the Death Watch open. Exclamations of surprise. Flechette pistols fired. Darts bouncing off metal. Wake would be advancing inside the Death Watch, tossing his small black cube into the room as he did so.

A bright flash of light drew the shape of the airlock on the opposite wall, confirming Felar's guess. That was her cue. She ran through the airlock, Maxar right beside her. Inside, they found Wake standing in the center of the antechamber. He had his flechette pistol aimed at a stunned opponent.

The cube had been a weapon of Wake's own design. He'd taken a module from the worm generator and made a slight modification. "It will overload when it hits a hard surface, discharging a flash of light. If they look directly at it, it will burn out their retinas."

"Why aren't you shooting?" Felar demanded, dispatching one of the Death Watch's crew. Maxar did the same.

"She's defenseless," was all Wake could answer.

"They were just shooting you," Maxar said, finishing off the last of the three.

"We don't have time for this," Felar yelled. "They are going to shut the airlock at any second." She could hear yelling outside the antechamber. *At least they don't seem to have any Marines on board.* "Move up!" she yelled back through the airlock.

Felar rushed forward, knowing that seizing the command deck was critical. *Can't let them signal the rest of the fleet.* She rushed forward, taking cover beside the hatch leading into the main deck of the Death Watch. Maxar slid into cover across from her, Beowulf just behind him.

Checking the progress of the rear guard, Felar watched Jaydon come through. A yellow warning indicator above the airlock began to flash. "They're closing it," Felar screamed. *If it shuts,* she thought, cutting herself off before she finished.

"I can handle this," Wake said, stepping into the airlock. He put his arms up, stopping the hatch as it began coming down. As the weight settled on him, Wake grunted. Behind him, Felar saw Lothis and the Entho-la-ah-mines. *Tremmilly better be right behind them,* she thought, worried at the sounds Wake was making.

Felar locked eyes with Maxar, nodded, and they both rushed ahead. The compartment before them was full of large ammunition loading machinery. As they neared the opposite hatch, flechette darts whistled by their heads, followed instantly by the crack of the discharge.

Maxar and Beowulf charged ahead. Felar laid down suppressive fire. The two opponents were taking cover behind machinery on either side of the hatch. Felar emptied her weapon, dropped it, and drew another flechette pistol. As she did so, Maxar got an angle on one of the defenders and shot him in the head. Felar kept a steady stream of rounds directed at the remaining troop until Beowulf leapt in and tore out his throat. "Clear," Maxar yelled.

They opened the hatch and carefully peered through. Inside were minimal crew quarters, just a few bunks and a lavatory. No one was present. When they reached the wall at the other end of the passageway, they found no door. Felar scrutinized the environment and found a floor hatch behind them.

"You open, I'll clear." She grabbed the hatch handle and twisted. Maxar signaled his readiness and she tugged. Immediately, he jumped down through the hole. Flechette pistols cracked, and Felar watched darts ricochet off Maxar as he fell. *That's some blightheartedly-advanced nano-tech,* she thought, shaking her head.

Maxar landed lightly on his feet and began returning fire. Crack. Crack. He spun around. Crack. "Clear!" he yelled and Felar slid down the ladder into the engine room. Three bodies lay sprawled out amongst the machinery. Maxar had excellent aim.

Beowulf whined above them. "If you can't jump down," Maxar said, "then go back and protect the others." The wolf-dog cocked his head, then disappeared. "Forward or aft?" Maxar asked.

"Forward. We need to get control of the ship before the Captain does anything stupid. I'm sure he's already transmitted that we are hostile." She shook her head. "We can secure the rest of the ship once the command bridge is under control."

Maxar advanced to the forward hatch and opened it. Terminal screens surrounded the room. Targeting info and tactical information displayed inside a seamless 360-degree video display. Four chairs sat in the center of the space, each covering a 90-degree arc. No one was present to greet them.

"Fancy stuff," Maxar said.

"You should see one of these in action. With skilled gunners, it can dominate large amounts of airspace. They are also unparalleled in ground support."

"Good thing we are about to have one for ourselves," Maxar said, a smile on his face.

Felar guessed the next hatch would lead to the command deck. They both took up positions and tried to open it. A passcode prompt flashed on the door display.

"Blightheart," Felar cursed. It would take too long to hash the control, even if she could figure out how. *Lothis,* she thought. "Wake, did everyone make it in?" Felar transmitted.

"Yes!" he replied breathlessly.

"Good. I need you to get Lothis to a terminal as soon as possible. Tell him we need the hatch to the command deck unlocked." The boy had taken his ENS off, losing his ability to communicate via radio. He'd complained the suit was too much of a distraction.

"Will do," Wake responded.

Felar began looking at the tactical readouts on the targeting displays. It showed the battle between the Ashamine and the Breakers was still in full force. When she looked closer, she could see a contingent of gunships and fighters had broken off the main Ashamine force and were heading towards them. "The Captain is bringing in other ships," Felar said, pointing towards the display.

The hatch started to open and they both assumed firing stances. Accurate shots would be a must. Damaging anything on the command deck could render the ship inoperable. "Either of you move through that door and I will scuttle the ship," a voice said. Felar found the source of the words, the Captain, and aimed her pistol at him. Maxar had the XO in his sights. She did a quick scan of the rest of the deck and found no additional crew. "If my heart ceases, the ship will automatically destroy itself. Your deception worked, but it ends here. Put down your weapons." He raised a pistol in his left hand, and Felar shot him in the head. Immediately, a loud alarm began to go off. A thirty-second timer appeared on the main terminal screen.

"Turn it off," Felar said coldly, shifting her aim to the XO.

"I don't know how," the XO replied, sounding shaken.

"If you don't, we all die," Maxar yelled.

"OK, OK, I'll try." The XO walked over to a terminal and began typing. He input code after code. The ship denied them all. "I told you," he said, turning to them. Felar checked the timer: ten seconds. Then it clicked down to nine and stopped. The alarm ceased and the timer disappeared.

"What happened?" Maxar said, looking puzzled.

"Lothis said to say you're welcome," Wake said, a chuckle coming through the end of his transmission. "You guys were riding the edge there, but Lothis had you covered."

"Good try," Felar said to the XO, aiming for his head, "but we can't have any security risks on board."

"Wait," he yelled, "I can help you. I can call off the Ashamine ships. I can tell them we have everything under control." Felar's eyes narrowed. His body language seemed to say he spoke truth, but could she trust an Ashamine officer?

"And if you are successful? What do we do with you then?" Maxar had a hard look in his eye and Felar could tell that he was even more skeptical than she.

"Shoot me out in one of the escape pods," the XO said. "I'll be out of your way and you can take this ship wherever you want."

Felar noticed a patch with the name "Smath" attached to the front of his flight suit. "Officer Smath," she said, "you have one chance to get this right. Any deceptions and you're dead."

"OK, I understand," Smath replied, a small smile on his face. His blue eyes shifted around the room, and Felar wondered what he was up to. Smath walked between them to a terminal near the hatch. "Ashamine Fleet," he said, transmitting, "this is XO Smath. The Death Watch no longer needs assistance. Return to combat with the traitors immediately. Authorization code 4-8-4-6-Kilo-Delta."

Something about that sequence of numbers caught Felar's attention. It wasn't a regular authorization, but she couldn't remember what it meant. Then, it came back to her: it was code to notify that the speaker was under duress.

Felar squeezed the trigger on her pistol, but Smath was already moving. He ducked through the hatch, and she lost sight of him. Maxar lunged towards the door. Felar followed. *Empty.* The engine room was clear as well. Smath had vanished.

"I'll go check behind the machinery," Maxar said. Felar looked around the targeting room. Smath couldn't have gone more than a few feet into this space before Felar and Maxar entered. How had he hidden so quickly?

A red indicator flashing on the main view screen caught Felar's attention: *EP-2 AWAY.*

"He's not back here," Maxar yelled from the engine compartment.

"Smath somehow got to the escape pods. He just jettisoned."

Maxar returned and began examining the targeting room. "There has to be some type of hatch or chute that gets you to the pods." Then he found it. Buttons on the side of the targeting officer's chairs were labeled "Escape Pods." When pressed, the floor in front of the chair opened to reveal a chute.

"Damn it," Felar cursed.

"Well we aren't really any worse off than before," Maxar said. "Smath tricked us and got away, but we still have the ship." Felar supposed he was right. She just didn't like falling for deception.

"You finish clearing the rest of the ship. I'll get us headed out of the gravity well." Maxar agreed and set off aft. Felar checked the tactical readout. "Jaydon, the command deck is clear. Cut the Revenge loose and get up here. You've got some fancy flying to do."

45 – TREMMILLY

"The ship is clear," Maxar announced, looking into Tremmilly's eyes. She had to think for a moment to realize what he'd just said. Wake, Lothis, Jaydon and the Entho-la-ah-mines left the cannon loading room as a group, heading for the command bridge. Except for Beowulf, she and Maxar were alone.

"That's great," Tremmilly replied, her emotions almost overwhelming her. She just wanted to forget everything that had happened in the past few hours, to lose herself in Maxar's eyes. So many people had died: Captain Malesis, his crew, Elth-eo-lan. Tremmilly felt responsible. *We could have stayed down on the surface of Eishon-2. Elth-eo-lan would still be alive. Captain Malesis and his crew obviously had a safe place, I forced them out to help me.* She knew Lothis, Felar, and Wake would be dead right now if she hadn't acted though, further increasing her inner turmoil.

No matter what you did, people would have died. That was a new voice in her mind, the one that had developed over the past few weeks of struggle and danger. *You did what you had to, and did it the best you could. You have to quit mourning sometime. Move on.* She knew that was sound advice, but she didn't understand how to do it. And what did she move on to? The Ashamine had obliterated her home world. *Can't go back there.* Everyone she knew, who was alive, was on this ship. *At least now you know what the Breakers are.* That was true, and they terrified her. The things she'd seen on the Justice were far beyond understanding.

"What?" Tremmilly said, realizing Maxar had been speaking to her.

"I said: You should find a place to sit down. You look tired."

Tremmilly nodded slowly in agreement. "Are there any beds on this ship?"

"Yeah, just through the next hatch. They don't look comfortable, but they are better than the garbage piles on the Revenge."

Another dagger of emotion stabbed Tremmilly. "You should have seen

179

Jaydon when he uncoupled the Death Watch and the Revenge. He looked like he was going to cry. I felt so bad for him. Jaydon had a lot of emotion wrapped up in that ship."

"I think it will be good for him to let go," Maxar replied gently. "That ship is part of the reason his daughter is dead, at least in his mind."

Tremmilly's emotion choked her up. "I feel like all of this death and chaos is my fault," she said in a rush. "If I hadn't left Eishon-2, maybe none of it would have happened." Tremmilly's vision blurred as tears welled up in her eyes. She looked at her feet, ashamed. Warm arms wrapped around her and she felt herself melt into Maxar's embrace.

"The Breakers and Ashamine brought this darkness," Maxar said, his voice soft. "You didn't cause it and you couldn't stop it." He paused for a moment. "If you hadn't left Eishon-2, the Ashamine would have killed you. If you escaped them, the Breakers would have found you soon after. If you hadn't come to the Bloodsport, I would be dead too. Jaydon would be stuck at the bottom of a bottle of booze. Felar would have been executed by the Ashamine, and Lothis would be back in whatever blightheart they have planned for him. Wake and the Entho-la-ah-mines would be dead or Breakers now too. You saved us all."

"But what do I do now?" she asked, trying in vain to keep herself from falling into an emotional well. "The prophecy doesn't say what happens next. We found everyone, but now what do we do?"

"We survive." Maxar paused for a moment, and Tremmilly wished he would keep talking. It made her calm. "We've seen the Breakers and the threat they pose to the Akked. They have abilities we can't explain. Maybe we can learn more about them. They have weaknesses, even if we don't know what they are, even if they seem unstoppable." Tremmilly leaned her head against his chest, finding comfort in his warmth and solidity. "Maybe the beings Lothis saw will help, maybe not. Either way, we have each other and that is enough." She couldn't tell if he meant just the two of them, or the group at large. "We keep fighting. We keep surviving."

"Maxar, Tremmilly," Felar's voice came over the ship's speakers. "We need your help with targeting controls." A spike of anger rose in Tremmilly before she could stop it. She didn't want to let Maxar go, didn't want to return to constant danger and death.

"Everything will be OK," Maxar said, looking into her eyes, "I promise." *He can't know that,* the hard, logical voice said. *True, but he will do his best to make it so.*

"Thank you," Tremmilly said, wiping the remaining tears from her eyes. "Let's go give them the fires of the dark star." Maxar smiled and led the way towards the targeting room. Tremmilly and Beowulf followed.

When they arrived, both Lothis and Felar had seated themselves in two of the four targeting control chairs. The Entho-la-ah-mines were on the command deck with Jaydon. "We figured out a plan while you guys were alone," she said, suggestiveness in her voice. Tremmilly blushed, but Maxar either didn't notice or ignored it.

"Good," Tremmilly said lamely.

"We are as fast as the Ashamine gunships in the squad following us, so we are square there. The fighters are gaining, and will likely be in range in ten minutes. Thankfully, we have way more firepower. The downside is, none of us have training on how to work these cannons. So we'll be learning on the job. Jaydon," she said, gesturing up towards the command deck, "thinks he can keep us pointed in a straight line towards the edge of the gravity well."

"I'm also learning as I go," Jaydon replied, sounding the happiest Tremmilly had ever heard.

"The Entho-la-ah-mines will be on watch for Breakers," Felar continued, "just in case they haven't given up. Wake is currently sending the previous crew out the airlock. When he is done with that, he will be our ordinance loader and damage control engineer."

"You just gave me this job because I couldn't shoot that woman," Wake said over the intercom, sounding frustrated.

"That's right," Felar replied. "You need to learn to be a soldier, to deal with death. Transporting those bodies and sending them out the airlock is a good first lesson." Tremmilly could tell Felar was almost laughing. Her friend definitely had a strange sense of humor sometimes.

"There," Wake responded, "the dirty work is done. I just cycled them out."

"Thank you," Felar said, smiling.

"Why do we need human targeting?" Maxar said. "Wouldn't the computers do a better job?"

"Normally, yes," Felar said, nodding. "In standard configuration, all targeting officers have to do is issue target priority commands. Unfortunately for us, the Watch's computers have a thing against firing on other Ashamine ships. Lothis tried to force the system, but it's hardwired somehow. We'd have to tear into unknown components to change it. There just isn't time. Lothis put everything into training mode, then hashed some variables to trick the computer into thinking we are using dummy rounds. Our displays will show targeting solutions, but we will still have to aim the actual cannons and fire them."

Tremmilly sat down in one of the two empty targeting chairs and looked at the wedge of space she would be attacking. Thankfully, it faced the front and she hoped there wouldn't be much to shoot in that direction.

Maxar took the other forward facing chair and smiled at her. "You'll do great."

"Better than you, I'm sure," she said, laughing.

"We'll see about that."

Felar snorted. "Both of you just do the best you can. The only competition here is between us and the Ashamine. Don't use all the ammo up on this first fight. There will be a lot of ships patrolling the edge of the gravity well. We still have to make a way through them."

"Yes, Enlightened Haltro," Tremmilly said in her best imitation of an Ashamine soldier. Everyone laughed, including Felar. Tremmilly felt more of her tenseness evaporate. She was glad to have Maxar, Felar and the rest of her friends.

Felar showed both her and Maxar how to operate their weapons systems, giving them as much detail as she knew and had time to explain. "Fighters will be within accuracy range in under sixty seconds," Jaydon said, his voice coming over the headset Tremmilly had put on.

"Go live on weapons," Felar ordered. "Wake, are you in the loading room?"

"Yeah. I think I have the systems figured out down here, but I'm not totally sure. I'll do the best I can."

"Acknowledged," Felar said, sounding like the Founder's Commando she once was. "That's all I expect."

Since the fighters were approaching from the rear, Tremmilly and Maxar both had nothing to do but wait. The remainder of the minute expired and Felar and Lothis began firing. If Tremmilly stretched her neck, she could barely make out what Felar was doing. She saw a large array of incoming fighters on Felar's display. They made her feel stupid for her earlier bravado. Things were about to grow more intense. Tremmilly wanted to ask if the Death Watch had armor, but the fighters were closing in and Felar was focused.

Tremmilly stared into her wedge of space, waiting. She could understand Wake's hesitancy to kill. It had been hard for her to pull the trigger, even on a Breaker. Only her desire to save Maxar had overcome the fear of becoming a killer. Now, she was once again willing to kill to protect her friends. *Hopefully this never becomes easy,* she thought, wondering how many fighter pilot deaths she would be responsible for.

"Tremmilly, three fighters passing into your low sector soon," Felar said, all business. "Be ready."

"Acknowledged," Tremmilly replied, trying to use Felar's terminology. Maxar chuckled, but said nothing.

"Maxar, eight ships high," Lothis said.

"OK."

"One enemy down," Felar exclaimed, sounding almost surprised.

Fighters entered Tremmilly's field of view, and if anyone else spoke, her focus was too intense to hear it. Tremmilly watched closely, waiting for her opportunity. Felar had explained that the computer calculated the distance to the target, the target's direction, distance, and speed, as well as the Death Watch's movement. When it thought the time to fire was right, the red box around the target flashed green.

She lined up a cannon on the lead fighter and waited for the box to change. Numbers fluctuated beside the indicator, and she imagined they would tell her something, if she knew what they meant. The fighters moved in irregular patterns, making her job harder. She hunched forward, concentrating.

Green. Tremmilly pulled the trigger, but the box had already switched back to red. Her round's orange ion tracer flew through the blackness. *Miss.*

Lining up her cannon once again, she waited for green. It switched, then switched back before she could trigger the round. *How am I supposed to do this?*

Her targets were getting closer. She had the feeling they would be sending their own cannon fire back soon. Sure enough, blue, green, and red tracers streamed towards the Death Watch. Tremmilly cringed, waiting for impact. All rounds missed, and she breathed easier. Maybe they were having troubles with their targeting computers as well.

All three fighters turned away, and Tremmilly felt frustration boil up inside her. The fighter pilots had experience and would figure out how to hit the Watch. Tremmilly had to do something different. She needed to find a way to destroy them before they figured it out first. *Remember what Felar told you about shooting,* she thought. But that didn't have anything to do with this crazy targeting system. *You can do this. Calm down and pay attention.*

Tremmilly took a deep breath and closed her eyes. A voice inside of her screamed that she needed to start firing. *No,* she thought, imagining the calm woods of Eishon-2, Beowulf at her side. Peace enveloped her and she felt herself expanding. Seconds passed. The scream returned, demanding she defend herself. *Not yet,* Tremmilly thought, flowing, growing, reaching out. She felt the seat, the surrounding air, the ship. Reaching out further, Tremmilly experienced the radiation from the Eishon Primary, sensed the enemy fighters. *Now you are ready,* she thought. *Now you are one with all.*

Opening her eyes, Tremmilly saw the fighters were almost in range to start their strafing pass. She lined up her cannon on the lead fighter once again and waited. His movements were irregular, but that didn't matter. The targeting computer moved too quickly for her reaction time, but that was also irrelevant. Tremmilly couldn't explain what she was doing, but she pulled the trigger. Simultaneously, the box flashed green for a fraction of a second.

The orange ion trail blazed between the Death Watch and the fighter. A few seconds later, the round impacted on the enemy ship. It did not burst into flames or explode. All that marked the pilot's death was a small burst of orange light. Tremmilly felt sad for the loss of a life, but she would protect her friends, no matter the emotional cost.

Before she could target the remaining two fighters, they both fired. Blue and green tracers streaked towards her. Tremmilly could tell the pilots had adjusted their aim. The rounds were coming straight for the Death Watch and she could do nothing to stop them. Closing her eyes, Tremmilly hoped for a quick death. The Watch shuddered and she tensed, waiting to have the air ripped from her lungs.

"Tremmilly," she heard Felar yell, "this ship has armor, but we can't take too many hits like that." Tremmilly opened her eyes. Everything was normal. The two enemy ships had turned around, setting up to take another pass.

"They won't hit us again," she replied, once again reaching out to the flow. Tremmilly destroyed first one fighter, then the other, her orange rounds obliterating the small hulls. "I'm clear," she said, trying to get a view of Felar's screen. At first she thought she must be misinterpreting the readout. How could there be that many fighters?

"Good thing," Felar said, her voice grim, "because at least twenty more are headed your way."

46 – MAXAR

Maxar wished he could help Tremmilly with her targets, but the weaponry's design made that impossible. *Plus, you have your own fighters to deal with.* At any given moment, at least thirty enemies were in his sector. He would occasionally hit one, but Maxar guessed that was probably due more to luck rather than skill.

All four of Maxar's cannons fired simultaneously. He was targeting the best he could, but his main objective was to keep the Ashamine ships under pressure. One daring pilot flew in for a shot, but Maxar was ready. He aligned his cannons for maximum spread, fired, and watched as his blue ion tracers sped towards the target. A second passed and one of the rounds impacted, the kinetic force of the tungsten alloy round ripping apart the small ship. Maxar only had a second to watch the results before he had to resume firing.

Time passed and he continued to pound away at the fighters in his sector. The controls became like extensions of his body. Maxar felt lost in the flow.

AMMUNITION JAM flashed on his status screen, indicators denoting it was his second, third, and fourth weapons that were malfunctioning. *Blightheart,* Maxar thought, seeing he still had at least twenty or more fighters in his sector. One cannon would not keep that many at bay.

"Wake," he yelled into his headset, "I've got three jams."

"Already on it," the engineer came back, his voice sounding calm and efficient. "Looks like you are firing too fast for the auto loaders to keep up. One of the rail rounds got jammed in the main feed tube for three and four, another got hung up in the sub-feeder for two." While Maxar listened, he kept his single cannon firing, trying to dissuade the braver pilots from taking a shot. "If you don't slow down," Wake said, "you're going to bugger cannon one as well."

"If I slow down, we are going to have about twenty fighters taking shots at us."

"If you don't slow down," Wake said, starting to sound frustrated, "you aren't going to have any cannons at all." Maxar couldn't deny that logic, so he lowered his rate of fire.

"Good," the engineer replied, "I should have the jam on three and four fixed in a minute."

"Acknowledged," Maxar said, strategizing how to drive off the Ashamine fighters with his diminished capabilities. If he couldn't hold them off, perhaps he could lure them in. Maxar quit firing altogether, waiting for the boldest pilots to come at him. Sure enough, two of them turned and headed directly for the Death Watch. Still, Maxar waited. He lined up the targeting icon on the lead fighter, anticipating how he would move. Just as Maxar felt it was time to fire, the indicator went green and he squeezed the trigger.

While his first shot was streaking through space, Maxar acquired the second fighter and unleashed another round. The first shot impacted, then the second. He'd destroyed both pursuers before they could fire on the Death Watch. *They'll think I'm trying to draw them in now,* Maxar thought, noting that none of the other Ashamine ships had decided to attack. If they came in as a group, Maxar wouldn't be able to stop them all, but for now they appeared hesitant.

"How are the cannons looking?" he transmitted to Wake.

"Oh, pretty good. I'm just giving them a thorough cleaning." Maxar could tell the other man was joking and he took the hint to leave Wake alone. He'd bring the cannons back up as soon as possible.

Uh oh, Maxar thought, noticing a pattern developing amongst the Ashamine fighters. They were forming up, getting ready to do something as a group. After a moment, they were all in formation and heading for the Death Watch. "Wake," Maxar said, starting to feel the pressure of panic, "I've got over a dozen ships forming up to take a pass at me."

"Just a little longer," Wake replied, strain evident in his voice. "The round is wedged, and even with the strength of my ENS and a bar for leverage, it's stuck." More grunting came over the channel, and then a cheer. "Cannons three and four should be operational. Hopefully two won't be so wedged."

Aiming all the guns was difficult, a task made for a computer, not a human. Maxar focused, directing the aiming indicators back and forth across his wedge, waiting for a vessel. Then, all the ships were in range at once and Maxar began firing with his three functional cannons. He kept his rate conservative this time.

The fighters had a smaller effective range, but they were quickly closing the distance. Maxar knew instinctively they would fire at any moment. He took out one, then two of the enemies. If they got much closer, the group would send enough rail rounds to penetrate the hull.

Maxar could not let that happen. He took out another fighter, but then they were in range. Blue, red, violet, orange, and green ion trails streaked towards Maxar. The Death Watch had no point defense system, so he would have to try to do it himself.

Feeling overwhelmed, Maxar lined up on the quickly closing ion trails. *Too many to count, too many to hit before they strike us.* Something shifted in Maxar's mind, and his calculations and intuitions sped up. He simultaneously aimed and shot all three cannons, striking the incoming rounds and either obliterating or deflecting them. Maxar lost track of himself and barely heard Wake's voice telling him gun two was online and that he had to lower his rate of fire. *Can't slow down, not enough time,* a deep part of his consciousness thought.

Seconds passed, still Maxar targeted the rounds at a furious pace. The guns kept firing, and he realized no ion trails were coming towards him. *Now,* Maxar thought, *to keep them from firing again.* He turned his attention on the fighters, now under full thrust and heading away from the Death Watch. They were all space junk before they had a chance to get out of Maxar's range. His mind slowed back to a normal pace and he realized his wedge was empty. He scanned the tactical display. Nothing.

"I'm clear," Tremmilly said. "No more targets."

"Same here," Maxar replied.

"The remaining fighters are retreating," Felar said, "but it looks like they are still following."

"They are waiting to hit us until we get to the blockade." Except for two shots, which their armor had stopped, they'd gone unscathed from the fighters. The ships in the Ashamine blockade would be much more persistent.

"Do you guys have access to long-range sensors?" Jaydon asked over the intercom. His voice sounded frightened. Maxar began flipping through menus, but nothing came up.

"No," Felar said, "it doesn't look like we do."

"Well then you better get up here and look on my display."

Maxar got out of his seat and followed Tremmilly and Felar onto the command deck. Jaydon had the long-range sensors pulled up on the big tactical screens.

"Blightheart," Maxar uttered. Tremmilly nodded and Felar cursed under her breath. A huge disc of Ashamine ships stood between them and the worm boundary. Behind them, the Justice was forcing its way through the mass of Ashamine vessels. It was heading straight for them.

"They began forming up as soon as we headed in that direction," Jaydon said. "More arrive every minute." It was true. Ashamine ships were leaving their positions in the blockade to join the new formation. "There is no way we are going to blast our way past that. There are probably hundreds of gunships the same size as us, plus fighters. If we try to go around, they will just move into the new path."

"The Justice is also gaining on us quickly," Cazz-ak added. Felar let out a frustrated growl.

"Can you cloak us like you did on the Revenge?" Tremmilly asked.

"This ship is larger," Na-ah-co replied, "and there are many more minds to deceive. Without Elth-eo-lan's connection to the Great Thought, we may not be strong enough. Jaydon, tell us when we should begin cloaking. It will be a strain, so the less time required, the more effort we can exert."

"The power of the Breakers is growing as well," Cazz-ak added. "Crasor is back on the Justice, it would seem. I do not think we can hide from them at all. The more Breakers in one place, the stronger they grow. It appears much like we Entho-la-ah-mines and the Great Thought, at least in that respect."

"I'll keep us headed towards the blockade," Jaydon said, intently focused on the tactical readouts, "and let you know when cloaking is critical. They'll see us coming, but I can change course after you hide us. Hopefully, we can just slip through the Ashamine unseen and worm out of here."

Felar nodded tensely in agreement. "And maybe the Justice will cause some chaos within the blockade as well."

"That's a good possibility. ETA to worm boundary is forty-five minutes or so." Jaydon went back to monitoring the complex displays of the Death Watch. Everyone but Beowulf and the Entho-la-ah-mines walked aft. Maxar guessed they were still connecting or talking with the Great Thought. He didn't understand exactly what that meant, but it gave the Entho-la-ah-mines strength. They would all need as much as they could get.

"We get to breathe for a few minutes," Tremmilly said.

"Yeah," Maxar replied, sighing. "It would be a good time to get some sleep."

"We don't have that long," she said with a laugh.

"Good soldiers sleep whenever and however they can. You never know when you are going to have another chance."

Tremmilly smiled.

"I'm feeling too amped up to sleep," Felar interjected, standing next to Lothis. The boy was still seated in his targeting chair. "Lothis and I can help Jaydon keep an eye on things while you guys get some rest. I suspect Wake will be too interested in getting to know this ship to want to sleep." Maxar could tell Felar was letting them know they'd have the crew quarters to themselves. She was probably setting it up that way. Maxar liked Tremmilly, might admit to himself that he loved her, but now was not the time for romance. He knew that instinctively. It would complicate an already difficult situation.

"Thanks," Maxar said, tiredness hitting him now that the opportunity to sleep had presented itself.

"If any of you want a break," Tremmilly said, "I'd be happy to come help so you can rest." Either she wasn't picking up on Felar's cues, or she was choosing to ignore them.

"Oh, I'm sure we'll be just fine," Felar replied, raising her eyebrows and smiling. "You two should get some rest."

With that, Maxar set off for the bunks and Tremmilly followed after. He tried to think of something to say, but his mind felt like sludge. The words sank into murky depths before he could take hold of them. Tremmilly seemed content to walk in silence. They passed by Wake as they entered the engine room. He stared intently at some type of readout, not noticing their passage. Maxar and Tremmilly went up the ladder connecting the engine room to the crew quarters.

Once inside, Maxar picked out a bed and collapsed into it. The mattress was barely big enough and not comfortable, but overall the setup was superior to what he'd had on Bloodsport. Tremmilly took the one next to him, sighing as she stretched out.

"I'm scared Maxar," he heard, the words forcing their way through the haze of sleep descending over him. "I know you said that what we do is survive, but I'm not sure we can." Maxar wanted to sleep, felt himself holding onto consciousness by just a faint thread, but he could tell she was genuinely worried. She had a right. Things were looking grim.

"Tremmilly," he replied, pulling himself out of the fog, "all we can do is try. If you spend your time fearing death and worrying about the future, you'll never enjoy now." He tried to look at her, but the bunk blocked his view. "I know your life was peaceful and relatively safe before this, so I'm sure it is a big shock. For me, this is much calmer and easier to handle than Bloodsport. I have something to fight for, people I love and want to protect."

"I just feel like my life is going to end at any moment, like I'm going to lose everything I have left. I already lost Psidonnis and Eishon-2. Beowulf is all that remains from my old life, and even he was almost killed in the fighting. I don't want to lose anything else, I don't want to lose you."

Maxar felt something quicken in his heart. "We have each other for as long as we have. We can't know the future. You just have to make the best of today, enjoy each moment." He looked up and Tremmilly was there, standing over him, looking as tired as he felt. Maxar rolled on to his side, making room for her to lay down. Tremmilly had tears in her eyes. "Everything will be OK," he said, putting his arms around her. They embraced, enjoying each other's comfort. Maxar couldn't remember the last time he had been this close to someone without being there to kill them. He was glad Tremmilly was in his life, felt immense gratitude he could support her.

"Can I sleep here?" Tremmilly asked finally, her words faint.

"Of course," Maxar replied, a small smile on his face. Tremmilly rolled over, still in his arms.

"Will you protect me?" she asked, her words once again filtering through the haze.

"I promise."

"I'll protect you too," Tremmilly answered. Maxar took comfort in her words, somehow knowing she could, and would, do just that. Soon, blackness overtook him and he thought no more.

47 – LOTHIS

"Lothis," the boy heard in his mind, "we think there might be a way for you to help us."

"What can I do?" he replied, excited for the opportunity. Lothis didn't exactly understand how to convey emotion with his mental voice, but he tried to send his feelings along.

"Come to the command deck. We will show you." Rising out of the targeting chair, Lothis went through the hatch. Cazz-ak and Na-ah-co stood next to each other along one wall. "We do not think we have enough strength to deceive the minds of all humans in the blockade, at least not for long." The Queen's voice was soft, but firm. "Both Cazz-ak and myself are powerful, but the energy required is just too great. If we had more of our people here, perhaps it would work. Cazz-ak had the idea perhaps you could sense and connect to the Great Thought."

"Would that actually work?" Lothis replied excitedly.

"Maybe, maybe not," the Queen said. "We will not know unless we try. You are the first human we have ever met who is able to interact with the world in a way similar to us. We do not understand how that is possible, but you were able to mentally strike at the Breakers, so perhaps you can be a conduit to the Great Thought as well. It was you who saved us from the darkness, wasn't it?"

"Yes," Lothis replied. "I don't know exactly what I did though. I just tried to imitate what Cazz-ak did to the Hammer. And I ended up losing myself somehow, trapped outside. I had to be rescued."

"I would like to hear more about that when we have the chance," the male Entho-la-ah-mine replied. "For now though, we will guide you. Follow our direction, there should be no danger of separating from your body."

"Good." Lothis felt some of his tension lessen. Instruction from the Entho-la-ah-mines might help him safely discover more about his talents.

"Thirty minutes till the blockade," Jaydon's voice echoed over the ship's comm.

"Give me your focus," Cazz-ak resumed, his eyes intent on Lothis. "Look at me. Look inside me." Lothis tried to do so, but didn't understand exactly what Cazz-ak wanted. "No, you're looking with your eyes. Use your mind. Find *me*, my energy. It is deep inside." Lothis stretched his mind, attempting to do what they asked. He focused using the part of himself he feared connecting to since his incident. "Good," Cazz-ak responded, "you are on the proper path. Now, go deeper." Lothis did and he saw Cazz-ak, the essence of his being. It felt bright, warm, and welcoming. A thick filament came off the orb, stretching into a direction Lothis didn't understand.

"The strand is his connection to the Great Thought," Na-ah-co said. "It is the same in every Entho-la-ah-mine. It's how we communicate and what gives us energy. Cazz-ak can expand the connection, allowing more power to flow through."

"What we want you to do is follow the connection back to the Great Thought and try to establish your own link." As Lothis watched, Cazz-ak's filament swelled to the size of a rope. "Can you see where it leads?"

Lothis studied the connection, trying to trace it back. It went well until he reached a certain point, at which time, his eyes lost focus and it fell away from him. Once he stopped looking, the strand came back into focus. "I can't seem to trace it," he said, trying yet again. "It's like my eyes can only see it for a specific distance."

"Do not be discouraged." Cazz-ak responded patiently. "What you are attempting has never been tried or accomplished by a human before. Let your mind be at ease, relax. You will not be able to force your way to the Great Thought. Embrace stillness."

Taking a deep breath, Lothis once again traced the strand. The further from Cazz-ak he went, the more difficult it became. He tried to obey the Entho-la-ah-mine's instruction to relax, but Lothis could see no way to progress if he didn't exert more energy. Once again, he reached a specific point and the filament blurred into obscurity.

"I can't do it," Lothis said finally, feeling dejected.

"OK," Cazz-ak said, sounding disappointed. "Your mind must be unable to sense or use other dimensions in the same way ours can. Since connecting to the Great Thought requires that, it will not work. Some day you will grow and learn how, but for now there is not time. I will expand my connection to the Great Thought to give us enough power."

"You will die attempting a link that large," Na-ah-co said.

"What choice do I have? The humans are relying on us. You are the important one. Perhaps, I can hold the connection open long enough to get us to safety."

"There is another way," the Queen replied. "You are always so willing to sacrifice yourself, Cazz-ak. You are important to our people too. Do not be willing to die so quickly."

"As you say," Cazz-ak said, bowing his front legs in response. "I miss Elth-eo-lan. I should have been in her place. The guilt is overpowering."

"If not for Wake and Felar," the Queen responded, "we all three would have died. Her death is not your fault, therefore you should feel no guilt. It was chance that she was closest, chance that our friends arrived in time to save us and not her. There is no one other than the Breaker Aeron to blame for her death. If you are distracted by guilt or a desire for self-sacrifice, you will fail at the critical moment." Lothis could feel the fire of emotion backing Na-ah-co's words. "Honor her sacrifice by appreciating and using it for good. Your death will not bring her back."

Cazz-ak was silent for a long while and Lothis wondered what he was thinking. "Alright," he said finally, sounding stronger than Lothis had heard in quite some time. "I will do my best to take your words into my being."

"Good," Na-ah-co, replied, sounding relieved. "You are very important to us, both humans and Entho-la-ah-mines. I do not fully understand it, but you are on the edge of a discovery, of learning something that might just save us all."

Lothis felt Cazz-ak's doubt, and Na-ah-co must have as well.

"You are special Cazz-ak," she continued. "Elth-eo-lan saw it first. I thought it was bad, thought you would corrupt the Great Thought and destroy us all. But Elth-eo-lan showed me, convinced me of the truth. You are showing us a new way, bringing about a change our people require in this time of need."

"Because of anger?" Cazz-ak said, his tone skeptical.

"No, not just anger. You see the world differently, unite us with humans, and show us how to have power. You are an inspiration to our people and to me. I feel your strength. It empowers me."

Lothis could feel the Queen's pride in Cazz-ak. They had been through so much together. It reminded him of his feelings towards Felar. *How would I have survived all this without her? What would I do if she died?* He had to find a way to help, both for the sake of the Entho-la-ah-mines and for Felar.

"I'm just one of the hive, one of many," Cazz-ak said, "doing what any of us would do."

"Cazz-ak," the Queen replied, sounding amused, "you are most certainly not 'just one of the hive.' You cannot see it, but every Entho-la-ah-mine in the Great Thought can. No one else could have protected me through everything that has happened."

Lothis felt like he was intruding on their conversation, but they could have quit sending at any moment. They wanted him to know this information. His interactions with the Entho-la-ah-mines were limited, but from what he could tell, everything the Queen said was correct. Cazz-ak was different, more powerful, and unique. *I wonder if Na-ah-co realizes how similar she is to him.*

"Yet I am not strong enough to shield us from the eyes of the Ashamine," Cazz-ak replied to the Queen.

"Not by yourself," Na-ah-co shot back, starting to sound exasperated. "It is an enormous task. You need help. That is why we asked Lothis for assistance."

"He cannot connect to the Great Thought."

"Yes, but even so, he is extremely powerful in his own way. He may not understand how to guide it, but perhaps we can do that for him. I feel, based on what we saw of him during the first battle, that our combined energy might be enough to shield us from the blockade ships." The Queen's words struck fear into Lothis, not because of working with the Entho-la-ah-mines, but because he worried using that much power would send him back to the dimension of darkness. The confinement and helplessness there reminded him too much of his imprisonment in the research facility under Haak-ah-tar.

Panic rose inside Lothis, threatened to overwhelm him, to consume him. He wouldn't go back, couldn't. Images of monstrosities filled his vision, and the room started to close on him. Darkness crept in on the edges of his vision and Lothis felt Felar, the Entho-la-ah-mines, and the rest of the group's comforting presence drift away. His palms grew sweaty and a foul taste invaded his mouth. *I can't go there, can't lose myself again.* Cazz-ak was right, he didn't understand dimensions, couldn't make a way out. *The Arche won't find me and I'll be in darkness forever.*

"Lothis?" Na-ah-co said, her voice concerned. Her beautiful image, both that of her physical presence and her inner being, helped him refocus. Breathing deep, he compartmentalized his fears, boxing each one away. Before Felar had rescued him, that had been the only way for him to cope. *Breathe. Now you have a family.* It took several moments to regain his composure, but finally, Lothis felt calm.

"Tremmilly, Maxar," Felar announced over the ship's comm, "time for you two lovlings to come help me with point defense."

They need you, he thought, *they all need you. Cazz-ak will die if you don't, and he is much more important to his people than you are to yours. Felar will be captured or killed if you don't help. Do you want that?* Lothis took another deep breath, forced the remnants of fear away, and reached deeply into his mind.

"I'm ready to do whatever you need," Lothis said, resolute.

48 – CAZZ-AK-TAK

"Five minutes till we are in range of the blockade ships," Jaydon announced. "If you guys are going to cloak us, now would probably be a good time to start." Cazz-ak worried they might not be able to hold the deception long enough, but they couldn't delay any further. The time had come. It would either work, or it wouldn't.

Drawing in as much of the Great Thought as was safe, Cazz-ak prepared himself. Na-ah-co opened to him. He used her connection to embrace even more energy. The Queen had explained how she thought they would be able to utilize Lothis' power. Cazz-ak thought it was brilliant.

With Na-ah-co's assistance, Cazz-ak began creating small filaments of energy, making them wispy and thin. In the past, they'd always made them more substantial, but there wasn't enough energy for that now. Cazz-ak held his mental creation before the boy and said, "Now, Lothis." Using his own unique power, the boy began coating the Entho-la-ah-mine energy. It wasn't more than the thinnest of skins, but it would help reinforce the psionic ability of Cazz-ak's work.

He knew the task would be hard on Lothis, but they would all be dead if the ship wasn't cloaked. The Ashamine in front and the Breakers behind: escape would be impossible if they were visible.

"Two minutes till we are in range," Jaydon said. "How will we know if it's working?"

"They won't be firing at us," Na-ah-co said, a hint of a laugh in her mental voice. Jaydon simply snorted a reply.

The filaments were ready, and Cazz-ak began sending them out towards all human minds in the blockade. The task of shielding the Entho-la-ah-mine fleet when they had brought the Queen to Haak-ah-tar had been almost as great, but there had been thousands wielding the Great Thought instead of just two.

"They are firing on us," Jaydon called. "We are still outside accurate

195

range, but not for much longer." Cazz-ak saw red, blue, and orange tracers streaking towards the Death Watch, but they all went wide. He refocused his attention and sent the filaments out. "Inside range," Jaydon announced.

Cazz-ak wound the strands around mind after mind. Soon, he was deep in the flow, blinding first hundreds, then thousands of humans to their presence. He had no time to look up, no time to do anything but deceive the Ashamine.

And then he finished. Cazz-ak could sense no unaltered consciousnesses. Now he could do nothing but grasp the strands. Maintaining the deception was difficult, a heavy burden his mind had to hold on to. Cazz-ak felt the edges start to slip away, but he tightened his grip, focusing even harder.

"Almost to the leading ships."

Even with Lothis' help in allowing such fine filaments, the mental energy required was enormous. The Queen kept her connection to the Great Thought as large as possible, giving it all to Cazz-ak. Still, the burden was crushing him.

"You are doing an amazing job," Na-ah-co said.

"Heading into the main body of the blockade," Jaydon announced.

Cazz-ak felt his mind start to weaken. The strain of maintaining the deception was just too great. *No,* he thought, fighting to keep the filaments intact, *we are in their midst. I must hold on longer.*

Then, just as he was about to lose a huge swath of strands, Lothis increased the thickness of his overlay. The decrease in the energy requirement was instantaneous and Cazz-ak maintained control. "Thank you," he said, barely able to get the words out.

Lothis was shaking now, his body convulsing like he was hypothermic. "I must do my part," he said, between his tremors.

"Be careful," Na-ah-co admonished. "Do not injure yourself. We are almost to the other side."

Time dragged on for Cazz-ak. His ability to maintain the deception weakened even further still. Lothis again added power and his convulsing became more violent.

"What's happening back there?" Jaydon asked, unable to look away from the screen.

"We don't know," Na-ah-co replied. "Something is wrong with Lothis."

"Just a few more minutes and we'll be on the other side."

Cazz-ak bore down even harder. *Just a few more minutes. Just a few more.* He knew something bad would happen to the boy if he tried to add any more of his energy. Cazz-ak would have to carry them through the rest of the way.

"Do not try any harder, Lothis," Na-ah-co said, reading the situation the same way as Cazz-ak.

"I cannot let my friends die. I will sacrifice myself before that happens." Lothis' voice sounded far away and isolated, like he was speaking to himself. His words chilled Cazz-ak, both because of their finality and because they echoed his exact feelings.

"No, Lothis," the Queen said. "You will not do that. We are almost there."

Cazz-ak wanted to look up, wanted to use some attention to see how much longer they would be in agony, but he had none to spare. Another minute dragged by, and Lothis continued to shake.

"We are through the blockade," Jaydon said excitedly. Cazz-ak almost dropped the filaments, but he knew they were still in danger. They had to keep the cloak up until they were out of rail weapon range. It would be ten minutes till they reached the distortion zone.

Then, without further warning, the deception imploded. It slipped out of Cazz-ak's grasp, and he could not stop it. Cazz-ak looked at Lothis, concerned for the boy's wellbeing. He was silent and still, but breathing.

"The cloak is down. We held it for as long as possible," Cazz-ak told Jaydon.

"Thank you," he replied. "Can Lothis go back and crew the remaining targeting station?"

"No, I do not think so," Na-ah-co answered. "He is breathing, but is non-responsive otherwise."

"OK. The Ashamine has noticed us. The fleet is turning." Jaydon paused for a moment. "What in the fires of the dark star?" His voice was low, in awe.

"What is it, Captain?" Cazz-ak asked.

"I don't know how, but the Justice rammed through the Ashamine blockade. How did they catch up so fast?" He flipped past a few screens and let out a bellow of frustration. "The Justice is almost within range," he transmitted throughout the ship. "Either it has faster drives than I've ever heard of, or the Breakers are magic. The Ashamine are firing on them, but it isn't doing much."

"How long till we are out of the gravity well?" Maxar said from the targeting room.

"Too long," Jaydon replied. "The Justice will be firing on us before we can get out of the system."

"Move evasively and keep us headed towards the worm zone," Felar's voice answered. "We'll be on point defense for anything that gets too close."

Cazz-ak looked down at Lothis. The boy's eyes were open now, but he seemed dazed. Felar already had enough to worry about, so Cazz-ak kept silent.

"He seems to be recovering," Na-ah-co said, her words only going to Cazz-ak's mind.

"Yes," he replied, feeling exhausted. "Without him, I never would have been able to hold on that long."

"Lothis is very powerful. If he ever learns control, he might be the strongest single entity in the galaxy."

Cazz-ak agreed. Crasor wielded amazing amounts of energy, but Cazz-ak guessed that he drew on the strength of the other Breakers. Lothis required no one but himself.

"The dark one is coming," Lothis said, sounding dazed.

"We know," Cazz-ak replied. "Rest, and do not worry. You've done your part. Let others do theirs." Lothis nodded, blinked rapidly, then closed his eyes. Soon, his features relaxed and Cazz-ak guessed he was asleep.

On the view screen, glowing ion trails cut through the space surrounding the Watch. "They're getting us dialed in," Jaydon growled. He pulled hard on the controls, trying to keep them from being a predictable target. More rounds flew by, trails getting closer and closer.

"I don't know how much longer we can protect the ship," Felar yelled. "How far till worm zone?"

"Three minutes," Jaydon yelled back.

"Bugger it all," Maxar cursed.

Cazz-ak wished he had some way to help, but he felt too exhausted. He closed his eyes and waited. Either they would make it or they wouldn't. Cazz-ak felt comfort radiating from Elth-eo-lan. That was impossible. Reaching out with his mind, he tried to trace the source, and found Na-ah-co.

"She had a great impact on me, just as you have," the Queen said in his mind. "She was amazing, and I honor her." Cazz-ak mirrored the emotion, feeling the peace Elth-eo-lan had so often inspired in him. "No matter what happens," the Queen said, "we will be strong and calm. The humans, and now the Breakers, have taken so much from us, but they cannot destroy our people. We will not let them." The fire of conviction was in Na-ah-co's voice, and Cazz-ak felt himself buoyed up, riding the surge of positivity.

"One minute till worm zone," Jaydon announced, and then the ship rocked violently.

"Wake, status?" Felar barked.

"No hull penetration," he replied over the ships speakers, "but the armor is badly damaged. If we take another hit on the starboard quarter, it won't hold." The remaining minute passed, the far away humming of cannon loading machinery the only sound.

"We made it," Jaydon exclaimed. "Initiating worm generator. Drive ready. Destination Qi-3. Coordinates good. Worm opening in five, four, three, two—" The ship shuddered violently from another impact just as Jaydon called out the last number. Cazz-ak saw the blackness of a distortion open in front of the ship, and the Death Watch passed inside.

Darkness filled the command deck's view screen. Moments ticked by. "Something is wrong," Jaydon transmitted. "Why aren't we coming out of the worm?" Still, the blackness was complete. "Wake, what's going on?"

"I'm checking," the engineer replied hurriedly. Jaydon brought up a rear view on one of the main screens. It too showed darkness.

"We are stuck inside the worm," Jaydon whispered, so quiet that Cazz-ak barely heard even though the man was just a few feet away. Fear rose inside him. Cazz-ak tried not to think about the implications of Jaydon's statement.

Long ago, when the Entho-la-ah-mines first ventured into space, they'd had accidents. Interstellar travel, especially using distortions, was hazardous. The Great Thought honored those who had sacrificed themselves to further exploration and discovery, but it held the Entho-la-ah-mines lost in other dimensions in special esteem. No one knew what happened to them. One moment, they conversed with the hive mind, alive and vibrant, and then the exits collapsed and they disappeared. They didn't die, at least not from what the Great Thought could tell. None had ever returned. Whether that was because they lacked the energy to reopen the exit, had gotten lost, or because they ceased to exist, no one knew.

Cazz-ak searched for the Great Thought, but it had vanished. His thread drifted in space, untethered. There was nothing there for it to connect to. He had no harmony, no unity. His consciousness felt dim. All the color and vibrancy of life had drained away. Emptiness surrounded him, threatening to close in and erase his being. *I'm alone, all alone.*

"Be calm," Na-ah-co said. "You have me, and I have you. We have these new friends. All is not lost. The humans have a way to get us out. Be patient." Her words calmed him somewhat, but utter despair still threatened to overwhelm him.

"It looks like that last round hit in a different location than the first," Wake said over the ship's comm, "so the hull is still intact, barely. From what I can tell, the shock disrupted power to the worm generator's guidance computer. We slipped through the entrance just before it shutdown. The power to the guidance controller is still interrupted, so until we can fix that, we are stuck."

Cazz-ak wondered how long he could endure disconnection from the Great Thought. *What if it can't be fixed? What if we are stuck here forever?*

49 – CRASOR

"Shoot them!" Crasor yelled, slamming his fist down on the terminal screen before him. Everyone on the bridge of the Justice went silent. The first cannon round to strike the fleeing vessel hadn't been enough to stop it. Maybe a second would.

"Their worm generator just came online," one of the officers said. Crasor growled in frustration. A cannon round lanced through space, its orange ion trail blazing brightly on the view screen. *Come on, come on,* Crasor willed, feeling it was on target. The cannons on the Harbinger's ship fired, trying to act as point defense. Round after round missed the incoming projectile, until it finally slammed into the back of the Death Watch.

"Yes," Crasor cheered, as did the surrounding crew, but before they could celebrate the destruction, the Death Watch disappeared.

Crasor screamed in frustration, rage contorting his fine features. "Where did they go? Trace their worm signature." He'd come so close to destroying the entire group. *Just another minute more,* he thought. *Another shot.*

Each time the Harbingers escaped, Crasor grew more irritable. First, they had killed him and then fled the Justice before Crasor could revive. Then, they had reached the Ashamine fighter escort just as he had, forcing Crasor to return to the Justice. He'd pushed the huge battle carrier to its limits, killing some of his crew. The ship's designers had limited the in-system engines' output for a reason. Exceeding that upper threshold had caused radiation levels to spike uncontrollably. The magnetic shielding couldn't be boosted on such short notice and radiation streamed through huge swaths of the ship. Even the Breaker nanites couldn't save a body from that much energy. The overdrive tactic allowed them to catch up with the fleeing Harbinger ship, but Crasor had still been a little too late.

"Sir," Karoth said, "their worm signature is abnormal. We can't pinpoint an exit location."

"That isn't possible. They are in an Ashamine ship. You told me the Justice has the ability to track any Ashamine worm signature."

"Yes, that is true," the former Ascended replied, "but the computers cannot give us a destination. They show the entrance as Eishon, but the exit is blank. It looks like they went inside and had no way out." This information made Crasor happy, initially. If they were stuck inside a worm, they couldn't do anything. No one quite understood what happened to people who didn't come out, but surely they were either dead or incapable of influencing the universe.

But why would they go into a worm with no exit? It's tantamount to suicide. No, they had figured out a way to escape him yet again. This time they had concealed their destination. "Keep monitoring the signature. If it changes, or presents further anomaly, notify me at once."

"Yes, sir," Karoth said. Crasor smiled. *Perhaps we can still find them yet.*

"Sir," one of the tactical officers said, his voice clear of the early conversion stutter, "the Ashamine blockade ships are firing on us."

"Activate point defenses," Karoth ordered. Crasor leaned back into the captain's chair, letting his subordinate handle the situation. Ashamine Command already had the intel that the Breakers had captured and obliterated their Eishon fleet. The loyalists would have transmitted that long ago.

With the Harbingers gone, all Crasor wanted was to capture as many enemy ships as possible. He wasn't sure they would be able to fight all the Ashamine assets left in Eishon space, but he had to try. Each ship captured by the Breakers added more firepower and personnel to the ranks.

"Initiate full turn, maximum speed," Karoth continued. "Stay outside the gravity well and let them come to us." Karoth looked at Crasor and he nodded back at the Captain. Karoth was a great addition to the Breakers. His tactical instincts were superior. "Keep the worm generator ready, destination—" Karoth once again looked at Crasor.

"The Traynos system," Crasor answered, thinking it was as good a place as any. If things were going so badly that they had to jump, he didn't want to lead the Ashamine back to a Breaker controlled system.

"Worm destination is the Traynos system," Karoth ordered. "All fighters and gunships deploy. Target enemy fighters. Disable if possible, destroy if necessary. All local cannons, aim to disable enemy gunships. We need as many of these vessels as possible. Take them out of commission, but don't obliterate them." Karoth paused for a moment, looking over the command deck. "You have your orders, make our leader proud." The officers yelled an affirmative, and got to work.

With almost all the pilots and crew newly converted, Crasor worried at their effectiveness. Some individuals integrated with the Breaker nanites quicker than others, but they were still slower than the humans they'd be fighting against. What they lacked in individual speed and intelligence, Crasor hoped to make up for in the Justice's overwhelming force and Karoth's superior tactics. He'd never led a fleet, hence why he was leaving most decisions to the former Ascended. Even with the conversion sickness, Karoth was a better commander and tactician than any of the humans on the remaining Ashamine ships.

The former Ascended had also disabled the Ashamine targeting lockout. Karoth had explained only he could unlock that feature on the Justice. It was a mutiny protection protocol, allowing the captain of the ship to defend himself. The smaller vessels' computers were hard coded against targeting the Justice, and as such, their pilots would have to use entirely human control. Since the Ashamine forces outnumbered the Breakers, this was a crucial advantage.

"Integrate us into the ship," the Breaker mind ordered. "We can upgrade and optimize the Justice's systems."

You can do that? Crasor mentally asked.

"After all you have seen, you doubt us?"

No, of course not, I'm just surprised. Crasor held up his finger, watching as the tiny nanites welled up, creating a black droplet. *Why couldn't you integrate before, back when you opened those doors?* The droplet grew, spreading over the entirety of his palm.

"There were not enough of us, not enough time. Now that we have Karoth's codes and you have control of the ship, things will be much easier."

Crasor put his palm on the terminal screen before him. He waited for a moment, then pulled back. His black handprint was slowly fading as the nanites absorbed into the screen and its circuitry. Initially, nothing else changed. The ship functioned as normal. Another moment passed, and Crasor wondered if he needed to insert more nanites.

"Wait," the Breaker mind said. Then, all the screens flickered off, then on, the Ashamine interfaces replaced with the Breakers' own. At first, Crasor thought this would confuse the crew, but something about the setup worked better with their converted minds. On the tactical display, the accuracy score of the Justice and the rest of the Breaker ships began to rise. Crasor smiled and nodded. "We will continue to optimize and integrate. It will take time. We could go faster if the ship could be completely rebooted, but that is not possible right now."

Crasor continued to monitor the tactical display, watching as the Breaker fleet obliterated the Ashamine. Once this battle ended, his position in the Akked Galaxy would be stronger than ever before. The

Breaker mind felt pleased with his progress. "You must still destroy the Harbingers," it reminded him. "There is no ascension while they are alive."

50 – WAKE

Wake wondered if he had successfully hidden the fear from his voice. *We are trapped*, he thought, inspecting the casing of the guidance system. He had to find what was causing the power disruption. *But even if you fix it, how will the worm generator get us out?* Wake didn't want to think about that.

While getting his advanced engineering education, Wake had learned much about the physics of worm tunnels and how the generators created them. He'd forgotten most of that information over the years, but one thing stood out in this moment. *The computer has to know where you are and where you want to go to generate the worm.* In this case, it couldn't determine where they were at, because they weren't in normal space-time. The worm was a void, a featureless no-scape that lacked traditional dimensions.

The professor of worm drive physics had been explicit: "Even now, Ashamine scientists do not understand the properties of the dimensions the worm system utilizes. We have a basic grasp, know that it contains aspects very similar to normal space-time. However, it is unclear if this space truly exists at all times, or if it simply comes into being because we observe it. If both ends of the worm are uncoupled from nominal space-time with humans inside, it is unclear what happens to them. Perhaps they disappear, perhaps they are stuck forever in a dimension permanently uncoupled from our own, or maybe they are transported to an alternate universe. We have hypotheses, but none of them have enough evidence to be theory."

Wake remembered the lecture vividly because it had a chilling effect on him. Before that class, he'd never realized the perilous state of worm tunnel travel. From that day, no matter how many times he rode the worm, a tiny voice always reminded him of the professor's words. Now, he was getting firsthand experience of exactly what would happen. This same thing had occurred to many others, merchants and decrepit civilian ships whose drives malfunctioned at just the wrong moment. None of them had ever returned to tell the scientists which hypotheses were correct.

Pushing thoughts of eternal imprisonment out of his mind, Wake began tracing wiring from the worm generator's guidance system. The frame and internal components themselves looked undamaged. Its protected location in the center of the ship made him guess the fault was elsewhere. *You had better hope it isn't an internal short.* A limited selection of parts were available in storage, but none of them were for the worm generator system.

"How's it going?" Felar asked, making Wake jump. "Sorry, didn't mean to scare you. Just came to see if you could use a hand."

"I'm just looking for the power disruption. Nothing seems out of place with the worm system itself, so I'm hoping it's an easy fix, like a wire break or something."

"You think that with the guidance system back up, you can get us out of here?" Felar's voice was skeptical.

"No, not really," Wake admitted, "but what else can I do? Once I find the problem, then maybe we can power everything back up. It might work."

"I don't understand how worm generators function, but I've heard plenty of stories of people disappearing inside faulty ones and never returning. We're buggered." Felar paused for a moment, then smiled. "But hey, for the first time, in a long time, we are finally out of imminent danger. And you're right, maybe you will find a way out."

"Thanks for the optimism," Wake said, smiling.

"Anytime," Felar replied, her lips turning up in a grin as well. "You sure there isn't anything I can do to help?"

Wake thought for a moment, then shrugged. "I suppose you could wander around looking for anything out of the ordinary: scorch marks, cracks in wiring, anything that catches your eye. Most likely, since both the power and worm generators are in this room, the problem will originate here, but there may be some kind of secondary circuitry, sensors, or something that is causing the malfunction. The Justice hit us hard. The problem could be anywhere."

"I can look around," Felar said. "I'll also see if any of the others would like to help."

"Great. I really appreciate it."

Felar left the room. Wake returned to searching for the interrupt. Using a meter he'd found in the Engineer's tool area, he began scanning the wiring around the guidance system computer. They all lacked energy. *This will take some time,* Wake thought, beginning to follow the wiring back towards the power generator. Eventually, he ran into energized wiring, but everything was all so mixed and mingled he found it hard to tell exactly what the wires were for. *Damn Ashamine engineering.* He returned to the guidance computer.

"Wake?" Tremmilly's voice said.

"Yeah?" he replied, trying to figure out where she was. Her voice sounded muffled, but close by.

"I found something weird."

"Where are you?"

"In the escape pod room."

Wake walked over to the hatch in the floor and climbed down to the small area. Tremmilly stood in the space, looking up towards the ceiling. "What is it?" Wake asked, walking over to stand beside her.

"Right there," Tremmilly replied, pointing up towards a damaged section of circuitry on the side of a small rectangular box.

"Good eyes," Wake said, standing on the tips of his toes to get a closer view. "How did you manage to find this?"

"Beowulf and I spent a lot of time exploring on Eishon-2. Once you learn to look for small details, it's hard not to see them."

Someone had crushed the circuitry, perhaps with a fist. Wake saw traces of blood and skin. "Why would someone punch it?" he wondered, brow furrowed.

"Well, that probably depends on what it does. What is the thing it's mounted to?"

Wake walked around the box, looking for a label. "It says it's the 'Worm Generator Backup Power.' Probably a battery of some kind." Wake thought for a moment, putting the pieces together. He remembered some of his space vessel engineering class. It all made sense. "The output from the fusion reactor charges this battery. Then, the worm generator draws energy from it. In the event of a fusion disruption, there is enough energy to keep the worm open long enough to get through. Why didn't I realize that before? It obviously had to be a problem in backup power distribution."

"Smath," Tremmilly said.

"Huh?"

"Smath punched the circuitry, on his way out. He knew it would bugger our ability to escape." Tremmilly's use of profanity surprised Wake, but he supposed that hanging around with Felar would insert profanity into anyone's vocabulary.

"But his punch didn't complete the job." Wake said, looking at Tremmilly. "The circuitry was still intact enough to open a worm. Either that or the shock from the cannon round was enough to cause a fatal short."

"Can you fix it?"

"Maybe. It's pretty messed up, but I think I saw the right kind of spare components up in the engine room."

"Anything I can do to help?" Tremmilly asked, hopeful.

"Not unless you have an education in electronics that I don't know about."

"No, nothing like that." She looked crestfallen. Wake understood needing to do something and not just sit around. The quirky girl was starting to grow on him, and they had time, so why not include her?

"I think you'll make a great assistant. Hand me what I need and I'll show you what we are up against." Tremmilly stood next to him, waiting for her first task. "First, we have to figure out how to disable the power input. We don't want to get electrocuted."

Wake soon forgot about time, losing himself in the tasks of repair and teaching. Tremmilly was a great student, easily picking up the skills and information he showed her. Smath had badly damaged the circuitry and it took time to swap out all the faulty components. Wake enjoyed the project.

"That should fix the last of the damage," Wake said, using a diagnostic tool to check the connections a final time.

"Now we turn it on?" Tremmilly asked excitedly.

"Yep, and hope it doesn't short out again. We don't have enough spares to fix the circuit a second time." They both went up the ladder to the engine room. Wake walked over to the control panel mounted on the fusion reactor and slid the switch marked "WGS" to "ON." He waited tensely for the smell of burning wiring or the arcing of a short, but nothing happened. When Wake checked the diagnostic readout on the side of the worm generator, it indicated that all self-checks were nominal. Relief flooded over him.

"The worm generator is back online," Wake transmitted to the ship, using the engine room intercom. "We should probably have a meeting to discuss what to do now."

Jaydon replied. "Let's all join up on the command deck."

Tremmilly looked at him with a puzzled expression on her face. "What's wrong? You just said you fixed the generator. Why do you sound so negative?"

"I'll explain once we get everyone together."

"OK," Tremmilly said, catching some of his despair.

When they arrived on the command deck, Wake could tell everyone understood their situation just by their body language. "With the worm generator fixed," Felar asked, "is there any way to get us back into real space?"

"I don't know," Wake replied, sighing. He looked at Jaydon. "Does the computer give us any options?"

"No," Jaydon answered, looking down at his terminal screen. "All it tells me is that our location is unknown."

"Can't we just pick a destination and go?" Tremmilly asked.

"The physics don't work like that." Wake paused for a moment, thinking. "In theory, at least from what I can remember, the worm only exists as a connector between two regions of space-time. Since both ends closed while we were inside, we are in a location that no longer exists or has any spacial connection to the normal universe. And since worm generators work by connecting two locations in regular space-time, there is no way for ours to create a way out of the worm we are currently in."

Tremmilly nodded and her shoulders slumped. "Ahh," was all she said in response.

"We may have a way," Lothis added. "The probability of success seems low, but the Queen, Cazz-ak, and myself all feel we should try."

"Why not?" Jaydon said. "It doesn't seem like our situation could get any worse."

"It definitely can," Lothis replied, but didn't elaborate.

"Entho-la-ah-mines have been in this situation before," Cazz-ak began. "Like humans, none have ever returned. Now that I am in this place, I understand why. Our people use the power of the Great Thought to create the worm tunnels, or as we call them, distortions. However, as soon as the exits closed, both Na-ah-co's and my connection to the Great Thought ceased. I suspect it has something to do with the relations of the dimensions and the folding of space-time. I don't understand that aspect, but the lack of connection explains why none of our people ever escaped.

"Humans create machines that make the distortions in much the same way as the Entho-la-ah-mines do, but as you've said Wake, without an understandable location, your generator is useless. So, we Entho-la-ah-mines have a location, but no power, and your machine has power, but no location."

"I am the bridge," Lothis said, his orange eyes still unsettling Wake. "I will connect the Entho-la-ah-mines and the worm generator and be the interface between the two."

"Is it dangerous?" Felar interjected, her concern for Lothis obvious.

"We don't know," Na-ah-co answered, her voice light in Wake's mind. "This has never been attempted before. If we don't try, death is a certainty." Felar nodded, still looking worried.

Cazz-ak's explanation made sense to Wake, but he didn't understand how Lothis would be able to connect the two. Wake felt lost, in more ways than one.

"Despite the desperation of this situation," Cazz-ak added, "I feel we have an opportunity. We are all tired and have been pushed to the point of breaking. It would be good to rest and recuperate. We are safe from both the Breakers and the Ashamine in this place. If our plan works, we will be thrown back into danger."

Na-ah-co agreed. "We will have a better chance of finding our way out if we rest."

Silence descended over the room until Wake's stomach growled loudly. "I can't remember the last time I ate," he said with a laugh. Everyone joined in and the mood lightened. Wake could tell Felar was still worried, but she appeared a little more at ease.

"Well, let's go see what kind of food the Ashamine feeds its crews." Maxar had a relieved smile on his face.

"I'm going to try to sleep," Felar said, heading for the crew quarters.

"I think I saw some rations back in the ordinance storage area," Wake said. Maxar motioned for him to lead the way.

***

"I think it is time," Cazz-ak said in Wake's head. "We should all meet in the engine room." Wake secured his tools in their storage space and left the cannon loading deck.

He'd lost track of how long they'd been waiting in the collapsed worm. Wake spent his time eating, sleeping, and then doing his best to fix the Death Watch's damage. There wasn't much he could do while stuck inside the ship—*No way I am going outside while we are in this place*—but had established they weren't in immediate danger. He'd also reinforced the internal structure and felt confident they would be alright as long as they didn't take any further hits.

When Wake passed through the crew quarters, he saw Maxar and Tremmilly stirring, each in their own beds. He descended the ladder into the engine room, guessing they would come when ready.

Other than Jaydon, Wake was the first human to arrive. Maxar and Tremmilly finally came down, looking groggy. Beowulf whined above and Maxar struggled to help him down. Felar, looking completely exhausted, came in from the direction of the bridge. She collapsed into one of the crew chairs. Lothis followed, his orange eyes as bright and piercing as ever.

"Is everyone ready?" Na-ah-co asked. Wake nodded, as did the rest of the group. Cazz-ak's suggestion to stay in the worm had been a great idea. He felt much better after getting some food and sleep. The location and situation was eerie, but the lack of a Breaker or Ashamine threat had allowed him to relax.

"We should move closer to the worm generator," Lothis said, breaking into his thoughts. Everyone looked as sober as Wake felt, remaining silent. They gathered around the worm generator, the Entho-la-ah-mines and Lothis closest to the sleek machinery.

As he waited, Wake remembered something Lothis had said during the previous meeting. *What did he mean about the situation possibly being worse?* Wake didn't understand, and something deep inside him shied away from pondering it too closely.

51 – FELAR

The fear of losing Lothis again was nearly overwhelming Felar. When he'd been unconscious the first time, their situation on the Justice had kept her occupied. Now, if it happened again, Felar would have plenty of time to dwell on it. They'd all starve eventually if Lothis and the Entho-la-ah-mines couldn't get them out of the collapsed worm. That was the only reason Felar was letting him be a part of the plan. The Founder's Commandos had taught her sometimes even the worst odds are superior to certain death.

"Please," Na-ah-co said, "no matter what happens, stay silent. We all need to focus, and an ill timed distraction could be disastrous." Everyone agreed as Lothis, Cazz-ak, and Na-ah-co settled into a triangular formation around the worm generator. "We will share our communication with you all, as long as it is possible," Na-ah-co continued. "Jaydon, be prepared to pilot us out of the tunnel as soon as you can. I'm not sure how long we will be able to keep the exit open." Jaydon nodded and sprinted off towards the command deck.

"Lothis, you must allow us to deal with the dimensional folds," Cazz-ak instructed. "It is extremely complicated. Perhaps someday we can explain them, but for now, you must be content in ignorance."

"I understand," the boy replied, nodding. He looked ready, his face serene.

"Connect to the generator," Cazz-ak directed.

A few moments passed in silence and a far away look entered Lothis' eyes. "Connection established."

Felar's anxiety ratcheted up a few notches. *Stay calm. He'll be OK. He can do it.*

"Na-ah-co, do you feel my model of the dimensional structure is complete?"

"Yes."

"Let us see if this will actually work."

211

For several moments, nothing happened. Na-ah-co twitched and Cazz-ak shuddered. Felar wished she knew how to read Entho-la-ah-mine body language. Lothis still looked far away, but remained conscious and relaxed. More time passed. *See, everything will be fine.*

Minutes dragged by, Felar's optimism battling with her feeling something might go wrong at any second. *Be patient. Wait.*

Finally, after several minutes had elapsed, Lothis looked at her and smiled. All Felar's anxiety vanished, and before she realized what she was doing, she picked the boy up. "I'm OK," he said, his voice a breathy whisper. Felar realized how hard she was embracing him and lessened her grip. "Cazz-ak and the Queen are OK as well," Lothis continued in his normal voice. "We did it. We reopened the exit." A loud cheer from the command deck confirmed Lothis' statement.

"Whatever you did brought us out where I had programmed earlier," Jaydon said over the intercom. "We are in the Qi system. It worked!" They all let out cheers. Maxar and Tremmilly hugged, then stepped away from each other, looking awkward. Felar smiled to herself, wondering how long it would take them to accept their mutual attraction.

"Nice work on repairing the worm generator, Wake," Felar said, slapping the engineer on the back. "You did a great job."

"Thanks," he replied, smiling ear to ear. "It was a team effort."

Before they could celebrate further, Jaydon's voice came over the intercom. "Felar, can you get up here." His tone was tense and worried. The joyous feeling in the engine room died immediately. *What's wrong now?* Felar wondered, wishing they could have some blighthearted luck for once.

When she arrived on the command deck, Jaydon was intently studying one of the tactical displays. "What's up?" she asked, sliding into the chair next to him. Everyone else stood behind them, waiting for the bad news.

"There are three Ashamine ships approaching us," Jaydon answered, pointing towards a cluster of vessels on the display. "None of them have sent any type of signal. Is that normal?"

Felar thought for a moment. "No, it isn't. Protocol is to exchange authentication codes, unless you are on a black op." She studied the display more closely. "They are in formation with several civilian ships?"

"Looks that way," Jaydon replied.

"I'm from Qi-3," Felar continued. "The whole system is known for its hostility towards the Ashamine. It's a place where criminals and outlaws govern and hold power. I doubt the Ashamine would make a move against them with just three ships. It wouldn't be enough."

"If they are hostile towards the Ashamine and have the strength to back it up," Maxar said, "why did we come here in an Ashamine ship?"

"I figured maybe we could sell them the Death Watch," Jaydon answered, "then buy a less conspicuous vessel. They always have bounties out for Ashamine weaponry. I've never actually dealt with them before, but you hear things around the black market."

"So maybe the incoming ships aren't really Ashamine controlled?" Felar said, trying to find an explanation.

"The government here has a protocol just like the Ashamine." Jaydon sighed. "They would have transmitted a code, and I would have sent one back to confirm that we are not hostile."

"So if they aren't Ashamine, and they aren't locals, then what are they?" Tremmilly's question hung over them like a cloud. Felar knew, but she didn't want to say it.

"Breakers," Maxar said finally, giving voice to what they were all thinking.

52 – TREMMILLY

"How can we be sure?" Tremmilly asked, wondering if something else was going on. She didn't want to believe there were any more Breakers than the ones they'd encountered in the Eishon system.

"We can't," Jaydon answered, "until they tell us, or one of our group can feel them."

"We cannot sense anything," Cazz-ak said, "but unless they are very strong, we would need to be closer."

"And I don't think any of us is willing to get that close," Felar interjected. "We should just worm to another system."

Status messages popped up on the terminal screens and an alarm began to sound. "Proximity warning. Evasive action required," a voice declared loudly.

"What in the blightheart?" Jaydon asked, looking down at his screen. A view of space behind the Death Watch flashed up on a large overhead display. The Justice was there, looming over them.

"How did they find us?" Felar yelled, heading for the targeting room. Maxar and Lothis were close behind her. A small voice in Tremmilly's head wondered if she should go back to help, but the weight of terror kept her enthralled.

"Maybe their Qi friends told them." Jaydon was quickly paging through options, his moves frantic and almost out of control. Tremmilly wondered if they would be able to create a worm and get out before the Breakers put a cannon round through them.

There is no way to escape, she thought, returning her gaze to the image of the Justice. *Give up. It's easier. They will give you back Eishon-2. They'll give you back your parents.*

"Don't listen to them," Cazz-ak said in her mind.

"They tell nothing but lies," Na-ah-co added. Tremmilly felt comfort and tranquility sweep over her.

"Thank you," she replied, breathing deeply. Knowing her help would

214

be needed, Tremmilly ran for the targeting room. As she got further from the Entho-la-ah-mines, her anxiety returned. *How were the Breakers able to influence me like that?* she wondered, settling in to her chair. *What if next time the Entho-la-ah-mines are too busy or unable to protect me?* Dread welled up within her, extinguishing what little sense of peace remained.

"Blighthearted fires of the dark star," Felar cursed, snapping Tremmilly out of her thoughts. She looked towards the back of the ship and her breath caught in her throat. A fusillade of point defense rounds streaked towards the Death Watch, lighting up the space between the two ships.

"They're moving in to ram," Jaydon yelled.

"Get us out of here," Maxar yelled back.

"I'm programing the worm generator as fast as it will let me." The smaller point defense rounds impacted the hull, the sound like a rain forest deluge on a metal roof. Tremmilly could do nothing. Her guns pointed forward and the Justice was aft. "Worm generator spooling up," Jaydon yelled. "Come on!"

Tremmilly watched as both Felar and Lothis fired their cannons as quickly as possible, trying to deflect the steady stream of point defense rounds. "Hull integrity at impact sites down to forty percent," Wake's voice said over the intercom.

"Worm created," Jaydon interjected. "We're heading in." Tremmilly watched from her targeting chair as they entered the blackness once again. The hail of projectiles ceased, creating an eerie calm.

"Where are we going?" Felar asked.

"Psinar," Jaydon answered.

"That's an Ashamine world."

"I know, but it was the first place that came to mind." Jaydon sounded defensive.

"Blightheart," Felar cursed, standing up violently from her chair.

"We'll figure it out," Tremmilly said, trying to calm her friend down. "Even if it's Ashamine, we can still make a worm and leave."

"No, no," Felar said. "I just thought of something. Maybe the Breakers do control the Qi system, and maybe they told Crasor we were there, but regardless, we are still leaving an obvious worm signature. The Justice will be able to read it without a problem. We will never be able to get away as long as we are leaving a truthful trail. Lothis," she said, heading towards the engine room, "I need your help." Tremmilly followed them both out of curiosity, hoping she might be able to lend a hand.

"The Justice is following our worm signatures," Felar announced over the intercom. "Jaydon, keep us moving. As soon as we get into a new system, get the generator started on the next worm. Wake and Lothis will be working on a way to hide our true destination."

"Acknowledged," Jaydon replied.

"How are we supposed to leave a fake worm signature?" Wake asked, caught off guard.

"You are an engineer, and Lothis is a genius," Felar snapped back. "Make it work."

"OK, well let's get started then." Wake and Lothis began talking and Tremmilly quickly lost the thread of the conversation. She'd never even heard most of the terms they were using.

"Justice is in system," Jaydon intercommed, "but we are on our way out." Tremmilly hoped they could remain one step ahead. Lothis and Wake kept working, first accessing a terminal, then looking around in the storage locker for components.

Three worm tunnels later, Wake held up a box. "It's rudimentary, but will work." He began attaching the device to the worm generator.

"We can't remove the true signature," Lothis explained, "but we can add fake trails into it. If we had more time, we could come up with a complex device, but for now, we will be able to inject ten false signatures each time we generate a worm."

"Good," Felar said, nodding. "That will slow them down."

"If they are as resolute on destroying us as they seem, we will need to come up with a more permanent solution."

"I'm going to the command deck to talk with Jaydon and Maxar about a strategy," Felar said, heading for the door.

Always on the run, Tremmilly thought. She briefly considered staying in the engine room, but she didn't understand what Lothis and Wake were doing. *Someday things will calm down again.* Tremmilly didn't know if she believed that or not.

The image of Beowulf popped into her head, and Tremmilly worried if he was OK. He was recovering from his combat with the Breaker Aeron, but she kept a close watch over him. Tremmilly had last seen him in the crew quarters, so she decided to check there first. She climbed the ladder and opened the hatch. Beowulf's head popped up in the bunk right in front of her, the same one she and Maxar had shared. "Hey, Beo," Tremmilly said, sitting down beside him. The wolf-dog licked her hand. He looked happy and less in pain than before.

Tremmilly closed her eyes, imagining a soft wind blowing through the woods on Eishon-2. Running her hands through Beowulf's fur, she conjured up the image of them both sitting in soft grass. Immediately, the tension of constant flight began to subside. Tremmilly breathed deeply, feeling the light of Eishon Primary warming her skin. Looking around, she realized it was the same clearing Psidonnis had told her the prophecy in. She missed him greatly, but with what had happened,

Tremmilly felt glad he'd died peacefully before the Ashamine could kill him.

Feeling a weight in her lap, Tremmilly looked down. *A book.* "Odd," she said, opening it. The title, printed in big block letters was: "What Happens Next." The rest of the page was empty.

"I don't remember reading this one, Beo, but it looks interesting," she said, looking over at her friend. Beowulf pulled his lips up in a sneer. Tremmilly had never seen him do that before, and the sight disturbed her. A sound in the wood stole her attention briefly, and when she looked back, Beowulf was normal. Tremmilly wondered for a moment what was happening, then she remembered it was all just her imagination. She laughed, and returned her attention to the book.

Turning through several blank pages, she found an image. It was of the Death Watch, floating in blackness. On the next page, she saw the Justice poised behind the smaller ship, but the image showed no ion trails between them. The following page was the Watch inside a hangar, surrounded by Breakers. "Is this book going in reverse?" she wondered aloud. Turning the page, she saw the horrible creatures leading all her friends out of the Watch's airlock. The Breakers had bound and gagged them, and blood ran down their faces. Tremmilly didn't want to see anymore, but she couldn't stop looking at the images. Each successive page showed Crasor stabbing one of her friends in the chest with his pointy fingers.

"No!" she screamed, trying to throw the book from her. Beowulf growled, and when she looked at him his eyes were as black as deep space and he had bared his teeth at her. "What's happening?" she stammered, trying to crawl away from her oldest friend. The sound of static emanated all around her and the grass began to writhe, turning black as it did so. Soon, the darkness had covered everything but the small patch of dirt she crouched on.

The mass undulated and swarmed, mounding up to create a humanoid shape. The form was rough, but she recognized it. *Crasor,* she thought. He began walking towards Tremmilly. She wanted to run, but had nowhere to go. The black mass surrounded her, and to touch it was death. Crasor said nothing, just kept walking, his gait easy and unhurried. Tremmilly looked around for Beowulf, but he had vanished.

"There is nothing left for you, girl," the shape said, stopping at the edge of Tremmilly's circle. She wanted to fight back, wanted to spit in his face, but felt paralyzed with fear. *Maybe he can't hurt me,* she thought. Crasor grabbed her by the throat and laughed. "No one can protect you," he continued, squeezing. "The Dawn will soon be broken, and you'll all be dead."

Tremmilly tried to strike him, but every blow simply passed through his black shape. When she pulled her fist out, it had caused no damage or change. Blackness was creeping in on the edges of her vision.

"See," Crasor said, "that is true darkness. It's where you are headed. If you come to me, I promise to save you from it, promise to give you more power than any Dawn could." Her vision had narrowed to pinpricks, and she knew she was about to pass out. "You think they are your friends, but you'll soon see the truth." Crasor released her, but before she could do anything, his hand was over her mouth. "I will be deep inside you, always." Before she could stop herself, Tremmilly inhaled, a huge breath full of dark particles. She breathed in again, her body crying out for oxygen. More particles entered, burning her lungs.

Tremmilly writhed on the ground, trying to scream. The blackness poured through her body, consuming and erasing her. She tried to cough, wanting beyond anything to expel the invaders, but she couldn't. Her airway was blocked. The edges of her vision began to blacken and her senses dimmed. Darkness engulfed her.

Air exploded into Tremmilly's lungs. She opened her eyes and looked around desperately. *The bunk,* she thought, frantically trying to free herself from the sheets. She was sobbing, panting, covered in sweat. When she finally got free, Tremmilly sat on the edge of the small bed. Beowulf had gone.

What happened to me? Tremmilly wondered if it was just a dream, or if it had been more. An icy dagger of terror forced its way into her heart. The Breakers had influenced her mind earlier, injecting thoughts and emotions. What if they could do more than that? The Entho-la-ah-mines had protected her in that moment, but maybe they had let down their guard or weren't strong enough.

Tremmilly got to her feet and looked around the crew quarters, wondering if Crasor saw it too.

53 – MAXAR

"We should go to Lith-elo-hi-rosh," Cazz-ak said. "It will be safe from both the Breakers and the Ashamine. We have been able to keep it concealed so far."

"It won't be hidden for long if we lead the Justice back to it." Maxar liked the idea of going to an Entho-la-ah-mine world, but the risk was just too high.

"I think I've figured out a way to make it statistically unlikely to follow our path." Wake began drawing in the air with a crimson gauntleted finger. "First, we choose five–no, eight–worm locations," he said, making eight circles only he could see. "Then we quickly move to each one and then back to where we started," he continued, drawing imaginary lines. "At each remote location, we will be leaving eleven worm trails: one true, which leads back to the start, and ten false. When finished, our origin point will then have 88 trails, essentially leading nowhere. We then transition to a new origin point, leaving 11 more trails in the original, for a total of 98 false paths and one true. Once we arrive at the new origin, we do the same thing we did in the first, just to be safe. That makes a really tangled mess of decoy trails. The chance the Justice even picks the single correct worm tunnel to our second origin is about one percent." He smiled. "We'll be creating..." Wake was obviously running the math in his head, but Lothis beat him to the answer.

"374 possible outbound trails total. Each worm is 0.26737 percent of the whole."

"That sounds right," Wake said, caught off guard. "If they had enough time, I'm sure they could try them all, but the signatures will fade too quickly for them to get very far. It is possible they could pick the right one at both origins on the first try, but it's only a..." Wake trailed off again, only this time he looked at Lothis for the answer.

"A 0.010203 percent chance."

"Seems pretty remote," Maxar added. "Is that an acceptable level of

219

risk?" The Entho-la-ah-mines both said it was, and Maxar's last reservation about the plan vanished.

"But can't they just follow the freshest signatures?" Felar asked.

Wake shook his head. "If we move quickly enough, there shouldn't be a discernible fade between any of them."

"Do you think the worm generator repairs can handle that kind of repeated use?" Jaydon asked, not turning away from the ship's controls.

Wake thought for a moment. "Yes, I think so. I had the correct replacement parts and everything looks solid."

"Well then," Jaydon replied, "let's get started."

As Wake began giving instructions, Beowulf, previously sleeping under the command console next to Maxar, looked towards the hatch and whined. A moment later, Tremmilly came through it on to the command deck. She kept her head down, not looking directly at anyone. "Maxar," she said quietly, her voice horse, "come with me." Beowulf stood next to her, looking anxious. Maxar didn't know what to make of their strange behavior, but he followed as she led him out into the targeting room. Still, Tremmilly kept her eyes pointed towards the floor.

"What's wrong?" Maxar asked.

"Don't speak, just listen."

Beowulf continued whining.

"OK," he replied, eyebrows rising. He'd never seen her act like this before.

"Don't tell me any updates or plans or anything." Tremmilly sounded like she was about to cry, and Maxar tried to gently lift her chin up with his hand. "No!" she whispered, shoving his hand away. "Something happened while I was sleeping. There is no time to explain. You have to kill me."

"What?" Maxar felt dumbfounded. "Tremmilly, what's going on?"

"No time," she continued, eyes still locked on the floor. Maxar bent down to try to see her face, but only caught a glimpse of tear filled redness before she turned away. "You have to do this for me. If you love me, care for me at all, you will do it."

"Even if I could, which I can't, why would I?"

Tremmilly looked up finally and locked eyes with him. "Because I'm infected, Maxar. Crasor found me, invaded my mind somehow. He's inside of me."

Maxar's breath caught and a shudder ran through him. "How is that possible?" he replied, gaining his composure.

"I don't know," Tremmilly said, her eyes falling back to the floor, "but I can't take the risk of him seeing our plans and following us. You have to kill me before he takes my body over like those things in the hangar."

Maxar had killed for money on his home world of Noor-5. The

Ashamine had forced him to kill on Bloodsport. Since his rescue, he'd killed for the survival of himself and his friends. Despite all that—or maybe because of it—he could never kill Tremmilly. Even if she became Crasor incarnate, he still couldn't do it. "We will find another way," he replied. "Maybe the Entho-la-ah-mines or Lothis can do something."

Tremmilly began sobbing, her whole body shuddering. Beowulf leaned against her, and she ran her hand through his thick fir. Maxar took Tremmilly in his arms, squeezing her tight. "Just—kill—me," she moaned.

"Cazz-ak, Na-ah-co, Lothis," he yelled towards the command deck, "I need your help in here."

"What is wrong?" Na-ah-co asked, rushing in.

Maxar waited for Tremmilly to answer, but all she could do was sob, so he told what had happened.

"As with everything related to the Breakers," Cazz-ak replied, "we have very little information. Perhaps it is possible for Crasor to do this, perhaps not. One thing we do know, however, is we can sense their presence, at least at close range. We can delve into Tremmilly and see if she is infected."

Tremmilly looked lost in emotion, so Maxar nodded his agreement. "Do it."

"Lothis," Na-ah-co said, "join us, but be soft. We will guide your energy."

The Entho-la-ah-mines and Lothis formed a triangle around Tremmilly and Maxar. Now, everyone but Tremmilly was silent. Her sobs echoed off the display screens, the sad sounds piercing Maxar. He couldn't stand to see her suffer this way. *I tried everything I could to protect her,* he thought despondently, *but I failed.*

Minutes passed. Felar came in from the command deck, brows furrowing when she saw the group. She looked at Maxar and he shook his head. They had both been around the Entho-la-ah-mines long enough to know they should stay silent.

Finally, Cazz-ak moved, his iridescent exoskeleton reflecting the low lighting of the targeting room. "We did a very thorough search. Unless the Breakers have found a new way to hide, Tremmilly is free."

Maxar smiled and hugged Tremmilly even tighter. Beowulf ceased whining, as if he too could hear Cazz-ak's words. "Everything is OK," Maxar said. "Crasor didn't do anything to you."

"What's going on?" Felar said, coming into the middle of the triangle.

"I went to the crew quarters to look for Beowulf," Tremmilly answered, her voice tired and raw. "I sat down on the bed and started daydreaming about Eishon-2. I don't know if I fell asleep or was having a vision, but there was a book. It showed our future, that you would all be converted to Breakers. Crasor came and he started choking me."

A chill ran down Maxar's spine even as rage boiled up inside him. Whatever Crasor was, no matter his power or abilities, Maxar would kill him, again.

"I tried to fight back," Tremmilly continued, "but it was like hitting smoke. I couldn't hurt him. Just as I began to black out, he put his hand over my mouth. My reaction was to breathe in and particles of him went into my lungs." She began to cry again. Maxar rubbed her back.

"You're OK now," Felar replied. "If the Entho-la-ah-mines say he isn't in you, then everything is alright."

"When the Justice was near us," Cazz-ak said, "Crasor had some type of influence on Tremmilly. It wasn't very powerful, most likely due to the distance. When Na-ah-co and I sensed it, we were able to block him fairly easily. Since then, we've felt nothing from the Breakers. With the Justice in an entirely different system, I think their influence is unlikely."

"So you think I just made it up?" Tremmilly shot back.

"No, that's not what they are saying," Felar said gently. "You just had the worst nightmare ever. I had horrible ones after what happened to Lothis and me on Haak-ah-tar. I still have them sometimes."

Maxar nodded in agreement. "I dream about Bloodsport regularly. I'm sure the Breakers will make it in there sooner or later."

Tremmilly sighed, drying her eyes on her shirt-sleeve. "I'm sorry I didn't handle it well. The dream just felt so real."

"There is nothing you need to apologize for," Maxar replied, looking into her green eyes. "I often wake up screaming. There is nothing you can do about it."

"We will watch over you," Na-ah-co said. Maxar felt calmness wash through him as she continued. "Cazz-ak and I cannot influence your dreams, but we can protect you from the mental influence of the dark one."

"Thank you," Tremmilly replied, finally sounding like her normal self. "Did you guys figure out where we can hide from the Breakers?"

54 – LOTHIS

"Lith-elo-hi-rosh," Felar answered, "it's a hidden Entho-la-ah-mine world." Just hearing the name of it again excited Lothis. Haak-ah-tar and Eishon-2 were the only planets he'd ever been to. *And neither of those is an Entho-la-ah-mine world, at least not anymore.* Seeing a whole planet full of the hive minded insectile race would be a new experience.

Cazz-ak and Na-ah-co were amazing. He greatly appreciated their guidance and mentorship. *Without them, you would be lost or useless,* he thought, remembering all the things they had shown him. Lothis was still wary of using his mental powers without their oversight, but now he had a better grasp of where the boundaries were.

"How long will it take to get there?" Tremmilly asked. Lothis looked at her, both with his eyes and with his mind. The Entho-la-ah-mines were right about not seeing any traces of darkness in her, but Lothis wondered if the Breakers were stealthier than any of them believed. There were countless unknowns. Lothis was unwilling to rule out that the enemy had done something to Tremmilly. She was a friend and an ally, but he would keep watching until he satisfied himself nothing was wrong.

"I don't know," Felar said, breaking into Lothis' thoughts. "Wake came up with a plan to disguise our worm signature, but it is complicated and involves a lot of tunnels."

"We'll need to show you coordinates, Lothis," Cazz-ak interjected. "Since Lith-elo-hi-rosh is unknown to the Ashamine, it will not be in the ship's database. The Entho-la-ah-mine way of noting a location in space-time is different from human, so it is not as simple as inputing our data. We will need you to convert it. Is that possible?"

Everyone looked at Lothis, waiting for his answer. He felt their eyes and became uncomfortable with the attention. *They are your family,* he thought, trying to calm himself. "With your help, I can try."

"Let us go to the command deck," Cazz-ak said. "We can check the progress of Wake's plan."

Once on the deck, Felar explained to Jaydon and Wake what had happened to Tremmilly. The focus shifted away from Lothis and he relaxed.

"Even though you cannot connect to the Great Thought," Cazz-ak said, his voice only in Lothis' mind, "we should still be able to establish a link to each other. It will be similar to how you gave us your power when we cloaked the Death Watch, but much deeper. We Entho-la-ah-mine use it to connect during ceremonies. Typically, the entirety of the Great Thought is enough to bring us all together, but there are events that require a deeper melding." Cazz-ak stopped, but Lothis waited, sensing he had more to say. "Since you have a human mind, we must be careful. We learn from our youngest age to be part of the whole, while still being an individual. It is at the core of our species. You have not learned how to give yourself to the meld and then take yourself back. It would be very easy to become lost, to lose yourself with me. I will do my best not to allow this to happen, but this type of connection has never been done with a human before. You must exercise caution."

Lothis nodded, some of his fear returning despite the presence of Na-ah-co and Cazz-ak. *You can do it,* he told himself. *Maintain focus and clarity.*

"It's going to take a couple hours to get through the sequence of tunnels Wake has outlined," Lothis heard Jaydon say. "We all have some time to rest, unless there happens to be an Ashamine or Breaker patrol out in one of the mining areas we are tunneling between."

"Seems unlikely," Felar noted. "The surviving Ashamine fleet from Eishon will head back to the core system. Once they report the Breakers, I bet Fleet Command pulls in to defend the primary worlds. They've never seen anything like this before."

"That's assuming they believe the story of the remaining captains," Maxar added. "They might just kill them all as mutineers."

"True," Felar replied, "it is a strange tale, but unless the Founder is in a very bad mood, they will at least investigate first. With no wreckage of the Justice in the Eishon system, the loyalists will have a strong case."

"Do you know if there are any kinds of transponders or beacons on this class of ship?" Wake asked.

"I don't think so," Felar answered, "but that was not my area of expertise. We should probably look before we make our jump to Lith-elo-hi-rosh. Lothis and I can go through the computer systems while you check the hardware?"

"Sounds like a good plan," Wake replied.

"Actually," Lothis interjected, feeling nervous, "I need to help the Entho-la-ah-mines first." Immediately, Felar looked worried.

"Is this going to be safe?" she said, coming to stand next to him. "It isn't going to be like when we were stuck in the tunnel, is it?"

"No, no," he answered, shaking his head. "It won't be like that." He didn't really know for sure, but neither Cazz-ak nor Na-ah-co disagreed with him, so he guessed it was true.

"OK, well I think I can look through the Death Watch's systems on my own, but when you are done, would you mind coming to double check?"

"Sure," Lothis replied, smiling at her.

"Be careful."

"I will."

Cazz-ak led Lothis and Na-ah-co back through targeting into the engine room. A small door at the back of the compartment opened into the ordinance storage area. It was silent here, at least while they weren't in combat. Large containers of rail cannon ammunition were sitting on conveyor systems, belts of rounds feeding up into the loading machinery above. Lothis hadn't been back this way yet, and he marveled at the large slugs. They were color coded according to the ionizing component of the tracer. Blue, green, red, orange, yellow, and more could have made the room look festive, but the mass and purpose of the rounds took away all joy.

"Are you ready?" Na-ah-co asked.

"Yes," Lothis responded, hoping it was true.

Cazz-ak turned to face Lothis, his insect like body language unreadable to him. "Reach out with a small portion of your mind." Thankfully, Lothis could sense emotion through their mental communications. It was still calm and embracing.

He did as instructed, sending a small sliver of his mental power out towards Cazz-ak. The Entho-la-ah-mine did the same and their two wisps touched. Immediately, Lothis could feel even more of Cazz-ak, could see his thoughts and memories.

"Good," he heard through the connection. "It is working. Now, we will both increase the strength of the bond, feeding in more power simultaneously." Lothis did so, beginning to feel overwhelmed. "Not too quickly," Cazz-ak cautioned. "We are in no hurry."

Lothis felt his memories smear across the palette of his mind. They mixed and mingled with a spectrum of thoughts and sensations he'd never known before. Memories of unknown places jumped out at him. Gorgeous vistas of both stellar and terrestrial space pulled at his attention.

"No more," Cazz-ak said, his voice stern. "We cannot increase the connection any further."

Nodding, Lothis fought to maintain his own identity and memories. "What now?"

"Take this," Cazz-ak said. A thought floated up through the sea of *other* that enveloped him. At first, its structure made no sense. It wasn't an equation, wasn't even numbers. "Don't worry about that now," Cazz-ak instructed, "just hold on to it and slowly disengage the meld."

At first, Lothis' task was easy, but as the connection began to decrease, the thought became harder to hold on to. It began to dim and lose its shape, fading away. "Be calm," Na-ah-co said, "everything will be fine." Lothis relaxed, the thought brightened. This helped him relax even further, and the information became as bright as when Cazz-ak first sent it to him. After a few more moments, their minds separated.

"All is well?" Cazz-ak asked. "You still have the information?"

"Yes, but how do I interpret it?"

"That, I do not know."

Lothis tried to make sense of the thought, to understand how it could be the location of Lith-elo-hi-rosh. The information was more of a feeling than it was a sense of place. An idea tugged at the edge of his mind, and he shifted the image to a different angle, and then another, and another. *There it is,* he thought, *just a matter of perspective.* It was a beautiful planet, full of mountains, plains, and lush ecosystems. Another piece of the image slid into place and Lothis could feel its location.

"I think I know where it is," he said in wonder.

"Good," Cazz-ak replied.

"Well done," Na-ah-co added.

"I will need to do some calculations to figure out human coordinates." Lothis headed towards the command deck and the Entho-la-ah-mines followed. Once there, he used a terminal to get the current location of the Death Watch. With that information, Lothis carefully worked out Lith-elo-hi-rosh's location and entered the coordinates into the screen.

"You figured it out?" Felar asked, looking happy.

"Yes," Lothis said, glad she was no longer worried.

"Good job," Felar praised, taking him into a warm hug. "I knew you could do it."

"Thank you," he replied. It was something he had only recently learned to say. He was proud of himself, proud he had been able to help his family.

"We still have a lot of time to get through the worm tunnel sequence. Why don't you go get some sleep?"

In the past, Lothis had never required much rest, but with all the mental exercise he'd been getting, he felt tired. "That sounds good," he replied. "Will you wake me before we make the tunnel to Lith-elo-hi-rosh?"

"Definitely," Felar answered.

***

Lothis woke from a dreamless sleep to find Felar tapping his shoulder. "We are generating the worm tunnel to Lith-elo right now."

"OK," he said, sitting up. "Did you get any sleep?"

"Nah, but I'm a soldier, so I don't need it."

"You know that isn't true, right?"

"It's a joke, Lothis," Felar replied with a laugh. "I'll get some sleep once we get planet-side. There was just too much for me to do."

"I could have helped." Lothis felt surprised she had so easily talked him into sleeping when many tasks needed completion. *I must have been exhausted.*

"Sure, but you probably would have passed out. Don't worry about it. We got everything done. No sign of hostiles. No trackers or transponders to give the Ashamine a signal. We made too many worm trails for the Breakers to search before they all fade away. I think we are clear for a while."

Lothis was glad to hear that. The whole group could use some down time. "Let's go up to the deck so we can see the planet."

"Alright," Felar replied, moving towards the floor hatch.

When they arrived at the command deck, Lith-elo-hi-rosh was on the main view screen, as beautiful as the image in his memory. The feelings coming from the two Entho-la-ah-mines were that of excitement, joy, and wonder. "I never thought we would make it back here," Cazz-ak said.

"You are stronger than you know," Na-ah-co replied, her voice like the tinkling of bells.

Then Lothis felt them, the millions of Entho-la-ah-mines on Lith-elo-hi-rosh. At first it was overwhelming, bright and full of energy, but as Lothis took more of it in, he realized it was a song. The whole species was singing with joy that their Queen had returned safely to them. Without understanding exactly why, Lothis stood before Na-ah-co and bowed. "You, and your people, are amazing. I feel gratitude to be in your presence."

Na-ah-co laughed, a strong sound that made Lothis feel good. "Lothis, it is you and your friends who are amazing. Without you all, our species would be without a queen and her general. We owe you more than we can ever repay."

"There is no debt," Lothis said, feeling tears well up in his eyes. He'd seen others cry, but had never done so himself. "It has been our pleasure." He shut his eyes, reached out his mind, and sang with the Entho-la-ah-mines as he'd never sung with his physical voice. No matter what the future held, Lothis would hold on to this joyous memory forever.

55 – CAZZ-AK-TAK

Stepping onto the surface of Lith-elo-hi-rosh was an amazing sensation. Cazz-ak breathed in the atmosphere and reveled in the radiation of the primary star. The planet's gravity felt right. He was home, at least as home as he could be. This was one of the last remaining Entho-la-ah-mine planets. Cazz-ak didn't want to think about what would happen if their distortion signature obfuscation didn't work.

All around him, Cazz-ak felt his people. They were still singing, had been since the Death Watch had come through the final distortion. He felt like he'd been gone for years. In truth, it was only a few standard weeks since his departure, leading a fleet of bi-pyramid ships towards Haak-ah-tar. Now he had returned, bringing just one of his species back.

"But you brought me through all of that." Na-ah-co said, interrupting his thoughts. "Sometimes sacrifices must be made, and sometimes the cost is higher than we believed possible."

Cazz-ak knew she was right, but he wished there had been some way to avoid it. He didn't want to face his people, didn't want to leave the area around the Death Watch. The Great Thought celebrated him as a hero, but he didn't feel like one. It considered Cazz-ak a grand leader, a warrior, and the first of his kind. "I'm not who they think," he told the Queen.

"Who am I?" Na-ah-co's question caught him off guard and it took Cazz-ak a moment to gather himself.

"You're Na-ah-co, the Queen."

"Do I know you? Have I been with you throughout this entire journey?"

"Yes."

"Cazz-ak, you are a warrior. You are the first of your kind. No other has done what you have been able to do in our history. I have seen it, have lived it, have been by your side. It is foolish of you to doubt the Great Thought, but you cannot ever disbelieve me." Na-ah-co was right,

228

and Cazz-ak knew it deep down. "If there is one thing you should know from human history, it is war means death, mostly of the innocent, and sometimes of the guilty. We are at war, Cazz-ak, a war getting increasingly complicated. Entho-la-ah-mines will die, and some of them will be under your leadership. It is our responsibility to ensure our species survives. Everyone understands that. Our survival as a race is more important than any one individual."

"You speak wisdom," Cazz-ak replied. "I'm sorry for my stubbornness."

"There is no need for you to apologize," the Queen said in a lighter tone. "Be proud of yourself."

Turning to face the humans, Na-ah-co addressed them. "Friends, we appreciate your help immensely. Cazz-ak and I wouldn't be here if not for your generosity and kindness. We would like to help you in return. Lith-elo-hi-rosh and any other Entho-la-ah-mine world are open to you. We will try to shelter, protect, and hide you to the best of our abilities. Thankfully, we all share a similar gravitational and atmospheric preference. Unfortunately, our living spaces would not be comfortable for you, so it is probably best to sleep in the Death Watch.

"Tonight, we celebrate, both for our survival and for the making of new friends. We can learn much from each other. In unity, we have strength, and perhaps through deeper understanding, we all might withstand the Breakers and the Ashamine." Their friends nodded and smiled. Cazz-ak felt grateful he had met such good people. It gave him hope that someday the Entho-la-ah-mines and humans could peacefully co-exist.

"Follow me," Na-ah-co said, setting off through the waving grass. A gentle breeze blew, swaying the nearby grove of palos trees. Another wave of joy overcame Cazz-ak. It just felt so good in this safe and familiar place.

The humans followed Na-ah-co, with Cazz-ak bringing up the rear. "Beware the calath plant," he said, motioning towards a small bush with sharp leaves. "Many life forms on this planet are sensitive to the chemical they secrete. I'm not sure how it will affect humans, but it could be fatal."

"Good to know," Maxar said, stepping carefully around the plant.

"This is such a beautiful place," Tremmilly announced. Everyone else nodded in agreement.

When they reached the edge of the narrow chasm, they stopped. "We have to go down," Cazz-ak said. "That is the way to access our city."

"Do you all live underground?" Lothis asked.

"No," he replied, "but it is our natural habitat, so we are most comfortable there."

"How do we get down?" Jaydon sounded shaky.

"Using the Great Thought," the Queen answered, stepping off the edge. The humans let out a cry of alarm, and then surprise, when Na-ah-co simply floated in the air. Cazz-ak could see the large platform of mental energy she had created, but none of the humans could, Lothis being the exception. "Come stand around me," she said, mirth in her voice. They tentatively followed, marveling at how they hovered over the dark void. Jaydon hesitated at the lip.

"I don't think I can do it," he said, turning away. "I'm afraid of heights."

"It will be OK," Tremmilly told him, stepping forward to take his hand. "Just close your eyes and pretend you're inside a starship." Jaydon followed her instructions, and soon they were all on the platform. Na-ah-co lowered them into the blackness. When they reached the bottom, everything was dark except for the thin slash of light far above.

"Does your species use illumination?" Felar asked. "If not, we may need to go back to the Watch and get some lights."

"We normally don't," Cazz-ak answered, "at least not here. A few places in the city have artificial lighting, but most is natural. The memories of those who've gone before us show the path in this place." The humans cautiously picked their way through the dark, rocky terrain.

"If we'd worn our EN suits, we would have lights," Wake bemoaned.

"You can't wear an ENS to a celebration," Felar shot back.

"It's not like any of us have nice clothes anyway."

"They are better than that crimson battle armor of yours. At least we don't look like we are coming down as conquerors."

Cazz-ak didn't understand why, but he had learned Felar and Wake liked to bicker. The emotion he picked up from them felt light, a stark contrast to when most humans acted this way.

"What is that blue glow up ahead?" Tremmilly's voice quietly penetrated the darkness.

"It's the entrance to the city," Na-ah-co answered. As they drew closer, the bioluminescent algae became more visible, its light allowing the humans to move faster.

"We made the city in a network of tunnels and caverns," Cazz-ak explained. "The algae are native to Lith-elo-hi-rosh, but we cultivated it in our living areas. While we can sense each other in the dark, it is nice to use our eyes." The group passed into the tunnel which marked the entrance.

"Does the city have a name?" Tremmilly asked.

"No. We have not decided on one yet. The settlement of Lith-elo-hi-rosh is recent. As some of you know, the Ashamine have been attempting to exterminate us. They steal our worlds for resources and perpetuate myths about us to humanity. We fled our origin planet, Haak-ah-tar, as well as our main worlds, for the colonies. The hope was that the Ashamine would not follow, but they did. We abandoned the colonies, trying to establish ourselves on places such as Lith-elo-hi-rosh: out of the way, hidden, and safe. The Entho-la-ah-mine species once numbered in the trillions, but is now down to millions."

"I'm sorry for what my kind did to yours," Felar said, her voice sad.

"It was not you, nor was it your kind, who did these things," the Queen replied. "There are many types of humans, and you are different from the Ashamine. You never abandoned us, never left us for dead, never turned us over." They were almost to the meeting place. Cazz-ak could feel the emotion of those gathered rise as he and Na-ah-co approached. "Now is not the time for sorrow or regret," she continued. "Now is the time for joy and celebration." As she finished, they entered the meeting cavern. It was a huge place, the ceiling stretching far above. Entho-la-ah-mines packed the entire floor, a vast sea of excited and joyous beings who wanted to glimpse their new Queen.

A mental cheer erupted, the sound deafening. Cazz-ak passed it along to the humans, attenuating it for their benefit. He wanted them included, not overwhelmed. As they took the view in, Cazz-ak watched their faces. Amazement, joy, and wonder were all there.

"My people," the Queen said, her light voice rising above the exultation of the masses. Instantly, silence came over the group. Cazz-ak could feel them listening, could sense the eagerness of every Entho-la-ah-mine participating on every hidden world they inhabited. "It is a joyous day," Na-ah-co continued, "a time for celebration. I left here unborn, inside an egg, and return as your Queen. Cazz-ak-tak, our new allies, and all of our brothers and sisters who sacrificed themselves made this possible. We celebrate and honor them. Just as important, Cazz-ak-tak and my governess, Elth-eo-lan, who also sacrificed herself to protect me, made some crucial discoveries about the Great Thought, emotion, and who we are as Entho-la-ah-mines.

"We have more enemies now, than ever before. The Ashamine wants to exterminate us all. And now the Breakers seek to dominate and assimilate our people. We must evolve to meet these changing conditions. No longer can we hide and hope our enemies will forget us. Our species must fight back, must protect the Great Thought, must preserve what we have left.

"Some philosophers will say this is a perversion of the Entho-la-ah-mine way of life—and that may be true—but if we do not go on the offensive, we will have nothing left. We have lived in our static, docile, peaceful way for millennia. Now, the universe has changed. We must adapt. We will not lose our principles, but we cannot allow ourselves to become extinct or assimilated." The Queen paused for a moment, allowing her words to settle in the minds of her audience. Cazz-ak simultaneously felt elation and dread. He was part of this change, central and integral. Both his use of anger and of his mental abilities as weapons were revolutionary. Now, the Queen of the entire species encouraged further change. Cazz-ak wondered what this would do to the Entho-la-ah-mine race.

"The humans gathered around me are proof they are not all evil and seeking genocide," the Queen continued. "We must find more of these allies and unite to fight both the Ashamine and the Breakers. This will not be an easy war. We, as a species, are far behind the humans in technology, and the Breakers in mental abilities. There will be many deaths, but I believe we can survive, that we can someday go back to being the peaceful species we once were. We will teach our children and their children about this war, about how to exist with humans, about how to defend themselves.

"If we do nothing, we will become nothing. We will be pushed into the oblivion beyond existence, forgotten as children of the universe. We were made by the stars, and we have a right to live amongst them, a right neither the Ashamine nor the Breakers can take away from us. Our evolution gave us a disadvantage in this situation, but we are strong, adaptable, and quick to learn. We can decide our own path, forge our own evolution, be who we choose to be. We are Entho-la-ah-mines."

Silence greeted her last statement. Cazz-ak couldn't tell what the Great Thought was thinking. It was in a state of flux. A moment later, a cheer burst from the crowd gathered in the cavern as well as the Great Thought. *They will fight,* Cazz-ak decided, hoping Na-ah-co's statements would all come to pass.

56 – CRASOR

"The w-w-worm impressions are t-t-too weak to decipher," the sensor technician said, confirming what Crasor already suspected.

"The Harbingers got away," the Breaker mind seethed within him. "This is an immense setback. They were all within reach and you failed to destroy them." Crasor felt furious about the defeat as well, but managed to control it.

Somehow, the Harbingers cloaked their destination when they first tunneled out of the Eishon system. They hadn't committed suicide by going into a worm with no exit, as Crasor first thought. Thankfully, his Breakers on Qi had notified him of the Death Watch's arrival, allowing the Justice to continue pursuit. Whatever they had done to cloak their first worm failed on subsequent tunnels, and Crasor had followed them. Unfortunately, the Harbingers had been able to stay ahead of him, despite his best efforts. Crasor would generate a worm, but by the time he got there, all he found was another signature.

He was content to continue the chase, knowing they would make a mistake at some point, but the Harbingers had deployed a new technology. Eleven worm signatures were in a space where there should be just one. Initially, the tech told him it was due to other ships using the same area, but that didn't make sense. Why would eleven ships tunnel out within minutes of each other? No, the Harbingers had discovered a way to throw him off the trail. Crasor had ordered the generation of worm tunnel after worm tunnel, checking each signature. It turned into a convoluted mess, especially once he discovered multiple destinations had eleven tunnels each.

Now, the hunt was over. The signatures had faded, and the Harbingers had escaped. *But just for now,* Crasor told the Breaker mind. *I will find them. It will take time, but they can't hide forever.* He sensed the Breaker mind calming.

"Three tasks you must complete in order for us to be secure," the

Breakers responded. "Destroy the Ashamine, subjugate the Entho-la-ah-mines, and kill the Harbingers. If you fail any one of these, the Dawn will rise and our kind will be eradicated or sent back to hibernation. That is unacceptable. We will continue to evolve and strengthen you, as we will do with the rest of the Breakers. Soon, we won't have to hide on the fringes of the Akked anymore. We will dominate the core worlds."

Crasor liked the sound of that. He sat down in the Captain's chair of the Justice and thought about what it would be like to rule the entire Akked. Closing his eyes, Crasor inhaled deeply.

The vast plain of faceless humanoid forms stretched out before him. Ever since his resurrection, Crasor was linked with the Breaker dimension. He couldn't travel there of his own will. That was fine because it was a horrible place, full of energy and pain. Crasor hadn't conjured it up in his mind, but it came anyway. The Breakers were drawing him in. "We must show you," the overwhelming voice of the One said. "You must know what has happened." Crasor felt himself slipping, felt the Breakers tearing away the fragile connection to his body. Dread filled him as his consciousness winked out.

***

Crasor regained his senses in a place that pulsed and surged. He looked around, trying to figure out where he was. "Where is not as important as who," the voice of the Breakers said. The surrounding room was luminous and felt charged with energy. It simultaneously seemed large and small, and his eyes couldn't estimate how far away the walls were.

Shimmering shapes surrounded Crasor, masses of energy he understood were Breakers. "This is not a normal reality, nor is it a separate dimension in the way you understand space-time." The forms began running towards the other end of the room. A door was there, one Crasor hadn't seen earlier. He ran with them, unable to control the movements of his body. "The dominant force of this time is a species called the Arche, a vain race who believe they are the progenitors and controllers of life in the universe. They are wrong."

Crasor and his group reached the door. Before they could smash through, the opening began to fade, merging into the wall. "This is the Arche's home, a quantum computer spanning entire worlds." Crasor's hand rose of its own accord, shimmering fingers elongating to points. He stabbed the wall, probing it. Images of sunny days, family, light, happiness and love filled him. The people in the images weren't human, but bore a striking resemblance.

"This is how they fight," the voice of the Breakers said, "but you are impervious to their emotional manipulation. They will not win you over with their feigned goodness or righteousness." More images flashed across Crasor's mind as he began slicing the wall apart: the terraforming of worlds, the manipulation of biology, the creation of species. They took pride in their accomplishments and felt it would protect them from Crasor. *Wrong again,* he thought, leading his shimmering Breakers through the hole he'd created.

Inside stretched a space Crasor's mind could not define, filled with innumerable beings made of light. Standing between him and the Arche were six entities, brighter and larger than the rest. *The Soldier and the Convict,* Crasor thought, recognizing them not by shape, but by their energy. "The other one of them you have seen before is the Protector," the Breaker voice stated. "The remaining three are the Boy, the Girl, and the Engineer. They comprise the Harbingers. They are here to convert the Arche to the philosophy of the Dawn, to turn them against us."

Crasor knew what to do. He stiffened his arms and raised them up to shoulder height, drawing in power from the Breakers as he did so.

"Stop," the voice of the Soldier said.

"We can reunite," the Girl yelled. "The Elrah can become one people again."

"Never," Crasor replied, confused by what she meant, but knowing it was the right answer. He swung his palms together, releasing all his stored up energy simultaneously. The resulting shock wave swept out in front of him. Before it could strike the Harbingers, they disappeared. Crasor screamed in rage even as the shock wave swept through the Arche, shattering and disassociating them.

"How can I follow the Harbingers?" he asked of the Breaker mind.

"You cannot, because this is all just a memory of things that happened long ago."

The energy around Crasor spiked sharply and he felt himself thrown into blackness. When he opened his eyes, he was back in the Justice. Crasor felt confused, not understanding what had happened.

"We showed you the memory so you might understand," the voice said. "Now is a critical time. The conditions of the universe, particularly in the Akked Galaxy, are prime for our ascendancy. There is much physical matter and genetic material available. There are many psyches inclined towards us.

"When we destroyed the Arche, it was the only time we've ever had the chance to strike at the Harbingers. They are crafty, staying with the rest of the Dawn race in whatever dimension or place they hide in. Last encounter, they kept their distance, not maintaining more than a token physical form. Now, as you've seen, they inhabit the bodies of humans and an Entho-la-ah-mine. The Harbingers cannot vanish as they did before. They are vulnerable now. They are weak.

"Your service has pleased us, Crasor, despite your recent failure to destroy the Harbingers. We have time. Our power grows with each new convert. You can still break the Dawn."

57 – WAKE

The days since the Death Watch had arrived on Lith-elo had been enjoyable for Wake. It was the first time in a long while he was not running or scared for his life. He still felt a dull fear deep in his mind concerning the Breakers and the Ashamine. As time passed, he became more and more secure in his belief the false worm signatures had thrown the Justice off course.

Wake had turned the engine room of the Watch into his workspace, spending most of his time there. It wasn't that he didn't like the other humans or the Entho-la-ah-mines, but he needed time to himself. The group seemed to understand and left him alone while he worked. They liked it out in the surrounding prairie or down in the Entho-la-ah-mine city.

His current project was the Clothing of the Iconoclast. The interior circuitry was fascinating. Felar laughed at how much time he spent examining the crimson suit, but Wake knew he could discover more. The beam weapon he'd used against the Breakers was just the beginning.

Captain Malesis had told him Calthis Brightwing, the name inscribed on the back of the suit's helmet, had been an important historical figure. She had been a battle commander and warrior. Wake once again wished Malesis was still alive. The man had been a good friend and full of information.

If they had access to the Ashamine Network, Wake could search databases for any information pertaining to Brightwing. Malesis had mentioned she was a part of the government preceding the current one, and the Ashamine didn't make information about that time available to the public. They had no desire to glorify anyone but themselves. *Perhaps the Network wouldn't be much help after all.* Brightwing was also connected to the Brotherhood of Azak-so somehow, but Wake didn't know if any members of that organization were still alive.

Wake mourned the loss of the Brotherhood. They'd saved him from death and the Ashamine. He'd joined the organization, but his time with them had been so short. If he ever ran across another Brother, Wake would try to help them as much as possible. He owed them that much. *Perhaps I can find the other bases Malesis mentioned.* If Parick Olvold, the Brotherhood's leader, had escaped Eishon-2, the group would keep on fighting.

A small circuit chip caught Wake's attention and he stooped down to examine it further. The suit had many such components, but this one wasn't wired in to the board below. It simply sat there, attached only by some type of non-conducting adhesive. Wake carefully pried it off, making sure not to damage anything.

Upon closer examination, he noticed a small port at the base of the chip. "Perhaps it is some type of data square," Wake said excitedly. Maybe it was specifications or design data for the suit. The interface technology was old and nothing on the Death Watch was compatible. Wake spent several minutes painstakingly crafting a wiring harness for the tiny chip. It took even longer to troubleshoot which wire was for what, but he finally succeeded in connecting it to a portable terminal screen.

When he scanned the data on the chip, only one file came up. The terminal listed it as "Untitled." It was a video. A dark skinned woman appeared on the screen. Blood caked her blond hair and weariness filled her blue eyes.

"For any who may find this, I am Calthis Brightwing, wife of Orick Brightwing, commander of the Akked Planetary Forces, descendant of the house of Azak-so." The woman looked past the camera for a moment and nodded. "It's as we suspected. Pull back to the inner perimeter. Protect Orick and the council members until I can evacuate them." She sighed and her attention returned to the camera. "I am making this recording so a part of the history of the Akked Planetary Council might survive the Ashamine coup. Our situation here on Amaz is grim. They started with a blockade and are now pushing through to our final ring of defenses. We should be able to hold them there for a while, but really, we lost the battle when the traitors arrived in system. Their numbers are too many, their support too great. One of their leaders, the one who's calling himself the Founder, is personally leading this latest push. He and Orick grew up together and were once friends." Calthis raised a red gauntleted fist. "I hope to have the chance to meet him in single combat.

"The Akked Planetary Council will not survive much longer. I had hoped the outer planets would send aid, but they are either dead or engaged in their own war with the Ashamine. Part of me says they allied with them, but I don't want to believe it. I will keep making plans and try to keep the Council safe as long as possible, but unless we get outside assistance, we'll all be dead soon. The Ashamine traitors don't take prisoners.

"One positive, amongst all this blightheart, is my new combat armor is working better than I ever could have expected. The master engineer has created something wonderful. Why he made it red, instead of the standard blue, is beyond me. Maybe it's his idea of a joke." She touched her blood matted hair and let out a tired laugh. "The helmet only works if you have it on though."

Calthis' mood sobered and her gaze left the camera. "Everything the Council has done for this galaxy will be upset by this new government. I'm not a futurist, but I think humanity is headed down a dark path. Perhaps I am wrong, and perhaps the outer worlds are amassing an army to rescue us, but I don't think so. I don't know when, or if, anyone will ever find this video, but if Alnos Azak-so is still alive, please tell him I love him and he will always be my little brother. His uprightness and character are constantly my guide." When Calthis looked back at the camera, Wake could see tears running down her face. "May light find you in the darkness, whoever you are, and may the stars never cease to shine on the Council." The video ended and Wake stared at the screen.

The Ashamine had slaughtered her, Orick, and the entire Council, of that Wake had no doubts. He didn't need to read a secret history to know. They had taken Calthis' battle armor, named it the Clothing of the Iconoclast, and began using it to execute their enemies. The Ashamine had twisted everything, and, as Calthis predicted, had led humanity down a dark path. Now, the Breakers were invading and the path had grown darker still. Wake sensed a connection lay between them, but he couldn't quite identify it.

Tremmilly's prophecy came to mind, confusing his thoughts further. Initially, he was skeptical, especially when Lothis had told them about the Arche. Beings of light who lived inside a computer didn't fit his image of omnipotent gods. *But they don't need to know the future, even if they act like they do,* Wake mused. *They only know possibility and probability, but it's all calculable, given the correct input.*

And what about his own dream, the one where he saw all these people before he'd even met them? Was it connected to the Arche somehow? That these individuals were the same people from Tremmilly's prophecy could not be chance. *So maybe the Arche had experience with the Breakers in the past somehow, and are bringing us together to stop them.*

"That blank screen is really interesting, huh?" Felar's voice said, startling Wake.

"Uh, yeah," he replied, setting the portable terminal down. "I was just thinking."

Felar laughed. "Haven't you had about enough of that lately?"

"I needed time to process everything, to wrap my head around it."

"I understand," Felar replied, nodding. "We've all had a lot to think about."

"Look at this," Wake said, restarting the video. After it finished playing, Felar had the same reaction as Wake.

"You can tell she really loved her government," Felar said. "That used to be me, if you can believe it."

"I can. You're very honorable. I bet you were a great Commando and soldier."

"I did things right, and I did things wrong. Thankfully, I was never involved in any action against the Entho-la-ah-mines, otherwise I don't think I would be able to stand myself."

Wake nodded. "Yeah. I only built things on one of their former planets and I feel guilty enough. It's sad what we've done to them."

"And now they have the Breakers to deal with. But the Breakers will divert the Ashamine's attention away from the Entho-la-ah-mines, so it isn't all bad."

They lapsed into silence, thinking. Wake's mind returned to thoughts about the Arche. "For what it's worth, I think I believe the prophecy now."

"It's kind of hard not to," Felar replied. "Where I get stuck is on what to do next. The prophecy identifies us, but says very little about our course of action. It is a lot of fluff and very little substance." Wake nodded as Felar continued. "There isn't a lot to believe in, actually, other than we are the group identified and something called the Acclivity is potentially in our future. It doesn't say what those things are though. Honestly, I think the prophecy's usefulness has ended with our coming together as a group. We are on our own now."

"What about the Arche?"

"Other than the prophecy and potentially your dream, they've been very little help to us. If they have any power or ability beyond those actions, they are choosing to withhold it. They seem the enemy of the Breakers, but I still don't trust them. I believe in my blades, and the group of us who came here on the Death Watch. That's about it." Wake felt honored he was in her trusted circle, something he didn't think possible before. "I suppose the rest of the Entho-la-ah-mines are trustworthy as well," Felar continued, "but I don't know them well enough to say for sure."

"Do you think there is any way we can find out more about the Arche?"

"Lothis might be able to tell us more. I worry about asking him though. He is extremely eager to help and might do something reckless. Thankfully, the Entho-la-ah-mines have been able to guide him, otherwise I think he would have killed himself by now." Wake had seen the boy's vacant body when they'd been on the A'Tal's Revenge. It had been disturbing. Felar loved Lothis, but Wake doubted she would be able to protect the boy from himself.

"Can you see any way for us to defeat the Breakers?" Wake asked. Felar was their strongest tactician and military mind, with Maxar a close second.

"You want my honest opinion or some blightheart to make you feel better?"

"I can deal with the truth."

"OK," Felar replied, looking grim. "You, Tremmilly, Jaydon, and I are normal for our species. Maxar, Lothis, and Cazz-ak are special. They possess abilities giving us a big edge if the Ashamine were our only foes. But we aren't fighting humans, we are fighting some sort of advanced race who possess all the abilities of our champions, with the addition of rising from the dead and converting anyone they don't kill. We don't understand them, don't know their history, don't know anything about their command structure other than it seems focused on Crasor. We have almost no intel about him. They obviously know about us, and want us dead. Overall, we are in the dark being blighthearted."

Wake nodded. He'd figured as much, but hearing her say it drove the point home.

"But that isn't the whole picture," Felar continued. "We are alive and have each other and the Entho-la-ah-mines. We also have the potential for the Acclivity, which may end up being a huge advantage or just some blighthearted prophetic jargon. We are hidden for now, which is a big plus, and have time to figure out a plan."

Wake felt down and useless despite Felar's positive additions. How could he stand against what was coming? *I'm just an engineer,* he thought, *wearing the armor of an executed hero. This is not my place.*

"The Ashamine might slow the Breakers down and buy us some time," Felar said thoughtfully, "but I don't think they will be able to stand against them. Even with the warning from the remains of the Eishon fleet, an enemy who can convert your troops to their side will always have the advantage. If the Founder's Light is finished and the Breakers make some mistakes, the Ashamine might stand a chance. It's a lot of ifs and maybes though." She trailed off, glancing at Wake.

"Hey, it's OK to be afraid," Felar continued, smiling. "In fact, I think the Breakers should scare us all, but we cannot underestimate ourselves. Whatever happens next, we need to be confident and ready to do our jobs."

58 – FELAR

"True," Wake replied, sitting up straighter in his chair.

"Why don't we go outside?" Felar stood and stretched. "The air is so clean here, the purest I've ever breathed."

Wake nodded, setting down his portable terminal. "Being with others would be good for me. I've been in my own head too much lately."

"That's easy to do. Maybe Lothis will be around and we can ask him about the Arche. He's been spending so much time with Cazz-ak that I've barely seen him." Felar felt her bond with the boy was weaker than it had been, but she knew Lothis loved her. It made her glad he was learning about his abilities.

When Felar and Wake stepped out of the Death Watch's airlock, the bright blue light of the Lith-elo Primary dazzled them. It took a couple of moments for her eyes to adjust, but when they did, the view of the groves of trees and far off mountains was exquisite. The wind was calm today, and the surrounding grass was still.

"Where is everyone?" Wake asked.

"Tremmilly and Beowulf went exploring somewhere. Lothis is with Cazz-ak, but I'm not sure if they are on the surface or in the city. Maxar is drilling Jaydon in combat skills somewhere nearby." The sound of a rail weapon discharging drew her attention. "Guess they are on the other side of that hill."

Felar fell silent. She'd sought Wake out because she needed someone to talk to, but now that she could share, Felar felt hesitant. Time passed, and her emotions churned. *Just get it out,* she thought, feeling ashamed.

"I'm worried about my parents," Felar blurted finally.

"Why?" Wake asked, sounding concerned.

"They are on Qi-3." She had to fight hard to keep from crying.

"I see," Wake said. "You're worried the Breakers are there."

Felar nodded.

"When we wormed to the Psinar system," Wake continued, "I

242

wondered if my parents were still there, if the Breakers had converted them. I didn't realize your parents were in Qi. Are you close?"

"As close as you can be with my schedule as a Commando. I tried to send them as many Ashcreds as I could spare, but it wasn't much." She hurriedly wiped away a tear. "Probably doesn't matter now."

"I once heard someone say: 'You can't let the chance of a bad tomorrow ruin the beauty of today.'"

Felar closed her eyes and turned her face towards the light of the star. She felt Wake's arm go around her shoulder in a friendly hug. Felar's mind calmed as she enjoyed the moment of support. "My parents were underclass. They did the best they could for me though. I was a handful, so it was good I was a single. I think they were the only reason I had the grit to become a Commando. They taught me to be strong, helped me see the potential in myself." Felar laughed. "Good thing I wanted to join the military. There were few options available on Qi-3. Most of my friends became whores, addicts, or both. A few managed to find a way off-world, but they had to sell body parts. I lost track of all of them as soon as I joined the Ashamine Forces."

Another rail shot boomed and Felar opened her eyes. She bit her lip and smiled. "Maybe we can go show Maxar and Jaydon how to shoot."

Wake laughed. "Have you seen my marksmanship? I'm probably the worst one here."

"You need more practice."

As they headed towards the base of the hill, Felar's mixture of emotions returned. Until she learned otherwise, she would have to assume her parents were dead or converted Breakers. Without an Ashamine communications relay or one of their large battle vessels, there was no way to communicate with them from Lith-elo-hi-rosh. Tremmilly had also been on her mind lately.

"I hope Tremmilly is doing alright," Felar stated, leading Wake by the base of the small rise. She didn't know in what direction they were firing the pistol, so going around the rise seemed like the safest option.

"She knows how to handle herself in wild places."

"Yeah, I know, but that's not what I mean. I'm worried the pressure of this whole situation may be too much for her. The death of her adopted father, the loss of her home world, the nightmares, the surrounding death: Tremmilly's experienced so much trauma. I'm barely coping with it and I'm a trained and experienced soldier. We are all doing the best we can, but I think it wears most on her. Hopefully, her time out exploring will be a rejuvenating experience, or maybe Maxar can help. I've tried to be there for her, but I'm not sure how useful I've been."

"You've known Tremmilly longer than me. What's going on with her and Maxar?"

Felar laughed. "I wish I knew. Certainly seems like something's happening."

"It's a crazy time to start a relationship."

"Agreed, but as you said: 'You can't let the chance of a bad tomorrow ruin the beauty of today.' Maybe they will do something about it, maybe not. In the end, it's good they can support each other, no matter how awkward they act." Wake chuckled. His laugh was infectious and they both started giggling.

"If you're trying to sneak up on us," Jaydon's voice came from behind a rock, "you're doing a blighthearted job of it."

"Actually, we were trying to do the opposite," Felar called back, trying to stifle her laughter. "I came to show you all how to use a rail gun."

"Is that so?" Maxar said, rising out of the grass directly beside Felar. Her right fist flew out in a reflexive strike, but Maxar deflected it.

"Bugger you," she cursed, laughing. "Nice concealment work."

"Thank you," Maxar replied with a bow, a huge smile on his face. He began removing the grass tufts camouflaging him with the surrounding prairie. Jaydon joined the group after a moment, and he too was laughing. His face was almost unrecognizable to Felar. Happiness was becoming on him.

"I think we should have a marksmanship competition," Wake said, a devious smile on his face. "Obviously, Jaydon and I are in a much lower category, so we can just eliminate ourselves."

Jaydon nodded heartily in agreement. "I'm certainly no match for the two of you," he said, gesturing towards Maxar and Felar.

"So," Wake continued, "it will be head-to-head between the two best marksmen of the— well what do we call our group? The Accliviters? That doesn't sound right. The Prophecy—something? The Death Watchers? Help me out."

Felar had no ideas, but then something entered her mind. "How about the Forerunners, or the Originators, since we are the beginning of the Acclivity?" The words were close to the idea she was trying to express, but were still slightly off.

"Hmmmm," Wake said.

"We're actually choosing a name for our group?" Maxar laughed. "We're not a military unit or something."

Felar was so close to the right term, but it kept skittering away. *Progenitor? No. Precursor? No.* Then she had it. "Harbingers!" she burst out. Maxar and Wake stared at her, eyes wide. Felar felt it too. Power was in that word. It connected them somehow, bound them together.

"I think you found it," Wake said, still looking at her in shock.

"It's a good name," Maxar added.

"What's going on?" Jaydon asked. "You guys look like you just dropped some narcs."

"I don't know," Felar answered. "There is deep meaning in the word Harbingers. Just saying it brings up images of vast stretches of time and space, of unity and destruction, of life and death."

Jaydon nodded. "Definitely sounds like you dropped some narcs."

"We should talk with Tremmilly, Lothis, and Cazz-ak," Wake said. "Maybe they will feel it too."

"And the marksmanship contest?" Maxar asked.

"Oh," Felar said, cocking an eyebrow, "there is plenty of time for me to beat you first. Interested in a wager?"

"You do realize I was rank one for accuracy on Bloodsport, right?" Maxar said flatly, reciting a fact.

Felar snorted derisively. "Do you know the accuracy requirements for a Founder's Commando?"

"Can't say I do, but I think I can outshoot you. If I win, you quit making insinuating comments about Tremmilly and I."

Felar thought for a moment. A wicked smile curved her lips. "And if I win, you have to tell us the extent of your relationship with Tremmilly."

Maxar sighed. "Fine. Rail pistols, human sized targets, begin at one hundred meters and add fifty after each successful shot?" Felar nodded her agreement.

"Lame bets," she heard Jaydon grumble as he and Wake propped up a large log.

"You first," Maxar offered as they walked the prescribed distance from the target.

"OK," Felar said, barely taking any time to aim. The ion trail of the round streaked across the prairie. It exploded through the wood and buried itself in the hill on the other side. The boom rolled across the plain, sounding like thunder.

Maxar raised his eyebrows. "Nice shot."

"Thanks."

They both waited as Wake and Jaydon propped up another hunk of log. Once they'd moved to a safe distance, Maxar took aim and fired. His round also hit the mass squarely. Felar led him back fifty meters and they repeated the process. Another fifty, and both became silent. She'd never expected the competition to go on this long. Maxar was a better marksman than she gave him credit for.

At two-hundred and fifty meters, Felar lost confidence. This was further than she'd ever accurately shot a rail pistol, even in perfect, windless conditions. Now, there was a crosswind blowing. Felar cleared her mind as she tuned into her heartbeat. She allowed emptiness to fill her, becoming one with her surroundings. Normally, these techniques were only used for sniping, but she hoped it would help with the pistol.

Lining up the sights, she synced her heartbeat and breathing. She adjusted slightly for the wind and waited. When her breath was out and she was between beats, Felar squeezed the trigger. The log exploded.

"Your turn," she said, not letting Maxar see how relieved she was.

59 – TREMMILLY

Tremmilly lay flat on her stomach in the tall grass, Beowulf beside her. Someone or something was coming towards them. She'd heard it approaching earlier and had concealed herself. In the past, her focus usually prevented her from noticing such things. Now, she constantly felt aware of her surroundings, even if she was studying a leaf or a bug.

"Tremmilly?" Maxar's voice said. She relaxed slightly. It wasn't that she believed Lith-elo contained real threats—other than the calath plants—but she didn't feel comfortable enough to let her guard down. "Tremmilly?" Maxar yelled again.

The situation with Maxar was complicated. After everything they'd been through, she had a close bond with him. He'd always protected and been there for her. *So why is it so hard to be around him?* Tremmilly only had a little experience with love or romance. Most of the boys she had grown up with thought she was weird. There were a few who showed interest, and initially she found the relationships exciting. A few even lasted a couple months. Eventually though, they became boring and unattractive to her. Now, she'd found someone who she really liked, felt interested in, and also seemed to have mutual feelings. *Am I just going to get bored again?*

Since their nap together on the Watch, Tremmilly felt awkward when Maxar was around. She played their conversation over and over in her head, wondering if it was truth or just delirious exhaustion. *You know you meant what you said,* she thought, her logic not letting her off easy. *Is this real love?*

Tremmilly noticed she hadn't heard Maxar for several minutes. Had he given up? Just as she was about to call out for him, something grabbed her leg.

"Hah!" Maxar said. Tremmilly let out a little scream. Maxar plopped down beside her. "I'm two for three today. If Felar ever offers a bet over marksmanship, don't take it."

"Blightheart you," Tremmilly cursed, her initial fear changing to laughter. "How did you find me?"

Maxar looked a bit sheepish. "Well," he said pausing, "you kind of left a very obvious trail."

"Very obvious?" she objected, trying to sound as indignant as possible. "I was careful."

"And I am good."

Tremmilly shook her head, bemused. "I guess I still have a lot to learn."

"We all do." She didn't understand what Maxar meant, but he continued on before she could ask. "What are you doing out here? Other than trying to hide from me?"

"Not much. Just exploring. Studying the plants and wildlife." She picked up a huge leaf and held it between them. It was as big as her torso. "This is one of the palos tree leaves. Can you believe how large it is?"

"Definitely the biggest leaf I've ever seen."

"Stop making fun of me!" Tremmilly punched him playfully on the arm.

"I'm not, I promise. It seriously is the biggest leaf I've ever seen. I've not been to many wilderness worlds though."

"I haven't either. The similarities and differences between this place and Eishon-2 are incredible. Have you ever heard of Dearadoth's Hypothesis?"

"No," Maxar said, laying down in the grass beside Tremmilly. Her heart began to beat faster. She tried to ignore it. "But I want you to tell me."

"Dearadoth, a scientist who lived before the Ashamine existed, stated there are two ways to explain the biological and ecological similarities between undisturbed planets. One is to say the universe selects for whatever those likenesses are: plants and trees have fractal structures, insects have exoskeletons, and ecosystems support a wide variety of life. The universe selects them because it is the optimum form for life's existence. Yes, there are other planets with strange, divergent organisms, but they only exist on one world.

"The other half of Dearadoth's Hypothesis says that similarities exist because those planets share a common ancestor. He didn't go so far as to say that intelligent beings created those environments, but that's the only real possibility. Sure, asteroids or comets could have carried genetic material throughout different systems, but that seems too complex and unlikely to me."

"So which one of the sides do you believe? Universe selection, or intelligent creators?" Maxar asked, staring into her eyes.

"I don't know," she replied, trying to focus on the conversation. "I read all this in a book the Dygars had. The author was analyzing the hypotheses, and wasn't Dearadoth himself. His conclusion was the hypotheses could never become a theory because no one could find evidence for or against either half or had a way to devise an experiment to find out more. The one thing he did say was that humanity would always have the chance that some type of creator would make themselves known. We could then verify or disprove their claim."

"It would take a very advanced race to modify that many worlds. And why would they do it anyway?" Maxar asked, sounding skeptical.

"We just ran into a very advanced race, more powerful than we understand."

"You don't think the Breakers seeded life throughout the Akked do you?"

"I've been thinking about that," Tremmilly replied, "but no, I don't. They seem focused on destruction and death, and unless they changed character dramatically, I don't think creation has ever been their desire."

"There is also the Arche."

"Yeah, I thought of them as well. We just don't know enough. They have power and influence, but unless more of them are somewhere, it seems unlikely." Tremmilly yawned. "Sorry, I haven't been sleeping well lately."

"Nightmares?" Maxar asked, concern evident on his face.

"Yes," she replied hesitantly. Tremmilly didn't want him to know her weaknesses. He'd seen enough of them already. She worried he might look down on her, that he told her he had bad dreams just to make her feel better. He was so strong, so in control.

"It's nothing to be ashamed of," he said, seeming to read her mind. "Like I said before, I have them too. It's a result of traumatic situations, of witnessing horrible things. Your brain is trying to process it all."

"You're not just saying that to make me feel better?"

Maxar laughed. "Of course not. I don't lie to you."

"I think the last time I slept well was our time together on the Death Watch." Tremmilly's cheeks began to burn and she wondered how brightly she was blushing.

"I slept well that time too, even if it was just a half hour."

"Maybe if we did it again I could get some real rest." Tremmilly wanted him close, needed his touch.

Maxar closed the distance between them, and Tremmilly's heart sped up even further. She rolled over, facing away from him. Maxar put his arm around her and pulled her close. The grass was soft and springy, making a perfect bed.

"You sleep as long as you need to," Maxar told her. "The others won't worry about us." Tremmilly wondered why that was the case, but didn't want to spoil the moment by asking. She was so comfortable, so at peace. When she tried to close her eyes and fall asleep, her heart was still beating a rapid rhythm in her chest. *You're not even sleepy anymore,* the logical voice said. Tremmilly realized it was true. *You want something different from sleep now...*

60 - MAXAR

"Tremmilly," Maxar said, scrambling for a way to handle the situation, "I don't think now is the right time for this." He tried to create some space between them, but every time he did, she closed the gap. Her body felt warm and inviting. It took every bit of self-control he had not to give in.

When Maxar was 17, he'd begun his life as a professional assassin and thief. Over the next 8 years, he'd had few romantic encounters. Most of the women in the circles he had been part of were either ice-hearted criminals, Ashcred seeking sluts, or narc dropping addicts. Some were all three. Noor-5 wasn't a place that good people survived long in.

Bloodsport had been an emotional wasteland. In his three years there, he'd barely made any friends, let alone lovers. It had been so long since Maxar had given or received any affection. Now, he felt awkward and lost.

"Why not?" Tremmilly asked, breaking into his thoughts. Her eyes were intoxicating, but he could see she was beginning to feel rejected. "You don't like me? What about what you said on the Death Watch?"

"No, no," Maxar replied hastily. "That's not it at all." He didn't know how to slow things down. His mind spun. "It's just that we've been under a lot of stress, and our emotions aren't normal."

"Stress or not, I want you."

"What if I infect you with nanites or something?"

Tremmilly laughed. "I'm not worried about that. Besides, it wouldn't hurt for me to be as strong or as fast as you."

Maxar felt himself losing the battle. She leaned forward to kiss him and his heart began to race. Everything within Maxar wanted her desperately, but he couldn't stop worrying she would regret her decision later.

Her lips were soft, just as he'd imagined they would be. She tasted like a warm spring day. Maxar closed his eyes, feeling his nervousness and worry begin to fade. Tremmilly embraced him, pulling their bodies

251

together. He opened his eyes, taking in the beauty of her face. Her warm, green eyes gazed at him lovingly. As she smiled at him, his remaining reservations vanished.

***

When Maxar and Tremmilly finally returned to the Death Watch, he felt like everyone knew what they'd done. After missing his shot at two-hundred and fifty meters, he'd had to tell them about their relationship, about how they'd napped together. Felar had been ruthless, asking lots of questions, digging for lurid details that didn't exist. Jaydon and Wake just looked awkward. *At least they all approve of the relationship,* Maxar thought. He felt a little ashamed, not for what he and Tremmilly had done, but just for it being so obvious.

"Glad we are all together now," Felar said as they stepped into the crew quarters, seeming normal. Maxar expected an embarrassing comment at any moment. "Have you asked Tremmilly about the name yet?"

"No," Maxar replied, trying to think of a way to explain their long absence.

"What name?" Tremmilly interjected smoothly before his silence became awkward.

"We came up with a name for the group," Wake said.

"It took me a couple tries, but the word I came up with is 'Harbingers.'" Felar was looking intently at Tremmilly, obviously seeing if the word would impact her the same way it had them.

Maxar dove forward and caught Tremmilly as her eyes rolled back into her head. He carefully lowered her to the ground. "What the blightheart?" Felar cursed, kneeling down on the other side of Tremmilly.

"She's still breathing," Maxar observed. "How could a word knock someone out?"

"I don't know," Felar replied, "but it isn't having the same effect on me as when we first said it." Maxar agreed, as did everyone else.

"I've looked into Tremmilly's inner mind as deeply as I can," Cazz-ak said. "She seems safe. I'm not as familiar with the human psyche as I am the Entho-la-ah-mine, but it appears her conscious mind is still within her, but is not connected to her body."

Maxar didn't understand what Cazz-ak was saying, and didn't find his words comforting. "Is there anything we can do to help her?"

"I don't think so," Cazz-ak said. "Whatever she is experiencing, it seems connected to this Harbinger phenomena. The effects passed for us, so perhaps they will for her as well."

Maxar wished he could do something to help. *What if she never wakes up?* Cutting off that line of thought, he focused on Tremmilly's face. The curve of her cheeks and jaw were so graceful. He smoothed a lock of her short black hair out of her face.

"She'll be OK," Felar said, patting Maxar on the back. He nodded in response, afraid that if he said anything, he'd lose control of his emotions.

Time passed. Maxar waited. The minutes stretched on, and he lost track of time. He vaguely noticed everyone but Felar had left.

"What if she never regains consciousness?" Maxar said, once again returning to his worst fear.

"That's not going to happen," Felar answered.

Just as silence was again reclaiming the room, Tremmilly's eyes fluttered open. Her face immediately locked on to Maxar's and she smiled. "That's the second time today I got to wake up to your lovely face."

Maxar tried to hide his embarrassment. "Are you alright?"

"Yeah, I'm fine," she said, looking around the room. "Where'd everyone go?"

"They wanted us to have privacy," Felar answered.

"Well, get them all back together," Tremmilly said, voice solid. "We need to talk."

Once everyone had returned to the crew room, Tremmilly addressed them. "I'm sorry to have scared you all. It's hard to explain what happened, but I'll do my best.

"I was in a memory, but I wasn't *me*, Tremmilly, not exactly. I had a vision once, before we all met, where I was inside Maxar's mind, seeing his vision and emotions. During that first experience, I felt united with his senses, but still separate somehow. This time, there was full integration. Anyway, I know these distinctions probably don't make much sense right now, but hopefully they will as I explain more.

"Maxar, Felar, Lothis, Wake, Cazz-ak: you were all there as well, but at the same time, you weren't *you*. You didn't have your present forms, but you felt like you do now. I'm not sure where or when this memory took place, but it was of a real event. I wished it had gone on longer, but I think I experienced what I needed to."

Maxar felt a chill run down his spine. He knew deep down her words were truth. Whatever she was about to say would change everything he knew about himself and those around him.

"I was telling you all it was the only way to stop them," Tremmilly said, fear filling her voice, "that the Breakers would consume the entire universe if we failed to act." A look of dread came over her, and Maxar sensed she was reliving the memory in vivid detail. "The Akked is at a critical point. The influence of the Dawn is not strong and the number of humans that can be turned to the Breakers is larger than ever. If they are dominated, the Entho-la-ah-mines won't last long. They've never had this much power before, and I don't think we have the ability to stop them, at least not with previous strategies. With the humans and the hive mind of the Entho-la-ah-mines converted, they'll have the ability to find the Dawn and destroy us all. Something about the Breakers has changed since our previous encounters. They have evolved, and we have not. We cannot use the same tactics of the prior engagements.

"I know it is a dangerous plan. We barely escaped the Breakers when they assaulted the Arche. If we take human and Entho-la-ah-mine form, it will trap us in regular space-time. We will be subject to all the weaknesses that entails, but I don't see another way. Our people are counting on us. If we do not save the species of the Akked, the whole universe will fall to the Breakers."

Tremmilly paused and seemed to return to herself. "Then you all expressed concern we'd forget who we were, that we wouldn't know what to do once we took on these bodies. I told you we would remember enough and said the remaining Arche would give us assistance. I knew there was no other way. We had to leave our hiding place and expose ourselves to danger."

Maxar's mind was spinning. Each word she spoke about the memory pulled strings in his mind. The vagueness of the connections was infuriating. Looking around the room, Maxar could see the rest of the Harbingers felt the same as he. Jaydon, the only one present who hadn't been in Tremmilly's memory, seemed dumbfounded.

"We all agreed to my plan," Tremmilly finished. "The memory faded away before I could remember anything else." Everyone was silent. Maxar tried desperately to conjure up his own images of the event. *Nothing.* His prior response to the word "Harbinger" and Tremmilly's recitation were all he had to tie him to his former existence. He didn't know if it was a good revelation or not. The nano-machines inside of him were horrible enough, and now he discovered he was—what? *Reincarnated? An extra dimensional being? A god?* It was all too much to take in.

"Does anyone think Tremmilly's memory is wrong?" Felar asked, looking at them each in turn. Everyone shook their heads. "I didn't think so." Felar sighed. "Blightheart, this is all getting complicated. That was the extent of your memory?"

"Yes," Tremmilly answered. "I tried to see more, tried to hang on, but the images just got fuzzier and fuzzier until I lost track of it. Then I woke up back in my body. Even now, the details of it are fading."

"We are lucky you remembered and were able to recount it," Cazz-ak replied. "None of us had a similar reaction to the trigger. It reveals how strong of a connection you have to our past."

"The name, Tremmilly's memory," Wake said, "it all feels right. If the

Arche are helping us, that would explain both the prophecy and my dream. I don't understand why they would use such obscure methods though. Why not just tell us outright who we really are?"

"The Arche are vain," Lothis answered. "They seem to believe they are gods, but they don't have as much power as they think. It could be an attempt to gain more influence somehow. They convince us to follow them, and we become their agents."

"The Arche obviously have their own agenda," Maxar added, "one we don't understand at the moment."

"I think I can find out more," Lothis said, "perhaps convince the Arche to tell us more about themselves and the Harbingers."

"How?" Tremmilly asked.

Lothis smiled, something the boy had gotten considerably better at since Maxar had first met him. "I'll just go and ask."

"Where does all this leave me?" Jaydon said. The man looked lost, and Maxar felt sorry for him. He was the only one not included in this shared experience. "I'm no longer one of this group."

"Of course you are," Tremmilly said, smiling. "Without you, none of us would be here. You were a necessary part of bringing us all together, a valuable member of the group. Just because we have this prior connection doesn't mean you can't be one of us. You are a Harbinger of the Dawn, Jaydon. You always will be."

61 – LOTHIS

"I'm going to find the Arche," Lothis told Cazz-ak. Over the past few days, he'd received much training from the Entho-la-ah-mine. He felt ready to use what he'd learned.

"And you feel confident with dimensional transitions?" Cazz-ak asked.

"Yes. You are a great instructor. I believe I can find my way to them and back again."

"Good. Be careful. You are putting yourself at great disadvantage by going into their environment. Return at the first sign of danger. There are many things left for me to teach you and I would like the opportunity to do so."

"The Arche are vain and obtuse, but I don't think they are actually dangerous. Why would they restore me to my body if they were just going to harm me later?"

"I believe you," Cazz-ak replied, "or else I wouldn't let you go, but their motivations are unknown to us. As a result, you must act carefully."

Lothis began drawing his mind inward, feeling the chatter of the group around him fade away. Through much practice, he had learned to find pathways between dimensions. It was dangerous and difficult, but worth the risk. The Arche could tell them more about who they were and what they needed to do to fight the Breakers.

Finally, Lothis disassociated his consciousness from his body. The action wasn't painful, but it was disconcerting. With his attachment to his bodily senses severed, he could no longer *see* those back on the Death Watch, but he could *feel* them. They were bright in this strange place, friendly auras that comforted him. *You're not strong enough to do this distracted,* he thought. *You're stalling because you're afraid. Focus!*

Letting go of his connection to Felar was hard, but it allowed his mind to adjust to the vibrancy of this new environment. It was akin to forsaking star-light for a vast, dark plain. Slowly, his consciousness began to adjust and pick out details. Cazz-ak had taught him that focusing too hard on too large an area would overwhelm him. *Be selective,* Lothis said to himself, over and over.

Time was strange in this place, flowing and twisting. *How long since I left the Watch?* Lothis shut out that distraction and continued his hunt for the path to the Arche. The surrounding space resolved. Everywhere he looked, there were threads and connections, all laid out in a confusing network. It was matter, energy, and space-time united, seen from a view even Lothis himself didn't quite understand. The entirety folded, enveloped, and cascaded, creating complex and ever shifting patterns. Frustration welled up within Lothis, both for his lack of ability and the difficulty of the task. *How do I find one path amongst this chaos?*

Cazz-ak had warned him that moving through dimensions would be like this, and he thought he understood. During practice, Lothis had been able to find specific threads, but now it felt impossible. *Your friends are relying on you. The Arche have the information you need. Believe in yourself, be patient, relax.*

Lothis let himself float amongst the network of pathways, observing the vast streaks of energy. Time flowed, twisted, reversed, crawled. A single strand amongst the innumerable pathways began to draw his attention. It was faint, but once he saw it, it became obvious. When the Arche had sent Lothis out of their presence, they'd tried to shield the connection, to keep him from finding the way back. *They underestimate me,* he thought, following the thread.

It could have been minutes, hours, or no time at all, but finally Lothis felt resistance to his progress along the Arche's pathway. The line began to blur, threatening to fade into the myriad connections of this place. *The dimensional transition,* he thought, his nervousness growing. Without giving himself time to think too much, Lothis streamlined his consciousness, forming an arrow. The line resolved and the resistance diminished. *Hold, hold, hold,* he thought, trying to keep the shape that would allow him to move through the tight fold of this part of space-time. The pressure rose once again. *Almost there.*

As Lothis transitioned into the new dimension, he felt a familiar sensation. It was the pulsing signature of the Arche, the first clue they were in some type of alternate environment. The throbbing grew exponentially as he approached. Realizing he'd successfully completed the dimensional transition, Lothis allowed his consciousness to return to its normal shape. The Arche stood before him.

"What is he doing here?" one of the beings of light said.

"How did he find us?" another asked. "He shouldn't have the ability to do that yet."

"It is too soon," the first voice stated. "We are not ready."

"Tell me about the Harbingers," Lothis ordered, his voice cold. He hoped his arrival would shock them into responding to his authority. No one answered, but Lothis could feel them communicating with each other. They were encrypting their direct messages, and it was so strong Lothis couldn't even begin to figure out how to crack it. With nothing else to do, he waited, nervously wondering if Cazz-ak would consider this a sign of danger. *You should go now,* he thought. *Something is not right.* Still, Lothis lingered, his curiosity compelling him. *I have no information,* he thought, *I cannot leave here without learning more.*

"How do you know about the Harbingers?" the deep voice asked.

"You're supposed to be helping me," Lothis replied. "You agreed." He hoped his bluff sounded confident.

"We did consent," the light voice responded, "but we already fulfilled our part. We brought you all together and you have found yourselves once again. What more do you expect of us?"

"I don't expect anything," Lothis replied, feeling he should switch to a different tactic. "We just need your help. We've discovered we are the Harbingers, but we don't know how to proceed. Please, give your assistance." Perhaps if he played to their vanity they might decide to help.

"You don't remember anything?" the deep voice asked. Something about the question put Lothis on edge. There was danger here and more of it than he'd anticipated. Lothis felt strong back on the Death Watch, but now he wasn't as confident. *I wish I'd brought Cazz-ak with me.*

"No," he answered. "One of us recalls a short time before we left wherever we were to come here, but it didn't show us the whole plan. We don't know how to fight the Breakers."

The light voice laughed, and Lothis' unease deepened. More flashes of encrypted communication sparked between the Arche. *Why are they hiding it from me?* Something was wrong. *Get out now!* He searched desperately for the exit, but it had vanished. They'd locked him in.

"Don't leave now," the deep voice chuckled, "we're not finished yet." Lothis continued searching in vain for an escape. Cazz-ak had been right: the Arche were the masters of this place. "Let us show you something."

A galaxy of stars shot out before Lothis. His mind spun, trying to make sense of the dramatic shift of perspective. All around him stars formed, lived, died, and were born again. As moments passed, the image before him began to look familiar. *The Akked,* Lothis thought, noting the distinctive spiral shape.

"Before the arrival of the Harbingers or even the Dawn race," the deep voice boomed, "our early biological form thrived. We were the first life to evolve in the Akked. Our path was very similar to humans. Not surprising, considering we planted the seed of their creation."

A dark planet loomed before Lothis, large electrical storms raging across its surface. He began plummeting towards the clouds, accelerating faster and faster. The crack and boom of thunder assaulted his ears as he passed through the weather. When he burst out under the storm, a vista of cities spanned below him, stacked almost to the height of the clouds.

"Surviving our technological advances was difficult, as was our transition to a multi-world species. Still, despite all our power, our science, our nano-technology, and our genetic engineering, we still died. We were flesh."

Time jumped ahead. The cities morphed into a solid mass of photovoltaic cells. The clouds were gone, opening the view to the system's three stars.

"But, we took control of our own destiny, of our own evolution. We moved the consciousness of our entire race into a network of quantum computers. This was the birth of the Arche."

Lothis dropped towards the landscape below and felt his perspective shift again. Now he was back inside the pulsing realm of his captors. Before him was an infinite plane filled with the Arche, bright beings emanating white light. A cluster of six figures, larger than the rest, drew Lothis' attention. They looked familiar somehow, but he didn't understand why.

"And then, after we gained our immortality, the Harbingers—you and your friends—intruded into our way of life. You claimed your species, the Elrah, had split into two races. One side used machines in the pursuit of the Acclivity and eternal life, and this had corrupted them. You told us what we were doing was dangerous, that we were on the same path as your enemies."

A darkness formed in one part of the plane, swelling into a malevolent mass. The Harbingers stood between the intruders and the Arche. As he watched, the blackness split open and dark blotches swarmed in.

"Before we could throw you all out of our beautiful world, the Breakers—who just happened to be the very people you warned us we would become like—came in and killed billions of us. In fact, they slaughtered everyone, all but five of our entire species. You did nothing to stop it, vanishing as everything we built was destroyed. We few survived, but only due to chance and the Breakers' haste."

The largest of the dark blotches swelled, imbued with dark fury. It became blacker somehow, sucking at the surrounding energy. Before the Harbingers could intervene, the dark entity exploded. The shock wave swept across the plane, shattering the Arche and sending them streaming outward. Before it could hit the Harbingers, they vanished. *Is this truth or another manipulation?* Lothis wondered. He had no recollection of this previous life or events, of anything before Haak-ah-tar.

The scene vanished, replaced by the five remaining Arche. "So, those few of us that remained wondered: Were the Harbingers really part of the grandiose, pretentious race called the Dawn, or were they really members of the Breakers they'd warned us about? The Harbingers obviously led the Breakers to us, but was it an accident or on purpose? Were they spies? Did it even matter?"

"Millions of years passed," a third, older sounding voice said, "and we lost track of time. We were abandoned, forgotten. Our star burned out, but geothermal energy kept our single surviving computer alive. With the destruction of almost everything we had built, we five were isolated, alone. The Harbingers never came, never tried to help or restore us."

"Then," the lighter voice continued, "you finally returned, saying you were trying to stop the Breakers once again and that you needed our help. It was a small request, to pass along a bit of information, to enlighten you after you had all forgotten yourselves. You said you had only recently discovered we were alive, that we were the only ones who could do this task."

"But this time, when you came, we knew the truth, and you put us in a position of power," the older voice said. "We knew helping you would do us no good. You were not friends. So we developed our own plan. For all your intelligence and power, Harbinger, there is something you don't realize. Not everyone is your ally, not everyone wants the Akked to evolve the way you do. We don't all believe your rhetoric.

"But we did as you asked, mostly. We fulfilled our agreement to you—we Arche do as we promise—but perhaps not in the exact way you expected. Giving you the information as a prophecy was a bit of fun, perhaps more obscure than you would have liked, but you found each other all the same. We watched you Harbingers give up your power in an attempt to stop the Breakers, knowing that at the right time, we would strike. Something went wrong when you transferred over, we don't quite understand what, but it gave us an even larger opportunity than we originally hoped for. Now, here you are, somewhat earlier than we expected, but developed and ready for harvest. The Harbingers, the Dawn, the Breakers: you are all responsible for our species near extinction. We were never part of your feud and wanted nothing to do with the Elrah civil war. You forced us into this. We will rise from our destruction, Harbinger, and we will be stronger than ever before." The energy around Lothis began to feel menacing, thrumming faster and faster. The white light of the beings grew, shifting towards a violet hue.

"But to destroy all the usurpers," the deep voice growled, "we need more power." Pain burst through Lothis, clouding his senses and making his head feel like it was about to explode. "What we want is for the Harbingers, the Dawn, the Breakers—all of you—to yield your energy to us." Lothis tried to force his way from their presence, but they held him fast. *No escape.* He tried to scream. Nothing. "We've waited many years for this time, cultivating the Akked to suit the Breakers, knowing this would draw the Harbingers out and cause a war. Now, the time has come." Lothis felt a violet dagger stab into his mind, sending cascades of pain throughout his consciousness. "Everything is aligning just as it should be."

Lothis tried to use every mental shield Cazz-ak had taught him, but nothing worked. The Arche continued torturing him. He couldn't even beg for mercy.

"We control this place," the lighter voice said, now full of hatred. "Try what you like, but we have you forever bound and silenced." The pain soared to a level Lothis didn't realize existed. "You will seek death, but will not find it. The pain will scour everything Harbinger, Dawn, or human away, leaving only your power. Then, we assimilate you."

As the pain rose to a throbbing crescendo, Lothis began to cry. He couldn't escape, couldn't fight back. He felt his personality and thoughts slip away as the Arche continued deleting him.

62 – CAZZ-AK-TAK

"Why has he been gone so long?" Felar asked, cradling Lothis in her arms. Cazz-ak felt worried about the boy as well. Perhaps they had underestimated the Arche.

"I know which direction he left from," Cazz-ak replied. "I believe I can follow to wherever the Arche are located."

Felar looked relieved. "Please Cazz-ak, bring him back to me. I should never have allowed him to go alone."

Cazz-ak focused on Lothis' trail. It was obscure, but he could still follow it. The path led into, then through, a folded dimension. As Cazz-ak's consciousness made the transition, he wondered what he would find when he reached the Arche. *They possess abilities I do not understand.* The idea frightened him, but he had to go on. Lothis needed him.

Then, the trail abruptly ended in a wall of crackling violet energy. Cazz-ak saw no way past it. He widened his connection to the Great Thought, pulling in more strands of power. Fashioning the energy into a thin wedge, he reinforced the implement until he felt it was strong enough. Cazz-ak drove the tool into the violet wall, creating a gap for his consciousness. He slowly worked his way through the opening, careful not to touch any of the hostile energy. He didn't want to find out what would happen if he did.

As he passed through the last bit, Cazz-ak's consciousness felt his connection to the Great Thought weaken, then sever. His wedge vanished and the wall snapped shut behind him. The surrounding room pulsed in the manner Lothis had described. *I'm trapped inside the Arche's computer,* Cazz-ak thought, dread creeping in on him. He once believed he would die or go mad if disconnected from the Great Thought, but this was the second time it had happened, and he maintained composure.

Across the space, Cazz-ak saw an exit. Since it was impossible to go back through the wall, he decided to go deeper. Once past the doorway, Cazz-ak found a room made of red energy, with several crimson doors

262

leading off it. He'd never seen a place such as this and he stopped, wary. *What if I get lost?* The concept was strange. *You must rely on yourself.* He chose the door to his left, and found yet another red room and more doors. *They are tricking me. It's a maze.* Everything looked identical.

What do I do now? Without his connection to the Great Thought, Cazz-ak was greatly limited. He began to despair of ever finding the boy, his mind trapped in this maze forever. His consciousness hurriedly walked through one red door, then another, then another. Each silent room was exactly the same as the one before it. A spark of anger ignited within him. Whoever the Arche were, they were not allies or friends of the Harbingers, Cazz-ak decided. They held Lothis and had trapped Cazz-ak in some part of their computer system. Even the dull red energy of the maze was hostile.

Before Cazz-ak realized what he was doing, he began drawing on his anger, magnifying it. The Arche were yet another enemy added to the growing list, but they would not control him, nor would Cazz-ak allow them to imprison Lothis. His mental focus became sharper, the sense of his surroundings amplified exponentially.

A small anomaly in the maze drew Cazz-ak's attention. One of the doors' hue shifted and flickered minutely as he scrutinized it. Passing through, Cazz-ak found another door with a similar energy in the next space. Perhaps he'd found a path, or maybe it was nothing more than his imagination, but either way, he had nothing else to try.

Cazz-ak lost count of the rooms. He always found the door with the slightly different energy than the rest. Room after room went by, and finally Cazz-ak felt Lothis. Something about him was different, however. His mind felt altered, changed. *No time to ponder,* Cazz-ak thought, hurrying through the obscurely marked sequence of doors. "I'm coming," he said, wondering if Lothis could hear him.

Bursting out of the final doorway, Cazz-ak found himself in the presence of the five beings of light. *The Arche.* Their bodies pulsed with the same violet energy of the wall.

"He found his way past the firewall," a light voice said. Cazz-ak saw Lothis a short distance across the room from him. The Arche had engulfed him in purple light, his face twisted in a rictus of pain. Above him was a faint cloud of energy, steadily growing larger.

"What are you doing?" Cazz-ak said.

"It is no matter," a deep voice replied to the lighter one. "Soon, the Boy will be consumed and we will have the strength to deal with the Protector."

"What are you doing to him?" Cazz-ak demanded again.

"Hold him in place," an older voice said. Violet beams shot out from the floor below Cazz-ak, engulfing him. Searing pain lanced through his consciousness. Cazz-ak tried to fight it, to shield himself, but nothing had any impact. "It appears without their hive mind, individual Entho-la-ah-mines are quite weak."

"It's as we expected," the lighter voice interjected. "The Breakers had the right plan: subjugate and convert the Queen, then the hive mind will fall."

"So much power for the taking," the deep voice marveled.

"And so many individuals," the elder voice said. "We will have the population we need to begin restoring our place in the Akked. Who knew that when we developed their sentience that the Entho-la-ah-mines would become so useful later, far more than humans."

The pain inside of him was almost unbearable, but Cazz-ak fought to focus on their conversation. He didn't understand what they were talking about, but at least he knew for sure they were hostile.

"NO!" Cazz-ak cried, drawing on every bit of his anger. He thought about what the humans and Breakers had done to the Entho-la-ah-mines, how the Arche were plotting against them. Cazz-ak drew on the rage inside, forging it into a heavy red cube.

"He is fighting our control," the light voice said.

"We are too powerful, even for two now-weakened Harbingers," the old voice said. "Finish deleting the Boy so that we can get this over with."

They are deleting him? Cazz-ak thought, amplifying his anger past any previous limit. "Damn you to the fires of the dark star, you blighthearted buggers!" he screamed, all the profanities he'd ever heard Felar say coming to mind. He swung the cube, hitting one of the light beams emanating below him. The violet energy shattered, shards of it exploding across the room.

"Amplify the dampening," the elder voice said hurriedly. Cazz-ak smashed another beam, feeling the pain decrease as he did so. "Do it now!"

The beams intensified, but Cazz-ak continued destroying them, the cube growing with his anger. "You will not control us," he said. "You were supposed to help." With the last beam of violet light destroyed, Cazz-ak began walking towards the Arche. The angry red cube hovered before him, ready to strike.

"We are not hurting Lothis," the deep voice said. "We are doing what you Harbingers asked of us."

"A lie," Cazz-ak replied scornfully. "I heard you say you were deleting him."

"Take the Boy and leave us in peace, Protector." The elder voice sounded like he had gained control of his panic. Cazz-ak sensed a craftiness in his tone, making him think the Arche was planning a trap. The humans sounded similar when they had promised peaceful co-existence on Entho-la-ah-mine worlds.

Cazz-ak had no time to waste, no time to ponder the consequences of his actions. He shot the cube forward, striking at the mass of the central member of the Arche. The projectile penetrated the light and stopped.

"You are not as powerful as you once were, Harbinger," the distorted voice of the elder said. Lothis let out a pitiful cry. "And we have learned much since you betrayed us."

Before the Arche could react, Cazz-ak sent every single bit of his remaining anger into the cube. Simultaneously, he shrunk the size of the weapon and bore down on it.

The red cube exploded, shredding the Arche. Pieces of energy flew everywhere, ricocheting off the walls, floor, and ceiling. The thrumming energy of the room cut off, replaced by a subdued buzz. As the violet light around Lothis vanished, Cazz-ak ran to him, hoping he wasn't too late. The boy seemed dazed, his eyes unfocused.

"We need to get you home," Cazz-ak said, wondering if it was possible for the Arche to put themselves back together. He didn't want to find out, at least not while he was in their dimension.

The cloud still hung above Lothis, but its size was stable now. *Is that the parts they deleted?* Cazz-ak had never encountered such a thing before. Not knowing of anything else to do, he encapsulated the cloud with his own energy. He would have to take it with them and try to restore Lothis once they were safe.

Cazz-ak put the boy on his back, instructing him to hold on. He was still in shock, but was conscious enough to obey. Tugging Lothis' cloud behind them, Cazz-ak set off, reversing his path through the maze of rooms. As he ran, the buzzing energy around grew louder and louder. It began oscillating, and Cazz-ak sensed the Arche would restore themselves soon.

Finally, they reached the wall, or where the wall had been before. Pale violet lines appeared in the air before Cazz-ak, growing. Before they could merge, he sprinted through a gap. The connection to the Great Thought flooded back into Cazz-ak, feeling like a welcome rain. Millions of voices cheered his safe return. Cazz-ak rejoiced with them. He never wanted to lose his people again, but was glad he could exist and fight without the connection. It seemed to be happening more and more lately.

Turning, Cazz-ak saw the Arche had restored the wall's solidity. "We made it," he told Lothis. "Just in time." Lothis didn't respond. The boy looked empty, disconnected from everything that made him a unique, thinking individual. The encased cloud still floated above him. Cazz-ak just hoped they could figure out a way to reunite the two.

The journey back to his body on Lith-elo-hi-rosh was arduous. When he reached the first dimensional fold, it took several moments to figure out how to shepherd Lothis and his cloud through it. Using concentration and careful manipulation of both his and the boy's energies, Cazz-ak was able to transition. He expected the task to get easier as he practiced, but something about managing entities other than himself prevented this. A mistake at one of the crossings would be disastrous, potentially marooning them in an inaccessible portion of existence. Time swirled, and Cazz-ak continued to work.

Finally, he arrived at the Death Watch and his body. Cazz-ak sent Lothis back into his mind and then returned to his own. He kept the cloud of memories and personality mentally encapsulated.

"I brought him back," Cazz-ak announced, "but something is wrong." He told the story of his encounter with the Arche and every word they said. The mood of the room shifted as he progressed, the other Harbingers growing more and more angry.

"How could they turn on us like that?" Tremmilly said. "We trusted them."

"That was the last time," Maxar said, fire burning in his eyes.

They all looked at Lothis, and then Cazz-ak.

"How do we restore him?" Felar asked.

Cazz-ak thought for several moments. "I do not know. They were using their computing power to erase him. It's unlike any type of damage I've seen. The Great Thought has no insights either." Felar began to cry. Tremmilly, Maxar, Jaydon, and Wake moved in closer, embracing Cazz-ak, Felar, and Lothis. Even Beowulf came to lay beside Cazz-ak. "All hope is not lost," he continued. "I have the parts they removed. I would like to take him down to the Queen. Perhaps she will have some wisdom."

***

"What you ask will be very difficult," Na-ah-co said.

"But not impossible?" Cazz-ak asked.

"No, it is possible, but there is much risk."

"I will do anything for him."

"The risk is not to you, Cazz-ak. It is to Lothis." Cazz-ak didn't understand how this could be. The Arche had already crippled Lothis. How could things become worse? "We do not fully understand the human mind. Through working with the boy, you and I have gained insights, but nothing this deep. I believe there is a chance if we simply return what was removed from him, the structure could be wrong. It might not restore him, and worse still, may kill him."

She was right. Cazz-ak hadn't considered that possibility. "Can we restore the pieces one by one?"

"Even with the entire power of the Great Thought, the task could take longer than any of us have to live. It's too complex and error prone."

"So all we can do is return the entire cloud to his mind and hope?"

"Yes," the Queen said. "I think it's the only way. It is risky, but Lothis is strong. He might be able to organize anything that is out of place. I just wanted you to be aware of the danger, Cazz-ak. He may be damaged forever."

"Alright, I understand. We'll do the best we can." Cazz-ak and Na-ah-co united, using the techniques they'd learned while mentally battling the Breakers. They opened a huge channel to the Great Thought, filling themselves with energy. Na-ah-co embraced the cloud, and Cazz-ak cradled Lothis' mind. They brought the two gently together.

"It is done," Na-ah-co said as they relinquished their increased connection to the Great Thought.

"You can come inside now," Cazz-ak said, knowing the rest of the Harbingers were waiting outside the Queen's chamber. Felar rushed in, her face red and blotchy from crying.

"Is he alright?" she asked, falling down beside the boy.

"We will soon see," Na-ah-co answered. The rest of the group entered, and came to stand next to Felar. Everyone waited, a caustic mixture of hope, fear, and tenseness eating away at them. Cazz-ak wondered what he would do if Lothis never returned. They had grown close, forging the bond of master and student. He loved Lothis like he loved his people.

After several minutes, Lothis' eyes began to twitch under his closed lids. Cazz-ak remembered from his studies that humans often did this when they were in the deepest part of their sleep cycle. *Is this a good sign?* It would seem to indicate he was having a dream, something the Entho-la-ah-mines didn't understand. Did that mean his mind was restoring itself, or was it an indication of discord? Knowing there was nothing he could do to help, Cazz-ak settled in to wait.

Time dragged by, the humans taking turns supporting Felar. Cazz-ak recounted the battle with the Arche to the Great Thought. Finally, Lothis' eyes fluttered open. "What happened?" he said, looking around at them.

"The Arche turned on us," Felar answered. "You were trapped in their computer."

"I remember that," Lothis said, smiling. The humans breathed out a collective sigh. "I don't remember how I got away though."

"Cazz-ak came to save you."

Lothis' brow furrowed. "I seem to recall that, but parts of it don't make sense."

"Do you feel normal?" the Queen asked. Cazz-ak sensed her reservation and knew she worried that perhaps everything wasn't as good as it seemed.

"Mostly. My mind seems fuzzy. I feel—" Lothis answered, hesitating mid-sentence. A look of horror came over him. "They are gone. Gone! I can't feel them! Where did they go?"

"What's gone, Lothis?" Felar asked. "We can help you. Tell us what is wrong."

"Everything is gone," Lothis said, despair and agony apparent in his voice, "I can't feel the Entho-la-ah-mines, I can't sense the galaxy, I can't sense anything. The signals are gone."

63 – CRASOR

Eishon-2, Taggardt-6, Qi-3, Crasor thought, listing off the names of Breaker controlled worlds in his head. *Eishon-2, Taggardt-6, Qi-3.* It was a good start, but he needed more. *Much more.* The Ashamine would know about the existence of the Breakers now, but it was a non-issue. With the Founder dead, the government would slowly implode. As it did, Crasor would be there, taking bites out of the empire.

The Harbingers and the Entho Queen had hidden somewhere, likely with the rest of the Entho bugs. That irritated Crasor, but he could do nothing about it at the moment. Eventually, he'd find and destroy them, just as the Breaker mind desired. *It's inevitable,* he thought, imagining what it would feel like to tear out the throat of the pole licker Soldier who'd shot him. He would kill them all, slowly and painfully if possible.

"Good," he sent to his group of nine Descended. "That is enough sparring for now. I have something to show you." They lined up in front of him, hulking frames bowed in deference. Their bulk made the expansive training area feel small.

Each day that passed saw the Descended and the rest of his Breakers develop greater strength and interconnectivity. Aeron was dead, but Crasor had found several replacements. He had scrutinized the Breakers, finding anyone who had the inclinations to become one. Their soul had to have a special receptivity, similar to Crasor's. As it turned out, this was a rare trait.

What would have taken humans years of training was implemented by the Descended in just days. The modification of the nanites and the intimate connection with Crasor accelerated their growth exponentially. They lifted weights, bathed in stellar light, studied tactics, and sparred with each other. Soon, they'd be tested in real combat.

Crasor also continued changing, his mind feeling sharper, his body stronger. *You're immortal,* he exulted, thinking about how the Breakers had revived him from death. As they'd promised, he wasn't the same as

269

before. He'd lost memories and now the Breakers were louder, closer to his mind. His skin was changing as well. Looking down, he saw the black, metallic flesh that had filled in his chest wound was spreading. It now covered large swaths. Crasor didn't mind. During his sparring sessions, he'd discovered it was far more durable than ordinary flesh. The skin was also peculiarly sensitive to the surrounding environment, giving him a stronger connection to his troops as well as better situational awareness.

"This is a cloak," he continued, folding space-time around himself. "You will be invisible, both to humans and Enthos. It is deception only, there is no protection in it. That is a more difficult warp." He demonstrated the shield, the space around him taking on an odd shimmering quality. "This will take time for you to learn and develop the strength to hold for any length."

As the Breaker nano-machines became more integrated into his biological systems, Crasor found it easier to perform these manipulations of space-time. What had once required all his concentration was now an offhand task.

"The ships are all in-system now," the Breaker mind announced.

Feeling ready to implement his plans, Crasor had summoned his fleets to meet him in Qi space. Hundreds of ships, ranging in size from Ashamine warships down to tiny courier vessels had been arriving over the past few days. It was a strange assortment, but they made Crasor happy.

Dismissing his Descended, Crasor headed for the command deck of the Justice. Karoth would be waiting for him there.

"This is still the beginning," the Breaker mind said as he walked. "All life will come under our dominion." Crasor nodded. It was happening, just as they'd promised. He controlled armies, space fleets, and planets. Soon, he'd control an empire, a species, a galaxy. Crasor knew the possibilities were infinite. "Once we reach critical mass, nothing will be able to stop us," the Breakers continued. "The more converts you make, the more power we have."

When Crasor arrived on the bridge, Karoth saluted. "All ships report ready for worm generation to the Psinar system," he announced. The time had come for the Breakers to take another, bigger bite out of the Ashamine.

"Give the order," he commanded. Crasor sat back in his chair, brown eyes blazing. A wicked smile twisted his fine features.

###

Want a free, exclusive Dawn Saga short story?

Subscribe to my newsletter, and I'll send you *Jaydon*. I'll also keep you updated on new Dawn Saga releases and short stories:

http://zachariahwahrer.com/jaydon

Dear Reader,

Thank you for investing your time in my fiction! If you enjoyed this book, I'd really appreciate it if you would share the experience with your friends and leave a review online at your favorite retailer.

If you'd like to get in contact with me, you can email: **zachariah@wahreroftheworlds.com.**
My website, **www.zachariahwahrer.com** *is a great way to find more of my writing. If you are more of a social media person, I'm on:*
Facebook: www.facebook.com/ZachariahWahrer
Twitter: www.twitter.com/ZachariahWahrer
and **Instagram:** www.instagram.com/ZachariahWahrer

May the fires of the black star be quenched in your life,
Zachariah Wahrer

***

ABOUT THE AUTHOR

Zachariah Wahrer spent the first twelve years of his adult life doing various jobs around the United States, such as eBay salesman, punk rock musician, horse halter craftsman, and rock climbing gym route-setter.

Near the end of 2014, Zachariah moved into a Honda Odyssey with his wife, Sarah, and began traveling the United States and Canada, seeking inspiration and adventure while writing and rock climbing full-time. His first novel, Breakers of the Dawn: Book 1 of the Dawn Saga, was electronically published in December of 2014.

When not deeply immersed in imaginary worlds, Zachariah loves to experience the outdoors as well as read about science, futurology, and trans-humanism. He also enjoys home-brewing and creating digital art to accompany his writing.

While writing this novel, Zachariah lived in: the Honda Odyssey; Las Vegas, NV; and Bozeman, MT.